TWISTED PREY

ALSO BY JOHN SANDFORD

Rules of Prey
Shadow Prey
Eyes of Prey
Silent Prey
Winter Prey
Night Prey
Mind Prey
Sudden Prey
Secret Prey
Certain Prey
Easy Prey
Chosen Prey
Mortal Prey
Naked Prey
Hidden Prey
Broken Prey
Invisible Prey
Phantom Prey
Wicked Prey
Storm Prey
Buried Prey
Stolen Prey
Silken Prey
Field of Prey
Gathering Prey
Extreme Prey
Golden Prey

KIDD NOVELS

The Fool's Run
The Empress File
The Devil's Code
The Hanged Man's Song

VIRGIL FLOWERS NOVELS

Dark of the Moon
Heat Lightning
Rough Country
Bad Blood
Shock Wave
Mad River
Storm Front
Deadline
Escape Clause
Deep Freeze

STAND-ALONE NOVELS

Saturn Run
The Night Crew
Dead Watch

BY JOHN SANDFORD AND MICHELE COOK

Uncaged
Outrage
Rampage

JOHN SANDFORD

TWISTED PREY

SIMON & SCHUSTER

London · New York · Sydney · Toronto · New Delhi

A CBS COMPANY

First published in the US by G.P. Putnam's Sons, 2018
A division of the Penguin Group (USA) Inc.
First published in Great Britain by Simon & Schuster UK Ltd, 2018
A CBS COMPANY

1 3 5 7 9 10 8 6 4 2

Simon & Schuster UK Ltd
1st Floor
222 Gray's Inn Road
London WC1X 8HB

www.simonandschuster.co.uk

Simon & Schuster Australia, Sydney
Simon & Schuster India, New Delhi

A CIP catalogue record for this book
is available from the British Library

Hardback ISBN: 978-1-4711-7483-4
Trade Paperback ISBN: 978-1-4711-7484-1
eBook ISBN: 978-1-4711-7485-8

Printed and bound by CPI Group (UK) Ltd, Croydon, CR0 4YY

TWISTED PREY

1

Tired?"

Porter Smalls looked across the front seat at the driver. The summer foliage was dark around the Cadillac Escalade as they rolled up the dirt lane. The South Branch of the Potomac River snaked along below them; the windows were down, and the muddy/fishy odor of the river filled the car.

"A bit—in a good way," Cecily Whitehead said.

Whitehead had taken a cold shower in the cabin's well water shortly before they left, and dabbed on a touch of Chanel No. 5 as she dressed. The combined odor of the two scents was more than pleasant, it was positively erotic.

"I'll drive, if you want," Smalls offered. He was a small man, like his name, thin and fit, looked like he might have spent time on a mountain bike. He had white hair that curled down over the collar of his golf shirt, too-white veneered teeth, and rimless made-for-television glasses over pale blue eyes.

"No, I'm fine," Whitehead said. She buckled her seat belt over her shimmery slip dress that in earlier days might have gotten her arrested if she'd worn it out of the bedroom. "You finished the wine—if we got stopped for some reason . . ."

"Right," Smalls said.

He kicked the seat back another couple of inches, crossed his hands across his stomach, and closed his eyes.

ABOVE THEM, in the trees, a man had been watching with binoculars. When the silver SUV rolled down the driveway, past the mailbox, and made the left turn onto the dirt lane, he lifted a walkie-talkie to his face and said, "I'll be home for dinner."

A walkie-talkie, because if nobody within three miles was on exactly the same channel at exactly the right time, there'd be no trace of the call; nothing for even the NSA to latch onto. Nor would there be any trace of the five rapid clicks he got back, acknowledging the message.

He was on foot, with his pickup spot a half mile away. He'd walked in on a game trail, and he walked out the same way, moving slowly, stopping every hundred feet to watch and listen. He'd never sat down while on watch, and had remained standing, next to the gnarly gray bark of an aging ash: there'd be no observation post for anyone to find, no discarded cigarette butts or candy wrappers with DNA on them. He'd worn smooth-soled boots: no tread marks in the soft earth.

He was a professional.

U.S. SENATOR PORTER SMALLS owned a cabin in the hills of West Virginia, two and a half hours from Washington, D.C.—close enough to be an easy drive, far enough to obscure activities that might need to be obscured.

He and Whitehead, one of his wife's best friends—his wife was back in Minnesota—had locked up the place and headed back to

D.C. as the sun wedged itself below the horizon on a hot Sunday afternoon. The timing was deliberate: they would enjoy the cover of darkness when she dropped him off at his Watergate condo.

Smalls and Whitehead had spent an invigorating two days talking, about political philosophy, history, horses, money, life, and mutual friends, while they worked their way through Smalls's battered '80s paperback copy of *The Joy of Sex*.

Smalls was married, Whitehead not, but she drove the car because of a kind of Washington logic concerning sex and alcohol. A little light adultery, while not considered a necessarily positive thing in Washington, was certainly not to be compared, as a criminal offense, with a DWI. Banging an adult male or live woman might—*maybe*—get you a paragraph on a *Washington Post* blog. God help you if Mothers Against Drunk Driving jumped your elective ass.

So Whitehead drove.

A fifty-year-old political junkie and Republican Party moneywoman, Cecily Whitehead was thin and tanned and freckled, with short dark hair so expertly colored you couldn't tell that it had been, the occasional strands of gray lending it a sly verisimilitude. She had a square chin, making her look a bit like Amelia Earhart. Like Earhart, she flew her own plane—in Whitehead's case, a twin-engine Beechcraft King Air. She owned a mansion on one of Minneapolis's lakes, and a two-thousand-acre farm south of the Twin Cities on which she raised Tennessee Walkers.

Smalls's wife didn't know for sure that Whitehead was sleeping with her husband, and the topic had never come up. For the past four years, Smalls's wife had been living with her Lithuanian lover, in a loft in downtown Minneapolis, a topic that had come up between them any number of times.

Lithuanians were known as the sexual athletes of Northern Europe. Smalls was aware of that fact but no longer cared what his wife did as long as she didn't do it in the streets. Actually, he hoped she was happy, because he was still fond of her, the mother of his children. He made a mental note to take her to dinner the next time he was in the Twin Cities.

"BE THERE BY TEN," Whitehead said.

"I've got that dimwit Clancy at noon," Smalls said, not opening his eyes.

"Dim but persistent," Whitehead said. "He told Perez that if Medtronic gets the VA deal, Abbott will have to cut jobs in his district. Perez believes him. It might even be true."

"Tough shit," Smalls said. "If Abbott gets it, Medtronic might have to cut people. That ain't gonna happen. Not when Porter Smalls knows that our beloved majority leader has that backdoor job at Rio Javelina."

"If you ever mention that to him, he'll find some way to stick something sharp and nasty up your rectum."

Smalls smiled. "Why, CeeCee . . . you don't think I'd ever actually mention it to him, do you?"

Whitehead squeezed his knee. "I hope to hell not. No, I don't think you'd do that. How are you gonna let him know that you know?"

"Kitten will think of something," Smalls said.

Whitehead smiled into the growing darkness, their headlights ricocheting through the roadside trees. Kitten Carter, Smalls's chief of staff, would think of something. She and Whitehead talked a couple of times a week, plotting together the greater glory of the U.S.A. in general and Porter Smalls in particular.

Whitehead was a lifelong yoga enthusiast and show horse competitor. She had a strong body, strong legs and arms, and, for a woman, large, strong hands. She wheeled the Escalade up the track faster than most people might have, staining the evening air with dust and gravel. She'd spent much of her life on farms, shoveling horseshit with the best of them, driving trucks and tractors, and knew what she was doing, keeping the twenty-two-inch wheels solidly in the track's twin ruts.

A half mile down the river, the track crossed a state-maintained gravel road, and with a bare glance to her left, she hooked the truck to the right and leaned on the gas pedal.

A FEW MINUTES LATER, they topped a hill, and in the distance, Whitehead could see a string of lights on a highway that would take them to the interstate that would take them into Washington. The river still unwound below them, below a long slope, the last fifty feet sharpening into a bluff.

A minute later, Whitehead said, "What an asshole. This jerk is all over me."

"What?" Smalls had almost dozed off. Now he pushed himself up, aware that the SUV was flooded with light. He turned in his seat. A pickup—he thought it was a pickup, given the height of the headlights—wasn't more than fifteen or twenty feet behind them, as they rolled along the gravel at fifty miles an hour.

He said, "I don't like this."

At the crest of the hill, the pickup truck swung out into the left lane and accelerated, and Smalls said, "Hey, hey!"

Whitehead floored the gas pedal, but too late. *Too late.* The truck swung into them, smashed the side of the Escalade, which went off the road, through roadside brush and trees, across a ditch and down the precipitous hillside. Instead of trying to pull the SUV back up the hillside, which would have caused it to roll sideways, Whitehead turned downhill for a second, then said, her voice sharp, "Hold on, Porter, I'm gonna try to hit a tree. Keep your arms up in case the air bag blows . . ."

Smalls lifted his arms, and the SUV bounced and bucked across the hill, heading sharply down toward the bluff below, as Whitehead pumped the brakes. He didn't actually think it, but Smalls knew in his gut that they only had a few seconds to live.

They hit a row of saplings, plowed through them, hit a tree that must have been six inches in diameter, breaking it cleanly off. The impact caused the truck to skew sideways while plowing forward, and now Smalls felt Whitehead hit the accelerator. The engine screamed as the oversized tires tried to dig into the hill-side, and he realized that she was *barking* with each impact: *"Ay! Ay! Ay! Ay! . . ."*

They were still angling downhill, but less steeply now. They hit another small tree, and the vehicle snapped around only to hit a bigger tree. The air bag exploded and hit Smalls in the face, yet he was aware that the truck was beginning to tilt downhill, toward the bluff. And suddenly the driver's-side window blew in. They'd almost stopped, not thirty feet from the edge of the bluff, but were not quite settled, and they blundered another few lengths backward and smashed into a final tree, which pushed up the passenger side of the truck. The Escalade slowly, majestically, rolled over on its roof and came to a stop.

Smalls, hanging upside down from his seat belt, half blinded by blood rolling down into his eyes, felt no pain—not yet anyway—and cried, "I smell gas. We gotta get out of here. Get out! Get out!"

He looked sideways at Whitehead, who also was hanging upside down from her seat belt. The overhead light had come on when the door came loose, and her eyes were open, but blank, and blood was running from one ear into her hair.

He called, "CeeCee, CeeCee," but got no response. Blood was still pouring down his face and into his eyes as he freed his seat belt and dropped onto the inside of the roof. He unlocked the door on his side and pushed it open a few inches, where it got stuck on a sapling. He kicked the door a half dozen times until it opened far enough that he could squeeze out.

As soon as he was free, he wiped the blood from his eyes, realized that it actually had been coming from his nose. As he cleared his eyes, he stumbled around to the back of the SUV, popped the lid, found his canvas overnight bag, and took out the chrome .357 Magnum he kept there. He tucked the gun in his belt and looked uphill: no sign of anyone. No headlights, no brake lights, nothing but the gathering dusk, the knee-high weeds and the broken trees, the natural silence pierced by the numerous warning and alarm beeps and buzzes from the Cadillac.

He hurried to the driver's side of the truck, wedged the door open as far as he could, unhooked Whitehead's seat belt, and let her drop into his arms. He had to struggle to get her out of the truck, but the odor of gas gave him the strength of desperation.

When she was out, he picked her up and carried her fifty feet across the hillside, then lowered her into the weeds, knelt beside her, and listened for a moment. Her scent, the Chanel No. 5 and the well water from the shower, now mixed with the coppery/meaty odor of fresh blood.

He heard and saw nothing: nobody on the hillside. The truck that had hit them had vanished.

He whispered, "CeeCee. CeeCee, can you hear me?"

No answer.

One headlight was still glowing from the SUV, and he dug out his cell phone and called the local sheriff's department—he had them on his contact list. He identified himself, told the dispatcher what had happened and that the incident might well have been a deliberate attack.

The dispatcher said deputies would be there in five minutes. "Be sure the emergency flashers are on," Smalls told the dispatcher. "I'm not coming out of the weeds until I'm sure I'm talking to the right guys. We'll need an ambulance; my friend's hurt bad."

When he got off the phone, he cradled Whitehead on his lap. The ambulance, he thought, wouldn't be in time: it was, in fact, already too late for Cecily Whitehead.

THE COPS CAME, and an ambulance, and when Smalls was sure of who he was dealing with, he called to them from the hiding place in the weeds. They told him what he already knew: Whitehead was dead, had sustained a killing blow to the left side of her head, probably a tree branch coming through the driver's-side window.

Smalls retrieved his government paper from the Cadillac as the cops and the EMTs took Whitehead up the hill in a black plastic body bag. Whitehead was put in the ambulance, but Smalls said he didn't need one. "A bloody nose, nothing worse. Give me something to wash my face."

The lead deputy asked who'd been driving, and Smalls said, "CeeCee was."

"We need to give you a quick Breathalyzer anyway," the deputy said.

"Yes, fine," Smalls said. "I had a glass of wine before we left my cabin, CeeCee didn't have anything at all."

The test took two minutes. Smalls blew a 0.02, well below the drunk-driving limit of 0.08, although Smalls was an older man, and older men were hit harder by alcohol than younger men.

"Be sure that's all recorded," Smalls told the cop. "I want this nailed down."

"Don't need to worry," the deputy said. "We'll get it right for you, Senator. Now . . . did you see the truck?"

Smalls shook his head. "He had his high beams on, and they were burning right through the back window of my Caddy. It was like getting caught in a searchlight. I couldn't see anything . . . And he hit us."

The deputy looked down the hill. "She did a heck of a job driving. Another twenty, thirty feet, and you'd have gone over the edge and hit that gravel bar like you'd jumped out of a five-story building. Makes me kind of nervous even standing here."

THE AMBULANCE LEFT for the Winchester Medical Center, Smalls following in a state police car. Whitehead's death was confirmed, and Smalls was treated for the impact on his nose. It had continued to bleed, but a doc used what he called a chemical cautery on it, which stopped the bleeding immediately. The doctor gave him some pain pills. Smalls said, "I don't need the pills."

"Not yet," the doc said. "You will."

When he was released, the deputies took him aside for an extended statement, and told him that the Cadillac would be left where it had landed until a state accident investigator could get to the scene.

When he was done with the interview, Smalls called chief of staff Kitten Carter and arranged to have her drive to the hospital to pick him up. She said she would notify Whitehead's mother and father of her death.

And when there was nothing left to do, Smalls asked to be taken to the hospital's chapel. The police left him there, and Smalls, a lifelong Episcopalian, knelt and prayed for Cecily Whitehead's soul. Less charitably, he had a word with the Lord about finding the people who'd murdered her. Then he cried. He finally pulled himself together after a while and began thinking seriously about the accident.

It had been no accident.

It had been an assassination attempt, and he thought he knew who was behind it. Justice, if not in a court of law, would come.

He said it aloud, to Whitehead: "I swear, CeeCee, I will get them. I'll get every one of those motherfuckers."

Whitehead hadn't been particularly delicate, nor particularly forgiving: if she were already experiencing the afterlife, he had no doubt that she would be looking forward to any revenge—and the colder, the better.

KITTEN CARTER arrived at the hospital. She'd been on her cell phone for three hours by the time she got there. The first news of the accident would be leaked to reporters who owed her favors and who would put the most sympathetic spin to the night's events.

". . . good friends and political allies who'd gone to the cabin to plot strategy for the summer clashes over the health care proposals . . ."

THE LOCAL DEPUTIES turned the crash investigation over to the West Virginia State Police. The second day after the accident, an investigator interviewed Smalls, in his Senate office, with Carter sitting in. Smalls, with two black eyes and a broad white bandage over his nose, and dressed in a blue-striped seersucker suit with a navy blue knit tie, immediately understood that something was wrong.

The investigator's name was Carl Armstrong. When he'd finished with his questions, Smalls said, "Don't bullshit me, Carl. Something's not right. You think I'm lying about something. What is it?"

The investigator had been taking notes on a legal pad inside a leather portfolio. He sighed, closed the portfolio, and said, "Our lab has been over your vehicle inch by inch, sir. There's no sign that it was ever hit by another truck."

Carter was sitting in a wingback chair, illegally smoking a small brown cigarillo. She looked at Smalls, then frowned at Armstrong and said, "That's wrong. The other guys took them right off the road—smashed them off. What do you mean, there's no sign?"

Smalls jumped in. "That's exactly right. The impact caved the door in . . . there's gotta be some sign of that. I mean, I was in a fairly bad accident once, years ago, and both vehicles had extensive damage. This one was worse. The hit was worse. What do you mean, no sign?"

"No metal scrapes, no paint, no glancing blow. The only thing we've found are signs that you hit several trees on both sides of the truck and the front grille and hood," Armstrong said.

"Then you're not looking hard enough," Smalls snapped. "That guy crashed right into us and killed CeeCee, and damn near killed me."

Armstrong looked away and shrugged. "Uh, well, I wonder if he actually hit you or maybe just caused Miz Whitehead to lose control?"

"She hadn't been drinking . . ."

Armstrong held up a hand. "We know that. She had zero alcohol in her blood, and we know she was driving because the blood on that side of the cab and on the air bag matches hers. We don't doubt anything you've told us, except the impact itself."

Carter: "Senator Smalls has provided a written statement in which he relates the force of the impact."

"There's a low gravel berm where they went over the side—we're wondering if Miz Whitehead might have hit that hard, and the senator might be mistaking that for the impact of the truck."

Smalls was already shaking his head. "No. I heard the truck hit. I saw it hit—I was looking out the driver's-side window when it hit."

"There's no paint from another car, no metal, no glass on the road . . . no nothing," Armstrong repeated.

Carter said to Smalls, "Senator, maybe we need to get some FBI crime scene people up there . . ."

Smalls put a finger on his lips, to shut her up. He stood, and said, "Carl, I'm going to ask another guy to talk to you about the evidence, if you don't mind. Kitten and I don't know about such things, but I think it'd be a good idea if we put a second pair of eyes on this whole deal."

Armstrong had dealt with politicians a number of times, and Smalls seemed to him to be one of the more reasonable members of the species. No shouting, no accusations. He flushed with relief, and said, "Senator . . . anything we can do, we'll be happy to do. We'd like to understand what happened here. Send your guy around anytime. We'll probably give him more cooperation than he'll even want."

"That's great," Smalls said, extending a hand. "I'll drop a note to your superintendent, thanking him for your work."

"Appreciate that," Armstrong said, as they shook. "I really do, sir."

WHEN ARMSTRONG HAD GONE, Carter asked, "Why were you pouring butter on him? He didn't believe you. I mean, Jesus, somebody killed CeeCee and almost killed you. If you let this stand, the whole thing is gonna get buried—"

"No, no, no . . ." Smalls was on his feet. He touched his nose, picked up the tube of pain pills, shook it like a maraca, put it back down; not many left, and he'd already taken one that morning.

His nose was still burning like fire from the chemical cautery. The doc had been right about needing the pills, not for the mechanical damage but for the cauterized tissue. He wandered over to his trophy wall, filled with plaques and keys to Minnesota cities and photos of himself with presidents, governors, other senators, assorted rich people, including Whitehead, and politically conservative movie stars.

Thinking about it.

Carter kept her mouth shut, and after a while Smalls, playing with an earlobe and gazing at his pictures, said, "I'm surprised by . . . what Armstrong said. No evidence. But I'm not really astonished. Remember when I told you the first thing I did was get my gun because I thought the guys who hit us might be paid killers? Assassins? Professionals?"

"Yeah, but I don't . . ."

"I was right. They were," Smalls said. "I don't know how they did this, but I'm sure that if the right investigator looked under the right rock, he could find someone who could explain it. We need to get that done, because . . ."

"They could be coming back for another shot at you," Carter finished.

"Yeah. Probably not right away, but sooner or later." Smalls left the trophy wall, walked to his oversized desk, pushed a button on an intercom. "Sally . . . get Lucas Davenport on the line. His number's on your contact list."

"That's the guy . . ." Carter began.

"Yeah," Smalls said. "That's the guy."

2

Lucas Davenport and Charlie Knight walked out of the Sedgwick County Regional Forensic Science Center into the bright Kansas sunshine, and Lucas took his sunglasses from his jacket pocket, slipped them on his nose, and said, "Move on. Nothing to see here."

"Could be worse," Knight said. He put on his own sunglasses. They were silvered and made him look like a movie version of a Texas highway patrolman, which he probably knew. His teeth, which didn't quite match—the two upper central incisors were white, the others various shades of yellow—made him look even more like a Texas cop. "The sonofabitch might've lived."

That made Lucas smile, and he said, "He wasn't as bad as his boss."

"Maybe not, but it'd be a goddamn close call." They'd been to look at the bullet-riddled body of a man named Molina.

"You want to write this up?" Lucas asked, as they walked out to the rental car.

"Yeah, I'll do it tonight," Knight said. "You'll be rolled up with your old lady by the time I get finished." Lucas's plane was going out that evening, Knight's not until the next morning.

"What about Wise?" Lucas asked.

"Fuck him. Let Wichita put him away," Knight said. "I don't

know for sure, but I suspect the Kansas state pen ain't a leading garden spot."

"I suspect you're right about that," Lucas said. "So, you thinking steak or cheeseburger?"

"Anything with beef in it that's not Mexican," Knight said.

"Yeah? Mexican's one of my favorites," Lucas said.

"I'm married to a Mexican, and we got gourmet Mexicano right there in the kitchen, so I ain't eating Mexican in Wichita. I'd like to get around a big bloody T-bone."

"You can do *that* in Wichita," Lucas said. "Did I ever tell you about the time I danced with a professional assassin in Wichita? No? Her name was Clara Rinker . . ."

LUCAS, WORKING OUT OF MINNEAPOLIS, but without a lot to do, and Knight, working out of Dallas, had hooked up to look into the murder of a Jesús Rojas Molina.

Molina, at the time of his death, was in the Federal Witness Protection Program, which was run by the U.S. Marshals Service. Both marshals now, Lucas and Knight had been chosen to look at the case because they both had histories in earlier lives as homicide investigators, Lucas in Minnesota, Knight in Houston.

Molina, the dead man, had ratted out his boss in a homegrown "cartel" that served the illegal drug needs of Birmingham, Alabama. After the boss was convicted and sent to prison forever, Molina was relocated to Wichita to keep him away from the boss's relatives, who'd promised to disassemble him with a power drill and a straight razor.

He believed them, as did the Marshals Service. As a Witness Protection client, Molina got a crappy manufactured home on the south side of Wichita, and a five-year-old Corolla, and a greeter's job at a Walmart Supercenter.

Not good enough for a man who liked rolling high.

A year after moving to Wichita, he was peddling cocaine to the town's higher-end dope clientele, meaning those who were afraid of methamphetamine or didn't like the way meth cut into their frontal lobes. He did that until Bobby Wise, whom he'd met as a fellow free enterprise enthusiast and whose wife Molina was screwing, put five shots from his .44 Magnum through Molina's screen door and into his chest and neck.

One would have done the job. Then Wise would have had the other four to use on his wife, who had promptly turned him in for the murder. But he loved her, so he simply cried when the cops came to get him, and he told her he still loved her.

The Wichita cops seized the .44, matched the slugs, confronted him with the evidence, and got a confession. Lucas and Knight were the Marshals Service representatives to the investigation, making sure that Wise was the one and only killer: that he hadn't been sent by the Alabama boss's murderous wife or equally murderous children.

They'd interviewed both Wise and his wife, who'd been confused about the whole Witness Protection thing—they had no idea that Molina had been in it. They were convincing.

Lucas and Knight were moving on: nothing to see here.

THAT HAD BEEN THE STORY too frequently with Lucas in his two years as a marshal. He'd had a half dozen interesting cases, most resolved in a couple of weeks, along with a half dozen tracking cases that were still open and two cold cases that might never be resolved. Lucas had joined the Service specifically to work on difficult cases—and he'd found something he hadn't expected.

The world was opening up to American criminals. The wars in the Middle East and the demand for American blue-collar workers in foreign jobs meant that the brighter crooks were disappearing into the confusion of war and irregular employment.

Others were crossing into western Canada, where the raucous oil sands industry provided income and obscure hideouts, as well as a familiar language. The disaster industry, helped by climate change, provided unregulated construction jobs and opportunities for scam artists in the Caribbean and Mexico.

In the U.S., even casual contact with the law often tripped up fugitives; when they went foreign, that didn't happen.

BUT THERE WAS ONE OPENING, one source of interesting investigations, which Lucas still wasn't sure would develop into a full-time gig. He wasn't sure that he wanted it to. The jobs were coming out of Washington, D.C. From politicians in trouble.

THE PREVIOUS SPRING, a Democratic congressman from Illinois had gotten in touch through the former governor of Minnesota, who was a friend of both the congressman and Lucas.

The congressman, Daniel Benson, had a college dropout daughter who'd gotten herself a flaming skull tattoo above the crack of her ass and a boyfriend in a sleeveless jeans jacket with a Harley. Benson hadn't worried about it too much until he learned that the boyfriend was an ex-con and a member of a neo-Nazi party and that the daughter had made a YouTube video with him.

She was largely unclothed in it, except for the fake German SS helmet and a red-and-black swastika armband. The congressman couldn't get in touch with her, either on her cell phone or by email.

The congressman thought she might have been kidnapped—or, if not exactly kidnapped, at least was being held against her will. Lucas was asked to take a look. The Marshals Service director was consulted, and he was more than happy to approve a quiet favor for a ranking member of the House Ways and Means Committee.

Lucas found the Nazi and the daughter in eight days, at their Ohio hideout. He and another marshal had retrieved the girl and had gotten her enrolled in a sex-and-drugs rehab center. The boyfriend had resisted arrest, and one of his legs had been broken in the fight. Because resisting arrest with violence is a crime, they were able to enter the rented hideout, where they found two thousand hits of hydrocodone in a plastic baggie and four semiautomatic pistols.

Charges of possession with intent to distribute and possession of firearms by a convicted felon were added to the resisting arrest charges, and the boyfriend was shipped off to a federal prison.

Lucas couldn't do much about the videos, which were out on the Internet, but the daughter was obscure enough, and the video was stupid enough, that the congressman thought he could probably let it go.

WORD ABOUT THE CASE got around, and that led to another. A U.S. senator from Wyoming had a sprawling ranch and a lot of cattle. The ranch backed up to an area of Yellowstone National Park that had wolves in it. Shot wolves began showing up on his property and then across the fence into the park. The senator had no problem with dead wolves personally but didn't like the idea of a criminal action that would have every environmentalist in the nation on his back, along with CBS and, worse, CNN.

"I'm not shooting the wolves, and my kids aren't shooting the wolves, and my hands aren't shooting the wolves, because I told them all we're a hell of a lot better off with a few dead heifers than we are with a few dead wolves, and that if I got even a hint that they were involved, I'd have their asses," he told Lucas. "I need this to stop, like, now."

He said the federal wildlife people hadn't been able to get anywhere because, basically, they weren't criminal investigators, and because everybody knew them by sight.

Lucas went out to Wyoming, spent a few days asking around, eventually found three brothers, all cowboys, who had a little sideline rustling cattle, spoke quietly to them about who might be doing what. They called it blackmail, but not wishing to have their sideline revealed, the cowboys were willing to speculate about the wolf shootings.

With a wildlife guy in tow to make everything legal, Lucas ambushed the senator's southern neighbor, who was stalking a decoy that looked a lot like a wolf, in the park. The senator and the neighbor had feuded over the years, some kind of complicated water dispute that Lucas didn't try to understand.

"That sonofabitch," the senator had said when Lucas called him. "He embarrasses the shit outta me and he gets rid of wolves that he don't want, neither. Two birds with one stone. I know for sure he's a fuckin' Democrat."

The neighbor didn't actually shoot anything, though, so wouldn't face much of a penalty, even if he was convicted. He claimed he'd been out for a walk and had taken his scoped semiauto .223 with him as protection against wolves . . . and bears and owls and chickadees and . . . whatever.

The senator told Lucas, "Don't worry your pretty little head about that, Lucas. That boy leases three thousand acres of BLM land to run his cattle on. I believe he's gonna find his contracts under review. That sonofabitch . . . Oh, hey, send me a couple of your business cards, would you?"

THOSE JOBS left Lucas feeling slightly corrupt—an ordinary citizen wouldn't get his kind of help. On the other hand, the confluence of crime, money, and political power did hold his interest. In both of the cases, the Marshals Service director had called him at home to hear what he had to say, and at the end of each report had said, "Keep up the good work. If you fuck up, I never heard of you."

AFTER THE ROUTINE WICHITA JOB, Lucas was sitting at the gate at Dwight Eisenhower National, reading an *Outside* magazine, when Porter Smalls called.

"I need you to come talk to me," Smalls said. "Soon as you can. Sooner."

"I saw a story in the *Pioneer Press* about the accident; sounded awful," Lucas said. "You okay?"

"Got a bloody nose from the air bag hitting me in the face, but

I'm not dead like CeeCee," Smalls said. "I called around and was told that you're not in town. When are you coming back?"

"I'm sitting in the Wichita airport right now. I'll be back home around eight o'clock tonight."

"Good. I'm getting on a plane at National in five minutes. We're supposed to get in at eight-twenty. Could you wait for me at the airport? A restaurant, or whatever? I haven't had time to eat."

"You know that Stone Arch place? We could get a beer. And if it's too crowded to talk, we could find an empty gate."

"See you there."

LUCAS WAS A TALL, tough-looking man, tanned with summer, a white knife-edge scar cutting across his eyebrow and onto his cheek, the product of a fishing misadventure. He had mild blue eyes, dark hair now touched with gray, and a smile that could turn mean. He liked to fight, not too often, but occasionally. The winter before, when he could no longer hold menus far enough away to see the fine print, he'd gotten his first pair of glasses, narrow gold-rimmed cheaters, that he hated but put up with.

"I look like Yoda or something," he grumbled to his wife, Weather.

"Yoda didn't wear glasses, as far as I know," Weather said.

"I don't mean the literal Yoda. I mean that guy from Tibet—you know, the religious guy."

"The Dalai Lama?"

"Yeah, that guy."

Weather looked at him, then said, "Yeah, you do kinda look

like him . . ." Which he didn't, but Weather refused to encourage whining. "Now, like the Dalai Lama, you can read the menu."

Although Lucas wasn't afraid of the occasional brawl, he feared flying. His rational mind forced his body onto airplanes, but his emotional, French-Canadian side told him that whole metal tubes flying through the air was a vicious scam that would end badly.

He tried to distract himself with *Outside*, but one of the cabin attendants was really, *really* good-looking, which meant that every time she passed he had to take off the reading glasses. The last time he did it, she patted him on the shoulder. She'd noticed, obviously familiar with male insecurities.

THE FLIGHT RAN LATE, as usual. As soon as the plane touched down, Lucas called Smalls, who answered on the first ring, and said, "I saw that you were coming in late. I got here five minutes ago. I'm heading over to the Stone Arch."

Lucas had no checked baggage. He grabbed his pack and his overnight bag and was on the Jetway ten minutes after the wheels touched down.

The bar was a typical airport restaurant, tables too close together, meant for singles or couples on their way to somewhere else rather than settling in for the evening. Smalls managed to find a table that was three down from the next closest drinker, who paid him no attention. Lucas spotted him, went over, dropped his pack and bag, shook hands, said, "Nice to see you, Senator," and sat down. "What's up?"

"Get a sandwich or something," Smalls said. "I've got a burger and beer on the way."

WHEN THE WAITRESS had come with Smalls's order and gone with Lucas's, Smalls leaned across the table and said, "This is going to sound insane, but that automobile accident? That was no accident. It was an assassination attempt. They were trying to kill me and they wound up killing CeeCee. I know who must've been behind it. You do, too."

Lucas said nothing for a moment, but when he did, it was: "Oh, Jesus Christ, Porter, are you sure?"

"Let me tell you about it," Smalls said.

HE DID, pausing only for the arrival of Lucas's Diet Coke and chicken sandwich, and when he finished his story, he asked, "See what I mean?"

"No sign of paint or metal from the other truck? None at all?"

"That's what the West Virginia accident investigator says, and he seemed competent. So, there's a mystery. People keep hinting that the mystery might be in my head. They ask if maybe the trauma of the event made me think we were hit when what actually happened was that CeeCee swerved to miss the truck and hit this little ankle-high roadside berm so hard that I thought the truck hit us. But that's not it. We *were* hit. Hard."

"You think the West Virginia cops are in on it?" Lucas asked.

"Oh, hell no. Well, not hell no, but it seems unlikely. That would make the whole conspiracy too big and unmanageable. You know, I never believed in hit men outside of the movies until Grant wiped me out two years ago. Sure enough, she had hit men. This is the same goddamn thing. She came after me again because I've been giving her a hard time."

"What do you want me to do?" Lucas asked.

"I WANT TO KNOW what happened, the best you can give it to me," Smalls said to him now. "Review the accident investigation. See if you can find the truck that hit us. West Virginia won't even be looking for it." Smalls's voice grew quieter. He glanced around the restaurant. "I want you to be very discreet. If it is Grant behind this, she'll probably try again. I oughta be dead right now. CeeCee did a hell of a job getting us into the trees that stopped us; I couldn't have done it."

Lucas nodded, and asked, "Is Grant going to run for president?"

"Yeah, probably. That's another problem, but I'm not asking you to solve that one. My first priority is staying alive." They sat and thought in silence for minute, then Smalls asked, "What do you think?"

"I believe you're telling the truth, but I'm not sure the truth is going to lead directly to Taryn Grant. I'll talk to the West Virginia cops, poke around, see what develops. Probably stay away from Grant, at least for the time being," Lucas said.

"I can have my staff line up anyone you want to talk to," Smalls said. "My chief of staff is named Kitten Carter. She's absolutely reliable and trustworthy. I'll have Kitten liaise with you, since she already knows about it."

"Good. I have to talk to my wife, but I can be in D.C. on Monday," Lucas said. He sat back and looked at Smalls, leaned forward and said, his voice as soft as Smalls's, "One more thing, though: if it's Taryn Grant, how did she get hooked up with another bunch of professional killers? She's only been in Washington for, what, two years?"

"I've got an answer for that," Smalls said. "She's on the Senate Intelligence Committee and she talks to spooks all the time. Then there's the fact that she could run for the presidency. She's young, great-looking, richer than God and willing to spend that money. It looks like we'll have a seriously unpopular president in two more years who might either take a chance and run again and risk getting blown out or leave it to some other guy who'll still be carrying that unpopularity on his back. So, she's a real possibility. When the people in Washington sniff out a real possibility . . . well, they can't climb on the bandwagon fast enough. Everybody's got to have a bandwagon going into a presidential election."

"Even killers?"

"The intelligence community," Smalls said, sitting back and simultaneously turning to look down the concourse, as though he might spot a spy. "Listen, Lucas, there are literally hundreds of trained killers out of the military and working as contractors with the private intelligence organizations. Most of them are fine people. Patriots who have risked their lives for the country. But some of these guys aren't so fine, and I've had a few of them testifying before committees. They don't have any real limits, moral or otherwise. They live on risk. They love it. You show them Grant's kind of money and the possibility that she might wind up in the White House? They'll be available. That's my gut feeling."

"Why you and why now?"

"Because I've been pissing on Grant ever since the election and some of it is beginning to stick."

"Maybe you shouldn't piss for a while," Lucas suggested.

Smalls grinned, and said, "I'm hiding out in town for now, and I've hired a couple of ex-cops to cover me. If you jump on this, maybe you'll be able to tell me how much trouble I'm in. Be nice to know, before I get back out in the open."

"Let me ask you a couple of uncomfortable questions . . . How's your marriage?"

"Well, you know . . ."

"You've got a few bucks yourself . . ." Smalls's financial disclosure forms, filed at the time of the election and printed in the Twin Cities newspapers, hinted at a fortune in the neighborhood of a hundred million dollars. "And if your wife thought you were about to, uh, move on . . ."

Smalls shook his head. "She knows I'm not."

"Your daughter once mentioned something about a Lithuanian lover. If you were to die, who inherits? Would the Lithuanian lover be in line for a payday? Directly or indirectly?"

"No. My wife's not stupid," Smalls said. "Besides, most of the money would go to the kids, after the government takes its cut. On balance, she's financially better off with me alive."

"Okay."

"Again, I would like to stay that way: alive."

"What about your friend Whitehead? Anybody want to get rid of her?" Lucas asked.

In exasperation, Smalls jabbed his index finger into the tabletop a half dozen times, hissing, "Lucas! Lucas! Pay attention! Keep your eye on the goddamn ball here! It was Grant! No, I can't think of anybody who'd want to kill CeeCee. She's been divorced for fifteen years, her husband is as rich as she is, and he's got a whole 'nother family. CeeCee has two adult daughters, nice girls, work in L.A., got all the money they need, they produce movies or some goofy shit like that. Listen: we decided to run up to the cabin at the last minute, nobody even knew we were going, somebody was watching us."

"All right, I need to eliminate the obvious possibilities," Lucas said. "I'll take a look at it. You might want to call the Marshals Service director and have a chat. Not about Grant, though. Tell him you want me to review the situation."

"I'll do that. First thing tomorrow. As far as Grant goes: if you have to poke a stick into that wasp's nest, be my guest. But be careful. Nobody seems to believe me, but these guys who tried to kill me, and murdered CeeCee, they're pros."

AS LUCAS DROVE HOME, he thought about U.S. senator Taryn Grant. Two and a half years earlier, she'd knocked Porter Smalls out of the Senate, beating him 51 percent to 49 percent, after what Smalls called the ugliest political trick in the history of the Republic.

Lucas had been virtually certain that Grant was behind it, working through a Democratic political operator known to be a bagman and sometime blackmailer. The man had planted a load of child porn on Smalls's computer at his campaign office, where it was "discovered" by an intern. Lucas had proven Smalls to be innocent, but too late: Grant was elected.

All of that was complicated by the fact that the man who planted the child porn sensed an opportunity and had tried to blackmail Grant. He'd been murdered for his trouble, and three more people had been killed by Election Day. After the election, Smalls had openly accused Grant of orchestrating the murders and planting the porn.

The people of Minnesota had begun to believe him. Two years after losing the first election, he had been voted back into the Senate in the next one. That was not good when you were dealing with a psychopath like Taryn Grant, Lucas thought. If Smalls was proving to be a threat, she would kill her way into the presidency as easily as she'd killed her way into the Senate, if she could do it without being caught.

The last time out, she'd beaten Lucas. He hadn't forgotten or forgiven. If Smalls was correct about an assassination attempt, he'd have another shot at her.

And that made him happy.

WHEN LUCAS GOT HOME, he kissed his wife Weather and his two kids, sent the kids to bed, told Weather about Smalls and that he'd be leaving again on Monday.

The next day was a Saturday, and since Weather wouldn't be working and didn't have to get up early—she was a surgeon who usually left the house at six-thirty—she took Lucas to bed and did her best to wear him out. Feeling pleasantly unfocused, they'd later sat, semi-naked, on the second-story sunporch with lemonades and looked out into the soft summer night, and she asked, "How long will you be gone?"

"Don't know—I have a couple of friends in Washington, but they can't help me with this."

"Not even Mallard?"

Mallard was a deputy director of the FBI who'd worked with Lucas on a couple of high-profile cases.

"Mallard is too political. He wouldn't want to get caught in a cross fire between Grant and Smalls. Besides, before I do anything else, I've got to make sure Smalls's story makes sense. If it does, I need to talk to somebody who's got an inside feel for the Senate. Somebody who could tell me who Grant might be talking to . . . who could hook her up with a professional killer. I need to know if there might be somebody who'd want to get rid of Porter even more than Grant does."

"Porter is an enormous asshole," she said. "You might have a lengthy list of candidates."

"He made you laugh, when we had dinner that time," Lucas said.

"He can be charming," Weather said. "He has a sense of humor. And he's got great political stories. But he's also doing his best to wipe out Medicaid. And ban abortion. And run every Mexican kid out of the country. And make sure every man, woman, and child has a handgun."

"Yeah, he's a right-winger all right," Lucas said. "But you don't get assassinated for that. At least, not yet."

"No, but if somebody did assassinate him, I probably wouldn't march on Washington in protest," Weather said.

"Shame on you," Lucas said. "I gotta tell you, not being a big political brain like some of the women I'm married to, I kinda like the guy, even if I don't care for his politics."

She let that go, and after a while said, "Great night."

"Yes, it is," Lucas agreed, looking up at the stars.

"Just try not to get killed, okay?"

3

When U.S. senator Taryn Grant heard that Smalls had survived, she got Jack Parrish in her basement SCIF and screamed at him for a while. SCIF, short for Sensitive Compartmented Information Facility, was where you went to discuss classified information, which this sure as hell was.

"You said it was a done deal," she shouted. "You said it was a perfect setup."

"It was," Parrish said, settling on a sofa. "I didn't tell you it was a done deal—I told you it was ninety-nine percent. Even a hundred-to-one shot comes in every once in a while, and that's what happened."

"Now we've got a murder on our hands," she shrieked. She was trembling with rage. "Instead of an accident, we've got a murder. You'll have the FBI on me. Smalls will tell the FBI that I was behind it, and he'll be right, won't he? You silly shithead . . ."

She went on for a while, and Parrish, still sitting on the sofa, looked at his watch. He had a meeting with the three guys who'd screwed this particular pooch and couldn't be more than fifteen minutes late. More than fifteen minutes and they'd be gone, as a routine precaution.

"Don't look at your fuckin' watch," Grant shouted, saliva flying across the room. "Don't look at your fuckin' watch!"

"Can't be late for a meeting," Parrish said. He yawned, then asked, "Are you done yet?"

"Am I done yet? No, but you might be."

"I don't think so," Parrish said, staying cool. He'd been screamed at before, and by senators with a lot more seniority than Grant. "We have way too many reasons to hang together, because, like the man said, if we don't, we'll hang separately. The fact is, the accident should have worked. If it had, we'd have taken a load off our backs and gotten rid of a major roadblock between you and the White House. Sometimes, things just don't work—but you wouldn't have gotten better odds—anywhere, anytime—on this one. And there's no evidence that it was a hit. There's nothing. The West Virginia cops think Smalls is a head case."

Grant's face was purple, but she struggled to calm herself. Parrish was right: even the best-laid plans failed sometimes. But he was wrong about the odds. She was extremely good at figuring odds, and there would have been a better way to do this. Example number one: find out where Smalls was going out for dinner and then shoot him in the back and take his money. That was simple enough, and nobody would be able to prove that it wasn't a robbery. Parrish's plan had had too many moving parts, and neither one of them had recognized that.

And she said so.

Parrish shrugged. "You could be right. On the other hand, if we'd shot him, the FBI would be all over the place and they'd never let go. The Senate wouldn't let them. They'd have had the director up on the Hill every goddamn week until he came up with the perp."

"You supply the perpetrator, dumbass," Grant shouted. "You don't have to supply a mountain of evidence! All you have to do is find some broken-ass Negro and put the gun in his backpack. That's all anybody wants."

"All right, I'll talk to the guys about what happened and get them thinking about some other possibilities. Smalls is a real problem. You saw what the Republicans did with Obama and that birth certificate. No evidence of anything, but they kept talking, and that bullshit stuck with some people. If Smalls keeps talking about what happened during your election campaign, I don't think you'll go all the way. He's got to be shut up," Parrish said. And, "By the way, if you *ever* use the word 'Negro' outside this room, you can kiss the White House good-bye."

SHE THOUGHT ABOUT IT for a couple of seconds—couldn't argue with that, Parrish was right. She had a stack of magazines on her desk. After she squared them, she picked up the top one, a *Vanity Fair*, and dropped it in the wastebasket. "All right. We went off half-cocked on this. You came up with an idea, you had the guys, and I bought it. If we try again, it's going to have to be something a little more subtle. Can't shoot him; not now. I need ideas."

"We'll work on it," Parrish said. Now that she'd calmed down, he realized that he could smell her, a smoky perfume that hung in the air like a Valentine's invitation. "Maybe . . . I don't know. Another scandal? I like that whole child porn thing that came up in your election run: that was cool. We'll think about it."

"Well, we can't do child porn, that's for sure. And this isn't the Middle East; we can't cut him down on some trumped-up bullshit that people will believe because they belong to some religious cult," she said. "Next time, it better work or you and I are going to have a major problem. A real serious major problem."

He may have sneered at her when he responded, "You know, you have to realize your limitations, Senator. Exactly what are you going to do? Report me to the police? You'll go right down with me. We're welded together. You go to the White House, I go with you. Get used to it."

GRANT MOVED BEHIND HER DESK and gave it a kick. Parrish thought for a second that she'd done it out of anger, or had stumbled, but she stooped, and when she came up, she had a gun in her hand. Parrish knew all about guns and recognized it: a Beretta. A big one, a military-style 92. Loaded with 9mm man-killers, it'd produce internal cavitation that you could fit a football in.

She was moving toward him, and he was pressing back in the couch. He heard the safety click off, and if he tried to get up, she might pull the trigger.

"Don't do that," he blurted. "I don't . . ."

"What am I gonna do? Who will I get to do it? Is that what you want to know?" She was shouting again, and there was a fleck of saliva at the corner of her mouth. "What if I get me? How'd that work?"

The muzzle was three feet from his nose, and he muttered, "That'd work fine, I guess. That'd be . . . Don't do this . . ."

Grant's finger was white on the trigger, and Parrish could plainly see that from thirty-six inches away, and he could hear her labored breathing . . . and then she stepped back, dropped her voice, and snarled, "Don't ever fuck with me. I know your background. I know you're a little crazy. Keep this in mind: I'm way, way crazier than you are."

He hadn't started to sweat until she backed away, but he was sweating now. "I see that," he said. The gun was still pointed at his nose, her finger was still white on the trigger. She looked like she wanted to pull it, he could see it in her glittering blue eyes. "I'm okay with it. I won't make a single fucking move without talking to you about it."

"Better," Grant said. She pointed the muzzle at the ceiling. "Now, is there anything we have to do about Smalls? I mean, right now?"

"Probably best to lay back in the weeds and not do anything," Parrish said, his voice trembling. He tried to smooth it out. "If we decide to take another run at him, we have time. I'll tell you what, though: he's got his oppo people digging around through your investments back in Minnesota. If you want to be president, there better not be much back there."

"There's not. Nothing illegal. Not that he could get at anyway." She stooped and dropped the gun in a desk drawer. Parrish noted which one it was in case he needed that information in the future. He would not be back down in this basement without a gun in his belt.

Though he probably wouldn't need one. Before this confrontation, he'd thought of Grant as a Minnesota blonde, with everything that might suggest: nice, sweet, maybe a little above average. But not too much above average. And certainly not dumb.

That had changed in the last two minutes.

Two minutes later, when he went out the door, still alive, he realized that he'd suddenly come to respect her, as much as any sociopath could.

She's crazier than I am . . .

WHEN HE WAS GONE, Grant remained in the basement, brooding about the mistake with Smalls and the possible consequences.

Would the cops figure out what had happened? Was there any way she could interfere without being tagged as responsible? Could Smalls somehow be blamed for the "accident"? If she got rid of Parrish—permanently, with a bullet—would that seal her off from any investigation? One other man knew about her arrangement with Parrish and had supplied the operators who went after Smalls. If she killed Parrish, he'd still be out there.

WHEN SHE'D BEEN ELECTED to the Senate, Taryn Grant had bought the mansion in Georgetown, which backed up to Dumbarton Park. The house was supposedly seventy years old, but if there were more than a few molecules left from the original structure, she hadn't been able to find them. Built of red brick, with a terrific garden behind eight-foot brick walls, everything had been "updated" to the point where the house might as well have been built a year earlier.

She had an eye for good houses, and as stately as this house was, and as well located, the major attraction was that it had been previously occupied by the outgoing secretary of defense. The basement had been reworked at taxpayer expense to be absolutely secure and was known as a SCIF space, she'd learned when she got to Washington. She'd had her own security firm go over it inch by inch and they'd found no faults. Sitting down in the basement, she might as well have been in a bank vault.

If she'd actually shot Parrish, her biggest problem would have been cleanup and disposal, because nobody outside the place would have seen or heard anything. And, she thought, it might still come to that.

GRANT WAS RICH.

She was also tall, blond, and physically fit. She controlled most of a billion dollars, her share of her family's agricultural commodities business, the fifth-largest privately held company in the United States, now run by an older brother. In addition, she owned two small but profitable Internet companies, run by remote control through CEOs as ruthless as she was, but with less money.

As a tall, blond, physically fit woman, there were rumors about her supposedly voracious sexuality, though nobody had the photos. The fact was, she was okay with occasional sex, if performed discreetly, with attractive men, but she was hardly voracious.

Power, not sex, was the drug she mainlined. She wasn't much interested in policy, or the Senate, or being on television: she wanted the hammer, the biggest one she could find. Barack Obama was her hero for one reason and one reason alone: he'd served a single term in the U.S. Senate before he became president.

"Madam President" had a nice round sound to it.

If everything went just right, Grant was two years out.

But not everything was going just right because Parrish's goons had failed on what had seemed a straightforward mission: kill Smalls and make it look like an accident. Parrish had stood in the SCIF and laid it out like a commando mission: "That's all these guys have done, for most of their adult lives. The people they took out . . . not all of them were from enemy countries. Sometimes, you need to remove a particular guy in a friendly country."

She'd asked, "Like Pakistan?"

"Yeah. And like Germany."

FOUR DAYS AFTER she'd pulled the gun on Parrish, Grant had him back in the SCIF. A blinking red light on her desk told her that he was armed. She opened the desk drawer where she kept the Beretta so it would be handy, but she didn't take it out.

She was angry all over again, though this time better controlled.

"You know that there was some controversy around my election . . . that people died," she said. It wasn't a question.

"Yes, I know," Parrish said.

"Then you know the name Lucas Davenport?"

"I read all the clips. He was the cop who led the investigation," Parrish said.

"A year or so after the investigation, he was appointed to be a U.S. Marshal," Grant said. "He got the job because Smalls and the former Minnesota governor . . ."

"Henderson, the guy who ran for vice president."

"Yes. They pulled some strings in Washington, got him the new job," Grant said. "I don't know what his position is, except that he was involved in a major shoot-out down in Texas last year. Anyway, guess what? Smalls has him on your accident case."

"He won't find anything," Parrish said. "There's nothing to find. I've read the West Virginia State Police files now—I had a guy get copies off their computers—and they've officially determined that it was a one-car accident resulting in minor injuries to one person and death to the other. No alcohol involved, no charges pending. Routine. Case closed."

"Happy to hear it. But I need to know what Davenport's doing," Grant said. "He is intelligent and he is dangerous. When I say dangerous, I mean a killer. You think your superspies can handle that?"

Parrish didn't like the sarcasm, but he said, "Sure. I'll need some money."

"We have a family office in Minneapolis," Grant said. "There's a man there named Frank Reese. I will send him a message, telling him to expect you or one of your associates. He will give you whatever amount you need, in cash, but I expect it to be accounted for. I'm not cheap, but I won't tolerate being chumped."

"I understand," Parrish said. "When you say send a message . . ."

"Thoroughly encrypted, to a site that only Reese and I know about," Grant said.

"Good. I'm impressed," Parrish said. "Look, if this gets complicated, would it be better to ask Reese for a big chunk all at once or better to go back to him several times?"

"How much do you need?" she asked.

"I don't know. If every time we go back, it could be tied to a particular . . . event . . . that could be a problem. We may need several events over the next couple of years."

She nodded. "I'll tell Reese to give you a half," she said. "How soon can you look at Davenport?"

"Half of what?"

"Half a million," she said. "Is that going to cover it?"

Impressed again, though Parrish didn't say so. "I'll fly out to

Minneapolis this afternoon. I'll want to handle Reese myself. Keep the loop tight," Parrish said. "I'll have somebody on Davenport right away, figure out where he's staying."

"He probably doesn't have a hotel yet. I've been told he won't actually get here until tomorrow or the next day."

"Where are you getting this information?" Parrish asked.

"I have a friend in the Smalls organization."

"Huh." Impressed again. "If Davenport's flying commercial, we can pick out his flight and spot him at the airport when he gets here."

"Do that." She waved him toward the door. "Stay in touch."

On the way out, Parrish paused, then turned. "You want to know everything, so I have a proposition that you might be interested in. Or, you can kill it."

"What?"

"If this Davenport guy wasn't investigating the incident, who would be?"

She thought about it, and said, "I don't know. Maybe nobody. Davenport has a personal problem with me. He thinks I had something to do with the murders around my election. He wants to get me. Nobody else, that I can think of, has the same incentive, except maybe Smalls himself."

"Still, he's a small-town cop, right?"

"Jesus, Parrish, it's not a small town," Grant said. "There are three million people in the Twin Cities metro area. Davenport was an agent for the Bureau of Criminal Apprehension. They've got the technical abilities of the FBI."

"Still . . ."

"Still, bullshit. I know a lot about Davenport. He dropped out of law enforcement for a couple of years, invented a computer software company, and sold out for something between twenty and thirty million dollars, and he's now worth maybe forty million. He built that company and sold it in two years, starting with nothing. If you underestimate him, he'll eat you alive."

"All right, I get it. If we had a guy who wasn't as smart and didn't have the incentive, that would be better for us, right? What if Davenport got mugged and hurt? Not killed, but hurt bad enough to take him out of it. Take him out long enough that the Smalls accident is old news. Antique news."

Grant leaned back in the office chair, pursed her lips. After a while, she said, "That has some appeal. For one thing, I'd like to see him get hurt. He does have a history as a shooter, though. It'd be dangerous."

"My guys could pull it off. Abort at the last second, if something doesn't smell right. They'd rob him, so it'd look just like a mugging."

She considered for another moment, and said, "Let's take a look at him first. See what he's up to, whether it'll go anywhere. Then we can consider taking him down."

Parrish nodded. "I'll have somebody look at his hotel room. Tell your man in Minneapolis I'm on my way."

WHEN PARRISH HAD GONE, Grant closed down the SCIF, found the housekeeper, told her to bring a fried-egg sandwich with ketchup and onions and a glass of Chablis into the breakfast room.

She had homework to do, constituency stuff, boring but necessary. She read through notes from her chief of staff and her issues team, but when the sandwich came, she put the paper aside and ate, peering out into the backyard garden. Three huge oaks, three smaller hard maples, a Japanese maple specimen that would turn flaming red in September, a ginkgo tree, all surrounded by a rose garden.

She thought about Davenport. She'd told Parrish that she was crazy; and she'd heard that Parrish was a couple of fries short of a Happy Meal himself.

In her mind, there were all kinds of crazy, including a couple of kinds that could be useful if they didn't take you too far out. A touch of OCD helped you focus obsessively, when you needed to do that. A bit of the sociopath was always helpful in business: you took care of yourself because nobody else would.

Grant was all of that, a little bit of OCD, a little bit of sociopathy . . . and she thought Davenport was as well. He was surely a sociopath, given his record of killings, she thought. How could he live with himself if he weren't?

The problem was, he was also seriously intelligent. She wasn't sure that Parrish appreciated that. Davenport had made that big wad of software cash, but instead of trying to work it, he'd gone back to hunting.

He was nuts, she thought, like she was. He was coming for her.

Something had to be done.

4

Lucas flew early on Monday, a blessedly short flight from Minneapolis into Washington. One of Smalls's Minnesota aides had dropped a map and a key at his house on Saturday.

He was carrying two substantial bags with him, one with neatly layered summer suits and shirts, underwear, socks, and Dopp kit, as well as a couple of pairs of gym shorts, several heavy T-shirts for workouts, a pair of cross-training shoes, and three burner phones he'd bought at a Best Buy on Sunday.

The other bag, a heavy-duty Arc'teryx backpack, contained his laptop, an iPad, yellow legal pads and mechanical pencils, a compact voice recorder, a Sony RX10 III camera, and all the associated chargers, cables, batteries, and memory cards. The camera was a chunk, and he was tempted to leave it behind, but Weather had bought it for him when he joined the Marshals Service, so he felt bound to take it.

Getting the rental car was a minor hassle, but an hour after he landed, Lucas headed out of Washington in a rented black Range Rover Evoque, with a back window about the size of his hand.

Hot day: the mountains ahead were covered with a blue haze of humidity that shimmered like a gauze curtain above the interstate. The car's navigation system took him on twisty highways through the mountains and most of the way to Smalls's cabin.

The nav got lost the last two miles, and he went the rest of the way with the paper map.

He was aware that he had driven past the place where Smalls had gone off the road, but he ignored it—he wanted to start from the cabin and experience the drive out as Smalls and Whitehead had.

The cabin sat a hundred feet back from the road, hidden by a screen of trees, which opened to a grassy lawn that spread up a short slope to the cabin. And it was, indeed, a cabin—bronze-colored logs with pine-green-painted steps leading to a front porch. A pickup had backed up the driveway with a flat trailer behind it, and an elderly woman with tight white hair was riding a John Deere lawn mower around the yard. When Lucas got out of the Evoque, she turned the mower off, took off her earmuffs, and asked, "Y'all lost?"

"Not if this is Senator Smalls's place."

"It is," the old woman said. "But he ain't here."

"I know. He's in Minneapolis," Lucas said. He showed her his marshal's badge, and said, "I'm a U.S. Marshal, working on a case with Senator Smalls. He gave me a key."

"You investigating that wreck?" she asked.

"Yeah, checking it out."

"Tell you what, marshal, that was one fucked-up Cadillac. I went over to Bill Bunson's yard and took a look at it."

"Where's that at?" Lucas asked.

"Up to Green Spring," she said.

"Still there?"

"Unless the cops hauled it away. Or the senator did," she said.

"Maybe I'll go up and take a look," Lucas said.

LUCAS WENT into the cabin, which was hot and stuffy, punched Smalls's code into the security system, turned on the air-conditioning, peeled off his jacket, got a bottle of Fat Tire from the refrigerator and a sack of pretzels from the cupboard, and went back out and sat on the porch.

The old woman had moved around behind the cabin, still mowing, and five minutes after Lucas got outside she drove the mower back around to the front lawn and onto the trailer behind her pickup truck. She killed the mower's engine, pulled up the loading ramp, and locked it, and said to Lucas, "Good hot day for a beer."

"There are a few more in the refrigerator. Help yourself."

"I'm not sure the senator would be okay with that." But she didn't walk away from the offer.

"I'll tell him I drank two," Lucas said.

The old woman nodded, and said, "My name's Janet Walker, and I thank you kindly."

She went inside and a minute later came back out with another Fat Tire, sat down on a wicker porch chair. "You getting anything good on the accident?"

Lucas shook his head. "Got to Washington about three hours ago, from Minnesota. I'm waiting for a West Virginia highway patrolman to show up. He's gonna tell me all about it."

"The rumor around here is, the senator got drunk and drove off the side of the road and blamed it on his dead girlfriend," Walker said.

"Girlfriend? I thought she was a political aide."

"Yeah, well, I don't doubt she was aidin' the senator, one way or the other . . . Don't tell the senator I said that, I need the work."

"You're safe with me," Lucas said. "You know anything about the accident?"

"Not a fuckin' thing," Walker said. She tipped her head back and took a generous swallow of beer, and when she took the bottle down she said, "Nothing like an ice-cold beer after you mowed yourself some weeds . . . Don't know nothing about the accident, but I heard that the senator told the cops that they was run off the road by a pickup truck. There *was* a couple of strange guys going through here with a pickup that weekend. Seen them around the day before the accident and not seen them since."

"Is that unusual?"

"Well . . . no, maybe not. Maybe you remember that kind of thing when something like the accident sets you off. These guys seemed to be looking around, but not doing anything in particular. Saw them myself, and my boss saw them, too. The kind of guys who are in really good shape. Those black razor sunglasses and ball caps, squared-away, military-looking."

"Huh. Anybody tell the cops?"

"Tell them what? That we saw some guys in a pickup truck?"

"What kind of truck?" Lucas asked.

"Black Ford F-250. New," she said. "Or almost new,"

"Local plates?"

"Didn't notice."

WALKER DIDN'T HAVE much else to say. She finished the beer, and headed up the road in a cloud of yellow dust.

Lucas went back inside the cabin and poked around for a

while. There were four smallish bedrooms, the master with a king-sized bed, the other three with two beds and bathroom each.

Lucas owned a cabin himself and recognized the layout: it was more or less a dormitory meant to sleep as many people as possible inside a fairly spartan envelope. The living room was separated from the compact kitchen by a breakfast bar, with a dining table and eight chairs parallel to the bar. A poker table was sitting in a corner, and there were scratches on the plank floor where it'd been pushed into the middle of the room when needed. A couch and four overstuffed chairs faced a sixty-inch TV.

He'd been looking around for ten minutes—he'd spent two of those minutes with *The Joy of Sex*, which he found under the bed—when a car pulled into the driveway. He went back out on the porch as Carl Armstrong was climbing out of a state police vehicle, a blue-and-gold Chevy SUV. Armstrong was Lucas's age, a heavyset man with a red face and a gray flattop haircut, wearing tan slacks and a blue dress shirt. He raised a hand to Lucas and walked around to the passenger side, popped open the door, and came out with an old-fashioned leather briefcase.

"You Marshal Davenport?" he asked, as he came up to the porch steps.

"That's me," Lucas said. "You're Carl?"

"Yup. Damn, it's hot."

"I got a key from the senator, turned the air-conditioning on. Come on in. You want a beer?"

ARMSTRONG DIDN'T drink on duty, so Lucas got them two Diet Pepsis. They sat at the dining table, and Armstrong produced an accordion envelope from his briefcase that contained a stack of paper, several sheaves held together with spring clips.

He peeled them apart and shoved them across the table at Lucas. "Photos of the car, reports from the lab, photos and reports from the scene, transcripts of interviews with Senator Smalls, a transcript of the 911 call. It's all yours."

"Senator Smalls said you seemed competent," Lucas said. "I'll go through the paper inch by inch, but what I want is your best judgment . . . off the record . . . What happened here?"

Armstrong had an accent that Lucas could only think of as wiry, something like an early Hank Williams recording on vinyl. He said, "I do appreciate the senator saying that. He can be scary if you're sitting on the far end of some federal funding, you know what I mean? Wouldn't want him pissed off at West Virginia 'cause of something I said."

Lucas nodded. "I was with the Minnesota Bureau of Criminal Apprehension for years before I took this job. People would get seriously puckered up around federal grant time."

"Exactly," Armstrong said. He put his elbows on the table and linked his fingers. "Anyway, nineteen out of twenty accident investigators would give you the same story about what happened that night: maybe the senator's girlfriend got careless, or maybe there was another pickup that scared her and she drove off the road. Or—don't quote me on this—the senator reached over and gave her a little pluck, and over the side they went. Because there's no physical evidence of anything else."

"She wasn't on her cell phone?"

"No—one of the first things we checked. The senator wasn't, either. They both made calls earlier in the afternoon, but nothing after about four o'clock, when the senator made a call to a woman in Washington who works as an aide."

"A Kitten Carter?"

"Yes. Miz Carter said it was a routine business call. I didn't ask what it concerned because that has no connection with the accident."

"So, nineteen out of twenty would say Senator Smalls's story about the other truck was wrong, one way or another. That nothing hit them. And what would the twentieth accident investigator say?" Lucas asked.

"That would be me," Armstrong said. "I've filed all these reports, and if anybody looks at them, they'll get the same conclusion as the other nineteen. But I'll tell you, marshal, there's something not right about it. They went off the road where it's perfectly straight, at the top of a hill, at a place with the biggest drop into the river. Wasn't any reason for Miz Whitehead to jerk the steering wheel to the right. Not unless she was trying to kill them both. The way she fought that truck going down the hill, it sure don't look like she was trying to kill herself. If somebody was trying to kill them, and if they tried to do it by ramming that Caddy, that's the exact spot they would have picked. The road is narrow, and gravel don't give the best footing, and if the truck was overtaking them and gave them a good whack . . ."

"Over they'd go," Lucas suggested.

Armstrong bobbed his head. "Senator Smalls's story felt strong to me. You couldn't fake a story like that and sell it to me: I'd sniff it out, if he was lyin'. With the senator, I had the feeling that he was telling the truth. Or, at least, thinks he was. Why would he lie? Neither one of them was drunk, and she was driving. No crime there. Now, he says that when they left the cabin, he sort of dozed off. He woke up when Miz Whitehead said something about the jerk coming up behind them. Is it possible that he thought they were hit, that he believes they were hit, when what actually happened is that Miz Whitehead got scared and yanked the wheel over? I mean, there's no physical evidence that they were hit by another truck. How do you pull that off?"

"Don't know, off the top of my head. If they were professionals . . ."

"That's where I get off the bus," Armstrong said. "I don't believe in that kind of thing. Professional killers."

"I understand that," Lucas said. "Look, I don't know anything about accident investigation, but you'd say . . . that it seems completely unlikely, that there are much better alternative explanations, but your gut tells you something unusual happened."

"That's it," Armstrong said. "My gut don't write the reports, though."

"Let's go look at the scene," Lucas said.

LUCAS TURNED ON the security system, locked the cabin, and on the way out to their vehicles he told Armstrong about his chat with Janet Walker, about the men with the sunglasses and the black Ford F-250. "If one turns up with some unusual dents . . ."

"I'll make a note," Armstrong said. "Maybe even spend a couple of hours sniffing around."

ARMSTRONG LED HIM up the track that went out to the state road and down that road to the point where Whitehead and Smalls went over the side. They pulled well off to the left, and Lucas got out and looked down toward the river.

"South Branch of the Potomac—real nice river," Armstrong said. He pointed to a notch in the thin roadside berm. "That's where they went over. You can still see the busted-up brush, and the tracks where Miz Whitehead steered along the hillside until they hit the trees."

Lucas looked down the hill, at the tracks. A hundred and fifty feet down, the hillside suddenly steepened, not quite to a ninety-degree drop, but close enough. If they'd gone over, they might have bounced once, but they would have been mostly airmailed right into the river.

"Hell of a job, getting over to the trees," Lucas said.

"Almost saved them. Should have," Armstrong said. "Car rolled over . . . We think that's when Miz Whitehead was killed, at the very end of the incident. They were crashing down through those trees, some of them pretty big—it looks to me like she was deliberately trying to hit them, to slow the car down—and a branch or part of a tree come through the driver's-side window and hit her in the temple, poked a hole right through her skull and into her brain. The medical examiner found pieces of bark inside her skull. His report is in the file."

He went through the sequence as reported by Smalls, and he and Lucas walked down along the hillside through knee-high weeds and grass to the spot where the Cadillac rolled over. Lucas could still see black patches of dried oil on the pale grass. "According to Senator Smalls, he crawled out of the pickup, which was upside down, got a pistol out of the back, because he thought the people in the truck might be coming down after them, and then dragged Miz Whitehead out. Nobody came down the hill. If there was a truck, it kept going. Sheriff's deputies took about eleven minutes to get here, from the first 911 call. The ambulance got here a minute later. First state police car got here ten minutes after that."

"Is that fast or slow?" Lucas asked.

"Not real quick . . . probably average. The deputies got a lot of territory to cover out here."

LUCAS WALKED SLOWLY back up the hill, along the scarred earth and brush left behind by the Escalade, and asked, "No sign of another vehicle's tracks?"

"Not in the loose gravel," Armstrong said. "If there were any, the responding deputies drove over them. Didn't find any broken glass, either."

"How far to the nearest highway from here?"

"Couldn't tell you precisely. Maybe a few miles. Maybe a bit more, maybe a bit less. We could do a Google Earth, if you want."

"I can do that," Lucas said, "if I need it."

THEY WERE BOTH sweating heavily by the time they got back to the cars, and Armstrong asked Lucas if he'd be staying overnight at the cabin. Lucas shook his head: "I've got some interviews to do in Washington. I'll give you my cell phone number in case you need to reach me."

"Wouldn't count on us coming up with anything new," Armstrong said. "With the senator involved, we pulled out all the stops on this one."

"I'd like to look at the Cadillac myself," Lucas said. "I understand it's still around."

"Yeah, the truck was pulled up the hill by the local towing service. Hell of a job, too: took two trucks four hours. If you want to follow me, it's probably twenty minutes from here."

LUCAS FOLLOWED.

Bunson Towing was run out of a junkyard set in a patch of trees that butted up against a railroad right-of-way. The truck had been parked under a tin-roofed shed and wrapped in a blue plastic tarp. A man Armstrong introduced as Lawrie Bunson came out of the yard's office and helped Armstrong pull the tarp off.

The truck hadn't been cleaned up, and the blood on the front seat had gone seriously bad in the heat. Flies were crawling all over it, buzzing around them after the tarp was off. Lucas didn't look, but he was sure that if he stuck his head inside, he'd find a mother lode of maggots.

"Stinks," Bunson said. To Armstrong: "When you think they're going to move it?"

"You seen an insurance agent yet?"

"Not yet. Some chick called from Washington and said State Farm would be out, but I ain't seen hide nor hair of nobody from State Farm," Bunson said.

"You will, I'm sure," Armstrong said. "This machine is too pricey to let it go."

"I'll talk to somebody, get them out here," Lucas said.

"Don't make no nevermind to me," Bunson said. "I get twenty dollars a day for storage."

They walked around the Escalade, looking at the damage, which was worse than Lucas had imagined it. The truck had probably sustained fifteen or twenty separate impacts, both sides, the front and the back, even the roof, had taken a pounding. The left front wheel had folded under the truck, with the frame sitting on the side of the tire, and the driver's-side window had been smashed entirely out of its frame. All the rest of the glass was cracked, including the glass in the mirrors, as well as the head- and taillights.

Lucas checked the side, where there were four wide marks that looked like they could have been made by trees. Armstrong said, pointing them out, "We took biological samples off here . . . and we matched them to the trees down the hill. The bark is right."

Lucas walked to the Evoque, got the Sony camera, and took several shots of the Cadillac's driver's side.

"All right," he said after a few more minutes, brushing a fly away from his face, "I'm done here. Thank you both. Carl, you see or hear anything more, or figure anything out, call me. About anything, no matter how small, anytime."

Lucas gave Armstrong a card with his cell phone number on it, they shook hands, and Lucas headed back to Washington. He was sure he was imagining it, but the stink of the rotting blood seemed to cling to his clothing, maybe permanently. He pushed a few buttons until he found the one for the sunroof, opened it wide, and breathed in all the great weed- and flower-scented country air.

5

Lucas checked into the Watergate Hotel because Smalls owned a condo in one of the Watergate complex buildings and Kitten Carter had an apartment in another. The hotel was okay, if a little heavy on the sixties décor in the lobby. Lucas got a small suite, jumped in the shower, brushed his teeth, put on slacks, a pink golf shirt, and a blue jacket, and called Carter.

"Are you available?" he asked when she'd answered the phone and he'd identified himself.

"I am," she said.

"You want to come to me or should I come to you?"

"I could meet you in the hotel restaurant in twenty minutes. Should be fairly quiet tonight." Her contralto voice had a slight growl to it.

"That'll work," Lucas said.

"How will I know you?" she asked.

"I'll be the guy in the blue jacket and pink golf shirt. Probably not too many of those."

"Not with a gun under the jacket."

LUCAS DID HAVE A GUN under his jacket, a new one, a Walther PPQ, the same .40 S&W caliber as the Glock pistols issued to most U.S.

Marshals. Lucas had one of those, too, but didn't like it and didn't carry it. He'd begun to carry the new pistol on his left hip, in a cross-draw position, which made it easier to get at and less obvious than the .45 he'd carried for most of his career.

When he was checking into the hotel, he'd been eye-checked by a security man in a gray suit. Lucas nodded at him, and, after he got his keys, walked over with his badge and ID case. "Just so you know," he said.

"I suspected, but thank you," the security guy said. "You gonna be here long?"

"I don't know," Lucas said. "I'm working."

"I'll pass the word to our other security people. Nobody will bother you."

Lucas patted his shoulder, and took the elevator up.

LATER, IN THE RESTAURANT, Lucas got a table for two, a beer and a bowl of nuts, and had been waiting for five minutes when Carter showed up. She was a short bottle-blond woman with arched thin black eyebrows who looked like she might work hard to avoid anything resembling a gym. She was in her mid-thirties, Lucas thought, and was wearing a jade-green dress with open-toed leather sandals. She spotted Lucas, twiddled her fingers at him, walked over, and took the chair opposite him.

"Beer guy, huh?" She had a soft Southern accent.

"Yeah . . . hot day."

She ordered a dirty martini with three olives, and, when the waiter was gone, asked, "Well, do you believe Senator Smalls?"

"Yes. He has no reason to lie to me. I believe he'd be reluctant to see me investigating something he was lying about."

"Ooo," she said. "You *do* have a good opinion of yourself."

Lucas shrugged, and said, "I get things done. That's why the senator invited me in."

"Well, the West Virginia investigator doesn't believe him," she said.

"That's not exactly correct," Lucas said. "I talked to the guy this afternoon and he thinks something about the accident smells wrong. He doesn't have a single piece of evidence, but his gut tells him that Porter was telling the truth, that there was another truck."

He went through what he'd learned from Armstrong, including the cop's personal judgment. "That won't show up in his written reports, because he has no support for it."

"Okay . . ." The martini came, and she took it, fished out two olives, munched on them, nodded at the waiter, and when they were alone again, she asked, "What do you need from me?"

"Tell me what you do," Lucas said.

"What the senator tells me to. I used to do a lot of research, but now I mostly manage the office, figure out what research we need, and make sure the research gets done. I read everything I can find, on all sides, about various policy options. I do liaison work with other senatorial aides, or House aides, or White House aides, and talk to media people. This week it's mostly been damage control."

"Is Cecily Whitehead's death going to hurt him?"

She thought about that for a minute, then said, "No. The fact that she was killed makes the story harder to control. But there's no definite proof that they were out there for sexual reasons . . . The medical examiner was kind enough not to look."

"Kind enough?"

"Sort of encouraged to believe it wasn't necessary."

"I see."

She shrugged. "Even if he had looked, that kind of thing happens all the time around here. Sex—adultery, I guess. Nobody wants to talk about it because too many powerful people do it. Politicians, staff, lobbyists. Even if there were proof that Porter and CeeCee were sexually involved, it wouldn't make the news here in Washington—I suppose it might back in Minnesota, but I doubt even there. The fact is, half the newsies are sleeping with somebody they shouldn't be sleeping with, so sex doesn't get reported. If word got out, in the papers, to the public, it might get a little embarrassing at Senate cocktail parties, with all the senators' wives from Idaho and Utah and such, but that'd be about it."

"If the senator was killed, would it derail anything? Any important legislation, anything like that?"

She thought again, and said, "This summer it might have. If Porter had been killed, and you've got a Democratic governor in Minnesota—he'd be appointing a Democrat to replace Porter. The Senate's balanced on a knife-edge. If Porter were replaced by a Dem, it'd be even tighter. So . . . there's that. Then, if the senator was carrying a particularly important piece of pork, and somebody was desperate that it not get passed . . . maybe then killing him might stop something."

"Gimme an example?" Lucas asked.

She pulled the bowl of nuts closer, took a few of them, crunched them, and said, "Okay. Say Porter had a widget factory in his district and he planned to sneak a few lines into an appropriations bill that would give that factory, and no other widget factory, a tax break. That would give the factory a price advantage over all the other widget factories. The folks who own those other factories could get upset."

"Enough to kill somebody?"

"Suppose the widgets were actually electronics suites and critical to construction of the Navy's new Ford class of aircraft carriers. Say the suites sold for seventy million each, and the Navy wanted six for each carrier, and there'll be two more carriers after the Ford. Could you get somebody killed for a billion dollars?"

"Know the right guy, you could get somebody killed for the keys to a five-year-old Prius," Lucas said.

She grinned. "There you are," she said.

"But you couldn't get anybody good," Lucas amended. "You couldn't get a serious pro."

"But for a couple of hundred thousand, plus an office at the White House?"

"Okay. Was Smalls carrying a bill like that? Anything that important?"

She took another scoop of nuts, and said, "It'd be an amendment, not an entire bill . . . but, no. I'll review what we're doing this session, I can get back to you tomorrow, but there's nothing I can think of. And I'll tell you, this kind of stuff goes on all the time in Washington. Tight votes, preferential tax rates, and nobody gets killed. Not for that kind of stuff."

"Smalls had a particular person in mind for this . . . attempt . . . accident . . . whatever it was," Lucas said.

"I know." She reached out to the bowl of nuts again, pushed it away. "Don't let me eat any more of those things. They make me fart."

"Okay." She had made him smile.

"I've been thinking about that particular person, reading up on her," Carter said. "She hates Porter like rat poison, of course, because Porter won't keep his mouth shut about what happened in that election. If he keeps talking, he could queer her presidential ambitions. You could consider that a motive."

"Yes."

"About means. She's on the Senate Intelligence Committee, and she has an aide who does nothing but committee work for her. He worked for the CIA for five or six years before he moved over to the Hill; he was in the Army before that; and he has contacts all over the intelligence community, both public and private. He is a pit viper of the first degree. A fixer, a sneak, maybe crazy. He would know people who'd take the job. Our particular person has all the money in the world to pay for it."

"Motive, means, and, of course, with Porter out wandering around the backwoods with his friend from Minnesota, plenty of opportunity," Lucas said. "I'll need this guy's name."

"I'll get you a whole file on him tomorrow," Carter said.

Lucas said, "Don't get killed before then."

"I'll try not to. But it's Porter they want, not a humble farm girl from Tifton, Georgia."

NEITHER OF THEM wanted a second drink, and Lucas walked Carter back to her apartment building. She lit up a thin, dark cigarillo with a stainless-steel Zippo, leaving a scent trail of cigar smoke and lighter fluid behind them.

As they walked, she said, "About that whole motive/means

thing. What worries me is, the motive is there, but does it seem strong enough? To me, it doesn't. She's been quite good at fending off Porter. She's had people talking about Porter being a little unbalanced, maybe senile. That has an effect, too, enough that I told Porter he ought to back off. He hasn't, yet, but he will. I mean, he's back in the Senate, so what's the point?"

"Hate?"

"The thing about senators is, they learn when to cut their losses," she said. "Porter knows that better than most. He'll figure out that a knife in the back is better than hitting her with a ball-peen hammer. I mean, maybe she's twisted enough to murder him or have somebody else do it, but I'm not happy about the motive. I'll grant you the means, but the motive seems weak."

"I'll make a note," Lucas said. *"Need more motive."*

"Do that." At the door to her building, she said, "I hope you're as smart and mean as you obviously think you are—this is a different league here."

Lucas smiled his wolverine smile, and said, "Another thing we'll have to disagree about. I know people from Washington think that, but from the outside D.C. looks like a pile of shysters and hucksters and general-purpose hustlers. If you were warning me about New York, or L.A., I'd say okay. But Washington? Washington I can handle."

"I hope you don't learn otherwise," Carter said, and went through the door.

Lucas walked back to the hotel, quietly whistling the opening riffs of J.J. Cale's "Fancy Dancer."

Washington, D.C.

He was going to kick ass and take names.

HE WOKE UP the next morning feeling less confident, having slept on what Carter had said. If Smalls and Whitehead had been attacked by professionals—and it certainly seemed that way—then there was a real danger. The killers were unlikely to go after a marshal because that would attract too much notice. They could go after Smalls, though, and if they gave up on subtlety . . .

It wasn't that hard to shoot somebody in the back, he thought, as he shaved. Gangbangers did it all the time and walked away. Former SEALs, Delta, Rangers: all were thoroughly trained and inured to killing. America had somehow gotten itself in the position of creating thousands of efficient professional killers and, at the same time, had provided them with easy access to the weapons needed for the job: you could get a perfectly adequate Savage .30-06 at your local Walmart for less than four hundred dollars. His neighbor at the lake cabin had done that, and the rifle could make a minute-of-angle shot all day and all night.

HE'D GOTTEN OUT of the shower and was trying to decide between a pair of bright red Jockey shorts and a more subdued pair with horizontal green stripes when his phone rang. He picked it up, looked at the screen, clicked on, and said, "Hey, Rae."

"Lucas, what are you doing?"

"I'm on a highly secret mission in Washington," Lucas said. "If you were here, I'd tell you all about it. How's Bob?"

Rae Givens laughed. "You know what the Stump is doing?

Wind sprints. Honest to God, it's like watching a tractor-trailer trying to drag race. But he's good. Good to go."

Rae and Bob Matees were marshals assigned to the Special Operations Group located in Louisiana. They'd been with Lucas as they chased a hard-core holdup man and multiple murderer across the face of Texas. Lucas had killed him in the town of Marfa, but not before Bob had been shot through both legs by an accomplice.

Lucas asked, "Good to go, but where's he going?"

"Well, I called up the Minneapolis Office to see what you were up to, and they told me you were in Washington, but they couldn't say why. I thought I'd call you up and see if we could help."

Lucas walked over to his window and pulled back the curtains as he said, "Tell you what, Rae, right now I'm looking at files. Not even quite doing that yet. I'll be looking at them later today. This could get tense, and it could get political, and it might not do your careers a lot of good to get involved."

"C'mon, man, this is Rae you're talking to . . ."

"Okay, Rae, let me ask you this: what if our targets turn out to be CIA? Or military guys?"

"Oh-oh."

"Yeah."

There was a moment of silence, then she said, "You know what? I'd still be up for it. Bob would be, too. Right now I'm trying to find this dude who walked out of a federal lockup in an ID mix-up, but he's about as dangerous as a head of lettuce. I'll get him, maybe, but I've got to pretend like I care. C'mon, tell me what you're doing. Give me some specifics."

"This is going to sound a little paranoid, but I'm not going to tell you on the phone," Lucas said. He was looking out at the Potomac, a nice view to the west, a forest on the far bank; if you didn't already know it, you'd never guess that a major city was at your back. "Let me look at these files, talk to a few people. If I need help, you're the one I'll call."

"All right. Well, shit. Back to tracking Warren Beasley, who, if he has any brains at all, ditched a couple million bucks where we can't find it and has already crossed the border and is now drinking pink cocktails with umbrellas in them."

"That kind of guy."

"Yeah, pharmaceuticals," Rae said. "Sold about a ton more hydrocodone to doctors than the doctors actually got . . . Skimmed maybe eight mil. Got five years at Club Fed, skipped on a presentencing bond."

"Good luck."

"Call me, damnit."

HE HAD ORDERED BREAKFAST, and was drinking the first Diet Coke of the day, when Carter called. "I've got several files for you. Are you carrying a laptop?"

"Yes."

"I've had everything reduced to pdfs, so you should be good. I'll come to you, if you're still at the hotel."

"I am, eating breakfast. Same table."

"Fifteen minutes."

Lucas was working his way through a *Washington Post* when Carter arrived. She was wearing an upscale tan business dress and heels, oversized Prada sunglasses, and carried a burgundy leather satchel over her shoulder. She waved at a waiter, ordered coffee, sat across from Lucas, dug into her bag, and slid a thumb drive across the table to him.

"The man you want is named Jack Parrish. I got a serious file on him, but I had to hint to the guy who gave it to me that we might have a romantic future together, which we don't. Read it fast so you can tell me if I have to go back to the guy before I turn him down."

"Not even going to give him a shot?" Lucas asked. "You ever hear about working a source?"

"You haven't met the guy," Carter said. "Does Brylcreem addiction suggest anything good to you?"

"Ouch. On the other hand, we may need as much help as we can get. Where'd the guy get the files?"

"Background checks for the Intelligence Committee," Carter said. "The committee has its own set of files on its personnel. I wouldn't have access to these myself, except for my Brylcreem buddy who works in the file room. So, speed-read and get back to me."

Lucas told her that his self-confidence had waned over the evening, but that he was more worried about Smalls than about himself. "While she might hate me, she can figure the odds. Killing me might feel good, but eventually it'd come back to bite her in the ass."

"When do you think you'll know something? Anything?"

"I don't know. I'll call when I do . . . In another case, a year ago, I had some strange experiences with cell phones." He reached in his pocket, took out a burner phone, and handed it to her. "I bought a couple of burners before I left St. Paul. I'll call you from mine before you leave here so you'll have my number. Only use the burner to call my burner . . . never call my burner from your regular phone, and don't call any other number from your burner. This is strictly for you and me."

"You think they're monitoring us?"

"I don't think anything in particular. Like I said, my last case had some weird turns because of cell phones. I don't trust them as far as I could spit a rat," Lucas said.

WHEN CARTER HAD GONE, with Lucas's secret cell number in her new burner phone, Lucas went back up to his room. There, he traded his jacket and slacks for a pair of soft cotton athletic pants and a T-shirt, jacked up the air-conditioning, plugged the thumb drive into his laptop, and opened Carter's files.

Jack Parrish was a thin, coffin-pale man with close-set eyes who used too much gel in his dark hair, enough that you could see the tracks left by his comb; he wore suits that were too dark and too sharp, like he'd picked them out of the pages of *GQ*. The photos in the file were all head and shoulders only, the type used for passports and security cards. He'd always faced the various cameras with the same hard glare.

Parrish was thirty-eight. He'd graduated from Ohio State when he was twenty-two with a B.S. in economic geography, served four years as an Army intelligence officer, and joined the Central Intelligence Agency when he finished his active military service. He spent four years with the CIA, worked for a private company called Heracles Personnel for three more years, then took a job as a researcher for the Senate Intelligence Committee and later became an aide to Taryn Grant. He was still in the military Reserve, currently with the rank of major.

That would, Lucas thought, give him a broad range of contacts both in the Pentagon and in the wider intelligence community. The file included a list of publications, some of which were marked as classified, although the level of classification wasn't specified.

At the CIA, Parrish seemed to have specialized in aerial and satellite photo interpretation, and had written a number of papers on the subject; he'd also written two papers with obscure titles that seemed to be mathematical studies of where "irregular fighters" could be found.

That all sounded like desk jobs to Lucas, but Parrish had a Bronze Star with "V" device and a Purple Heart. Lucas didn't know what a "V" device meant, and when he looked it up, it turned out that a Bronze Star could be awarded for general meritorious service, even to a civilian—a news reporter had gotten one once—but a "V" device indicated "Valor" and was a combat award. Lucas knew the Purple Heart meant that Parrish had been wounded, but there were no details on the wound. Other military awards included ribbons for service in both Afghanistan and Iraq.

So Parrish had been shot at and apparently hit. Nothing in the files indicated that the Army had any doubts about him.

He'd been married and later divorced, and currently seemed to be not married. His ex-wife was named, and had a security clearance, but the level of the clearance wasn't mentioned. Parrish got consistently high evaluations as a Senate researcher and later as an aide to Grant.

A second file contained Parrish's divorce decree. The divorce had been in Maryland and had apparently been by mutual consent. His wife got the house but no alimony. There was no testimony about abuse or anything else, other than their agreement that the marriage was "irretrievably broken."

A third file contained a list of companies that would incur economic impacts, both bad and good, under Senate bills that Carter expected to receive bipartisan support. Heaviest impacts were on businesses and communities that supported now-obsolete military bases that were facing closure.

Smalls supported all of the closures except one on the West Coast. Carter noted that he wanted that base kept open as the possible site for an atomic power reactor, but since all of the California delegation, both Republicans and Democrats, opposed the idea of a reactor on the coast, Smalls's opposition to the closure was seen as idiosyncratic and garnered little support. There was no reason to kill Smalls for any of his Senate activity, as far as Lucas could see.

A fourth, even shorter file contained nothing but a list of four names, with addresses and telephone numbers, and a note from Carter that said "These people don't like Parrish and might talk to you. Call me when you're done with this."

WHEN HE'D FINISHED with the files, Lucas knew all kinds of things he hadn't known that morning, but nothing that pointed in any particular direction. If anything, Parrish seemed like an accomplished bureaucrat, somebody who'd always been good at what he did.

Lucas closed the laptop down and called Carter on the burner phone. She answered on the third ring, and he asked, "Can you talk?"

"Sure."

"I've read the files, and Parrish doesn't seem like a terrible guy, but you said he was a snake. Why's he a snake? And what's with the list of names?"

"He *is* a snake, and part of his snakiness is that he doesn't seem like an awful guy to most people. He's a sociopath, in my opinion, but a cautious one. He doesn't care who gets hurt as long as it's not him."

"A good match for Grant, then," Lucas said. "I think the same thing about her, although she might be darker than a simple sociopath; she could be a full-blown psycho."

"Whatever—I'm not sure how much definitions help," Carter said. "Anyway, that list of names . . . those are people who have reason to seriously dislike Parrish and who might be in a position to give you some information about him. He has made some enemies getting to where he is, and I listed them in the order that would reflect the intensity of their dislike. Joe Rose, the first guy, probably likes him the least—hates him, actually. And so on. That's something I keep track of."

"Okay. Thank you."

"Lucas, you scared me this morning," she said. "The secret phones and all that. If you read those files, you can see that there's not much detail in them—you can remember everything you need to know, about Parrish and his wife and his jobs. I'd appreciate it if you'd get rid of that thumb drive: if somebody got that drive from you, they might be able to figure out who copied the files, and, from that, who got them: me."

"I'll get rid of it," Lucas said. "I mean, really get rid of it, everything but the names."

He did just that when he got off the phone. He copied down

the names, addresses, and phone numbers of Parrish's supposed enemies, smashed the thumb drive with the sliding shower door, and flushed the pieces down the toilet.

That done, he went back to the desk, looked at the notepad with Joe Rose's phone number on it, and punched the number into his phone.

6

Joe Rose had a voice that sounded like gravel being shoveled from a truck—too much whiskey, cigars, or both. Lucas only told him he was a U.S. Marshal, that he was investigating an auto accident only peripherally involving Mr. Rose. He didn't mention either Jack Parrish or Porter Smalls.

Rose told Lucas he lived in Bethesda, Maryland, and that he'd be around all day. "I work at home now."

Lucas retrieved his car from the valet, followed the GPS through tangled traffic to Bethesda, which was northwest of the District. The distance couldn't have been more than ten miles but took him almost forty minutes to drive.

Rose lived in what was probably an expensive house, half brick, half white clapboard, of a style that Lucas thought of as confused—it had a bunch of overlapping roofs, a truncated clapboard turret, two single-car garage doors that probably fed the same double-car garage, a cobblestone driveway, and a manicured front lawn. The front door gave onto a tiny covered porch, good only for keeping the rain off visitors while they waited for a ride.

Several black cables led from a telephone pole near the street to the house—power lines, maybe a hardwired phone, maybe cable television/Internet . . . but a couple of more as well, although Lucas didn't know what function they might serve.

Lucas parked in the driveway, stepped out into a humid, nearly wet heat, and rang the doorbell. As he waited, he looked up and down the street: no people, no cars, nothing moving, not even a cat.

A bedroom community.

THE DOOR OPENED, and a man who was probably Joe Rose stood in the doorway and asked, "Do you have some ID?"

"I do," Lucas said. He showed Rose his badge and ID card, and Rose stepped back and said, "Come on in. Uh . . . I can't think of any reason that I would, but should I have a lawyer here?"

Lucas shook his head. "No. The investigation doesn't involve you in any way, except as a possible source of information."

Rose was Lucas's height and build, but older, retirement age, gray-haired, large-nosed, with a pair of inexpensive computer glasses pushed up on his forehead. Close up, his voice sounded even harsher than it had on the phone—an injury of some kind; he hadn't gotten it singing. He was pale, like an office worker, and freckled, wore tan slacks and a golf shirt, loafers but no socks.

He said, "Okay, I got the time. You know I don't have a regular job anymore."

"No, I didn't know that," Lucas said, as he followed him into the house and down a hallway. The hallway opened into what had probably been designed as a family room but now was being used as a spacious office, with three separate computer monitors on a library table.

"Yeah, I'm a contract researcher now. You know what's *not* on the Internet now?"

"I thought everything was."

"Nope. There's tons of government stuff that isn't—stuff that's still important but that was recorded before 2000 or so," Rose said. "Internet people don't know how to do paper research, courthouse research, so I'm doing fairly well. I'm praying it keeps up, because I can use the money."

"Cool. You invented your own job," Lucas said.

"Yup. So . . . what's up?"

Rose pointed Lucas at a leather club chair and took an identical chair facing Lucas across a fuzzy brown-and-tan rug. Not married, Lucas thought: women generally didn't allow big fat leather chairs or brown fuzzy rugs in their family rooms.

Lucas: "I'm told you don't much care for a man named Jack Parrish. I need to know more about Mr. Parrish. About his character."

Rose responded with a grunt, then asked, "What does that have to do with an auto accident?"

"I don't want to talk about that," Lucas said. He softened things with a smile. "I know it's horseshit, but . . . I can't right now tie two things together with somebody I don't know."

"Got it," Rose said. He sighed, and said, "Parrish is . . . I mean, calling him an asshole or a sonofabitch doesn't do the man justice. Even in Washington, he's something special. And, believe me, we've got a glut of assholes around here."

Rose had worked for the CIA at the same time Parrish had, both as middle managers in "parallel departments," as Rose put it. "I can't tell you what we were doing, but it was technical."

"I saw a file that said Parrish did something with photo interpretation."

"He did, but . . . let's just leave it there. If you got that information by seeing a list of his so-called publications, he stole most of those things from his subordinates," Rose said. "Anyway, he was there for five or six years—I overlapped him on both ends, in terms of employment. During that time, I watched him undermine anyone he thought might someday challenge him—bad personnel reports, that kind of thing. He was an attention junkie and an ass-kisser. What I'm saying is, he stepped on a lot of good people and tried to crawl up the org chart over their bodies. Eventually, people began to catch on, it caught up with him . . . and he got out. Moved over to the Senate as a staff member."

"Leaving you . . . where?"

"Where I was. I had an obscure job, important but not flashy. At least, I thought it was important, and I was good at it. Then, we had a situation come up . . . uh . . . that I don't want to talk about yet. Parrish advocated one kind of response, we advocated another. My boss and I went over to SIC—the Senate Intelligence Committee—with some, mmm, documents that suggested that Parrish was bullshitting them on behalf of a faction over at the Pentagon. He and the Pentagon got their way, and what happened later was a goddamn disaster. Too big even for an effective cover-up."

He looked up at the ceiling, both hands in the air, grinned at Lucas, but leaned forward and whispered, "People died. People who shouldn't have. Lots of them."

Lucas: "Who got blamed?"

Rose tapped his chest. "I did. Not for the disaster but for the fact that some of it got out to the press. One of the senators brought the deputy director over for a closed-door meeting, and, the next thing I knew, I was talking to our security people about leaks. Shit, I didn't even know a reporter. I said so. But they kept after me—this went on for a year—and I got what they called a lateral transfer to a nonsensitive position, pending resolution of the leaking case. I had thirty-three years in, and I said fuck it and retired. When I was going out the door, a pal of mine, higher up the line, took me aside and said that be believed the whole thing was a dirty trick engineered by Parrish, who'd been telling people that I'd been leaking and that me leaking might even have caused the problem—that I'd been leaking before the action, somebody overheard me, and word had been passed to the Syrians . . . Damn lie, every bit of it. I found out later he'd gone to work for the senator who'd been asking the questions."

"Taryn Grant," Lucas said.

Rose nodded, and asked, "You want a Pepsi or a beer?" After asking the question, he nodded vigorously, a pantomime nod.

Lucas said, "Yeah, I could use a Pepsi. I haven't had anything to drink since I left the hotel . . ."

"C'mon, I'll get you one," Rose said.

In the kitchen, he opened the refrigerator, took out two Pepsis, handed one to Lucas, and said, "Let's go out and sit by the pool. I got an umbrella out there."

Outside, he led the way past the pool to the end of the backyard. "I'm probably overcooking things a little, but I worry about surveillance. Especially since I know what can be done, if they want to do it," he said. "I doubt anyone's actually watching me . . . If they are, they wouldn't be bugging us out here."

Lucas said, "Okay . . ."

"Anyway, what I don't understand is, why did Senator Grant

jump into this with both feet? Stick a bullshit investigation on me and on my boss? She didn't have to do that. What would she get out of it?"

Lucas had an answer to that question, but he didn't say what he thought: that Grant was buying Parrish's loyalty. Instead, he said, "I need to know the dimension of this . . . disaster. I won't talk about it to anyone, but I need to know. I will tell you that the matter I'm investigating is extremely serious . . . more so than you can probably imagine."

Rose looked around the yard, took a hit on his Pepsi, and said, "I don't even know if you're really a marshal. You could be spoofing me."

"You could look me up on the Internet. There's a lot of stuff there, going back years."

"I'll do that," Rose said. "In the meantime . . . I'm not going to say anything more. We're talking about federal prison."

"I don't think so," Lucas said. "If all this works out the way I suspect it will, they'd be afraid to go after you."

"You don't know," Rose said. "I don't believe that they're afraid of anybody."

"You'd be wrong about that," Lucas said.

"Give me your email," Rose said. "Maybe I'll get back to you."

"Tell me one more thing—I'm sure it isn't classified, but it's something you'd know," Lucas said. "Parrish was an active duty military officer, stayed in the Reserve, and is now a major, and he's moving up to lieutenant colonel sometime soon. Would his service with the Army and the CIA, and now with the Senate, give him access to, you know, people with an ability to do violence?"

Rose squinted at him, licked his lips: "Who'd he get shot?"

"Nobody. But if he wanted to get somebody shot, would he have the connections? I'm not talking about a military shooting, a terrorist shooting, but a civilian shooting here in the U.S. Could he get a couple of names?"

Another hit on the bottle, and a quick nod. "Oh, yeah. In about five minutes. And now I am done."

Rose refused to say anything more. Lucas left him standing by the pool and walked around the house and out to the street.

THE SECOND, third, and fourth entries on Carter's list all lived in Virginia, on the other side of the District. He'd get them later in the afternoon, he thought, and could stop at the hotel on the way.

The first time Lucas had encountered Grant, she'd worked through two ex-military security men, whom she'd paid to kill for her—and one of them she'd bound to herself with the pretense of loving him. Grant would do what was necessary to recruit people she thought she needed—political favors, money, sex—whatever she thought it would take.

If she needed Parrish's particular kind of expertise, she'd probably bought his loyalty by protecting him from criticism; maybe even saved his job. There was also the prospect of the White House . . .

BACK AT THE HOTEL, Lucas washed his face and went to the laptop, clicked on his email, expecting a note from Weather, and maybe from his daughter Letty, who was in her third year at Stanford. There was nothing from Letty, but he did have a brief note from Weather, with school news, and another email from Rose, hiding behind the name Donald R. Ligny, with a subject line that identified him: "Looked you up on the Internet."

Scrolling down, Lucas found a *Washington Post* story about the bombing of a Syrian nerve gas warehouse that turned out to be a *souk*, or marketplace, instead, with a small school for girls at one end. The Syrians claimed that ninety-four people had been killed, most of them women or children, a claim verified by a religious charity and with photographs. The school had been wiped out.

Under the story, there were six added words:

"We told them. They didn't listen."

YEARS BEFORE, Lucas had seen a Tom Clancy movie—he couldn't remember the name of it, but Harrison Ford was in it. He remembered one scene in particular, in which a British SAS team had wiped out a terrorist training camp someplace in North Africa. The scene had stuck in Lucas's head because he'd spent his life working murders, murders which had often horrified him. In the Clancy movie, the SAS attack had been monitored by satellite, and a group of CIA suits had casually watched the attack and conducted a running commentary. "There's a kill," one had said while leisurely drinking a cup of coffee.

The scene was chilling, as it was intended to be. There were people down there, dead, executed while they slept. They were terrorists, probably deserved what they got, but they were still people, snuffed out in an instant.

The *Post* story, combined with what Lucas had been told by Rose, reflected the same kind of bureaucratic attitude as the Clancy scene: people more interested in taking care of their operational lives, their political lives, than the fact that a whole lot of people died at their hands.

Parrish and Grant hustling around to shift the blame . . . Forget about the women and children blown to bloody rags in a split second.

LUCAS GOT HIS CAR BACK, and let the navigation system guide him across the Potomac to a neighborhood of neat brick homes and crooked, elderly trees on a blacktopped lane in Arlington, Virginia. Another bedroom community, but at least a hundred years older than Rose's place in Maryland. Of the three additional names on Carter's list, Lucas had gotten no answer with two of his phone calls, but the third call had been picked up by a woman named Gladys Ingram. She was a partner in an Arlington law firm, and said she could be home for an hour or so.

"If I'm going to talk to a marshal about anything, I'd rather it not be here," she said, referring to her office. Lucas looked up the firm, found that it had two dozen partners, and more than eighty associates, and did a lot of lobbying.

Ingram's car, a silver Mercedes SL550, was parked in the driveway when Lucas arrived. The street was so narrow that he pulled in behind her car to keep from blocking it.

Like Rose, when she came to the door, Ingram asked to see Lucas's ID.

Unlike Rose, after Lucas's original call, she'd gone straight to a computer and looked him up on the Internet. There were several hundred references to his time as a cop, with two different Minnesota agencies, and there was a brief note in a *Star-Tribune* gossip column that he'd moved to the U.S. Marshals Office. There were also a dozen photos taken over a twenty-year span of Lucas at various crime scenes. Not content with that, she'd used a law office code to check his credit rating.

"Okay, if you're spoofing me, you've gone to a lot of trouble to do it," she said, still standing in the doorway. "I have to say, you're apparently the richest marshal I've ever met."

"I got lucky with a computer start-up when I was between police agencies," Lucas said. "You're the second person I talked to today who worried about being spoofed. 'Spoofed' means, like, a fraud or a deception, right?"

"Yes," she said. She was a gawky woman, with reddish brown hair that barely escaped being mousy. She had brown eyes, looking at him through tortoiseshell glasses, and wore a dress that was conservatively fashionable. Lucas thought she might be forty. "It's 'Net slang. So, what are we talking about here? You said you were investigating an automobile accident that has nothing to do with me—but that I might have some information about. I don't know about any automobile accident."

"Like I said, your information might be important, but it's . . . peripheral to the accident."

"What accident?"

"An auto accident involving Senator Porter Smalls," Lucas said.

"Was there something unusual about it? I thought that was all settled," she said.

"He's a U.S. senator. We're taking another routine look at it," Lucas said.

"Okay." She nodded.

Lucas said, "Now, I understand you know a man named Jack Parrish . . ."

She said, "Oh boy . . ." then stopped and put two fingers to her lips.

Lucas: "What?"

"Oh my God. Did Parrish try to kill Porter Smalls?"

Lucas, astonished, smiled. "I see why you're a partner."

"Well, did he? I mean, Smalls's accident . . ." She stopped again, gazing past him at the street, thinking. They were still standing in the doorway, and she suddenly said, "Come in. Come in. This is interesting."

INGRAM'S HOME was simply but expensively furnished. One living room wall held a single painting, but it looked a lot like a painting that Lucas had seen at the Minneapolis Institute of Art when Weather made him go to a reception there. He bent to look at the signature: RD.

Ingram, standing behind him, said, "Richard Diebenkorn. Do you know him?"

"I think I saw something by him at the Minneapolis museum," Lucas said. "Looks nice."

"Well, yeah!" Her tone suggested that of course it looked nice because it was a fuckin' masterpiece. "Part of the Ocean Park series."

"Cool." Lucas had never heard of the guy, but what else was he going to say? He turned and gazed at her for a few seconds, and asked, "What's your opinion of Parrish?"

"He's a bad man," Ingram said. "You must have gotten my name through the Malone case."

"I don't know the Malone case," Lucas said.

"Then how'd you get my name?"

"I can't tell you. I got it from a confidential source who's involved with the government. If you say there's a Malone case, that could be where she got it."

"Hmph. She, huh? I'll think about that. Anyway, the Malone case involved one of my clients, Malone Materials. Malone lost a military procurement bid to another company and didn't understand why since the other company had no expertise in the required area, which involved retrofitting certain military vehicles with lightweight side-panel armor as protection against improvised explosive devices. We sued. There was never any absolute proof, but it became quite clear to me and others who were handling the case that Parrish had been involved in discussions between the Army procurement people and a number of members of both the House and the Senate. Their discussions ended with the other company, Inter-Core Ballistics, getting higher procurement grades despite its lack of experience and markedly higher prices for the panels. I believe money changed hands in a variety of ways, and some of it stuck to Parrish's hands and probably the hands of some members of the procurement team. A good bit probably wound up in reelection funds."

"Bribes," Lucas said.

"Not only bribes—but bribes that channeled money to a company with no experience in a mission critical manufacturing operation and so risked the lives of American troops," Ingram said.

"That's . . . ugly," Lucas said. "Parrish seems to be doing quite well in his continuing military career. In the Army Reserve."

"I didn't know that, but, now that I do, I'll ask around. Do you really think that he tried to kill Smalls?"

"That's a conclusion you jumped to."

"Don't bullshit me, Davenport, it won't work. I saw your face when I mentioned the Smalls accident." She turned away, thinking, snapped her fingers, turned back, and said, "Got it: Smalls and Taryn Grant. Parrish now works for Grant. That is very, very, interesting. Very."

"Don't jump to more conclusions . . . And don't try to use that," Lucas said.

"I don't think I'm jumping to anything," she said. "You've got something about the accident, don't you? What is it? I'd love to get something good on Parrish and/or Grant."

Lucas said, "Miz Ingram, let me suggest you forget about all these . . . speculations. I'm afraid if you go somewhere with them, somebody might come to your nice brick house and hurt you."

"Really." Skepticism, not a question.

"Really," Lucas said. "Listen, we're looking at a . . . at a bare possibility. The most likely thing that happened in the Smalls accident is that he and the driver both had a little to drink, she lost it and went off the road. We need to check, and that's what I'm doing. I've gotten the impression from . . . other people . . . that Parrish is a dangerous guy. If you try to stick it to him, or he thinks you will, you could have a problem."

"I will take that under advisement," she said.

"Sit tight for a couple of weeks—that's all you have to do," Lucas said. "By that time, I'll have figured out whether Parrish was involved in the accident. If he was, I'll handle it. If he wasn't, I'll let you know. No point in taking risks that you don't have to."

"I will take that under advisement as well," she said. "Boy—Taryn Grant and Jack Parrish. That's a mix 'n' match, huh?"

"They actually—" Lucas cut himself off.

"Are well suited to each other, that's what you were about to say," Ingram said. "I don't know much about Grant, but I do know about the controversy when she was elected. Were you involved in that investigation?"

"I led it; for the state," Lucas said.

"Now you're a federal marshal. There wasn't any political influence involved in that, was there?"

Lucas shook his head. "I didn't know you were a trial attorney."

"So, I'm starting to see it. U.S. senator gets jobbed by an opposition candidate, who takes his seat. He gets himself elected again and immediately begins peeing on his opponent's shoes—or, in Grant's case, her Christian Louboutin pumps. Grant is a murderous witch who lands on the Senate Intelligence Committee, where she connects with a hustler who has ties both to the military and the CIA and does her a favor by trying to kill the U.S. senator who's peeing on her presidential chances. Smalls, who has used his influence to get the man who saved his bacon an appointment as a federal marshal, gets the marshal to investigate the witch," Ingram said, finally taking a breath. "Man, is this a great country or what?"

LUCAS SAID he'd stay in touch, and Ingram said, "Oh, do. I'm fascinated." Back in his car, he tried to call the other two people on the list and again got no answer, so he headed back to the hotel.

After leaving his car with the valet, he was walking through the lobby when the security chief, who he'd met when he was checking in, flagged him over. He'd learned the man's name was Steve Schneider.

"Did you . . . have a friend in your room? A male friend, maybe another marshal?" Schneider asked.

"A friend? No . . . what happened?"

"One of my guys was doing routine floor checks and he heard a door close. A guy was coming down the hall, and my guy got the impression he'd come out of that stub hallway to your room. There was no reason to stop him, so he went on his way. There's nobody in the other room on that hall. I thought I should mention it."

"Thanks. Any sign he'd actually been inside my room?"

"No, no. We would have stopped him if we thought he had been," Schneider said.

"Can I talk to your guy?"

"Sure. I think he's down in the parking structure, if you want to wait in the bar . . ."

LUCAS GOT A DIET COKE, and Schneider and his guy showed up five minutes later. The second security man was named Jeff Toomes, white-haired with a ruddy face, in a gray suit—an ex-cop, Lucas thought.

"There wasn't any reason to stop him, at first," Toomes told Lucas. "What happened was, I was doing my checks, and I came out of the stairwell and started toward the hallway that goes to the rooms. I heard a door close as I turned the corner and there was a guy walking toward me. I'd say six feet, maybe a half inch either way, close-cut brown hair, brown eyes. Looked to be in very good shape. Clean-shaven, decent pale blue summer suit, polished lace-up shoes. If he was carrying a gun, it would have been in the small of his back—no gun sag on the sides, and the suit wasn't cut for a shoulder rig. I suppose he could have had an ankle wrap, but who has those?"

"And he was by my room," Lucas said.

"That's what I realized as I was walking by. I think he had to come out of your hallway. There's only two rooms down there, and when I checked later I found out there's nobody checked into the other one."

Lucas said, "You heard the door actually close."

"Yes. Another thing . . . you're on four, and I realized that I didn't hear the elevator bell, the one that rings when the doors open. I went back: I was going to see what room he was in or who he was visiting, but he was gone. He had to have taken the stairs. That'd be unusual, unless you were in a hurry. I called Steve, but nobody saw him again. He would have gotten lost in the lobby."

"He'd have been in a hurry because he'd been surprised by a guy he recognized as security."

"The thought crossed our minds," Schneider said.

Lucas said, "Well, hell."

SCHNEIDER CAME UP to the room with him. Lucas popped the door, and they both eased inside. Lucas looked at his luggage and briefcase, but nothing seemed out of place, missing, or added. Schneider tipped his head toward the door, and Lucas followed him into the hall.

"I know a guy who could sweep it for you," Schneider said. "Or, better, I could move you across the hall but leave you registered in this room."

"Let's do that," Lucas said. "Then if somebody else shows up, I'll actually be behind them. I might even hear them going in."

"If you shoot somebody, try not to hit any guests," Schneider said. "Unless it's an old lady with a mink hat carrying a rat."

"A rat?"

"Okay, a Chihuahua. That'd be Mrs. Julia Benson, grass widow. She lives here. Eighteen thousand a month, and she doesn't care—she likes servants. I'm apparently one of them. Biggest pain in the ass in the building. I wouldn't want you to kill her, but wounding her a little would get you some free drinks."

"I'll keep that in mind," Lucas said.

7

Lucas settled into his new room, across the hallway from his previous one and without the view of the Potomac. He struggled briefly with a spasm of paranoia: did guys in nice suits break into hotel rooms occupied by U.S. Marshals? In Washington, D.C., in a place called Watergate? Really?

When that moment had passed, he called Smalls, who blurted, "Can't talk at this exact minute, call me back in . . . four minutes."

Lucas called back in four minutes, and asked, "You were with somebody inconvenient?"

Smalls said, "No, I was standing at a urinal. I'm at a luncheon. Try not to call when I'm taking a leak."

"All right." He told Smalls about the possible illegal entry, and asked, "Have you told people that I'm looking at the accident?"

"I had to tell a couple of people at the office. I trust them, and I told them not to talk to anyone else. I took my wife to lunch and I didn't even tell her."

"There's a leak somewhere, Senator, and it's probably Grant. You might think about that," Lucas said. "Now I'll be working out in the open, I guess. If this was an entry and not a mistake by the security guy . . . If it's not a mistake . . . I mean, they knew where my room was."

"I think a mistake's most likely—though given the shot they took at me, the attack, you can't know for sure, can you?"

LUCAS CARRIED a Sony voice-activated recorder in his pack, a unit only five inches long and less than an inch and a half wide. He dug it out, checked the battery, found a place to leave it—tucked under the mattress at the head of the bed, with only the microphone sticking out. He recorded precisely ten seconds of sound from the room television, a CNN news report. If somebody found the recorder and erased it, or simply took it, he would know as much as he would if it recorded somebody coming and going.

HE CALLED the last two names on Carter's list, still got no answer. Since both numbers were supposedly good, and both supposedly to cell phones, he suspected that the calls were being ignored. He'd decided to drive back across the river, find the houses, hang around until someone showed, when a call came in to his cell phone from an unknown number.

He said, "Lucas Davenport."

"Marshal Davenport? This is Carl Armstrong, the accident investigator."

"Hey, Carl. What's up, man?"

"You mentioned that lawn mower lady saw a black Ford F-250 going through town. There's a nursery there with a video camera that covers the street. I asked them to let me take a look, and I spotted the truck and got the tags. It's outta Virginia. But there's a problem."

"Like what?"

"The truck I saw on the video was black, like the lawn mower lady said, but when I looked up the registration it says the truck is blue."

"So what do you think?" Lucas asked.

"If I was gonna do something like run another car off the road, and I thought somebody might see me or remember me, I'd steal the plates off another 250 and change them."

"I would, too," Lucas said. "Give me the details, I'll look into it . . . What about faces? Could you see the guys in the truck?"

"You can see them, but you can't quite make them out. I could see sunglasses and black hats."

"Could you send me the video?"

"Sure, I got it here—I'll email it to you. I had our computer guy make it the highest resolution he could."

"This is good stuff, Carl."

THE VIDEO CAME IN, but it wasn't much to look at. The black pickup rolled past the camera, but the two people in the cab were obscured by reflections off its windows. Lucas agreed with Armstrong that the men were wearing sunglasses, but he wasn't sure about the hats. To Lucas, it looked more like one of the men had long dark hair.

The truck was registered from a place called Centreville, which Lucas found on a Google map. A D.C. suburb, it was straight west, across the river, in Virginia. He turned on the tape recorder, tucked it into the mattress, put the "Do Not Disturb" sign on the doorknob, and went down to get his car.

The afternoon was getting on, but Lucas was in front of the

first wave of the outgoing rush hour and made it into Centreville in a half hour, following the Evoque's GPS. The license tag had gone to a Gerald and Marie Blake, who lived in a town house complex off I-66. The complex didn't have a parking lot, as such, but instead nose-in parking right off the street.

Lucas cruised the Blakes' address. The truck was parked out front—blue Ford F-250—but the plates no longer showed the number that Armstrong had given him. There was no sign that the truck had ever been involved in an accident.

Lucas considered for a bit, then pulled in, popped the restraining strap on his pistol, walked up to the front door, and pushed the doorbell. A minute later, the door opened, and a teenage girl looked out at him.

Lucas: "Are your parents home?"

Girl: "Who wants to know?"

Lucas took out his ID case with the badge. "U.S. Marshal Lucas Davenport . . . I need to talk to Gerald or Marie Blake, or both of them."

Girl, turning: "Mommm . . ."

MARIE BLAKE came to the door a minute later, peering at him nearsightedly through computer glasses. She took them off as the girl said, "He says he's a U.S. Marshal. He has a badge."

"What's going on?" the woman asked.

Lucas explained what he was doing, and she said, "We've never been to West Virginia, even passing through. We moved here from Delaware . . ." Her husband, she said, was at work; he was a bureaucrat with the Bureau of Land Management.

Lucas asked, "Do you know what your license plate number is?"

"No . . . There's an insurance card in the cab; that should have the license number on it."

Lucas knew what would happen, but they went out and looked anyway. The number on the truck didn't match the number on the insurance card because the tags had been stolen off the Blakes' truck and replaced.

He got back on the phone to Armstrong. "Do you have access to a database of stolen license plates in Virginia?"

"Sure. Take me a minute."

Lucas gave him the tag number, and a minute later Armstrong came back and said, "Those plates were taken off a blue F-250 probably at the Fair Oaks Mall a week ago. They weren't replaced with anything else; they were simply gone. The owner saw they were missing as soon as he came out of the mall, so he called the cops and reported it."

"The day before the accident," Lucas said.

"Yes."

"They didn't want the Blakes to notice that their tags were gone so they replaced them with another stolen set. That way, it'd take two steps to catch them—a cop would have to stop the Blakes and report the Blakes' tags as missing, then spot the bad guy's truck. Which nobody did."

"Looks like it," Armstrong said.

They were stuck. Lucas rang off, told Blake she had a problem with the license plates, that hers had been stolen and probably dumped somewhere after a crime had been committed. She needed to get new ones. He gave her a card and told her that if anyone at the Virginia DMV gave her a hard time to have them call him.

HE STILL HAD two more people to talk to from Carter's list. Since he wasn't far from where they lived, he decided to drop in. At his first stop, he saw somebody working inside James T. Knapp's house, so he leaned on the doorbell until a heavyset woman came to the door. "What?"

Lucas identified himself, and said, "I'm looking for Mr. Knapp?"

"I'm the housekeeper. What'd he do?"

"Nothing, as far as I know. I'm checking up on somebody Mr. Knapp knows."

"Huh." The woman scowled at him, as though judging his genuineness, and finally admitted, "He's gone off to California on some sort of mission."

"He's in the military?"

"No, he's a preacher. He's gone off on a preacher mission. Supposed to be back next week, but he paid me in advance for the week after that, too."

AT THE NEXT HOUSE, a stand-alone ranch-style painted blue and gray in a quiet neighborhood of similar houses and trees and small lawns, he was walking away from the front door when a black five-liter Mustang pulled into the driveway. A thin, rangy, heavily tanned man in a blue Army uniform got out. He had lieutenant colonel's silver leaves on his shoulders. "Hello?" he called out.

Lucas walked over and identified himself, and the colonel said, "Horace Stout. What can I do for you?"

"I need to talk to you about Jack Parrish."

Stout grimaced, and said, "Better come inside."

Stout was single but kept a neat place that included a studio grand piano, a Model M Steinway, in a corner of the living room with a pile of piano music on its closed lid. Lucas said that his wife had a similar model, and Stout said, "That's what I got out of eleven years of marriage. That and a sick dog, which died last year."

"Sorry about that," Lucas muttered.

"Can I get you an orange juice or a vitamin water?" Stout asked. "I don't keep any alcohol."

"Juice would be fine," Lucas said.

They sat at Stout's kitchen table, and Lucas assured him that anything he said about Parrish would be kept confidential. "I'm not taking testimony, I'm trying to get a grip on the guy. Who he is, what he's like, what he does."

"Right now, he works for Senator Taryn Grant," Stout said, "but you know that."

"I do."

"My experience with him was in Iraq—our tours overlapped. He did two, I did five, working basically with logistics out of Kuwait into Baghdad."

"He has a Purple Heart and a Bronze Star," Lucas said. "I assumed he had a combat role."

Stout sighed, and finally said, "I . . . You know, Marshal Davenport, it's not right to speak poorly of an absent officer."

"It could be important," Lucas said. "I assume you could speak poorly if you wished?"

After a short silence, Stout looked away, and said, "Some people . . . get medals. Guys get minor but real wounds, and a local medic bandages them and gives them a couple of pills, and they never see a Purple Heart. Other guys get what you might call *owies* and they get the Purple Heart. Same with Bronze Stars. Nobody in the military will talk about it, but there's sometimes a political component to the award."

"You're saying that Parrish—"

"I'm not saying anything specific," Stout said. "I'm saying it happens with some people."

Lucas said, "The reason I'm talking to you is, I heard you didn't care for Parrish. When we're doing investigations, we try to talk with people who—"

"I know, I know . . . I know what you're doing," Stout said. "I don't care for Parrish. Not at all. You know when you're working in logistics, in a war zone, stuff has to be done in a hurry, and sometimes material goes . . . astray."

"Parrish stole stuff?"

Stout ticked a finger at him. "I'm not saying he stole stuff, I'm just saying . . . an inordinate amount of material went astray after it passed through his unit. He had an E-8 working for him . . ."

"I'm sorry, I don't know military ranks."

"E-8, master sergeant. It's no big secret that the Army has some crooked NCOs, but I believe that man was one of the crookedest I've ever encountered. He retired to a rather lush lifestyle down on the Gulf Coast, as I hear it. But even that . . ."

He paused, thinking it over, and Lucas pressed him: "What? Nobody else is listening."

"There were a lot of private military contractors roaming around Iraq. Our security guards were contracted out of Africa, for instance. Uganda, mostly, although they usually worked for stateside-based companies," Stout said. "I'll tell you, marshal,

Parrish was way too close to these guys, the stateside managers. Most straight-up officers stayed well away from those assholes. Not Jack. Jack seemed to think they were romantic warriors. He liked hanging with them. I suspect, but I can't prove, that some of the missing material went out to these guys."

Lucas said, "That's interesting. Is he still close with them? These companies?"

"That's the word. He went to the CIA after he left the Army, and the CIA uses a lot of the same contractor organizations. After the CIA, Parrish worked for one of them for a while. I don't like him, and he doesn't like me, thinks I'm a prig." He glanced at Lucas, as if trying to figure out whether Lucas knew what a "prig" was, then continued. "What I don't like is, he wasn't . . . a professional officer. He's a hustler. He was a hustler in the Army, a hustler in the CIA. People are talking about Senator Grant running for the presidency. So now he's hustling that."

"That word gets used a lot when people are talking about Parrish," Lucas said. "When he was with the Senate Intelligence Committee, there was a stink about the bombing of a marketplace in Syria . . ."

"I know about that," Stout said. "If the place is full of poison gas, he's a hero. If it turns out there's nothing but a bunch of dead towelheads, who cares? A typical Parrish operation, in my opinion."

"Was there any particular military contractor he was especially tight with?"

Stout nodded. "There's the one I mentioned where he worked for a while . . . Heracles Personnel," he said. "Don't tell anyone that I told you that. They're big in the military contractor world. They've got a private army, along with the usual support staff."

They talked for a bit longer, and when Lucas said good-bye, Stout shook his hand, and said, "Listen, marshal, give me a call when you're done with this. I'd like to know what happened."

"If I can," Lucas said.

HE WAS ON HIS WAY back to the hotel when Armstrong called again, from West Virginia.

"I don't mean to bother you," Armstrong said.

"You're not bothering me, Carl," Lucas said. "What's up?"

"I've been thinking. That F-250 is a common truck, but more out in the rural areas than in urban places. Whoever switched those plates found the two trucks close to each other, which maybe means they scouted them out in advance. Which might mean that they actually live or work in that general area."

"Yeah, possibly."

"So I got to wondering, how many F-250s are there in that zip code? The Virginia DMV can sort vehicles by zip code—I checked," Armstrong said. "If you could get a list and compare that list with driver's license photos and then run those guys through the Internet, you might come up with something. Not that I'm saying there's anything to come up with . . ."

"Carl . . . you're a smart guy."

LUCAS HAD SEVERAL THINGS WORKING: somebody may have tried to break into his hotel suite and may actually have succeeded; he had a name, Heracles Personnel; and now he had an idea of how to find the F-250.

His nominal boss worked out of the Marshals Service

headquarters no more than a few miles from where he was, but telephones were faster. As he drove back toward Washington, against rush hour traffic, he got hold of Russell Forte, who was about to leave for home.

Lucas asked him to get whatever information he could on Heracles Personnel and to see if the Virginia DMV could produce a list of black F-250s around the area where the plates had been stolen and driver's license photos of the registered owners.

"Well, hell, I didn't want to go home and talk to my wife and kids and go to all the trouble of cranking up the barbecue and cooking up those ribs my wife bought this afternoon . . ."

"Go home, Russell," Lucas said. "Tomorrow's fine. I've got a couple of places I want to visit in Washington anyway. I'll check with you in the morning. Not too early."

"Thank you," Forte said.

WHEN LUCAS GOT BACK to the hotel, he ate dinner, went to his room, took a quick shower, then dressed carefully in a medium blue summer-weight suit, with a checked dress shirt, a slender Hermès necktie, and black John Lobb shoes.

He thought about taking the Walther, but the gun messed with the drape of his jacket. He finally locked it in the room's safe, although he happened to know how to open any hotel room safe in approximately eight seconds. When he was ready, he called down to the front desk to get a cab, and ten minutes later was on his way up New Hampshire Avenue to Figueroa & Prince, a men's tailor shop that he'd read about, done research on, and finally called before he left St. Paul.

The shop was on N Street, on the bottom floor of what looked like a New York brownstone even though it was constructed of red brick, a three-story building with only a small silver sign next to the door designating it as a commercial establishment. When Lucas tried the door, it was locked, although he'd been told they were open until nine o'clock.

He took a step back, spotted another small sign, this one saying "Please Ring for Entry." He pushed the doorbell button, an apple-cheeked young man looked out the window at him, and a buzzer sounded to let Lucas in.

The young man did a quick eye check on Lucas's suit, smiled, and asked, "Can we help you?"

"I'm looking for autumn and winter suits . . . I was told to ask for Ted."

TED WAS A THIN MAN, older and balding, with a shy smile and a soft voice. Lucas introduced himself, and Ted said, "Oh, yes, the gentleman from Minnesota."

After that, it was forty-five minutes of looking at fabrics and talking about colors, not only of the materials but of Lucas's eyes, hair, and complexion. There was also a subtle interview about where Lucas had bought other suits, accessories, and shoes. Next came forty minutes of measurements, after which Ted said, "This should be good enough for the preliminary work; you will have to come in again for the next fitting . . . probably in two or three weeks?"

"That'll be fine," Lucas said. "I'd like to get them before it gets cold back home."

"We should have them finished by mid-September."

Lucas spent an absurd sum on the suits, put it all on his American Express card. When it had cleared, Ted called a taxi, and Lucas shook his hand and said, "This was a nice experience."

"Happy to be of help," Ted said, as he walked Lucas to the door. "There aren't that many men who take your interest. Mostly, they want something dark that won't wrinkle too badly and they want it quick."

Lucas smiled, went out the door, heard the lock click behind him, and walked down the stoop to the street, where the pleasant evening came to an end.

THREE MEN. At a casual glance, they might have been street people—funky dress, too heavy for the heat, with weird headgear. But the funky dress was too clean and too uniformly funky, as though it had been manufactured that way. None of them had beards. And they didn't move with the halting gait of longtime street people, they moved like well-fed athletes. They were coming in hard. And they weren't carrying anything in their hands.

In addition, there were a few more salient aspects to the approach: (1) The jackets looked heavy, as though they might be covering armored vests, which would be good protection in a fistfight. (2) They were all wearing hats pulled low on their heads—one wore a ball cap, and the other two wore tennis hats. Tennis hats on bums? Don't think so. (3) Lucas could feel them focus on him. One was hurrying in from his left, one was crossing the street straight toward him, one was coming in from his right.

No gun. Couldn't get back inside, the door had locked behind him. In the two seconds that it took him to scan the three of them and discern their intention, he made a snap decision.

Run.

The guy on the right was the bulkiest, and maybe the slowest, and Lucas ran right for him, then swerved to the right, and when the guy moved to block him, Lucas cut left, the guy swung at him, Lucas blocked his fist and with the heel of the same hand hit the man in the face, under the nose, jamming it up into the ridge of his brow, sending him staggering and down on his back.

As Lucas hit him, he realized he couldn't see the man's mouth: he was wearing a tan knit face mask. The impact turned Lucas enough that he could see the other two were almost on top of him. He pivoted and went left, which meant that the farthest one would be behind the closer one, and Lucas'd only have to fend off one man.

The closer one pulled a flashlight from his pocket as he came in, a Maglite, as good as a billy club. Lucas dodged him but then was open to both of them again, and he turned away and the man with the flashlight swung it at him, hit him in the back below his left shoulder, above his shoulder blade, and he stumbled and half turned and nearly stumbled over the first man, who was back on his hands and knees.

Lucas cleared him and the flashlight man came in again and Lucas dodged the light and grabbed the man's face mask and wrenched it sideways, enough to see the man's face, for an instant, from the eyes down. The man wrenched free, and the mask slipped up over his eyes and blinded him; he collided with the third man, and they reeled away. Lucas took advantage of the break to jump over the man on the ground, digging a heel into his back in the process, and Lucas was off and running.

Lucas had a step on them, probably not enough . . .

Then there was a burst of light, and another, and Lucas

thought maybe he'd been shot at, but there was no sound, and the lightning flash came from across the street rather than from behind him. He glanced that direction and saw a tall, thin Asian man holding a cell phone and a briefcase, and it registered in the back of Lucas's brain that the Asian man had taken a cell phone photo of the fight . . .

The flash also diverted the attackers. One of them took several running steps toward the Asian man, but another of the men shouted, "No! No! No!" as the Asian man turned and sprinted down the street. Lucas followed, slower than he might have if he hadn't worn dress shoes to buy a suit.

And Lucas began screaming: "Help! Help! Help!"

He was loud and moving fast, and though there were few people on street, heads were turning their way. Lucas continued running for another hundred feet before risking another glance back . . . and saw the three men running in the opposite direction, before disappearing down a cross street.

The Asian man had stopped ahead, and Lucas ran toward him and called out, "U.S. Marshal. Wait! Wait!"

The man slowed, and Lucas got his ID from his jacket pocket and held it in front of him. Gasping for air, he stuttered, "I'm a . . . I'm a U.S. Marshal . . . Did you take a . . . a photo of that fight?"

The Asian man nodded, and said, in perfect English, "Yes. Two pictures. Who were those men?"

"I don't know," Lucas said. "Maybe muggers."

"I don't think so," the Asian man said. "They all wear masks. They all look the same. I don't think muggers."

Lucas nodded. "Could you please send those photos to my phone?"

"Yes, I will. Of course."

The photos came in: they were sharp enough, but all you could read from them were shapes and sizes. Lucas got the man's name and address in Japan. He was staying at a Washington hotel, on a business trip.

AS LUCAS shook the man's hand, a cab came around the corner. Lucas jumped in front of it, and the driver ran his window down, and said, "I've got a call," and Lucas said, "If it's Figueroa & Prince, it's me."

He was still breathing hard and sweating, and the driver looked at him doubtfully, said, "Well, okay, that's where I was going."

Lucas got in the back, and said, "Watergate Hotel."

The driver pulled away, saying, "I could be wrong, but in my opinion it's too goddamn hot to jog in a suit and tie."

"Gotta get your cardio where you can," Lucas said. They passed the spot where he'd last seen the trio of men, but they were gone. He wouldn't be going out again without a gun, but even if he'd had one, he didn't know if he could have gotten it out in time. The three men had been closing fast, and looked competent, and maybe were armed. If he'd pulled a gun, they might have shot him. Still, he was . . . embarrassed. He'd had to run, and he'd been screaming for help like a little girl.

"So how about them Nationals?" the driver asked.

"I'm from Minnesota," Lucas said, sinking back in the seat. "I'm a Twins fan."

The driver thought for a few seconds, and said, "Then I got nothin'."

AT THE HOTEL, he checked the recorder. Nobody had been in the room, as far as he could tell. And he called Rae. "How soon can you and Bob get here?"

She said, "Oh-oh."

Lucas said, "Yeah."

WHEN HE GOT OFF THE PHONE, he was still high on adrenaline. He eventually put on some gym shorts, a T-shirt, and athletic shoes, went down to the fitness center, and ran off the high on the elliptical machine.

Back in his room, he showered, concentrating on his back: he'd have a major bruise where the Maglite hit, he thought. Out of the shower, he watched the end of a Dodgers game from the West Coast, flopped on the bed, and thought about getting old. He'd barely cracked fifty, but he'd lost at least a step in the past ten years, and maybe two steps. The three muggers would have beaten the shit out of him.

He spent some time brooding, and finally managed to get to sleep at two in the morning.

He'd gotten up the next morning, had shaved, showered, and was about to go to breakfast when Forte called and said, "You're not fucking around with this Heracles place, are you?"

8

Forte said, "These are bad guys, Lucas. Mercenaries. There have been a dozen complaints filed against them by military people in Iraq and Syria, and more by the Iraqi and Libyan governments. They shoot first and ask questions later, but it appears that we continue to contract with them. By 'we,' I mean the Defense Department and contractors working with foreign governments. Can't tell about the CIA, but probably there, too."

"Do they work here in the U.S.?"

"They've got no special status here," Forte said. "They poke a gun at somebody, and that's ag assault, and they go to jail. They're not LEOs. Not law enforcement officers, no way, shape, or form."

"If they jumped me on the street . . ."

"Did they do that?"

"Somebody did," Lucas said. He told Forte about the problem he'd had the night before, and described the three men; he left out the part about screaming for help like a little girl.

"Well, there you go," Forte said. "It sounds like what I imagine the Heracles guys are like, though I've never actually seen them myself. Most of what they call action executives are former SEALs, Delta, Force Recon, Rangers, that sort of thing. You didn't see a gun?"

"No. All three were wearing jackets that had some bulk—like they were wearing light armor, or maybe thick shirts, or padding of some kind, like they were ready for a fight," Lucas said. "I suspect they were planning to take me down but not kill me. Killing me would cause somebody a much larger problem than what might pass as the mugging of an out-of-towner."

"You're sure that's not what it was?" Forte asked.

"Yeah, I'm sure. They were all too neat. Uniform. They wore masks. They didn't look like raggedy-ass muggers; they looked like . . . cops, actually."

"Here's what I want you to do," Forte said. "Write it up, all the details. Put those cell phone photos with it. I'll file it as 'Attack on a U.S. Marshal, Unsolved.' Then if you identify one of the guys, we grab him, file charges. With you as the only witness, we might not get far with it, but we might be able to squeeze the guy while we've got him . . ."

"Probably should have done that last night—or called the D.C. cops."

"I'll call the cops, inform them. I can somewhat mask the time of your report. If they think you reported it immediately . . . well, let them think that. That way, we're on record with two different agencies."

"All right."

"So, sounds like life is getting complicated, but that's why you were hired," Forte said. "What else are you going to do about it?"

"Called Bob and Rae, for one thing. They'll be talking to you guys about coming up here."

"We'll clear them through. Now, about that Ford F-250 . . . There are forty-seven black F-250 short beds of last year's model registered in the three zip codes surrounding the area where those plates were stolen. Black is a popular color, but the F-250 is pricey, so there weren't as many as I expected . . ."

Lucas: "The West Virginia cop I talked to . . ."

"Armstrong,"

"Yeah, he said the truck was new, but didn't specify a year, so maybe we should look at this year's, too."

"Nope. I talked to him this morning, soon as I got in, and he sent me some grab shots from the security video," Forte said. "The taillights changed between the two years—it was last year's model, not this year's."

"Did you get the driver's licenses and run them?"

"I did. Got a whole bunch of hits, but nothing that went directly to Heracles. Several military people—more Navy than Army, but that could include SEALs. Criminal activity is all minor stuff. A few drunk driving arrests, domestics, like that."

"Can you get me the license photos?" Lucas asked.

"We're queuing them up now—my assistant is. You'll have them in twenty minutes."

"Russell, thank you. I'll keep you up to date."

"Stay safe," Forte said. "I don't like the sound of that thing from last night."

LUCAS TOOK the elevator down, ate breakfast, took the elevator back up, and found forty-seven driver's license photos attached to an email. Twelve were women, which, if not irrelevant, wouldn't match any of the faces either he or the hotel security man had seen.

He flipped through the forty-seven, returning a couple of times to the image of a James Harold Ritter, age thirty-nine. He resembled the man whose mask he'd pulled down. He'd been wearing a green tennis hat low on his forehead, so Lucas wasn't positive about the ID, but the chin and mouth looked right. He got on the phone and called Schneider, the hotel security chief, and asked if Jeff Toomes was on duty. Toomes had seen the man he thought might have come from Lucas's hotel room.

Toomes was in the hotel, and Schneider said he'd send him up. He arrived ten minutes later, smelling faintly of onion rings. Lucas let him in, sat him at the desk in front of Lucas's laptop, and let him scan the photos.

"I don't think so," he said eventually. "Photos aren't so great, but none of them ring a bell."

AS LUCAS took him to the door, Toomes turned, and said, "Let me show you something."

He swerved into the bathroom, where a box of facial tissue sat on the sink counter. He pulled out a sheet, tore off a quarter-sized piece, dropped the rest of it in the toilet, touched the small piece to the tip of his tongue, wetting it, wadded it into a small spitball, and pressed it into the peephole of the door.

"These peepholes work both ways," he said. "There was this freak who'd go around making movies of famous women who were walking around their room naked. He was shooting through the peephole. I'm told that you can buy special lenses for that specific purpose, on the Internet. Unless you want to take the chance that somebody's looking at you, keep the spitball in it."

"I'll do that," Lucas said. "You're good at this hotel security stuff, huh?"

"Yeah, I am," Toomes said. "A lot of weird shit happens in hotels. It's interesting."

WHEN HE WAS GONE, Lucas called Forte. "I need everything you can find on James Harold Ritter. You've got his license info, so that's a good start. Nothing's too small."

"I'm in a meeting. Give me a couple of hours."

"Fine. I'm going to go scout his house, see what I can see," Lucas said.

"Easy, boy."

He did not leave immediately. Instead, he called Smalls, and said, "You've got a woman working for you at the cabin. Janet Walker . . ."

"Yes, she runs a caretaking service for absentee landowners."

"I need her phone number," Lucas said.

Smalls went away for a while, then came back for the number. "Her cell phone; she usually answers right away."

She did. Lucas identified himself, and asked, "Do you have access to the Internet?"

She said, "I live in West Virginia, not on the friggin' moon."

"Great. Do you have it handy?"

"I'm in the yard. I'd have to walk into the house."

"I'm going to send you eight or ten photographs. Tell me if any of them look like the guys you saw driving the F-250."

The whole round-trip with the photographs took five minutes. Lucas sent ten, and, after examining them, Walker said, "The third photograph—that looks like the driver. I'm not sure I could swear it was him, if it went to court, but it looks like him."

"Thank you," Lucas said. "Keep this under your hat, if you would."

JAMES HAROLD RITTER.

Lucas had three markers pointing at Ritter: his impression of the attacker's face on the street; Walker's identification; and the fact that he owned a black F-250. Could be a coincidence, with a little bit of a stretch, but Lucas felt he was on a roll, that Ritter was the one.

Like most of the other people Lucas was trying to find, Ritter lived across the Potomac in Virginia, in what turned out to be a neatly kept condominium complex not far from where the F-250 plates had been stolen. The complex had individual covered parking spaces at the back of the building. Although Ritter's driver's license hadn't included an apartment number, Lucas spotted the black Ford pickup, which *did* have an associated apartment number; the apartment number apparently included a vacant space beside the pickup.

Lucas parked in a visitor's lot and walked back to the F-250. There was nobody around in the noon heat, so he walked into the covered parking area and took a close look at the truck.

Smalls had said that his Cadillac had been hit by the passenger side of the attacker's vehicle, and when Lucas squatted at the back of the truck bed, he thought he could see a subtle distortion in the truck's sheet metal. He checked the driver's side for a comparison, and when he came back to the passenger side, the distortion—nothing as clear-cut as a dent or a tear—seemed even more apparent, like a quarter-inch wave in the flow of the metal.

He walked down the side of the truck, to look at it from the front. The same distortion was visible, and the front right headlight cover had a small crack on the right side. He peered in the passenger-side window, but there was nothing visible on the seats. He pulled out a shirttail, used it to cover his hand as he tried all four doors. All four were locked.

The truck had been recently washed, Lucas thought, dragging his shirttail-covered hand across it: it was virtually spotless, and even a heavy forensic examination might have trouble placing it in West Virginia. Still, the truck had been involved in an unusual impact: he wasn't sure he'd found the truck that had taken Smalls and Whitehead off the road, but he'd found a solid candidate. Proving it would be another problem, a greater problem than simply knowing it.

But what kind of impact would leave both trucks without obvious damage while still being violent enough to knock one truck right off the road? He thought about it . . .

His first thought: what if Ritter and his friends had rigged a lattice of freshly cut tree trunks and hung it off the side of their truck? They would have had to put padding under the trunks, against the side of the truck, to prevent damage, but they'd want the raw timber to hit the Cadillac.

It'd be simple enough. When Lucas was in the Boy Scouts, his troop had built rafts out of dead wood and rope and had floated down the Rum River on them. Hung on the side of a truck, the rafts would have worked well as protection against impact, and, even better, would have left evidence of wood contacting metal.

But who would think of that?

People who thought about killing other people in undetectable ways, Lucas figured. Professionals who were given a problem: knock a car off the road and down a bluff without any metal-on-metal contact. Given that dilemma, the tree-trunk-lattice idea would pop right up.

LUCAS WALKED BACK to the Evoque, cranked it up, pushed the air conditioner to max, and called Carl Armstrong, the West Virginia accident investigator.

"I may have found that F-250," he said when Armstrong was on the phone. He described the truck's condition, and asked, "Since you can see there was some impact, but since it's been washed . . . is there going to be anything there for you?"

"If we can show there's been an impact, we could question him about when it happened and why it is that the damage was both extensive yet subtle, and whether he reported the accident. That kind of damage would be uncommon—in fact, I've never run into anything like it. Be hard to explain."

Lucas told Armstrong about the tree-trunk-lattice idea, and after a moment Armstrong said, "That seems kinda unlikely. Not to say . . . stupid."

"I've given you an explanation," Lucas said. "Do you think my idea could result in the kind of damage I've seen?"

"Well . . ."—Lucas could visualize Armstrong scratching his head—"it could, I guess. If it was padded on the back side. Maybe something like a good solid rubber mat, that would do it. As far as finding hard forensic evidence . . . Sounds unlikely. For one thing, everything you find driving around eastern West Virginia you'll find driving around Virginia. Pollen, and all that."

"Okay. I don't want to do anything with it now, but I may be calling you to take a professional look, after we're out in the open on the investigation."

"Happy to do it," Armstrong said. "But, really, a lattice?"

LUCAS WALKED AROUND to the front of the condominium complex and went to the glass front door, which turned out to be the first of two doors. He could get inside the outside glass one, but the interior door was locked. There was a phone on the wall, with a sign that boldly said "DIAL 1 + APT. NUMBER," and, below that, not so boldly, "Dial 1+00 for Management Office." A domed security camera in the ceiling monitored the door and the phone.

He called the office, identified himself to the woman who answered. "I'll buzz you in. Take the first left and walk all the way down the hall to the end. We're the last door on the left."

She buzzed him in. Inside the door was an enclosed booth for mail, with mailboxes on the outside for the residents and an enclosed area behind them that would allow the mail carrier to insert mail in the open backs of the boxes without needing keys to open them. No camera was monitoring the booth's door.

Lucas tested the door: locked, but the lock was crappy, and the door rattled in its frame. He continued on into the building, took the first left, walked down to the end of the hall and into the office, where a woman sat at a desk behind a service counter. She looked up from her computer and asked, "What's going on?"

Lucas flashed his ID and badge at her, said, "I'm a U.S. Marshal. We are trying to talk to Thomas D. Pope, who we understand lives here."

She looked puzzled, and said, "I know everybody who lives here. There's no Thomas Pope."

Lucas said, "Huh? Are you sure?"

"Absolutely positive," she said. "Are you sure you got the name right?"

Lucas scratched his head. "I got the name right, but I might have the wrong apartment building . . . I'm navigating with a description and don't have an exact address, as such."

"You need an address," the woman said. "There are about a million apartment buildings around here. This is a nice one, but there are quite a few that look like it."

Lucas rubbed his nose. "Well, shoot, I guess I'm going to have to do it the hard way. Getting an exact address is a little harder than it usually would be, since the guy moves around a lot."

"I wish I could help you . . ."

"Well, not your fault . . . Have a good day."

LUCAS WALKED BACK toward the main entrance, but, instead of going out, he passed the elevators and then took a staircase up to the second floor. Hallways stretched in both directions from the landing, burgundy carpet in one direction, blue in the other. Nobody was in the hallway; the complex was white-collar, and residents were at work. If he needed to black-bag Ritter's apartment, there wouldn't be a lot of people around, and he saw no security cameras. He went back down the stairs, headed toward the exit.

At the mail booth, he checked for movement inside and out, grabbed the doorknob and put all of his weight against the door, pushing it sideways toward the door hinges, and with an additional punch from the shoulder, the door popped open. He looked around again, stepped into the booth. The backs of the mailboxes were all identified by name and apartment number. Lucas scanned them, found Ritter's. A half dozen pieces of mail sat inside it, and he quickly thumbed through them while listening for footsteps. Three ads, an electric bill, and a bank statement.

He stuck the bank statement in his jacket pocket, replaced the rest of the mail. The lock on the door had a turn bolt on the inside, and he unlocked it, stepped outside, and pushed the door shut behind him. Maybe the mail carrier would think he'd forgotten to lock it.

He walked outside, let the stress fall away in the sunshine. Mail theft: a federal felony, if anybody found out about it, but nobody would.

He hoped.

HE WALKED BACK around the building. The heat was stifling, and though he'd only been out of the Evoque for a few minutes, the interior was already intolerably hot. He started the truck, stood outside briefly, peeling off his jacket while the air conditioner took hold, got back in, and opened Ritter's bank statement.

The statement listed routine payments to fifteen or twenty different places—gas, electric, water, cable, Visa, Amex. The incoming money was more interesting. He found what appeared to be weekly paychecks from a company called Flamma Consultants.

He stuck the letter in his hip pocket: he'd shred it and flush it down the toilet back at the hotel.

AS HE WAS HEADED BACK across the Potomac, he took a call from Rae Givens. "We talked to your man Forte, and we're on our way down to New Orleans right now. We'll be flying back straight into D.C. He got us rooms at the Watergate Hotel. I said, 'Are you kiddin'?' and he said, 'No, why would I be?' I said, 'Okay' . . . So we'll see you there tonight."

A second call came from Forte himself, with information about Ritter. "There's not much on him in the files; we're not allowed to see his income tax returns, but we did take a look at his Army records and his passport. He did three tours in Iraq, got good evaluations, landed a job with Delta and looked like he was in there for life. Instead of reenlisting a third time, he dropped out. His passport would suggest he's been out of the country, in Iraq, Kuwait, Afghanistan, and Pakistan, for most of the time since then."

"A guy who knows his way around. A hard guy."

"Yes . . . Did you get anything?"

"I did. I'll tell you, Russell, I'm going back to the hotel to write this up, but, basically, Smalls's accident was no accident. It was an assassination attempt and a murder, and Ritter was in it up to his neck. His truck was used to run Smalls and Whitehead off the road."

"Lucas, you gotta be sure," Forte said. "It's too hot to be wrong."

"I am sure now, but I can't prove it yet. Between us, we have to figure out where to go with this. Think about it."

"Write it all up, in detail, don't leave a single fuckin' thing out of it. If they smell you coming for them, they might not try to beat you up again. And next time they might come with guns."

"Bob and Rae . . ."

"Are a good idea, but might not be enough. I need to know everything you get, in case you have a problem."

Like getting shot, Lucas thought, smiling to himself. "I'll send you an email, Russell. Later this afternoon."

AT THE HOTEL, Lucas made a few notes, then shredded Ritter's bank statement and flushed it. That done, he kicked off his shoes, dropped onto the bed, and used his burner phone to call a St. Paul friend named Kidd, a painter and an expert in computer databases. Kidd's wife, Lucas believed, was a jewel thief, but that was another story.

Kidd came up, and Lucas identified himself—"Oh-oh. Using a burner?"—and asked Kidd what his favorite charity was.

"Other than myself? The Minneapolis Institute of Art. Weather's a big deal over there, I understand," Kidd said.

"I will give a thousand dollars to the institute if you can dig up some stuff on the Internet and tell me how I could have done it myself," Lucas said.

"What's it all about? That you have to use a burner to even ask me the question?"

"It's about a murder and an assassination attempt . . ."

Kidd had helped Lucas with the original investigation of Taryn Grant. Like Lucas, he believed that Grant was a murderer and that she had gotten to the Senate through a murderous political trick. Lucas explained about the accident, and what he'd found about Ritter, and told him about Jack Parrish and Heracles.

"I, uh, would have a hard time explaining how I came up with the connection between Ritter and Flamma," Lucas said. "I need to be able to make the connection on the 'Net. You know, like I did some research, and there it was. I need it quick."

Kidd said he'd start looking. "I'd like to see you get Grant. She's your basic fascist thug, but with great tits," he said.

From the background, Lucas heard Kidd's wife, Lauren, shout, "Hey! I'm standing right here."

"Call me at this number," Lucas said. "Don't use my regular one. I worry about being tracked."

"As you should," Kidd said. "Give me an hour or two."

LUCAS SPENT AN HOUR putting together an email to Forte, explaining how he'd tracked Ritter, leaving out the part about stealing the bank statement. He saved the email to his laptop but didn't send it. He went back to the bed, closed his eyes, and thought about the case.

So far, he had nothing on Grant or Parrish. They were the ones he needed to get to. If he could nail Ritter for the murder of Whitehead, he could talk to the West Virginia cops about a prosecution. Looking at life in a West Virginia prison would be a powerful incentive to talk about Grant and Parrish.

Of course, Ritter might be one of those hard-nosed stoics who'd take pride in not talking, who'd go to prison first.

KIDD CALLED BACK.

"You said you already knew about Heracles. If you look at the company's incorporation papers—I'll send you a link—you'll find the list of officers. If you run the officers, you'll see that they're also the officers of two other companies, Flamma Consultants and Inter-Core Ballistic Products."

"Wait—there's a direct connection among Heracles, Flamma, and Inter-Core?"

"Not technically direct, but, yeah, they're all run by all the same people."

"Kidd . . . this is serious shit. I'm throwing an extra ten dollars at the museum."

"Thanks, ol' buddy. Anyway, if you run Flamma Consultants, you'll find an online article published in last September's *Combat Tech Review* magazine called 'CanCan Dancers.' In the gun world, suppressors—silencers—are called cans. In that article, you find a picture of Ritter and a couple of other guys all geared up, testing some big-bore silencers at a rifle range in Virginia . . . and Ritter is ID'd as an employee of Flamma. That's how you tied them together."

"Excellent," Lucas said. "I owe you."

"Actually, you owe the museum. A thousand and ten dollars. The original Flamma, by the way, was a famous Roman gladiator, which fits with the whole Heracles *We read the classics* thing. Oh, and let me encourage you to look at that magazine article. Ritter was testing that silencer on an M2010 sniper rifle, which is like a .300 Winchester Magnum and has an effective range of twelve hundred meters. In other words, they can shoot you in the back from more than half a mile away."

"Thanks for the tip," Lucas said, "I'll go hide under the bed. Listen, this Inter-Core Ballistics . . . I met this lawyer out here who told me an interesting story about a Pentagon bid . . ."

He told Kidd what Gladys Ingram told him about a company that had outbid her client on a contract for lightweight side-panel armor for military vehicles. Lucas was checking his notes as he described his meeting with Ingram: "Her client was Malone Materials. If you could check around and see what happened with that particular lawsuit . . ."

"I hate that kind of shit. Good guys die because of it," Kidd said. Lucas knew Kidd had served in an unusual military unit as a young man. "I'll get back to you—I've got extensive resources at the Pentagon. You go hide under the bed."

Rather than hiding under the bed, Lucas called up the text for the email to Forte, added the information about Flamma, which he supposedly found himself on the Internet, and sent it off.

GRANT AND PARRISH: time to look at where they lived.

He got his jacket and went back out, spent the afternoon cruising their houses, which weren't far apart, in Georgetown.

Grant had a mansion, as was fitting for a billionaire, while Parrish lived in a town house. Lucas pulled out his iPad and entered Parrish's address: it popped up on Zillow, which showed it sold three years earlier for $1,450,000. Three bedrooms, three baths, "close to M Street shopping."

Not bad for a guy who'd never worked for anything other than the federal government and maybe two or three years at a private business, Lucas thought. It would be interesting to see if he had a mortgage and, if so, how large it was.

In the meantime . . .

He drove over to M Street to see if that was a big deal—and it was, he supposed. It was like Madison Avenue meets Greenwich

Village, mixing high-end clothing boutiques with burger joints, bars, and yuppie-oriented bicycle shops.

He got a decent burger, drank a couple of Diet Cokes, watched the Washington women walking by, almost all of them clutching cell phones. He asked the waiter where he might buy a book. The waiter had no idea, but a woman who overheard the question told him there was a used-book store three blocks down the street.

He spent a half hour browsing there, found a Carl Hiaasen hardcover novel, *Skinny Dip*, selling for $5.98, bought it and took it back to the hotel.

HE'D LEFT the burner phone in the closet safe, and when he checked it he found a call from Kidd that had come in twenty minutes earlier. He called back, and Kidd said, "Okay, it's as bad as you thought. I've got some ways to check on information . . . that most people wouldn't be able to use. The information is public, and it's out there, so I worked backward through a lot of it."

"I don't know what that means," Lucas said.

"It means that after you find some information, after you know what you're looking for, you can usually find some other way to get to it. Something you could have at least theoretically gotten to. For example, if you know that a company did X, you can often find references to X as the nine hundredth entry on a Google search. Nobody looks for it there—it would take forever. But if you know it's there and you've got specific search terms . . ."

"Got it," Lucas said. "So what was nine hundredth on the list?"

"The guys who run Heracles and Flamma invented Inter-Core Ballistics after the Army began looking for bidders on the armor panels. When they won the bid, they paid another company down in Florida, Bishop Composites, to make the armor. Inter-Core was the middleman on the deal. When I looked up Bishop, it turns out that their stuff had failed earlier tests for shrapnel resistance. They recycled their product through Inter-Core, and, this time, they passed the tests."

"Was it different armor or the same?"

"As far as I can tell, it appears to be identical. Let me make that a little stronger: it *was* identical. After they failed the earlier tests, they were stuck with a lot of the plate, so they gave Inter-Core a cut-rate price. Bishop looks to have sold around thirty-five million in plate, and, from looking at their financial statements, it appears that Inter-Core took about twenty percent of that."

"Twenty percent? Seven million for doing nothing?"

"Not for doing nothing: Inter-Core had to fix the deal."

"Tell me how I get to that," Lucas said.

KIDD DID, with explicit directions of where and how to search legally. Lucas understood most of what he found, although only a forensic accountant could pull it all together. He thought about it, and called Gladys Ingram.

"Marshal Davenport," she said. "Nice to hear from you. How's the investigation going?"

"After you told me about your Malone Materials lawsuit, I went looking for information about Inter-Core Ballistics and found that it tied in to my investigation. I'd like to pass some computer links to you. You probably have much better information resources than I do, so I thought . . . you could take a look, and if you found anything interesting, you might pass it back to me."

"Sure. We still represent Malone, and I have an intern who was born with a silver computer in her mouth . . . What'd you find?"

Lucas gave her a few of Kidd's key discoveries—she'd find the rest herself, or her intern would. Then, Lucas hoped, it would appear that the information was flowing from her to him rather than from him to her.

When she had Lucas's notes, Ingram said, "I'm impressed. I see why you made money on the Internet."

"Yeah, well, it isn't all that hard," Lucas said modestly. "If I had more time, I think I could probably find even more . . . Anyway, get back to me."

"I will."

"And soon."

"Yes."

9

Parrish was let into Grant's house by a housekeeper who told him that Taryn Grant was in her "study": the SCIF in the basement.

Grant was standing behind her desk, talking into a hardwired phone. She used a yellow pencil to point him at a chair.

He sat, and while she talked to somebody about developing a new line of Samsung cell phone apps—it sounded crooked to Parrish, but what did he know?—he considered lying to her about the attempt to mug Davenport.

And decided against it.

Grant was saying, to someone, "Look: I don't want you to copy the code. I want you to look at what the code produces and I want you to produce the identical fuckin' app with a different batch of code and I want you to translate it into fucking Zulu. Are the fuckin' Zulus writing their own apps? Then find out. Call me back tomorrow. I want numbers."

Grant was wearing a white blouse and an ankle-length white skirt, both with cutouts that looked like lace and offered peeks at what lay beneath. What lay beneath, Parrish thought, was either nothing at all or a body stocking that precisely matched her complexion.

Either way, it wouldn't affect him much. Like Grant, he found power more compelling than sex. A quiet deal meeting at the Pentagon or the Senate Office Building, with serious people, was far more compelling than a piece of ass. Anybody's ass.

Grant put the phone on the hook, and said to Parrish, "I mean, Jesus, how hard can it be?"

"What are you trying to do?"

She inspected him, rolling the yellow pencil between her fingers like a baton, and decided to take ten seconds for the answer. "There are about a billion apps for the Samsung phone and the iPhone. The apps are mostly in the major languages. So you take the best ones and you redo the code so nobody can sue you for plagiarism, or whatever that would be, and put it into a non-English language that doesn't have that app. Like Zulu. There are ten million Zulu speakers, and I suspect about eighty percent of them have cell phones. Eight million phones times two bucks for an app is worth doing—especially if you can translate the same app into a whole bunch of other non-major languages that add up to a billion people or so, and if developing the app costs you ten grand."

Parrish considered this, and finally said, "You know, I might have some people who'd be interested in talking to you about that. About specialized apps. I wonder if there are military apps? Tactical apps? I wonder . . ."

Grant waved him off. "No, no, no. The problem with that is, you have to do research. Research costs money. The way we're doing it: we pay some nerd five grand to rewrite the app with different code and pay some college language professor another two grand to translate the language. No research. If it's already a popular app in fifteen major languages, the market research is done, too."

"I'll stick to guns," Parrish said.

"Good idea." She'd been rocking from one foot to the other behind the desk and now she stopped: "Speaking of which?"

"We missed him. We spotted him leaving the Watergate, but he grabbed a cab and took it all the way to a tailor shop, where he stayed for almost an hour and a half," Parrish said. "We set up to take him, but when he came out he spotted us . . . and he ran. He was screaming for help. Jim told me it kinda freaked them out—he was supposed to be a fighter. We were all set for that."

"He ran?"

"Yes. Hauled ass. Moore was coming up from one side, took a swing at him, but he blocked it and punched Moore in the face, and then he ran down the street, screaming for help."

The story made Grant smile—for a moment anyway—but then the smile vanished, and she said, "That's two fuckups. Are you sure you've got the right people? Do I have the right people?"

"Yes, you do. Delta, SEALs—you couldn't get anybody better. They can take a guy down. But this . . ."

"I told you he was smart. You need to spend some time looking him up on the Internet," Grant said. "He's also violent, and somebody's going to get killed if you miss him again. I think it's time to reconsider."

"Reconsider how?" Parrish asked.

"Maybe we lay low. Ignore him. If we see him following me around, we file a stalking complaint with the D.C. police and the Marshals Service, based on his investigation back in Minnesota. Let him die on the vine."

"Well, we could try that," Parrish said. "Still might be a good idea to keep an eye on him."

"You can do that—but don't fuck it up. Stay back. If you lose him, let it go, don't go running around like a bunch of idiots, where he'll see you."

THEY SAT LOOKING AT EACH OTHER across Grant's desk, and Parrish said, "Of course, there is the other problem."

She nodded. "Smalls."

"Smalls and Whitehead. If Davenport develops anything on that—we're talking about murder—the only way he could develop anything is to find the truck, which would get him to Jim, and Jim would get him to Flamma and Heracles, and from there to me, and then to you. If Smalls prepares the ground by going up to the Senate and tells people you tried to kill him . . . and murdered his friend . . ."

"He'd have no proof," Grant said. "Not a goddamn thing."

"He doesn't need proof: he's not taking you to federal court; he's trying to undercut your possibilities. How many people have figured out that if you lie enough, and loud enough, people will start to believe?"

Grant twiddled the pencil, muttered, "Goddamn that Davenport. I'll tell you something: he's not a bad-looking guy, and he's rich. I would have gone out with him, if he'd asked, before all the trouble."

"That's wonderful. Maybe you could say that on the floor of the Senate," Parrish said.

"Watch your mouth," Grant snapped. She went back to twiddling. "Maybe laying low is the way to go—but if he looks like he's getting close to anything, we need to remove him. Permanently or otherwise. Let me know before you move, I'll want the details."

"If we kill him . . ."

"Yeah, yeah, yeah, I know: all the cops in the world will be after us. But not cops exactly like him. Other cops, I can handle. He's the one I'm not sure about."

"He's your basic operator. He's Jim Ritter," Parrish said.

"But smarter. Goddamnit, Parrish, he's got me worried, and I've got other things to worry about."

"We'll handle him. One way or another."

WHEN PARRISH WAS GONE, Grant wandered around the SCIF. The room had unadorned polished concrete walls, floor, and ceiling, designed to make any alterations instantly visible. All the wiring for power and communications came through the ceiling in a single stainless-steel tube that ran through a safelike steel compartment on the first floor. If somebody wished to bug her, they would have to do it by first eluding one of the best security systems ever built and then getting into either the first-floor steel safe or through the steel basement door, all without making a mark. She'd been told that was, essentially, impossible with current technology.

The only way to get at her would be through a computer bug introduced into the dual computer systems by a visitor. Both computers also carried software designed to detect any attempts to do that. The secure computer accepted only encrypted messages, preceded by recognized keystrokes, and transmitted only encrypted messages. The other computer, which was isolated from the first, was considered nonsecure and was used for routine communications only.

Both computers had isolation capabilities: everything coming and going was captured in a software box, where Grant could check it before it was released to the rest of the computer. Anything not recognized would be burned.

She was still paranoid enough that she rarely used the computers and was careful to shut them down and kill the power when not in use. A minute's delay in powering them up was worth the security that step brought.

She found the uninflected gray concrete environment of the SCIF surprisingly conducive to thought. She thought about Davenport, about Parrish, about George Claxson and the Heracles operators, and about the presidency. Parrish and Claxson assured her that the operators didn't know her name, didn't know who they were indirectly working for. She didn't believe that. If they couldn't figure it out—Parrish, after all, was her paid aide—they were too dumb to be working for her.

Knowing or suspecting was okay, though, as long as they had no proof.

DAVENPORT'S INVESTIGATION could probably be derailed by one simple action: she could fire Parrish, call it all off, wait for six or ten years to run for president.

The cable news shows loved her—she was hot, sassy, well briefed, always prepared with a few quips about whatever the subject matter was, always willing to treat the producers and the talking heads as if they were actual movers and shakers, which they loved more than anything. She could go on her pick of cable shows and let drop that her only current political interest was serving the people of Minnesota, and, no, she wouldn't be a candidate for the presidency. Not now anyway.

Getting rid of Parrish, her connection with Claxson and

Heracles, and announcing that she wouldn't run for the presidency, removed all her motives for attacking Smalls, or anyone else.

She thought about that for a while.

Thought about how the newsies clamored after even the possibility of getting video of the President walking between the White House and his helicopter. About how they chased him around a golf course, about cameramen taking video of his friggin' airplane taking off. Because, you know, the President is in there.

That was more than celebrity: they treated the President like Caesar. Like Stalin. Like God.

And that's what she wanted. She could feel it, taste it.

To be the most important, looked-at person on the planet.

She was young enough, she could wait . . .

But she didn't want to.

10

After finishing the report, Lucas watched television for a while. And a few minutes after nine o'clock, there was another knock at a door—and, this time, it was his door. He removed the spitball from the peephole, checked, and saw Rae peering in at him.

"Man . . ." Lucas was pleased to see her, and him: Rae Givens, the tall, thin black woman, a former basketball player at the University of Connecticut; and her partner, Bob Matees, the short, wide former wrestler.

Rae was wearing a red pants suit that was loose enough to hide the Glock bump at her hip. Bob was wearing a blue cotton jacket over a knit golf shirt, and similar hip bump, and khakis. They were apparently happy enough to see him as well, Rae giving him a hug, Bob slapping him on the back, and Lucas, once he got the door shut, began cross-examining Bob about his leg wounds.

"All healed up. Still get some pain now and then, and they tell me that'll probably go on for a while, maybe forever," Bob said. "But it doesn't slow me down at all." He did a couple of squats to prove it.

"Not that he was all that lightning fast to begin with," Rae said.

"Our rooms are down the hall," Bob said, marveling. "Boy oh boy, the Watergate. Do we get one of those minibars?"

"Possibly," Lucas said, laughing.

In addition to personal duffel bags, they each were carrying a heavy tan canvas duffel stuffed with black rifles, ammo, armor, helmets, and everything else you needed to break down doors and bust gun-crazed fugitives.

"Tell us everything," Rae said, dropping onto the bed.

Lucas told them about Parrish and Grant, about Heracles and Flamma, about finding the Ford F-250, about the street attack, about checking out Parrish's and Grant's houses. "Pulling full-time surveillance on them would be difficult. They've got these former military operators hanging around, and there's no good place to set up."

He pulled up the addresses on Google Earth so they could check out the streets. "It's all choked up, there's no place to watch from where you don't stand out like a sore thumb."

They talked about that for a while, and Bob said, "You know, I don't think we'll find out much by trailing them around, Grant and Parrish. We need people we can talk to, voluntarily or otherwise. Might be better to figure out who knows about the bad stuff, might be willing to deal, and pick them up and squeeze them."

Lucas considered that, and nodded. "You've got a point. They already know I'm poking around, but they don't know that I spotted the truck."

"As far as we know," Rae said.

"Yeah, as far as we know. They might have been in my room, they sure as hell know I was in that tailor shop, but I never felt them watching me." Lucas walked around, scratched his head, and said, "Everything is up in the air. I'm almost certain that Parrish was involved in trying to kill Smalls, but that doesn't mean that Grant was. Parrish might have wanted to kill Smalls for his own reasons. He wants to ride Grant's coattails as a senator and maybe someday as president. Did she know what was going to happen? If she did, she's guilty of murder—"

"You told us that she's already guilty of murder. Back in Minneapolis."

"She is, but I couldn't prove it," Lucas said. "I don't want that to happen again. This time, if she's got her hand in it, I want to nail her."

Bob said, "Okay, then one of the first things we want to do is not talk like that. We're doing an investigation, not carrying out a vendetta. You and Rae and me might know that we're trying to nail her, but that can't go on the record. We're looking into what we think might be a crime, a murder, and guess what? Senator Grant pops up, much to our surprise. No way, no how, did we frame her. Never even thought about it."

"Of course not," Lucas said. To Rae: "You did say he was smarter than he looks."

"I also said that wouldn't be hard," Rae said.

BOB AND RAE went to check out their rooms, down the hall from Lucas, to wash their faces and use the bathrooms. Fifteen minutes later they were back, talking about how to proceed.

They worried about the Ford truck: it was a key piece of evidence, but not yet a very good one. They had to combine the truck with other evidence if they wanted to get any of it in front of a jury, and they had to do it quickly.

Bob said, "The problem with letting it go is, if Ritter takes it out and deliberately smacks it into another car or scrapes a bridge abutment, there goes the evidence. If he managed to do it right, he wouldn't even have to pay for it—his insurance would cover it."

"Yeah, I know, but what are we gonna do?" Lucas asked.

"How about if we got your West Virginia cop over there to document it, sometime when Ritter isn't around," Rae suggested. "We'd at least have a record of the damage, and somebody official who could testify to it."

"That might be something," Lucas said. "Be nice if we could do it somewhere besides his apartment complex. Even if he's not home, somebody could see us and mention it to him."

They talked about how that might work and then let it go—they'd make some kind of decision the next day.

"Is there any possibility that Smalls could prod Grant?" Rae asked. "You say he's already pissing on her. What if he made some kind of statement that hinted he thought she'd tried to assassinate him and wound up murdering Whitehead?"

"That could drive her underground," Lucas said. "She might freeze out everyone, tell them all to disappear. What we need to do is get her worried, get her moving around, get her trying to fix things. Get her boys more out in the open."

Bob: "I don't think we should mess with either Parrish or Grant—not yet. For our sake. Listen, we're messing with the U.S. Senate here. If that became public, we could lose our jobs."

Lucas: "But she's nuts, we need to get at her . . ."

Bob nodded. "Yeah, we do, but we have to come at it from another direction. We have to be *protecting* the Senate. Somebody tried to off Smalls, right? An assassination attempt. We try to find the assassins. That takes us to Ritter and Heracles, and Heracles takes us to Parrish, and Parrish works for Grant. We take that to the attorney general, maybe get a look-in from the FBI . . ."

Rae and Lucas looked at each other, and Lucas said, "He's right, of course."

Rae nodded. "He might be right, but where do we go with that?"

LUCAS MENTIONED that he and Smalls shared a theory about how Smalls's Cadillac could have been hit but show no signs of anything other than impacts with trees. "They'd have hung a grid of tree trunks off the side of the truck, like a Boy Scout raft."

Bob said, "So . . ."

"We know Ritter lives back here, in the Washington area, and his accomplices, whoever they are—another guy was seen in the truck—probably live here, too, working for Heracles. After they ran Smalls off the road, they'd have wanted to get those tree trunks off the truck as soon as they could. As invisibly as they could. I asked my West Virginia guy to talk to the local sheriffs, to have their deputies keep their eyes open for that, for the tree trunks, but that's probably a low priority over there. We need to light some fires."

Rae: "You think we should wander around West Virginia looking for tree trunks?"

"What the hell else you got to do, other than watch my back?" Lucas asked. "It has two benefits: if they're tracking me somehow and see what we're doing, they'll try to interfere, and we'll have a shot at them. If they're not tracking us, there's a fair chance we'll find the tree trunks. Then, if we wanted, we could take the whole thing public. Or talk to big guys at the Department of Justice. Or do something to drive Ritter and his pals out in the open."

"Like what?" Rae asked.

"I haven't figured that part out yet," Lucas said.

"I'd like to talk to the big guys at the Department of Justice anyway," Bob said, "to tell them what I think about everything."

"That's a real good idea," Rae said. "Remind me *not* to be there."

Bob yawned, and said, "Let's find a pancake place tomorrow morning and work it out. Pancakes, coffee, and West, by God, Virginia. They got pancakes in D.C.?"

"Haven't looked, but there's gotta be something. Maybe even downstairs," Lucas said. "We've got to move early. Before nine."

Rae: "In case somebody needs to tell you, nine's not early . . . Say, I wonder if they got grits?"

"Jesus, I'm not watching you eat grits. Or okra. Let's stick with pancakes," Lucas said.

"Waffles," Bob said. "Big scoop of creamery butter. They got cows in D.C.?"

"With all the bullshit that comes outta here, you'd think there'd be a cow around somewhere," Rae said.

"Let's talk more in the morning," Lucas said.

BEFORE HE WENT TO BED, Lucas went to his iPad and called up maps of Virginia and West Virginia. Because the mountains ran northeast to southwest, so did most of the roads. The quickest way out of the area around Smalls's cabin and back to the D.C. area was almost straight east. If they were right about the tree trunks, they would have been ditched in Hampshire County, West Virginia, or in Frederick or Shenandoah counties in Virginia.

But the killers wouldn't have wanted to drive in traffic with the logs on the side of their truck . . .

Lucas called up a satellite view of the area and made some notes on likely roads back toward I-66 into Washington. Avoiding towns and traffic . . .

He spent an hour at it, then did a search for the sheriff's contact emails in the three counties. He made up three emails, explaining what he wanted to do, asking for help, and telling them that he'd arrive with two other marshals by noon. He finally put away his electronics, read the Hiaasen book for a while, and went to bed at one o'clock.

Wasn't much of a plan, he thought, before the lights went out, but it was something.

THE NEXT DAY they did the pancakes and waffles, sausage links and bacon, at a greasy but otherwise decent diner off in the general direction of Capitol Hill, recommended by the hotel's concierge.

Lucas told Bob and Rae about the emails he'd sent to the sheriffs the night before and the follow-up calls he'd made that morning. He'd gotten some grumbling, but they agreed to meet at a country store at noon and supply a few cars to methodically cruise the ditches and side roads specified by Lucas and to search turnoffs or other likely dump spots.

"And what are we going to do?" Bob asked.

"Same thing. I've marked some places that I think would be good prospects—close to major roads, heavy cover, and so on," Lucas said. "I didn't have time before we left, but I saved the stuff on a thumb drive and I'll run down to the business center and print out maps before we leave."

"You are a paragon of efficiency," Bob said, "but it sounds really, really boring."

"Probably, but I've also figured out a small variation on the whole plan."

"What's that?" Rae asked.

"I'm going to tell these sheriffs and their deputies that the reason this is so important is, we believe somebody tried to assassinate Senator Smalls, and actually did murder his friend," Lucas said. "That this isn't some fishing expedition looking for a minnow. And it might be something they'd like to get credit for."

Rae stopped chewing on her strip of bacon. "Lucas, that'll wind up in the newspapers, sooner or later. Or on TV."

Lucas nodded. "For sure. Because if one of the sheriffs doesn't leak it, I will."

BACK AT THE HOTEL, Bob and Rae hauled their equipment bags down to their rented Tahoe, Lucas rolled out his Evoque, and at ten o'clock, dressed in jeans, long-sleeved shirts, and boots, on a day that was already sweating heavily, with thunderheads building to the southwest, they took off for West Virginia.

Included in the equipment that the two marshals had brought were radios with headsets so they wouldn't have to talk on cell phones. Lucas set the pace, and they rolled west on I-66 and, at ten minutes to twelve, arrived in the small town of Strasburg, Virginia. Since everyone involved was a cop, they'd agreed to rendezvous at a convenience store that also sold Dunkin' Donuts; when they arrived, the parking lot looked like a police convention, with seven sheriff's cars scattered around the blacktop. The store wasn't big enough to hold all the cops, so they got ice-cream cones and donuts and sacks of potato chips and gathered in the shade of an ash tree to talk.

Lucas introduced himself, Bob, and Rae. The sheriffs said that they already had deputies out looking, but without any luck at that point.

Lucas said, "Look, we appreciate your help. This is important: we have developed some evidence, which I'm not allowed to talk about, that this so-called accident was an assassination attempt aimed at Senator Smalls. The killers wound up murdering an innocent woman, but we believe she was what you call collateral damage."

They seemed skeptical. One deputy said, "You know how many trees we have in West Virginia? If somebody said a billion, I'd say that's probably low. Might be that many downed tree trunks, too."

Bob jumped in. "I know what you're thinking, that this sounds like some kind of federal horseshit, but I promise you it's not. We're not fancy federal cops. We're street guys; we make our living kicking down doors and kinda, you know, looking for trees. This might be the most important case we'll ever work on—and that you'll ever work on. Even if you have your doubts, I hope you'll work it hard."

Rae: "Lucas and Bob and I will all be out there, combing through the woods, right along with y'all. If we find what we're looking for, we'll have hard proof that this was murder."

After some more back-and-forth, and the purchase of massive numbers of additional donuts, Cokes, Diet Cokes, a couple of Pepsis, and water, the crowd broke up, still with some grumbling.

Lucas, Bob, and Rae caucused before they left, Lucas asking, "What do you think?"

"They'll look," Bob said. "At least for today. Maybe tomorrow. Not much longer, though. It's too goddamn hot out there."

Rae touched Lucas's arm, and said, "Don't get your hopes up, big guy. This is a needle in a haystack."

LUCAS EFFUSIVELY THANKED all three sheriffs before they left, including the two from Virginia, but believed that the tree trunks, if they were to be found, would be in West Virginia. "They wouldn't have gone far before they got rid of them. All they needed to do was get caught in somebody's headlights and they'd be dealing with witnesses."

Bob said, "They could have pulled over one minute after the accident, taken the trees, the lattice, whatever, taken it apart, thrown the trees in the bed of the truck, and taken them to a landfill somewhere."

Lucas was shaking his head. "No. When they made the lattice, they would have wanted to protect the entire length of the truck. I looked up the F-250, their model: it's almost twenty-one feet long. But they've got a short bed, and the cargo box is only like six feet nine inches long. If they put twenty-one-foot logs in a six-foot box, they'd have a fifteen-foot overhang. That'd be as noticeable as hanging them off the side."

"Then let's go find the needle," Bob said.

THEY STARTED where the accident took place, looking down the steep slope at the river below. Rae said, "Think about it: the accident happens, do they watch to make sure they go over the cliff or do they keep going?"

"For one reason or another, they apparently kept going," Lucas said. "Porter told me that he was afraid they'd come down the hill and finish them off, so he got a gun out of the back and hid out . . . nobody came down, and he never saw the truck again or even its lights."

Rae: "How far would they drive before they pulled over? They'd have to be thinking that there might be a witness, so it wouldn't be in the first two minutes they'd actually want to, you know, get away. Get out of sight."

"Look for places they could do that," Lucas said.

BOB AND RAE LED, with the Tahoe's wheels edging the road, Rae hanging out the window as Bob drove. Lucas edged the wheels of the Evoque off the other side of the road, looking in the ditches for any changes in the foliage. The ditch on his side was shallow, and there were occasional ripples in the weeds, but he saw nothing that looked suspicious. The going was brutally slow and hot, and Lucas had one arm hung out the window, the better to get his head out where he could see; by the end of the day, he thought, he'd be bruised from his armpit to his elbow.

When they got to the main intersection leading out, they saw a sheriff's car crawling toward them. They stopped to talk, and the deputy said he'd followed the road four miles out, both sides of it, and had seen nothing. "There were some woodlots back there, right along the road. I got out and looked, but there were only a couple of spurs back into the trees. I didn't see anything fresh."

"Nothing behind us," Lucas said. "So we go east? You're welcome to track along with us."

"More trees that way," the deputy said. "We'll be taking it slow."

They again took it slowly, four or five miles an hour, getting out to walk in some spots. They had two false alarms but never did find anything good.

But another deputy did.

Her name was Marlys Weaver, and she found the logs fifty feet up a remote forest road, a place called South Branch Hills Drive, which crossed the mountains toward Virginia.

Lucas took the call from the sheriff on his cell phone. "Ol' Marlys says she's found them. I personally didn't think we had a snowball's chance in hell, but Marlys always knows what she's talking about."

"How do we get there?" Lucas asked.

LUCAS AND BOB AND RAE, in their two trucks, followed the sheriff's deputy cross-country, the deputy playing with his lights and siren though they rarely saw another car. Running hard on poor roads, they got to Marlys Weaver in twenty minutes.

When they came up to Weaver's patrol car—and saw the sheriff's car coming in from the other direction—Lucas piled out of the Evoque and joined Bob and Rae, and Bob said, "Man, we should have looked here first. If I was going to find a spot . . ."

They were fifteen miles from the accident scene, on a lightly used road that ran east up a shallow valley toward the top of the mountain ridge, and down the other side. On the right side of the road, a track cut off to the south, up the wall of the valley.

The deputy, Weaver, was standing a hundred feet up the track and twenty or thirty feet above them. She shouted, "Don't let anybody drive up. We have some tire tracks."

Rae said, "No fuckin' way," and the sheriff came up, and Lucas, Bob, Rae, the sheriff, and the deputy who'd been working with them all walked up the middle of the track to Weaver. She was a stout young woman with short hair and glasses, dark patches of sweat at the armpits of her black-and-green uniform. As they left the road, she shouted again, "Watch your ankles. I might've kicked a copperhead out of there."

"Oh, that's good," the sheriff muttered. He was a broad, anxious-looking man with a red face and redder nose. "Somebody else walk ahead of me."

"The first walker only scares them," Rae said. "They strike at the second one in line."

"Good to know, young lady," the sheriff said. "Two of you walk in front of me."

THE TRACK had no apparent reason for its existence. It ran a hundred yards up the hill and then simply petered out. "There's an illegal dump back there, doesn't get used too much," Weaver explained, pointing on up the hill. "I didn't see the logs when I walked up, spotted them on the way back down. Right over here."

The track itself ran up a sloping spine, which rolled off to each side. To the west of the road, a patch of raspberries spread across the hillside. Weaver led them down a foot-wide track, and there, fifteen feet into the berry patch, were four logs, each at least twenty feet long and five or six inches in diameter.

"Got silver car paint on them." She looked at Lucas. "You said that Caddy was silver, sir . . ."

"That's right," Lucas said. He knelt by the logs, found scrapes of silver paint, and Bob, working beside him, said, "Look here."

Lucas looked, and Bob pointed at cuts that went horizontally around the logs. "That's where they put the chains, or the ropes, to tie them together."

Lucas looked at Weaver. "Great job. Great job. You said there were tracks?"

"Yes, sir. Only fresh ones up here and only about a foot long, but somebody ran right up into some softer dirt here."

She pointed, and all of them crawled out of the raspberry patch to look. The track wasn't entirely clean: weeds grew up out of the tread marks, but they were clear enough if you looked closely. The sheriff said, "Might have some more over here . . ." and they found another six inches of similar track. "Need to check the whole road out," the sheriff said.

Lucas: "I've got to make a phone call. Let's stay away from the logs completely, and out of that raspberry patch, in case they left behind some DNA. And let's try to stay away from snakes but work that track, see if we find more treads, coming or going. They must have turned around up here somewhere."

BOB, RAE, AND THE SHERIFF got everybody organized as more deputies rolled in, while Lucas got on his phone and called Carl Armstrong.

"Guess where I'm at," he said, when Armstrong got on the phone.

"Minnesota? You went home?"

"I'm on a mountain road here in West Virginia. We found the logs, with silver paint. We've got treads. We need an accident investigator." He looked up at a growing thunderhead to the southwest. "We need him quick in case it rains."

"I'm running out the door," Armstrong said after Lucas told them where they were. "But it'll be a couple of hours anyway."

Armstrong told Lucas to get to the nearest store and buy plastic sheets—"garbage bags, anything, the bigger, the better"—to cover the tread marks and as much of the logs as possible.

Lucas told the sheriff what was needed, and one of the deputies' cars went screaming away, lights and sirens running. "Back in twenty minutes if he doesn't kill hisself," the sheriff said. "Don't think that cloud'll hit us. Looks to me like it'll slide off to the east."

The deputy got back in half an hour with painter's plastic drop cloths. They wrapped the logs and covered the tread marks they'd found. One of the deputies trenched around the treads to drain water away. With an extra sheet of plastic, and the smell of rain in their noses, they tented the wrapped logs and anchored the plastic with sticks from the surrounding timber.

Then the rain hit, a downpour that would have given Noah a hard time. They sat in their cars, running the air-conditioning and listening to music, flinching at the nearby thunder and the lightning that flickered through the woods. The rain lasted twenty minutes and rolled off to the northeast. The sheriff, getting out of his car into the last bit of drizzle, said, "Like I told you, it was sliding off to the east."

"Too bad it wasn't a direct hit," Rae said. "Might of drowned the fuckin' snakes."

ARMSTRONG TOOK a bit longer than two hours to arrive. Lucas impatiently paced the road, calling him twice to make sure he hadn't killed himself. Eventually, Lucas, Rae, Bob, and the sheriff went out to a country store that sold microwave bean burritos, the same store where the deputy had bought the drop cloths, and had a nasty lunch.

"You still gonna talk to the newspapers?" Rae asked.

She kept her voice down, and Bob had moved in to block the sheriff out of the quiet conversation; he was having a noisy campaign chat with the store owners anyway.

"I've got to talk to Porter's top aide—she's in on this and she probably has a link to somebody I could call. I'm thinking we should drop a hint, anonymously, at one of the major news stations, and maybe the *Washington Post*, and give them the sheriff's name. He's a talkative sort," Lucas said, glancing over at him. "I don't want it out there before we've got an eye on that truck, though."

"Day after tomorrow would be soon enough," Bob said.

Lucas nodded. "I'll work it out this evening, after Armstrong shows up."

ARMSTRONG ARRIVED in a pickup with two crime scene investigators. The sky had cleared, and the three men carefully peeled the plastic off the logs. Armstrong looked at the paint scrapings, comparing them to a piece of metal taken from Smalls's Cadillac. After a moment, he muttered something to himself, stood up, and walked over to Lucas, Bob, and Rae.

"If that paint didn't come off the Caddy, I'll eat the logs. We need to take paint samples and transport the logs. You said there were some tracks that might be associated?"

They showed him the tracks, and the two CSI guys went to work with lights, cameras, and tape measures, eventually clipping the vegetation in the tread marks and making casts with a beige-colored liquid that quickly solidified.

As the sun dropped toward the horizon, the logs were wrapped in plastic padding and loaded one by one onto the pickup and tied down, with red flags hanging from the exposed ends sticking out of the back of the truck. Armstrong asked Lucas, "What about the truck? When can I look at it?"

"Day after tomorrow, probably," Lucas said. "We've got some prep work to do."

"So do I," Armstrong said. "I need to measure the logs and see what kind of impact marks they'd leave on an F-250 if they were used the way we think they were . . . although they were probably well padded. The formal lab results on the paint will take a while. And we need to go over the logs inch by inch to see if there's even a speck of black paint."

"When we decide to officially look at the truck, we'll call," Lucas said.

THAT NIGHT, Lucas walked over to Kitten Carter's apartment complex and took an elevator to the fourth floor. She was standing in the hallway and waved at him when he stepped off the elevator.

Carter lived in a two-bedroom unit, with the second bedroom converted into a compact, messy office with a desk and two visitor's chairs. Lucas saw the office as he walked by, but Carter pointed him into the living room and asked him if he'd like a glass of wine or a bottle of water. He took water, and she asked if he wanted bubbly or still, and he took bubbly. When they finally sat down to talk, he told her about finding the truck.

"Then we've got . . . something? What do we have?"

"We've got one end of the string," Lucas said. "If we find black paint on the logs, we could pick up Ritter. But I don't think they'll find any—I've looked at that truck and I didn't see a single scrape or mark of any kind. So we get Armstrong over here to go over the truck, we roust Ritter, but we don't take him yet. Let's see if we can create some cracks in their team."

"How?"

"Do you know anybody at the *Post*, or one of the major TV stations, who you could talk to off the record? Who would never give you up?"

She nodded. "Yes. Of course. I can always feed them a tip, if you can tell me what to say."

"I need you to give them the names of a couple of people. Russell Forte, over at the Marshals Service—and the sheriff we worked with—and Carl Armstrong in West Virginia. None of them might give much up, but if you give a good reporter a few details, he'll be able to pry a few more facts out into the open. Especially if he talks to the sheriff."

"Give me the details. In one minute." She got off the couch and went into her office and came back with a legal pad. "Okay. I want to make sure I get this right."

"Investigators from the Marshals Service found four logs with paint on them that match the paint from Senator Smalls's Cadillac. That's now being confirmed in a crime scene lab . . ."

He gave her the name of the sheriff and the deputy who found the logs, and Forte's name and phone number. He added, "Marshals Service investigators have reported to their superiors that they have a lead on the truck, based on video taken the day before the murder and assassination attempt."

"When should I feed it to them?"

"Depends on who you're going to give it to," Lucas said.

"Depends on when you want it out. I can give it to a friend at WJZ and have it on the air tomorrow night, or to a woman at the *Post*, who'd put it up the next morning . . . or both."

"Let's go with both," Lucas said. "We don't want them to miss it. Make sure you're totally off the record."

"What are you going to do?"

"We're going to look for reaction . . . We're gonna hope for one."

THE NEXT DAY wasn't quite a waste. Ritter's truck remained parked at his apartment, with the empty space next to it. Lucas did see Ritter, arriving back at his apartment at five-fifteen in the afternoon, driving a sporty red Mazda Miata. He left again at seven o'clock and drove a mile or so to a cocktail lounge called the Wily Rat, with Lucas following behind, and with Bob, who'd been about to take over the watch from Lucas, trailing in the Tahoe.

Ritter parked and walked toward the nightclub's entrance. Before he got there, a short, slender woman came out, looked both ways down the sidewalk, and spotted Ritter walking toward her. She trotted over to him, put her hands on his shoulders, jumped up and wrapped her legs around his waist. Ritter kissed her, and they spoke for a minute. Then she jumped down, and they walked into the club.

Bob followed them inside a few minutes later, got a beer, watched for a while, walked back outside, and told Lucas, who was waiting in the parking lot, "They're getting burgers and beers. Met some people in there, look like military folks. Yakking it up."

"Not much, then."

"Not yet. My turn to watch them. Do you want me to follow them home?"

"Be nice to know who the woman is," Lucas said.

"I'll see if I can spot her car, get her plates."

"Okay." Lucas yawned. "I'm going back to the hotel. Kitten said there'll be something on TV tonight about the assassination attempt, so . . . you might see something from Ritter. If anything happens, call. Gonna get up early. We should see something in the papers tomorrow, for sure, and all over TV."

11

Taryn Grant didn't see the original broadcast about the assassination attempt on Porter Smalls, but her chief of staff picked up an echo on CNN. Mabel Tate was at first bemused with the report, which was more than a little vague. Then, recalling the controversy surrounding her boss's initial election, and with the news reports' reminder that a woman had been killed, bemusement shifted to concern, and she called Grant at home.

Grant did not like to be called at home with anything less than end-of-the-world problems. She had a date that night with an Assistant Secretary of the Treasury (Legislative Affairs), who was on temporary career-building loan to the Treasury from JPMorgan Chase. She hoped to impress him with the plight of hapless billionaires facing unfair tax burdens.

He was a sleaze, she knew, the kind of government official who owned a specialized high-riding electric razor that kept him in permanent three-day-beard mode, and who wore custom silk dress shirts open at the throat to show off the mat of chest hair beneath, but . . .

He had his uses.

Grant definitely favored men who had uses.

WHEN HER PHONE RANG, she picked it up, saw "Tate" on the screen, and asked, "What?"

"Have you been watching the news?" Tate asked.

"Are we bombing somebody?"

"I wouldn't call you for that," Tate said. "This might be worse."

Grant knew Tate wouldn't call for anything trivial. She had a dressing stool in the bathroom, and she sat, and said, "Tell me."

"There are reports on CNN that a U.S. Marshal is claiming that Porter Smalls's accident last week wasn't an accident—that it was an assassination attempt," Tate said. "There's no comment from the marshal, but there's a comment from a West Virginia sheriff, who said the marshal and he and his deputies found some logs with silver automotive paint on them, which had been hung off the side of the truck that forced Smalls's car off the road. They say the truck has been spotted on video, a black Ford F-250. The logs were apparently an attempt to make it look like Smalls's truck hit nothing but trees. CNN says that Smalls is traveling to the CNN affiliate in Minneapolis to be interviewed later in the show, and that the truck is being sought."

"Shit! I didn't need to hear this."

"I'm sorry."

"No, no, I mean I didn't need to have this happen. But you did right to call," Grant said. "The problem is, it could dredge up all that old crap around the election. The marshal is named Lucas Davenport. Was he mentioned? Was he on the show? He's definitely out to get me."

"No, they didn't mention his name. They called somebody at the Marshals Service headquarters, who had no comment. A spokesman for the Justice Department said the matter is being reviewed at the highest levels, which means they don't have a clue. Since it's Smalls, and a woman is dead—and, even worse, she's a rich woman who gave lots of money to Republicans—I imagine there'll be a lot said tomorrow."

"Goddamnit. Listen, monitor this for me, all the channels, and call me at eleven o'clock. I've got a date, but I should be home before then—and if it's urgent, call me anytime," Grant said. "If you have to bring a couple of people in, go ahead. I'd like to see some transcripts of the major shows."

"We can do it. Because of the . . . controversy . . . what should I do if they start looking for a comment from you?"

"I'm not available. I have no knowledge of the incident. If you can, go deep off the record with reporters you can trust and suggest that Smalls has a history of alcoholism that he has successfully covered up. This might be part of another cover-up. If he was drunk when the woman was killed and he was driving, that would make him guilty of vehicular homicide."

"Do you think he was?" Tate asked.

"I don't know and I don't care," Grant said. "I know that he does drink a bit; I've seen him tipsy. The point is, to fuzz things up."

"You got it," Tate said.

WHEN TATE was off the phone, Grant went back to her mirror for a minute, working on her eyelashes, thinking about the news reports, and when she was done with the mascara, dabbed on a touches of Black Orchid perfume, and called Parrish.

He hadn't seen the news, either. When she told him about it, he said, "Give me some time to check around. I'll handle this personally. No blowbacks."

"I said it before: it's Davenport we have to worry about. If he goes away somehow, we're in much better shape."

"I'm handling Davenport. It's already under way."

IF THE TREASURY MAN thought he was going to get laid by a beautiful blond Minnesota senator, he was mistaken. He made some of the usual eye and touching moves that men thought were good ideas when dealing with desirable women, but Grant, as a long-legged blonde, and one of the heirs to a multibillion-dollar fortune, had been inoculated against that kind of bullshit from the time she was eight.

Still, the night developed profitably for the both of them. When the Treasury guy realized that Grant was looking for an insider, not a piece of his ass, he slid into negotiating mode, and they spent their time over cocktails, and cocktail napkins, where they outlined possible beneficial changes to the tax law.

Not really fun, but not uninteresting, either.

They'd finished dinner, and were drinking the last of a four-hundred-dollar bottle of white Bordeaux, when Grant's cell phone buzzed: Tate.

"I've got to take this," she said. She turned away from the Treasury guy, and said, "Yes?"

"An update. Smalls had a press conference. Every TV station in the Twin Cities was there. Parts of it will hit the major networks, and Fox and CNN. He didn't mention any names, but he said that violence had been used against him before and that he wouldn't let it shake him. Three different reporters tried to get him to say your name—they mentioned you, asked if that was what he was talking about. He smiled: might as well have said your name. He never did, but everybody got the point."

"Goddamnit. I'm going to have to say something. Work it for me. Remember what I said about seeing him tipsy, drunk—see if you can work that in. If he's going to get in my face, I'll get right back in his."

"I'll get some ideas together, but it might not be the wisest move. There are other ways to get in his face."

"Give me those, too."

She went back to the Treasury man with a smile. "Porter Smalls is getting in my face about his drunken accident last week. If you want to witness a traumatic castration, watch me on the news tomorrow."

He laughed, and said, "I believe you ahead of time. And I'll be watching."

GRANT WAS HOME at eleven when Tate called again. "Talked to my guy at PBS. They're sucking wind on the story, and they liked that thing about Smalls's drinking problem and the questions that might raise. I don't know if it'll do us a lot of good, but it will fuzz things up, like you said. I've also got them checking up on this Davenport's record—he sounds like a trigger-happy right-winger; he's killed a whole bunch of people . . ."

"I don't want to mess with a nice story line, but Davenport actually worked for Elmer Henderson." Henderson was temporarily out of office but had been the governor of Minnesota and the extremely liberal Democratic vice presidential candidate in the previous election.

"Oh . . . Well, basically, who gives a shit," Tate said. "We can still frame him as an attention-seeking killer. That should create more fuzz."

"I knew there was a good reason I hired you," Grant said. "Keep thinking about this. The more fuzz, the better. See you in the morning. I'll be making a statement."

She was tired but checked with Parrish. "Still working on Davenport?"

"We need to talk. Ritter got back to me a couple of hours ago. We've done some work . . ."

"Are you at your house?"

"Yes."

"Come over, we'll talk."

"Give me twenty minutes," Parrish said. "I'll come on foot."

PARRISH SHOWED UP, dressed all in black nylon, with a black-and-green-camouflage baseball cap and running shoes; he looked like a crow, Grant thought, as he came down the basement stairs. The housekeeper had let him in, and Grant watched the computer pad that showed the door sealed at the top of the stairs. And that Parrish was carrying a gun.

He dropped onto the sofa opposite her desk, and she could suddenly smell him: he'd jogged over.

"What have you got?" she asked.

"I'VE HAD JIM RITTER in St. Paul the last two days doing . . . observations. We've found a situation that may work for us and that will take Davenport out of Washington. If he's as bright as you say, he might suspect something, but he'd never be sure."

"The longer he's out of Washington, the colder the whole situation becomes. Two weeks, and it's cool. A month from now, nobody'll care."

"Exactly. We needed to find a particular guy in St. Paul or Minneapolis and we found him." Parrish outlined what he had in mind, and Grant closed her eyes as she listened, the better to visualize Parrish's proposal.

"If there are cops too close . . ." she said when he was done.

"There won't be: we'll be tracking them. Tracking them passively, listening only, not talking to anyone. All we need is ten seconds . . . fifteen, at the outside. If the cops are too close, we reset."

"Fifteen seconds, as long as your man doesn't get hurt. If he gets hurt, we're in trouble," Grant said.

"Handled."

"Handled how?"

Parrish laughed. "Well . . . the man we found is a fat guy. Ritter's coat will be stuffed with Bubble Wrap, and, of course, he'll be braced. He's done this before, actually, when they were trying to take down a guy without it being an obvious hit."

Grant sat back in her chair and thought it over. Parrish's operators, supposedly the crème of American hit men, had already screwed up twice. On the other hand, she had to get Davenport out of her business. If they knew the truck that hit Smalls's vehicle was a Ford F-250, she didn't doubt that he would eventually find it.

"All right," she said. "Let's do it. No fuckups. *No fuckups!*"

GRANT WENT TO SLEEP easily enough, unaffected by any anticipatory guilt, though she grew restless at six in the morning, an hour before she usually got up. There was one thing that hadn't occurred to her the night before and that Parrish hadn't considered. What if Davenport decided Grant was responsible for it all . . . and he simply killed her?

He could probably do it without being caught. And he was crazy, wasn't he? As crazy as she was?

She shuddered, tried to go back to sleep but couldn't get it out of her mind.

Tate called at seven, as Grant was downing a double espresso. "You've got the Senate studio from eight-thirty to nine-fifteen. I'm rounding up the usual suspects from the local media, and as many national people as I can find. We need to talk before you go on. You should wear your best TV stuff."

"Already there. Call Allison about hair and makeup."

"Done. You okay?"

"I'm fine," Grant said. "This will work for us."

12

Bob and Rae called early, waking Lucas, to tell him that they were going to work out before starting the day. Bob added that the girlfriend had gone back to Ritter's apartment in his car, so he hadn't been able to get a license plate number on her.

Lucas took his time shaving, didn't bother to look at the television, and went down to the restaurant for breakfast.

He was finishing his pancakes when he heard a man in a two-thousand-dollar suit ask a woman in a two-thousand-dollar dress, "Did you see her? Hot blond senator with a severe case of the red-ass?"

"I did," the woman said. "The shit has hit the proverbial fan. I like it."

SURVIVALISTS FANTASIZE about SHTF day, when Shit Hits The Fan—Mexico invades Arizona, the gasoline runs out, all the chickens get eaten, and anybody who doesn't have a root cellar in the backyard fully stocked with AR-15s, camouflage hats, hunting bows, and gold coins is doomed to a life of sexual slavery or death by cannibalism.

So far, that day hadn't happened. Except in the media.

There it happened about once a week, with the intellects at

Fox and CNN howling about "Breaking News" as if the real SHTF day had finally arrived.

When the rich guy asked the rich woman about a "blond senator," Lucas felt an eyebrow rise almost of its own accord. He'd been reading the *Washington Post* as he ate. There'd been a short, ambiguous article about "sources" saying that the Marshals Service was investigating the Smalls auto accident as a possible assassination attempt. Most of the story was simply recounting the accident, with not much on later developments.

But if Grant had jumped into it? That would raise more eyebrows than his. He waved at the waitress, got the bill, left money on the table, and while he didn't trot to the elevators, he wasted no time getting back to his room.

Both CNN and Fox had already gotten past the actual news and were asking their talking heads to opine on what the senators were saying about each other. Lucas went to his laptop, entered "Taryn Grant" in the Bing search window, and got back a half dozen hits. He found a replay available on C-SPAN and watched as Taryn Grant ripped a new one for Porter Smalls.

Lucas got on the phone to Smalls. "Have you seen Grant?"

"No . . . Has she said something? Anything she says will hurt her . . . Did you see me on 'CCO last night?"

"No, I didn't know you were on. What'd you say?"

"Look for it. It's all over the place," Smalls said.

"Just tell me, Senator."

Smalls cleared his throat, and said, "Well, I had some news media call me up and tell me that these tree trunks had been found by a U.S. Marshal and had silver paint on them. I assumed the marshal was you."

"Yeah, me, and two other marshals, and a West Virginia sheriff and some deputies."

"Good, good, lots of witnesses. Anyway, I started getting more calls, and then CNN and a Washington TV station asked me to go down to 'CCO and make a statement for them."

"Did you say Taryn Grant was involved?"

"No, not by name. I did say that I'd experienced this kind of thing in the past, although that was character assassination and this was real assassination, a dear friend being murdered. It didn't take a genius to put two and two together, which is a good thing, because geniuses are a little thin on the ground in the TV media these days."

"Anyway . . ."

"Anyway, the reporters started asking me if I was accusing Taryn Grant of trying to assassinate me. I told them that it was clear that somebody was trying to assassinate me, but I had no idea who it was. They kept trying to get me to say Grant did it, and I kept tap-dancing."

"But you never said it *wasn't* Grant."

"Of course not," Smalls said, "because it is."

Lucas said, "Well, she just went on TV here and said that you're senile and that everybody in the Senate knows it; that you were probably drunk when the accident took place, because you're also quite well known as a secret alcoholic; that you may well be guilty of vehicular homicide, if you were driving drunk; and that you'd sent your pet marshal to try to frame her, and she wasn't going to stand for it."

Long pause. "She didn't say that," Smalls finally said. "Not really."

"Look at a C-SPAN rerun."

"Sounds like one heck of a guilty overreaction to me," Smalls said.

"Given the context, that's not what the news analysts are saying," Lucas said. He was looking at CNN. "They're saying that you did everything but flatly accuse her of trying to kill you. How would she overreact to that?"

"I can't say I'm sorry," Smalls said. "It's out in the open now. Let's see what happens."

"As the 'pet marshal,' I wouldn't be surprised if I got fired," Lucas said.

"I would," Smalls said. "Try to remember which party is in the majority right now. I wouldn't be surprised if the Tweeter in Chief wades into it."

"Oh, shit . . ."

"Keep pushing, Lucas. You're doing good. If you or anyone at the Marshals Service needs help, call me."

LUCAS CALLED RUSSELL FORTE, and as he finished dialing, he heard a knock at the door. He walked across the room, took the spitball from the peephole, looked out, and saw Rae's face. He opened the door, waved Bob and Rae inside—they were still dressed in their workout clothes—and when Forte answered the phone, Lucas asked him, "Have you seen Grant?"

"Everybody's seen Grant," Forte said. "The shit has hit the fan."

"That seems to be the general opinion," Lucas said. "Are we in trouble?"

"Hard to tell," Forte said. "I've got lines out. There's a rumor that the FBI might want to talk to us."

"Kick us out? Take over the investigation? That'd be all right with me."

"Uh . . . I don't think so. This is becoming the hottest potato in Washington, and you don't often see the FBI stepping up to intercept hot potatoes. I have gotten a call from the director's assistant—our director, not the FBI's—and I'll be talking with him later this morning."

"What should we do here? We were planning to call you about a search warrant for this afternoon."

"Hold off on that," Forte said. "Let's see what the director has to say, see if anybody else gets into it. I'm sure the director will be talking with the attorney general . . . let's see what happens."

"You're telling me to lay low."

"For a few hours. Go climb the Washington Monument or something. Be a tourist."

"All right. Smalls told me if you need some support, to call him."

"If I need it, I'll call *you* to call him," Forte said. "I'd rather not talk to him directly, at this point. Not being a director."

LUCAS FILLED IN Bob and Rae: "It's not bad," he said. "It's a bureaucratic clusterfuck, but it has the effect of chasing these people out in the open."

"There's no way Grant or Parrish will do anything now," Rae said.

"We couldn't count on them doing anything before," Lucas

said. "They're operating through Ritter and Heracles. Once all the newspeople start talking about Whitehead being murdered . . . maybe we'll get a little panic. We could use a little panic."

"So what are we going to do?" Bob asked.

NOTHING.

Spend a day or two as tourists, and let the situation cook, as Forte had suggested. Keep an eye on the news.

They tried to do that but failed. While Lucas went for a walk around the Capitol, and to look at the White House, Rae went to the National Gallery, and Bob went to find an uncle's name on the Vietnam memorial, but by one o'clock they were back in Lucas's room, watching sporadic commentary on the news channels, and a few minutes after that, Gladys Ingram, the lawyer, called Lucas.

"I'm going to email you a bunch of links. You said this phone was safe?"

"About as safe as it gets, but, you know . . ."

"I'm going to give you a string of numbers. You'll need to write them down."

Lucas got his pen and a legal pad: Ingram gave him eighteen random numbers. "That string will open the email I sent to you. If you copy the email with a pen—it's quite short, but you'll have to be accurate—you can touch the burn tab, and the email will eat itself. I don't think, even if they're listening to us, they could interfere, but if you save the documents instead of burning them, they might be able to get at them later. So print out a paper copy and hold it close."

"I'll do it right now."

He did. There were twelve links, and they provided the same information that Kidd had . . . but now flowing from a different source. Lucas copied the twelve out on paper, then burned the email. If any investigator ever asked how he'd come up with all those links, he had an answer.

At two, Forte called and said, "Me, my boss—you met him, Gabe O'Conner—and a few high-level suits from the FBI want to talk to you."

"Where at?"

"Conference room at the FBI building. They'll take you to the conference room when you show up, at four o'clock sharp. Bring Bob and Rae."

"Gonna be trouble?"

"Doesn't feel like it. More like an ass-covering mission."

LUCAS TOLD Bob and Rae that they'd been summoned, and they spent half an hour speculating about what would happen; and, despite the heat and the suffocating humidity, they decided to walk the two miles to the meeting.

"We need to look professional," Bob objected. "If we walk, we'll be all sweaty when we get there."

Rae shrugged. "But it'll sort of let them know we're not too worried about things. They get all the media, but we're just as big a deal as they are. Sort of."

"So you're saying we should push them back with offensive body odor?" Bob asked.

"Walk?" Rae asked Lucas. "Or drive, and spend an hour trying to find a parking place?"

"Walk," Lucas said.

THEY STARTED WALKING by three o'clock, stopped on the way to get Cokes, paused at an Au Bon Pain across the street from the FBI to cool off, and arrived at the building, looking crisp and non-sweaty, although they might not have passed a sniff test.

"Goddamn building looks like it was built by fuckin' Joseph Stalin," Bob grumbled, looking up at the Hoover Building, as they crossed the street.

"Art history–wise, I would say you are correct," Rae said.

INSIDE, they found Forte and O'Conner waiting in the lobby with an FBI gofer, who escorted them to an elevator, up a few floors, and fifty yards down a hallway to a conference room. Other than the five of them, and the usual table and chairs, the room was empty.

"Everybody likes to be last because, that way, we know who's most important," O'Conner said. He was a beefy man, in a pale blue suit and white shirt, carrying an old-style leather briefcase. He took a sheaf of papers from the case, and said, "I understand you guys may be asking for a search warrant."

"Depending on how this comes out," Lucas said.

"I can tell you that in advance. You're to be cautiously aggressive. Or aggressively cautious. I've been told that the FBI is not anxious to get involved until they figure out who's the fall guy. There are several possibilities, including you three."

"Great," Rae said.

"The thing is, if you pull this off and prove there was an assassination attempt, it'll be a big feather in our cap. If you screw it up, then . . ." O'Conner was about to go on, but the door popped open, and a half dozen suits walked in—three men, three women—and everybody shook hands with everybody else.

THE MEETING took an hour. Lucas outlined the investigation, starting with the request from Smalls to finding the suspect truck to discovering the logs. He concluded by saying that the West Virginia accident investigators were looking at the paint sample with several different machines that he didn't understand and would provide solid evidence that the paint came from Smalls's Cadillac.

One of the feds said to Lucas, "We understand that you have a close relationship with the senator."

"We're not exactly friends, but I worked on an investigation that involved the Smalls–Grant Minnesota election two years ago, when Grant won Smalls's Senate seat," Lucas said. "He remembered me from then, asked me to work on this problem. I consulted with my superiors at the Marshals Service, and they concluded that the request was legitimate and that I could go forward with it."

Forte added, with a smile, "Seeing that it was Senator Smalls, and that the Republican caucus voted to restore the seniority he held before his defeat by Senator Grant."

"We're not, uh, affected by the influence of a single senator," one of the FBI suits said.

O'Conner said, "Really?"

The suit nodded, and said, "Yes, really," but nobody really believed him. He didn't even believe himself.

"Not even a senator who was the victim of an apparent assassination attempt . . . ?"

Another suit, this one a woman named Jane Chase, jumped in. "This isn't the time or place to debate questions of influence." She turned to Lucas. "You have a good deal of experience as a homicide investigator for the Minneapolis Police Department and the Bureau of Criminal Investigation."

"Bureau of Criminal *Apprehension*," Lucas corrected. "Yeah. Overall, I was the lead on about ninety murder cases, give or take, over twenty-five years or so. Most of them were straightforward enough, but some were . . . intricate. I've worked closely with a couple of your agents."

She nodded. "We know. Deputy Director Mallard vouches for you and recommends that we step back and allow the Marshals Service to lead on this investigation."

"Nice of him," Lucas said. And, "He's a smart guy."

"Yes, he is," Chase said. She looked around the table at the rest of the suits. "Does anyone have a problem with allowing Marshal Davenport and his colleagues to lead this investigation, at least for now?"

One of the men said, to Lucas, "You'll need to be cautiously aggressive. But aggressive."

All the feds nodded, and O'Conner said, "Listen, guys, thanks for the support. We think we've got an edge on this thing . . ."

Lucas held up a finger. "I have a couple more things. I was hoping I could get some FBI help. It wouldn't be anything you'd have to go public with at all . . . unless you wanted to."

They all knew what that meant: if credit and congratulations were being handed out, the FBI could get in the front of the line. If it were hellfire and damnation instead, they could pass and pretend they were in the cafeteria, buying Ding Dongs, when the trouble started.

"Go ahead and talk," Chase said, clicking her iPhone to look at the time without sneaking the move. In other words, *I'm busy* and also *I'm the one in charge here.*

Lucas outlined the problem with the vehicle armor provided to the Army by Inter-Core Ballistics and the problems with the bidding process. He also gave them the Internet links that demonstrated the problems.

"I think you'll find widespread corruption involving the bids—Army officers and enlisted men, a high-ranking Senate aide, a military contractor who also provides mercenaries to the countries we're involved in . . . all of that. Even worse, the products they provided, products that were supposed to protect our military people, had already been proven inferior," he told the agents.

There were glances around the table, and Chase said, "That would be something we could be interested in. But what's in it for you?"

"If you could take a quick look at this, and ask some questions that would get back to Heracles . . . that might provide me with a bit of leverage," Lucas said. "I could explain that I could come talk with you about who at Heracles gets hurt."

Chase pushed out her lower lip, more glances were exchanged, and she said, "I can't green-light you implicating us directly in any kind of a deal, but I would be willing to keep you up to date on what we might find . . . regarding Heracles."

"I seriously appreciate that," Lucas said. "Seriously."

"Seriously," she repeated, and, "If you lie about a deal, of course there's nothing illegal about that."

"Right," Bob said. "We know that. We do it all the time."

Chase eye-checked Bob, looking for possible cynicism, but

Bob's face was as innocent as the moon's. She turned backed to Lucas. "Was there something else?" she asked.

Lucas fished a thumb drive out of his pocket and slid it across the table to the woman, who didn't immediately touch it. "This is a video. I've seen—you know, on television—that you guys are good with photo enhancement. We think this is a video of the truck that hit Senator Smalls. We can see the plates, but the faces of the men inside are obscured by reflections off the windows. And they're wearing sunglasses. But if we could get a peek, get anything . . ."

Chase nodded. "We'll take a look."

Back on the street, Rae said, "Suits, but not uninteresting suits. We might actually get something done."

"If they can find a way to cover their asses while they're doing it," Bob amended.

O'Conner asked, "You're friendly with Deputy Director Mallard?"

Lucas said, "Yeah. We worked a couple of cases together, and we did okay."

"I'd like to hear that story sometime," O'Conner said. "The rumor is, Mallard has the AG's balls in his pocket."

"Since the AG's a woman, that would be unusual," Rae said.

"You obviously haven't met our beloved attorney general," O'Conner said. To Lucas, as they waited for a car to arrive for O'Conner and Forte: "Remember: Aggressively cautious."

Forte: "Or cautiously aggressive. Try not to get them confused."

13

Weather Karkinnen, Lucas's wife, was driving her dark blue Audi A5 convertible, the top down, in the soft summer evening, but with the windows up because she didn't want to tangle her freshly coifed hair.

A bag of groceries sat beside her on the passenger seat, as she drove home from the Lunds supermarket on the Ford Parkway in St. Paul. She was a small woman, her shoulder reaching barely to the bottom of the car's side window. She enjoyed the curvy ride down Mississippi River Boulevard; the A5 wasn't a hot car, but it was very driveable.

Weather was thinking about her kids, Sam in particular. Sam was in elementary school, and, unfortunately for a kid enrolled in school in these modern times, engaged in the occasional fight. He wasn't a bully—all the teachers said so—but he *was* the kid who stood up for the picked-upon, a role he may have enjoyed too much, according to those same teachers. Lucas had talked to him about it, and needed to talk to him more about it, she thought.

Weather caught a boy on a skateboard in her headlights, carefully arced around him, and continued on down the street to Randolph, still thinking about Sam, and . . .

WHAM!

She never saw it coming.

THE AUDI WAS BROADSIDED by an elderly Toyota Tacoma, accelerating out of the intersection of Randolph and Mississippi River Boulevard. The A5 jumped three feet sideways, the door crushing inward, all the air bags firing simultaneously.

Weather's head collided with the passenger-side window as it shattered, shards of glass sliced into her scalp, and then her head ping-ponged to the left, but she wasn't aware of that because consciousness had left the building. The violence torqued her neck, and the smashed-in door broke her arm and drove her elbow into her ribs, cracking several, sending the broken end of one of them into her right lung.

There were four witnesses: a couple out for an evening stroll, who were on the walkway that paralleled the boulevard; a St. Kate's student, heading back to the school on her bike after getting off her shift at a Ford Parkway restaurant; and the skateboarder.

All four saw the driver of the pickup, a fat man in a loose, short-sleeved black shirt and a bright gold ball cap, jump uninjured from the truck, stop for a second in the pool of light cast from a pole on the far side of the intersection, and run back up Randolph, across the street from the Temple of Aaron, and down an alley.

No one thought to chase him, during the first minute after the crash; they were all gawking, reaching for their cell phones, running to look at Weather. The skater had dropped his board when the driver ducked into the alley and had run after him, but never saw him again.

The St. Paul cops had a car there in two minutes; an ambulance arrived in six. Weather was still in the car, unconscious, when an EMT and a cop wrenched open the passenger-side door, slipped in the end of a stretcher, cut the safety belt still looped over Weather's chest, and eased her on the stretcher.

A moment later, she was on her way to Regions Hospital, the EMT advising the driver, "Drive fast, man . . . Let's get her there . . . Drive faster . . ."

A patrol sergeant recovered her purse and had opened her wallet, looking for an ID, when another cop hurried up to him and asked, "You know who she is?"

The cop looked at the driver's license. "Weather . . . Karkinnen."

"Yeah, and I ran the plates. The car's registered to her and her husband, Lucas Davenport."

"Ah, shit," the sergeant said. "Listen—get onto the BCA, get a phone number for Davenport. If they don't have it, get one for a Del Capslock. Tell him what happened. He's a friend of Davenport's."

"What are you going to do?"

"Get more cars here. Lots of cars. The guy's on foot; we're gonna track him down if it takes all night."

LUCAS HAD NEVER WORKED for the St. Paul cops but had lived in the city for better than twenty years and was well known around the St. Paul Police Department. He might not have been the best-liked guy, but a cop's wife is a cop's wife.

The sergeant got more cars to the crash scene, and the cops crawled the neighborhood with flashlights and dogs, but they never found the driver. They had his truck, though, and the license plate went to an Alice B. Stern. Alice Stern's house, on St. Paul's east side, was dark and quiet. There was no response to persistent knocking. A neighbor said Stern worked at a nearby bar, as a waitress. They found her there, serving drinks. She had been at the bar since four o'clock.

When questioned, she admitted owning the Tacoma. She used the old truck for cruising yard sales on Thursday mornings and for selling stuff at the flea market on Saturdays. For daily driving, she had a Corolla, which was still in the bar's parking lot.

She also had a boyfriend.

"I can't believe Doug would have taken it—he can't drive," she told the St. Paul sergeant. "I mean, he *can* drive, but he's not allowed to. He just got out of Lino Lakes on his last DWI."

The sergeant gave her a look, and she said, "Oh, no . . ."

THREE COP CARS went back to her house. She let them in, and together they found Douglas Garland Last in the garage, dead in a flea-market-bound office chair, a bullet hole in his head, a .38 on the floor next to his hand, along with a bright gold Iowa Hawkeyes ball cap. The sergeant called everybody. When all was said and done at the Medical Examiner's, Last was found to have a blood alcohol content of 2.1, well over twice the legal limit.

The same old story. Call Mothers Against Drunk Driving. Again. Not that it would do much good—Douglas Last had never been elected to anything.

Before they ever found Last, they'd found Capslock. Del knew exactly where Lucas was.

LUCAS WAS SITTING on his bed, paging through a tattered book of American haiku, when Del got through to him.

Del didn't screw around with preliminaries. "Man, Weather's been in an auto accident. She's on her way to Regions. She's hurt bad. I'm on my way now, but you better get back here."

Lucas, heart racing, was on his feet, looking for his pants. "What happened? Where'd it happen? How bad? Del . . ."

"She got hit on Mississippi River Boulevard, couple of blocks from your house. The other driver ran off, but they got his truck. That's all I know. I'll call you back . . ."

Lucas turned cold. He had to get back there.

The front desk hooked him up with an air charter service at Dulles International. He gave them a credit card number, he invoked Senator Smalls by name. The operator said they could leave as soon as the card cleared. He called the desk again for a cab, got dressed, stuffed his Dopp kit, all his various phones, his computer, and his camera in his backpack, did a quick survey of the room to make sure he had everything involving the case, and sprinted out the door. At the desk, he told them to hold his room, that he would be back but didn't know when, and to let Bob or Rae in the room if they asked.

During the forty-minute trip to Dulles, he called Bob, told him what had happened.

"I don't know how bad she is but she *is* hurt, from what I can tell. I'll be gone for a while. You guys stay. I'll let you know when I'm heading back . . . if I come back."

He next called his daughter Letty, at Stanford. He told her

what Del had said, and she said, "I'm on my way. I'll get back to you."

He called Del, who said, "I'm at Regions, I can't talk to a doc, they're all working on her. Anyway, she's alive. The EMTs who brought her in said she was still unconscious when they got here. I found a friend of my wife's, got her to snoop around." Del's wife, a nurse at Regions, wasn't on duty when Weather was brought in. "Weather was bleeding from some head cuts, but they don't think she's got a fractured skull, which is good. But she does have a collapsed lung and a broken arm. They're gonna run her through an MRI when they think they've stabilized her enough. They haven't had to give her blood yet, which is also good I guess . . . That's what I've got so far."

"I'm on my way to the airport," Lucas said. "What do we have on the other driver?"

"Don't know anything yet about the driver. I'm calling my friends in St. Paul; I know they've got every patrol cop in the city searching the neighborhoods for him. They told me that the guy ran the stop sign on Randolph and T-boned her in that convertible of hers. That's all I know so far, but I'm doing my best to stay on top of things. When you get on your plane, call me and tell me when you'll get in—I'll meet you at Humphrey."

LETTY CALLED BACK as Lucas's cab was approaching Dulles. "I'm on a red-eye out of SFO at ten, going through Denver. It's the only flight I could get. I'll rent a car when I get to Minneapolis. See you early in the morning. How's Mom?"

Lucas told her what Del had given him, and then they were at the airport. She said, "Dad, take care."

THE SMALL BUSINESS JET had two pilots, no cabin attendant. The pilot said, "We're told your wife was in an accident; sorry to hear it. We'll get you there in a hurry."

Lucas nodded, strapped in, and they were gone.

Lucas had seen movies in which people made phone calls from flying jets, but he wasn't able to get through on his cell. Two hours after they left Dulles, the jet put down at the Humphrey terminal at Minneapolis–St. Paul International, and Del was waiting.

"How much do you know?" Del asked, after Lucas had stumbled down the steps to the tarmac.

"Only what you told me—I couldn't get through on my phone when we were in the air."

"She's alive. She sort of recovered consciousness . . ."

"What the hell does that mean?" Lucas demanded. "Sorta?"

"She's got some short circuiting. The docs say that's not unusual with concussions. She's got a broken arm. Her lung collapsed when something . . . I dunno what, maybe a rib . . . punctured it, but the lung's been re-inflated. She has more cracked ribs, she's got major bruising, and she's probably got a soft injury in her neck tissue, although all her arms and legs and fingers and toes are moving. She's gonna make it it, but she's gonna hurt for a few weeks. Or months."

Lucas felt the boulder lift from his shoulders. "I gotta call Letty," he said. "She should be in Denver by now."

"I gotta tell you about the driver."

"They got him?"

"Sorta."

"Del, goddamnit."

"He's dead. He'd just gotten out of Lino Lakes on a fifth DWI. The last one, he managed to cross the centerline and hurt a couple of people," Del said. "He did a year in the treatment facility. I guess he wasn't completely treated because he's only been out for a month."

Lucas had nothing to say to that, except, "Wouldn't you fuckin' know it."

THE TWO OF THEM walked into Regions at two o'clock in the morning. Weather was in the intensive care unit, where guests were discouraged, but given Lucas's history and the fact that Weather was a doc, they'd pulled two chairs behind the ICU curtains around her bed.

When Lucas stepped behind the curtain, he wanted to stop and cry. Weather's eyes were open, but her face was horribly bruised, purple over the entire left side. Her neck was encased in a brace, her left arm in a fiber cast. Two bags of solution were hanging from a drip stand, with tubes snaking down to her arm; another emerged from beneath the bed covering, emptying urine into a bag hanging on the side of the bed.

Lucas had been in an ICU himself as a patient on a couple of occasions and had learned to hate the odor, which he could have identified anytime, anywhere: a mixture of the coppery smell of blood, raw meat, urine, several kinds of disinfectant, and what he thought might be iodine, a stink he remembered from his rough-and-tumble childhood.

He sat, leaned toward Weather, took her free hand, and muttered, "I'm here." He got no acknowledging squeeze, but her eyes moved toward him, and she said, through sandpapery lips, "Was I in an accident?"

A nurse behind Lucas whispered, "She keeps asking that."

Lucas said to Weather, "Yes, but you'll be fine. The docs say you're doing great."

Weather closed her eyes and seemed to drift away. Lucas sat holding her hand, and, a few minutes later, her eyes opened again, turned fractionally, and she again asked, "Was I in an accident?"

She asked three more times, and after the third Lucas tucked her hand under the covers and stepped outside the curtain and said to a passing nurse, "I need to talk to her doc."

"He's here, I'll get him."

Del had been waiting in the lobby, and he walked up and asked Lucas, "What's happening?"

"Gonna talk to the doc."

The doc showed up two minutes later, carrying an iPad. He was a tall man, thin, in a white physician's jacket, gray slacks, and steel-rimmed glasses perched on a beaked nose. "Mr. Davenport?" he asked, and, looking at Del, said, "Mr. Capslock, nice to see you again."

"Is she going to be okay?" Lucas asked.

"Yes. Most likely," the doc said, turning back to Lucas. "We've got all the obvious stuff handled, the open question at this point is the neck injury, which we can't fully assess until we can talk to her. The head injury appears to be a moderate-to-serious concussion."

"She keeps asking if she's been in an accident."

"That happens. There's no reason to believe it will continue, it should clear up. She may have some residual amnesia, and that might go away or may never go away. Typically, she could lose the few minutes before the collision or part of the day, or she might lose some of it and get it back later. Or she might not lose anything at all."

"Bottom line?"

"Bottom line is, she should be fine. The neck is the thing I'm most worried about—but it could be that there's nothing there. We know there's some swelling of the muscles on both sides of the spine, which means she's going to have some pain. But the specifics? We don't know yet."

"When will you know?"

"Best guess? Tomorrow. I expect that after she's had some good solid sleep, she'll be able to talk to us, and we can do some tests and get some responses."

"What can I do for her?" Lucas asked.

"Not much. What she needs most is physical rest. One thing—and this is hardest for doctors—she needs cognitive rest. Don't bring in magazines or her tablet or laptop. She'll be here for a few days, and we don't even want her watching TV. She needs to keep her brain quiet. For people like her, that's difficult. She's gonna get very bored."

"Bored is okay," Lucas said. "We can handle bored."

"That's what they all say," the doc said, with a smile. He turned to Del. "How are you doing?"

"I'm back at work, but it still hurts," Del said. "Can't run all that well."

"That'll take some time," the doc said. "Are you still doing the PT?"

"When I can . . ." Del's eyes shifted away from the doc.

"Hey! Do it all the time. Every time. Goddamnit, Capslock..."

"I know, I know," Del said.

The doc turned back to Lucas. "I had Capslock after his adventures down in El Paso. I can tell you, he was hurt a lot worse than Weather. And look at him now."

Lucas: "Do I have to?"

"I know it's hard."

Del had gone out to his car while Lucas was behind the curtain with Weather and now he handed Lucas a plastic shopping bag. "I went to Barnes and Noble while I was waiting for the plane to come in," he said. "Magazines. You owe me seventy-seven dollars."

"The doc said I can't give her magazines."

"They're for you," Del said. "When I was in here, my old lady almost went nuts from the boredom. Man, you sit there and stare at each other, and, every once in a while, a little pee trickles into the bag. That's about it for excitement."

"Take the magazines," the doc said.

LUCAS TOOK the shopping bag and sent Del home. "No point in both of us going nuts." As Del was walking away, Lucas called to him, and when Del turned, Lucas said, "Hey, you da man."

Del waved, and Lucas went back behind the curtain, and a second later Weather's eyes opened, and she asked, "Was I in an accident?"

Lucas said, "Yes," and she closed her eyes again, and he picked up a copy of *Outside* magazine and started with the last page.

She asked again, and again, and again—"*Was I in an*

accident?"—and after the last time, Lucas said, "Yes," and she asked, "Was anyone else hurt? Did I hit somebody?"

Lucas dropped the magazine: "Holy shit, you're back. Don't go anywhere, I gotta tell the nurse."

WEATHER'S BRAIN was working again, and she asked a hundred questions, and she was still asking questions when Letty pushed through the curtain, looked at Weather's bruised face, and blurted, "Oh my God."

"Just what I would expect from a college student," Weather said. *"Oh my God."*

Letty turned to Lucas. "She looks bad, but not so bad she can't give me a hard time."

Lucas said, "She's not good. She's gonna hurt a lot, and she's going to be bitchy for weeks."

"What about the asshole who hit her?" Letty asked. She was a lanky young woman, with striking dark hair and eyes.

"He's dead," Lucas said. "He shot himself. Had a whole string of DWIs, just got out of prison for the last one."

"Good," Letty said. "That keeps me from the inconvenience of killing him."

Weather said, "Letty, we need to get you some serious therapy."

AT SEVEN O'CLOCK, Weather drifted off to sleep, and a nurse said she'd be down for a while. "We get lots of concussions here. She's worn out, and she'll probably sleep until noon or later. You'd best go get some sleep yourselves."

They were inclined to stay, but the nurse, and then the incoming doc, shoved them out the door.

They were both back at noon, though Weather didn't wake until two o'clock, when she asked for her laptop. "I know all about concussions and I don't want to browse, I just need to notify patients . . ."

"That's all been taken care of," Lucas said. "You ain't getting a laptop until the doc says so."

"What am I supposed to do? Lay here until I go insane?"

"Exactly," Letty said. "Besides, they're planning to kick us out of here and do a lot of tests with you. You'll be busy until dinnertime."

LUCAS SPENT the next two days suffering a mix of stress and boredom. Weather's spine looked good, but she had several pulled muscles in her neck, chest, and rib cage, and she would be stuck with the neck brace for a while . . . "a while" being undefined. She couldn't cough or laugh without suffering a spasm of pain, her broken arm ached, but she said she could ignore it.

"Not being able to move my neck is driving me crazy. It makes my eyes hurt, looking around without moving my head. Not being able to read is worse . . ."

LETTY BEGAN TO TALK about going back to California—classes were about to start again—and Weather told her to go. Letty said she would . . . in a few days. She wanted to see Weather at home.

Lucas brought Sam and Gabrielle down to see Weather every afternoon; Weather fell into a routine of sleeping late in the morning, taking a nap in the afternoon, and staying up late with Lucas. She'd already determined that she wouldn't be working again for at least six weeks, and two months was more likely.

On the sixth day after the accident, they sat up talking until two in the morning. Lucas, the night owl, was still restless when he got home and spent another hour reading. At eight o'clock the next morning, he was sleeping soundly when there was a knock on the bedroom door, and Letty called, "Dad?"

He struggled to sit up. "Yeah?"

"There's a lady here to see you," Letty said.

"What?"

"There's a lady here to see you. I've got her in the kitchen. You better come down." Letty's tone implied significance.

Lucas felt like he'd been hit on the forehead with a five-pound ham. "A lady? What does she want?"

"You better come down," Letty repeated.

She turned away from the door and went back down the hallway to the stairs. Lucas got up, found his jeans and a T-shirt, pulled them on. He was barefoot but didn't bother with shoes, followed Letty down the hall and down the stairs.

THE WOMAN waiting in the kitchen looked like a refugee from Ukraine, but not the Ukraine of today, more like a year after World War II. She was short, with gray hair that might once have been blond; she was elderly, probably in her seventies; and she was overweight. She was wearing a cheap raincoat, though the day was bright and warm, and carrying a plastic purse in one hand. To complete the image, she was wearing a babushka. She smelled vaguely of boiled cabbage and sausage, or looked like she should. And she looked exhausted.

Letty was standing next to her, and Lucas asked the woman, "What can I do for you?"

She made a pacifying gesture with her free hand, and said, "I'm Mary Last. My boy is Douglas Last, who the police say was driving when your wife was in the accident. But he didn't do it."

Lucas looked at Letty, and said, "I don't think . . ."

Letty: "Listen to her."

There was that tone in her voice again, and Lucas turned back to Mary Last, and asked, "Why didn't he do it?"

"Douglas, he drank too much," Mary Last said. "I tried to tell him. And he's smoked since he was in high school. He ate cheeseburgers every day—every day of his life. Eggs and bacon in the morning, cheeseburgers all day, or pepperoni pizza. Even now. He never exercised. He was a fat man, and he had heart failure. The doctors said he would die in one year, maybe two, if he didn't change. He didn't. The food was like a drug. He was an addict. My boy, he couldn't run a hundred feet, but the police say he ran so fast nobody could catch him and he got away. This is impossible for him to do. Impossible. You ask his doctor."

Letty later told Weather that Lucas could have said any of a thousand things in response, but Lucas was feeling the world shifting around him. What had been simple and awful had suddenly become enormously complex and even worse.

He looked at the old lady, and said, "Sonofabitch."

14

Lucas had been a cop for more than two decades, and as soon as the words came out of the old lady's mouth, he knew that she was telling the truth, that she was right, Last couldn't run a hundred feet. Weather's crash had been set up to take Lucas out of Washington, and Mary Last's son had been murdered. Lucas had to check, but he knew it was true.

Lucas had been in the Cities for a week and had not talked to Smalls since the accident, other than to drop him an email, telling him what had happened. Smalls had simply answered back, "Take care of your wife."

After sending Mary Last away, Lucas called Smalls on his private cell phone. When Smalls answered, Lucas identified himself, and asked, "Do you still have protection?"

"Yes, but nothing . . ."

"Senator, I think Weather was taken out by the same guy who ambushed you and Miz Whitehead. I think they set up the guy with the DWI, Douglas Last, and then murdered him. I've got good reason to think this. The killers are still with us, and active, and they might be here in the Twin Cities."

Smalls didn't respond immediately, though Lucas could hear him breathing. Finally: "It's best if I go away for a while. I've got to be back after the recess, but for the time being . . ."

"Don't tell me where you're going. Or anyone else. You know how to get a burner phone?"

"Of course."

"These guys are very sophisticated. My last case, my cell phone was tracked by a bunch of dopers—everybody's got tech now. Get a couple of burners, FedEx one of them to Kitten, don't call anyone except her, and any business that you have to do with other people, do through her. I don't think they can break that—not easily anyway. I've got a private line to her myself, so we can relay anything we need to say to each other."

"I'll be gone tonight," Smalls said. "Are you going back to Washington?"

"I have to talk to Weather about that. And I have to hire some people to sit with her until this is done."

AFTER HE GOT OFF the phone with Smalls, Lucas called Mitchel White, the Ramsey County medical examiner, told him about what Last's mother had said, and asked, "Did you look at his heart?"

"Yes. He had advanced congestive heart failure. But, Lucas, he had a bullet go through his head, and the shot was fired from one inch away."

"The witnesses said he jumped out of his car after the accident, sprinted down the street and into an alley," Lucas said. "A sixteen-year-old kid ran after him but never saw him again."

"I didn't know that," White said. "Everybody was focused on the gunshot wound. I can tell you, though, he didn't sprint anywhere. For one thing, he weighed two fifty-two, his legs were bacon-wrapped twigs, and his heart was a lump of Jell-O."

LUCAS MADE ANOTHER CALL, asked an old political friend for a favor.

He called Roger Morris, at St. Paul Homicide, and told him what he thought. "Oh boy. All right, I'm on it," Morris said. "This shouldn't have gotten past us. I never heard a word about his heart."

When Lucas and Letty got to the hospital, Catrin Mattson, wearing a loose white overshirt to cover her gun, was already sitting in a chair next to Weather's bed, reading aloud a magazine story about shoes. Virgil Flowers was slumped in the second chair, cowboy boots up on the end of Weather's bed.

When Lucas came in, Mattson said to Weather, whose eyes were closed, "The lug is here. And your improbably beautiful daughter."

Weather said, "We've got a two-lug room. And hello, Daughter."

Lucas kissed Weather on the lips, and Mattson on the forehead, and said to Mattson, "You got here in a hurry," and to Flowers, "What the fuck do you want?"

"Sneaky way to see your improbably beautiful daughter," Flowers said. "The rest of you, I don't give a shit about."

Letty stepped behind Flowers and began massaging his shoulders. "You're such a manly man," she said. "You've even got muscles in your shoulders."

"Of course," Flowers said. "That's where I keep most of them, until they're needed. Ooo. That feels good."

Mattson watched the massaging, made a crooked smile, and looked up at Lucas. "Rose Marie talked to the director and he came up with my leave of absence in something like eight seconds."

Rose Marie Roux was the head of the Department of Public Safety and Lucas's old political friend. She was the one he'd called for the favor, asking, if Mattson agreed, that she be given an emergency leave of absence to watch over Weather.

Mattson worked for the state Bureau of Criminal Apprehension, Lucas's former department, as did Flowers, and she knew Weather well. The director reported directly to Roux and was unlikely to resist any of her suggestions.

The fix was in.

LUCAS HAD CAUGHT Mattson's crooked smile and thought, *Hmm. Catrin might have a thing for Virgil*, dismissed the thought, and said, "How long . . . ?"

"They told me to stay as long as I was needed," Mattson said, "though it's not my kind of gig."

"I know that, but this is complicated," Lucas said. "I asked for you because you can handle it."

"I could handle it, too," Flowers said.

Lucas: "Yeah, but I worry that that's not all you'd handle."

Letty rolled her eyes, and said, "Oh, Jesus."

Weather: "Since you haven't told me anything about what's going on, why don't you tell all of us at the same time?"

"It's crazy," Letty said. "But then, we've all seen crazier."

LUCAS TOLD THEM, and the two women listened quietly. "You're saying they almost killed Weather to move you off the job," Mattson said.

"Yes. Whether they were trying to kill her or only hurt her bad enough to get me back here, I don't know," Lucas said.

"They were *willing* to kill her, like they were Smalls's girlfriend," Letty said. "They killed that Last person in cold blood."

"That's right," Lucas said. To Mattson: "That's why I need somebody good in here. These guys are professionals. They kill for a living."

"They've messed up a few times," Weather observed. "Missed Smalls, killed his girlfriend. They tried to mug you but failed . . ."

"Would have worked with you, though, if Last's mother hadn't come to see me," Lucas said. "St. Paul cops said it looked for all the world like a suicide. Like he sat there and finished a bottle of vodka and then shot himself. The gun even belonged to his girlfriend, nobody's prints on it but his."

"Interesting," Flowers said.

Letty said, "Yeah. Almost worth staying for."

"No, no, no," Weather said. "You get on back to school. And, Lucas, when are you going back to Washington?"

"That depends on you," Lucas said.

"They're letting me out of here tomorrow, I think, if I promise to stay in bed for a couple of more days. Catrin can take me around, Helen can handle the house and the kids . . . you need to take care of this."

"I'll wait until you're home," Lucas said. "But, yeah—I oughta get back. These people need to be put away."

"These people need to get shot, is what they need," Letty said. She and Mattson slapped hands. Flowers only raised his eyebrows.

LUCAS TOOK Mattson aside before he left the hospital: "I need to make sure you're okay with this."

"Weather's a good friend. She helped me a lot after my . . . problem," Mattson said.

"How about a grand a day?" Lucas asked.

"Lucas, that's not . . ."

"Yes, it is," Lucas said. "You've taken a leave, I've got the money. Is that good?"

"That's better than good," Mattson said. "I'd do it for free."

"I know. It's nice for all of us that you don't have to."

SHE WENT BACK to Weather, and Lucas and Letty walked out of the hospital with Flowers. In the parking lot, Flowers said, "You need anything, let me know. Anything. I can always take some undertime. If Catrin needs somebody to spell her . . ."

Letty got a handful of Flowers's shirt and pulled him in and kissed him on the lips, and let the kiss linger. "Thank you."

Lucas said, "Hey . . . Hey! The guy's practically married."

"He could still fool around," Letty said. "I mean, God, it's like you don't even live in the twenty-first century."

"Hey!"

LUCAS FINALLY MADE a call to Rae Givens, told her to jack up Bob. "I'm headed back to Washington day after tomorrow."

"Ooo. We get to shoot somebody?"

"That could happen," Lucas said. "Try to pretend you're not happy about it."

LUCAS GOT Weather settled at home, watched her for a day until she got annoyed—"I'm unhappy enough about this neck brace that I'm going to take it out on you, and I'm too tired to fight, so go to Washington and fix this," she said.

Lucas and Letty went to the airport together, Lucas headed east, Letty west, and when they'd gotten through security, they sat at Lucas's gate until it was time for him to board the plane. She gave him a squeeze when he got in line, and said, "Call me every night and tell me what's happening. In case I have to come out there . . ."

"I'll be okay," he said. "I don't want you out there under any circumstances."

Letty could be as cold as anyone Lucas had ever known. She stepped back, and said, "There's only one circumstance that would take me out there. Think about it."

He thought about it on the plane. She'd be out to Washington if he were killed. She'd bring a gun. In some ways, she was a typical lighthearted college girl; in other ways, she wasn't.

Not at all.

BOB AND RAE were waiting when he got in, and they met in Lucas's room, where he told them all about the accident.

When he was done, Bob said, "This . . . You can't do this kind of thing out of your hip pocket. They had to do some intel work;

they must have had some computer access to spot the drunk . . . If he was living with his girlfriend, he wouldn't even have an address of his own. How'd they find him?"

"Probation records," Lucas said. "If they have a good computer guy, he could get into state files . . ."

Rae nodded. "We've had that problem on the federal level. The files are designed to provide a fast response to people who aren't computer jocks. For a serious hacker, getting in there would be child's play."

"And we're dealing with people who probably have access to federal computer systems," Lucas said.

"The safest bet here would be to make a hard move on Ritter. We know he used a truck once, so I have to believe he was probably there in Minnesota," Bob said.

"I agree," Lucas said. "We don't have enough for an arrest or a search warrant, but we can roust him, impound his truck, get Carl Armstrong to take a look at it. I'll get Russell looking for a way to put Ritter in St. Paul—run his credit cards, look at airlines."

"Put this Parrish guy in there, too," Rae said.

THEY'D MOVE the next morning, they decided. Bob and Rae had been watching Ritter's truck during the week Lucas was gone. They would continue with that the next day, while Lucas would work with Forte on a computer search of electronic records on both Ritter and Parrish.

When the other two had gone, Lucas called Forte and told him what he wanted to do, and Forte agreed to start pulling all the records he could think of, that might track the movements of the two men during the days before and after Weather was hit.

With that under way, Lucas called Carl Armstrong in West Virginia, to get the latest results on the logs they'd pulled out of the mountainside ditch.

"The news is mixed," Armstrong told him. "The paint on the logs came from the Cadillac, but we knew that was probably the case. The other side of the logs, the ones that would be on the attack truck . . . we've got white canvas fibers. I think they padded the logs, probably to minimize damage to the side of the truck. They must've taken the padding with them after they threw the logs in the ditch—we've got no paint on the logs themselves."

"Damnit," Lucas said.

"Well, you told me they were pros," Armstrong said. "That sounds professional."

"Talk to you tomorrow, Carl," Lucas said.

FORTE GOT BACK with the information that Parrish had probably been in Washington the night that Weather got hit.

"I pulled his credit card charges, and he uses his cards a lot. We have charges for most days leading up to the attack on Weather, on the day itself, and every day since, all around Washington. But Ritter . . . Ritter has MasterCard, Visa, Chase, and Amex cards, but he went dark three days before Weather was attacked and didn't pop up again until two days later. He doesn't use his card as much as Parrish, but he uses it every day or two. I couldn't find any other five-day periods when he didn't use one or the other. Not when he was in the States."

"He was trying to avoid anything that would put him in the Cities."

"I think so. That's negative proof, not so good for a jury. But now we know," Forte said. "No airline tickets, no trace of any cars rented in the Twin Cities, but we have George Claxson's private plane flying into Omaha the first day Ritter goes silent."

"Who's George Claxson again?" Lucas asked. The name rang a bell, but he couldn't place it.

"Ah, yeah—he runs Heracles. They call him the director," Forte said. "Anyway, there's no sign that any names that we know rented a car in Omaha. Probably used phony IDs."

"They fly into Omaha . . . What's that? Six hours from the Twin Cities?" Lucas asked.

"I checked on Google Maps. It's six hours if you pay strict attention to the speed limit. If you let it out, seven miles over the limit, drive straight through, with one gas stop, less than that."

"Cell phone?"

"Okay, there's a problem," Forte said. "Ritter placed a half dozen calls to various people around the D.C. area the day Weather was attacked. There were more calls the day before, and the day after, and every day since, all in the Washington metro area. Of course, everybody but a complete idiot knows that calls can be traced. His phone made the call; we don't know that Ritter did."

"You know who he called?"

"That's where it gets interesting. In the days before and immediately after Weather was hurt, he called only four different guys, including Parrish and Claxson," Forte said. "Parrish made quite a few other calls, but Claxson, Ritter, and the two other guys didn't call anyone but Parrish and each other."

"Tell me that again," Lucas said.

"They only called each other and Parrish," Forte said. "We

know that if Ritter was the driver in West Virginia, he had at least one other accomplice, because that old lady saw two guys in the black truck. There may have been a third if they had a spotter, and they probably did. Then there's Parrish and Claxson."

Lucas: "The other two guys, the accomplices, fly out to Omaha with Ritter and Claxson. They all leave their regular cells behind in Washington and take burners. Parrish uses the regular phones to call all the others to establish alibis. If that's what happened, we should have the names of the two accomplices, too."

"Yes, we do," Forte said. "I'm digging out their records right now."

FOR THE REST of the afternoon, Forte forwarded records to Lucas, including everything he could find for John McCoy and Kerry Moore, the other two men who were calling Ritter, Parrish, and Claxson around the time of Weather's auto accident. Like Ritter, both McCoy and Moore worked for Flamma, the Heracles subsidiary. And both had been in elite Army or Marine units before they went private.

Forte found photos of the other two, and Lucas was fairly certain that Moore, an ex-Marine, was the mugger he'd hit in the face.

He called Rae with Moore's information, including his apartment address in Virginia, and asked them to check him out. "I'm especially interested to know whether he has a black eye or a swollen nose," Lucas said.

"I'll go now—I'm looking at his address on my iPad, and it's only a half mile from Ritter's. I'll walk over, see if I can find a place to hang. If Bob's not seeing anything at Parrish's place, maybe you ought to switch him over here to keep an eye on Ritter's."

Lucas did. By the end of the day, neither Ritter or Moore had shown up at their apartments—but they were young and single, so that wasn't entirely improbable. At the same time, Rae couldn't hang out any longer at the Starbucks she'd found, and Bob felt he might be conspicuous if he continued to park and repark on the streets around Ritter's.

Lucas called them in.

THE THREE OF THEM had a late meal at the hotel, and Lucas laid out what he and Forte had found in the records.

"So they did it," Bob said. "If we can get this Armstrong guy to say he believes that Ritter's truck was involved in the West Virginia hit, would that be enough to get a search warrant for Ritter's apartment?"

"Maybe, if we found the right judge," Lucas said. "Forte may have some ideas about that."

Rae was shaking her head. "I have my doubts. We know, but it's weak on paper."

"The other problem being, Ritter might have pulled the trigger, both on Smalls and Whitehead, and on Weather, but I mostly want to get the people behind Ritter," Lucas said. "That looks to me like Grant, Claxson, and Parrish. We're nowhere near those guys."

"Rousting Ritter will stir things up," Rae said.

"Yeah. I'm counting on that," Lucas said.

WHEN THEY FINISHED DINNER, Lucas called Armstrong in West Virginia: "Can you make it over here tomorrow to look at the truck?"

"Yup. I'll call my boss right now, and I'll bring a tech with me," Armstrong said. "What time do you want me there?"

"How long will it take you to get here?"

"Five hours, if we drive," Armstrong said. "We could be out of here by seven o'clock, get there about noon."

"How about flying?" Lucas asked.

"Rather drive," Armstrong said. "We'd have to drive down to Charleston, wait for the plane, fly for an hour, get a car at the other end, and we've got some equipment—it would take almost as long to fly as to drive—and then we'd have to get back."

"So drive; we'll plan to look at our guy at noon."

When he was off the phone with Armstrong, Lucas called Weather, and told her what he'd figured out.

"Good. You learned a lot," she said. "You've got the names of the men who hit me and murdered Last. You've always said that knowing was a big deal."

"It is," Lucas said. "Now to bag them."

15

Lucas, Bob, and Rae went out for breakfast together, and Lucas called Forte to tell him about the day's plan. Forte thought the information they had was too sparse for a search warrant, but Lucas asked him to spot a friendly federal judge in case they found a bit more.

"If it would help, I could call Smalls and see if he'd talk to the judge. Explain the seriousness of the situation," Lucas said.

"Also explain the seriousness of getting confirmed by the Senate in case a judge should be nominated for the appeals court," Forte said.

"He might do that," Lucas said. "What do you think?"

A long pause. "Call Smalls. He's a lawyer, right?"

"Yes."

"Then he'll be aware that there might be some lines he wouldn't want to cross . . . when making the request."

LUCAS CALLED SMALLS on his burner and made the request. Smalls said, "I could do that. In fact, I know a judge down that way who'd probably give you a warrant with what you've got right now. Benjamin Park. Nice fellow. I'll give you a ring after I talk to him."

"Are you in a safe spot?" Lucas asked.

"I'm so safe that even I don't know where I'm at," Smalls said.

When Lucas hung up, Rae said, "Sometimes this inside baseball makes me nervous, speaking of things ethics-wise."

Bob shook his head. "You know better than that. Almost everything in Washington is inside baseball, ethics-wise. Been that way since the git-go."

"Didn't have as many lawyers at the git-go," she said.

SMALLS CALLED BACK at eleven o'clock, and said he'd spoken with the judge, who agreed to take an expedited look at a search warrant request.

"I believe you'll get it," he said.

They drove over to Ritter's apartment complex in two cars, and Lucas led the way around back, where the truck was still sitting in the carport. They didn't approach it until one o'clock, when Carl Armstrong and a technician named Jane Kerr rolled into the parking lot.

They all got out, shook hands, and walked as a group to the black F-250. Lucas pointed out the ripples down the right side of the truck, and both Armstrong and Kerr took a look, running their hands over the panels, and Armstrong asked Kerr, "Do you see it?"

"I definitely see it," she said. "I can feel it, too—at least as good as I see it."

Armstrong said to Lucas, "We've got templates from an undamaged truck just like this one, and when we fit the cutouts over the side of the truck, you'll be able to see the damage more clearly. We'll take photos in case we need the evidence."

"Great," Lucas said.

"In the meantime . . ." He jogged back to his SUV and pulled out a piece of what looked like white rubber. When he carried it back to the F-250, Lucas could see it was actually a cast made from the truck tire tracks they'd found on the mountainside where the logs had been dumped.

Armstrong squatted next to the truck, held the cast up to one of the tires, and they all bent over to look. "Same tires," he said. "They come as one of the standard options with the truck, but less than thirty percent are equipped with them. Not definitive, but supportive."

"Another straw on the camel's back," Bob said.

THE SIDES AND FRONT END of the truck bed had been fitted with a steel rack to give it more carrying capacity and better tie-down capability. Kerr walked along the side of the bed with a Sherlock Holmes–style magnifying glass. Halfway down, she stopped, looked more closely, turned to Armstrong, and said, "Carl . . . take a look."

Armstrong took the magnifying glass to look at what appeared to be nothing at all. He said, "Huh," and, "You guys want to look?"

Lucas took the magnifying glass, and Armstrong took a mechanical pencil from his pocket and pointed at the truck, and said, "Right at the end of the pencil point."

Lucas looked, and under the glass could see three or four wispy beige threads clinging to a tiny nick in the steel rail. "What am I looking at?"

"Those look exactly like the threads that were stuck to the

padded side of the log. I'll kiss your ass if they aren't identical. We need to find as many as we can and collect them; a lab will tell us if they're the same."

Bob and Rae both took a look, and Bob said, "That's the search warrant."

LUCAS CALLED FORTE. Forte wrote the search warrant application for Ritter's apartment and the interior of the truck and drove it over to the judge's chambers. Getting the warrant back to Ritter's place took three boring hours. Lucas, Bob, Rae, Armstrong, and Kerr hung out in their vehicles in the parking lot, making occasional individual runs out to a Safeway Supermarket for food, drinks, and magazines.

They didn't need the search warrant to fit the F-250 templates to the side of the truck, so Armstrong and Kerr did that while the others watched and waited. The photography was interesting, in a way, for a while, and then they slipped back into a hot, sweating boredom.

When Armstrong finished, he transferred his photos to a laptop and brought the laptop over to Lucas's Evoque. With Bob and Rae looking over their shoulders from the backseat, Armstrong ran through the high-res photos on the laptop's screen, and the impact dent was plain enough—Kerr had been on the other side of the templates with a flash, which fired when Armstrong took the shot, illuminating the space between the templates and the truck.

"It's what you'd expect if they did what we think they did with the logs," Armstrong said. "I bet they don't even know that the truck was damaged."

FORTE DELIVERED the warrant himself, bringing along four additional marshals. Two of the marshals were left in the parking lot to watch the truck; Armstrong and Kerr began collecting fiber samples from the truck and bagging them for the lab.

Lucas, Bob, Rae, Forte, and the other two marshals went to Ritter's apartment; the two marshals specialized in searches, the first man computers, the second safes and lockboxes. There was no answer to their knocks, so they showed the search warrant to the apartment manager and ordered her to open Ritter's door.

She squinted at Lucas, and said, "Hey, you're the marshal who got lost. You were lying to me when you were here before."

Lucas said, "Sorry."

He was lying again.

THEIR SEARCH WARRANT was sharply limited to records, both paper and computer files, and to weapons, since Ritter was suspected in the Douglas Last shooting in the Twin Cities. Last had supposedly been shot with his girlfriend's gun, a fact not mentioned in the warrant application. The warrant specifically said that they were allowed to search for records that might be hidden in the apartment, which, for practical purposes, meant they could look at everything, but if they found something criminal that was not openly visible, and was not a record or a weapon, it probably wouldn't make it into court.

Ritter's apartment smelled of almost nothing, except maybe pasta and kitchen cleaner. He lived a spartan life except in three areas: he had a high-end, high-definition television, which sat in front of a seven-foot couch; he had a high-end stereo system, with a turntable in addition to a CD player, and a load of fashionable vinyl records; and he had lots of guns.

The guns were in a gun safe, as opposed to a real safe, in a closet. It was bolted to the floor, and the locks-and-safes specialist took no more than five minutes to get it open.

Inside were fourteen guns—five rifles, a tactical shotgun, and eight handguns—none of them cheap, in a variety of sizes and calibers. Two of the handguns were equipped with screw-on silencers. The marshal noted the serial numbers on the silencers and checked with the ATF computer records and learned that they were both licensed to Ritter and so were legal.

"That's a shame," he told Lucas. "That would have been a nice round federal felony if they weren't registered."

They also found about a thousand rounds of ammo for the guns. The apartment had a small, tidy kitchen, with two tables. One table was for eating, the other was a gun repair and reloading station.

RITTER HAD an inexpensive Dell desktop computer and a small multipurpose printer/scanner. The computer had no password. All its software was the standard stuff that came with the machine, plus Microsoft Word and a privacy application called Win/DeXX.

That was it: there were no emails, there was no browser history, there were no documents, there were no cookies. The computer specialist marshal explained that Win/DeXX was a

Windows software package that could remove any trace of the computer's use at the end of each session. Click on the Win/DeXX icon, and whatever you'd been doing was lost to history.

"It all goes to where television pictures go when you turn off the TV," the marshal said.

Ritter also had three black, two-drawer file cabinets in the office: Rae worked through those, while Bob and Lucas prowled the apartment, trying the common hiding places and plugging a lamp into each outlet to make sure it was operable. Outlet caches were currently fashionable among the crooked.

Lucas found the first useful piece of information: Ritter had a modest selection of clothing, mostly athletic and outdoorsy, including camo cargo pants and jackets, along with a dark suit, suitable for funerals, three sport coats in varied textures and shades of blue, three pairs of gray or black slacks, four pairs of boots, and one pair of black dress shoes.

Lucas was patting down the jackets when he felt something stiff in the inside breast pocket of one of the sport coats. When he pulled it out, it was a plastic hotel key card. On the back was a logo of the Hilton Garden Inn Omaha East/Council Bluffs.

Ritter had been in Omaha.

"Bag that baby," Bob said.

"Think we can call it a record?" Lucas asked.

"Fuck yeah."

OF THE SIX file cabinet drawers Rae was working, two drawers were a jumble of office supplies and computer cables, the other four a collection of investment and bank statements and employment and tax records. "I'm looking at it, and he does have some money, about . . . maybe eight hundred thousand dollars in cash and investments, if I'm not missing anything. He seems to spend a lot of time overseas, and I wouldn't be surprised if he gets free food and housing along with a nice salary that he can't spend anywhere over there . . . so his investments don't seem outlandish. You'd need a good accountant to tell you for sure, and I'm not one."

Sitting on one of the file cabinets was an innocuous framed photo showing Ritter, with two male friends and two women, in what looked like a park. He had his arm around the shoulder of one of the women, who might have been who they'd seen at the Wily Rat nightclub. She was half turned away from the camera, her face obscured, but Lucas could see that she was short and dark-haired.

FORTE HAD LEFT with the computer specialist a half hour after they started the search. The locks-and-safes guy was helping go through the apartment inch by inch when he took a call from one of the two marshals who were at the truck.

He listened for a moment, then said, "Hey, Lucas, Ritter's down at the truck. He just showed up."

Lucas took the phone, and asked, "He's driving the Miata?"

"Yeah."

"Don't let him leave," Lucas said. "We'll be right down."

"He's already parked," the marshal said. "He's coming up, and he's pissed."

"Walk with him," Lucas said.

RITTER WAS at the door five minutes later. He was a bit shorter than average, but muscular, dark-haired, dark-eyed, dark-complected, with three parallel white scars on one side of his face that might have been inflicted by a woman's fingernails or, in Ritter's case, shrapnel. He was wearing a black T-shirt, tan cotton/nylon cargo pants, light hiking boots, and a black ball cap.

He picked out Lucas as the main fed, demanded, "What the hell is going on?"

Lucas said, "We believe you may be involved in the attempted assassination of Senator Porter Smalls that resulted in the murder of Mrs. Cecily Whitehead. We're looking for evidence in that case."

Ritter nearly did a movie double take. "What the fuck you been smoking, man?"

"Don't smoke," Lucas said. "We have a lot of questions for you."

Ritter reached down to one of his cargo pockets, and it was Lucas who reacted, moving a hand toward his side. Ritter froze, then said, "Wallet."

Lucas nodded, and Ritter extracted a trifold wallet from his pocket, took a card out, and handed it to Lucas. "I might ask a question or two myself, but I'm not going to answer any, not without an okay from my lawyer. That's my lawyer's name, address, and direct phone number. I'm going to call him now, unless I'm under arrest."

"Not yet," Lucas said, "but you will be. Go make your call."

"Can I leave the apartment to make the call?"

"Yes. You're free to go, but our search warrant covers your vehicles, so you can't take those until we're done with them. If we find any evidence pertinent to the case, the cars will be impounded."

"Goddamnit, that's not right," Ritter said. "Do I get reimbursed for the cost of a rental car?"

"I wouldn't hold your breath," Lucas said.

Ritter said, "There are two pistols in the safe with suppressors. Both are registered with the ATF."

"We know," Lucas said. "That was a disappointment."

Ritter held Lucas's eye momentarily, and said, "I'll remember you."

"I think you already met my wife," Lucas said. And Ritter blinked.

RITTER TURNED AND LEFT.

Ritter had committed at least one murder, and probably two, but he wasn't a professional or career criminal—he was essentially a soldier, a guy who killed people under orders, or even of his own volition, but who didn't have to worry about prosecution.

Stupid crooks would have reacted to Lucas's comment about Weather, but a professional would have allowed a puzzled wrinkle to appear on his forehead. Ritter had blinked; it was called a tell by poker players, and, as far as Lucas was concerned, it was as good as an admission of guilt.

Couldn't take it to a jury, but it was there.

Rae eased up, and said, "Decided to go with Mr. Subtle, huh?"

"I wasn't going to get anything from being Mr. Nice, and we don't have enough to bust him yet, so . . . a push never hurt."

AS THE SEARCH wound down, Lucas walked around the building and found Armstrong wrapping up his inspection of the truck. Kerr was working on Ritter's other vehicle, a fire-engine-red Mazda MX-5 Miata. A very nice car, Lucas thought; a driver's car, probably even more than a Porsche, at about one-fourth the price.

The interior of the truck hadn't produced anything. It did have a GPS, but all the history had been wiped clean. That was evidence of a kind but not useful.

"We got enough threads to braid a string," Armstrong said, "but only from the right side. I think we'll be able to produce some hard evidence that the fabric is identical to the fabric that was used to pad the logs."

"How soon will we know?"

"I'll squeeze the lab guy. I'll know something tomorrow, but we can go after DNA to nail it down, and that'll take a few days . . . or even a couple of weeks."

"Would it speed things up if a U.S. senator called and asked about it?"

"For sure," Armstrong said.

THERE WAS NOTHING IN THE MAZDA.

Bob had come along with Lucas, and said, "I gotta believe that the guy has a laptop. Everybody has a laptop, including Ritter. Nothing in his hands when he got out of the Miata, nothing in the car. I wonder where he ditched it?"

Lucas looked around the parking lot. The lot, behind the

apartment house, wasn't visible from the street. Ritter hadn't pulled in and pulled back out because somebody would have noticed a bright red sports car coming and going without stopping.

"Wouldn't have had a chance to throw it out the window," Lucas said. "Wonder if somebody tipped him off that we were here?"

"Mrs. Snyder?" Snyder, the apartment manager.

"We warned her. And she struck me as a woman who knew when to stay warned."

"Well . . . look at all those windows," Bob said, and they both looked up at the back of the apartment complex. "We know Ritter's got a girlfriend, and if she lives up there, she might have given him a ring."

"Probably what happened," Lucas agreed. "I'll ask Snyder; maybe she'd know something about a relationship."

"Be nice if we could find a laptop," Bob said. "The computer guys might be able to find out if it was used in either Omaha or Minneapolis even if the messages were erased."

RAE CAME AROUND, and asked, "What's next, boss?"

"We get the truck towed to the Arlington impound lot. We have the names of four people probably involved in hitting Weather, and those four are also probably involved in the Smalls attack," Lucas said. "Tomorrow, we'll track them down. Keep the pressure up."

16

Ten o'clock was a good time for a raid, even if this wasn't exactly a raid. At ten o'clock, the employees who were running late should be at the office, but it was too early for lunch.

Rae had filled out the return on the James Ritter search warrant the night before, and Forte would file it. There wasn't much to report, although the hotel key card was seized as documentary evidence in the case.

Lucas, Bob, and Rae walked out into a bright blue day and hit the greasy spoon at nine o'clock, talked about what they would do that morning, and a few minutes after ten rolled into the parking lot at Heracles's Virginia headquarters, in an area called Crystal City. Airliners were landing nearby, and Lucas thought they might be close to Reagan National Airport.

Heracles was only one of a half dozen tenants of a nondescript fifteen-story, green-glass cube that just as easily could have been a parking structure as an office building. The parking lot, landscaped with relentlessly green, unidentifiable bushes as nondescript as the building itself, was two-thirds full. An overweight guard in a dull-gray uniform was patrolling the parking lot, and when they pulled into visitor's slots, he walked over and asked Lucas, "Do you have an appointment here?"

"No, but we do have business here," Lucas said, holding up his ID. "We'll be speaking to some of the tenants."

"No problem, bub," the guard said. "I'd make sure nobody stole your hubcaps, if you had hubcaps."

"Keep an eye on the wheels, then," Rae said.

"I'll do that," the guard said.

As they walked up to the building's entrance, Bob said, "Gonna be hot."

"You mean, talking to Heracles or walking around outside?" Lucas asked.

"Outside," Bob said, wiping his forehead with his fingertips.

A RECEPTION COUNTER faced the building's front door, with a steel fence extending from the counter to the walls on either side. The fence was penetrated on the left by three steel turnstiles. A receptionist, wearing a kelly green dress, and a matching pillbox hat, sat behind the counter, while a guard, this one with a gun on his hip, stood between two of the turnstiles.

They again showed their IDs, signed in, and got badges from the receptionist that allowed them through the turnstiles. Lucas said to her, "You don't have to announce us," and she nodded but looked perplexed, since announcing was her job, so he clarified: "Don't announce us."

The guard asked, "You here to arrest somebody?"

Lucas said, "Don't know."

Heracles was on the second floor. Lucas and Rae took the elevator up, since the fire door on the stairway was one-way—out—and locked. Bob waited for the next elevator to keep an eye on the door, the guard, and the receptionist. Lucas always preferred showing up unannounced, to see the unpracticed reaction of the person he was interviewing. In this case, though, the search of Ritter's apartment might have served as its own notice.

The entrance to the Heracles office was a double glass door that faced the elevator. Lucas could see no other glass doors, or greeting signs, along the hallway that stretched in both directions to the end of the building. Heracles apparently had the whole floor, he thought. A young woman sat at an expansive desk on the wall opposite the glass doors; there were four red-orange visitor's chairs, two on each side of the reception lobby, none occupied. When Lucas pulled the door, it didn't move.

The woman spoke into what must have been a microphone embedded in the desk: "Can I help you?"

Speakers were set into the walls on either side of the door. Lucas said, "U.S. Marshals. Open up, please," and held up his badge. The woman hesitated, and Lucas said, "Open up now, please."

She reached out to a black object on her desk, and the doors unlocked with a quiet clank. Lucas pulled the door open, went through, trailed by Rae, and said, "We want to speak to Mr. George Claxson, Mr. John McCoy, and Mr. Kerry Moore."

The receptionist looked frightened. "Can I tell them what this is about?"

Lucas said, "No. I'll tell them. Just tell them we're here."

"Mr. . . ."

"Marshal Lucas Davenport and Marshal Rae Givens. Marshal Bob Matees will be here in a minute."

The woman nodded, picked up her phone, pressed a button, and said in a hushed voice, "There are three U.S. Marshals here to speak to Mr. Claxson, John McCoy, and Kerry Moore . . ." followed a few seconds later by, "They won't say . . ."

Bob stepped out of the elevator, and the woman unlocked the door for him. Bob said, "You guys got a lot of security."

The receptionist said, a nervous shimmer in her voice, "We have a lot of defense contracts."

THE RECEPTION LOBBY had two doors into the back, one on each side of the receptionist's desk. The one on the left popped open, and a middle-aged woman in a gray dress said, "Marshals . . . you wanted to see Mr. Claxson? Follow me, please."

They followed her through what might have been an insurance office, but not a heavily staffed one: a warren of perhaps fifty waist- and shoulder-high cubicles in a room the size of a basketball court. Each cubicle housed a computer, with perhaps a third of them occupied by either a man or a woman looking at the screen. A couple of the occupants looked up as the woman led Lucas, Bob, and Rae through the cubicle farm, but most paid no attention.

The woman half turned, as they were walking, and said, "I'm Mr. Claxson's personal assistant. Mr. McCoy isn't here today; he's at Camp Peary. Mr. Moore is here somewhere, maybe in Planning—I'll go find him. Mr. Claxson is waiting in his office."

The receptionist might have been surprised to see them, but this woman wasn't, Lucas thought. Their visit wasn't unexpected.

CLAXSON'S OFFICE was a two-room corner suite with views of the airport. The outer room had three secretarial-style desks with computers, two of them occupied by older women who watched the marshals with curiosity but said nothing. The third desk, a large one, probably belonged to Claxson's PA, who was escorting them.

In the inner office was a wide swath of thick blue carpet, the walls decorated with plaques, photographs, one wildlife painting on each wall, and two mounted deer heads. A wide walnut desk sat diagonally in the corner.

Claxson himself was seated at a computer that perched on its own stand to the side of his desk. He looked up as they entered, waved them toward a half circle of chairs facing the desk. There were two pistols lying on the desk, one a Model 1911 .45, the other a Browning Hi Power, with a foot-long Marine Ka-Bar fighting knife sitting between them. The knife had the initials "GC" stamped on its well-oiled leather sheath.

Claxson was a fast touch typist. He rattled through a paragraph of text while Lucas, Bob, and Rae were settling into their chairs. He checked the screen, touching it with the tip of an index finger, then hit two keys, and the text vanished. He turned, crossed his hands on his desk, and said, "Marshals, what can I do for you?"

Claxson resembled a character actor that Lucas had seen in any number of movies: thin, balding, with quarter-sized freckles spotting his shiny scalp, but with a soft face rather than one with athletic contours. He wore rimless glasses, a gray suit, white shirt, and a light blue tie with stars on it.

Lucas: "Did you fly your personal plane to Omaha two weeks ago, with James Ritter, John McCoy, and Kerry Moore on board?"

Claxson lifted his hands. "I might as well lay out the rules right now. I'm aware that you went after one of our employees,

Jim Ritter, yesterday afternoon, some ridiculous accusation that he was involved in an attempted assassination of Senator Porter Smalls. I spoke to our company lawyer. We take care of our personnel, and he will be representing Jim if you have any more questions. Our attorney has also advised me simply not to answer any questions that might . . . feed your conspiracy theories. Yes, I flew to Omaha. I was there for a week of business, more or less. I fly my own plane, and there was nobody else on board. I won't reveal the nature of the business because that's a private matter that would possibly reveal classified military information. So, I don't believe we have anything more to talk about."

"We understand that John McCoy is not here in the building, but Kerry Moore may be. We need to talk to Mr. Moore," Lucas said.

"He's here, you can speak to him, but he's taken advice from the same attorney that I have. He won't have anything to say," Claxson said. He looked out the door of his office, and said, "Here's Kerry now."

Kerry Moore, probably thirty-five years old, was a muscular man with short-cropped hair in what seemed to be a favored Washington paramilitary uniform: tan cargo pants, light-colored boots, and a light-colored long-sleeved pullover shirt. He nodded at Claxson, and said, "You rang?"

Claxson waved in the direction of the marshals. "These are the marshals Jim told us about."

Moore nodded at them, and said, "Well, Rick Brown told me that talking about anything might bring trouble, so I guess I don't want to talk with you. Unless there's an attorney in the room."

"Rick is our attorney," Claxson said to Lucas.

Speaking to Moore, Rae began, "You don't have anything to worry about—"

"Honey, you gotta know that's bullshit," Moore said. "You guys go on one of these snipe hunts and it winds up on CNN, where they're pulling apart every word looking for every possible meaning. The next thing you know, you got a noose around your neck and cameras chasing you down the street. If you want me to talk, we're gonna need a lawyer in the room."

"So you're not unwilling to talk," Bob said.

Moore considered, and said, "Not entirely unwilling, but you gotta know Rick Brown. He's going to say no as soon as you open your mouth."

Lucas looked at the two of them, and said, "Okay. Dead end, then. But I'll tell you guys, this isn't the end of it. You tried to kill a U.S. senator, and you murdered two people—"

"No! No! Did not!" Claxson said, slapping his desk. "I absolutely reject any such notion. You say one word about it in public, we will sue everybody in sight. Our livelihood depends on our reputation, and if you begin slandering us with that . . . We did not have anything to do with any of that."

Lucas said, "We'll see. In the meantime, I'll tell you that we haven't made any 'ridiculous accusations' against Ritter—those were the words you used. I will tell you that we have substantial evidence that he was involved in the assassination attempt. We believe we know why; we believe we know the others involved. We have a bit of lab evidence we're waiting to get back and then we'll be here with an arrest warrant."

"Fuck you," Claxson said.

LUCAS, RAE, AND BOB stood up to go. Bob nodded at the pistols on the desk, and asked Claxson, "Are those weapons loaded?"

Claxson snarled at him: "Of course they are. If they weren't, they wouldn't be weapons, they'd be paperweights."

They took the elevator down, and Rae said to Lucas, "That was embarrassing. They did everything but kick us in the ass. But you don't look all that unhappy."

"I'm not. All we've got is evidence against Ritter and he's not the guy we want," Lucas said. "We want to go up from there, and now we've put a skunk in with the chickens. One way or another, they'll react. Oh—we need to put a hold on their passports, in case one of them decides to run for it."

"Your man Forte should be able to handle that," Bob said.

"We wait for lab results? What do we do while we're waiting?" Rae asked, as they got out of the elevator. "Play pinochle?"

Lucas said, "Bob's a camera freak, and you like art, so Bob can go take pictures, and you can go over to the National Gallery and look at art. But keep your phone handy."

"We did most of that while you were gone," Rae said. "What are you going to do?"

"I've got a fitting with my tailor," Lucas said.

Bob and Rae both stopped walking to peer at him, and Rae said, "You're joking, right?"

"No, I'm not. We've got some downtime, so it seems like a reasonable thing to do," Lucas said.

Bob: "If one of these assholes kills you, you'll have a new suit to get buried in."

"There's that," Lucas said.

THEY WENT BACK to the hotel, where Rae took the rented Tahoe and headed for the National Gallery. Bob got his camera but asked Lucas if he could tag along to the tailor shop, and that was fine with Lucas. Parking was rare around the shop, so they took a cab.

At Figueroa & Prince, Lucas was met by Ted, who smiled, reached out to shake hands, and said, "Lucas, happy to see you back. We have a preliminary cut . . . There were some interesting discussions here about how to accommodate the pistol . . ."

Lucas introduced Bob, who took a chair to watch the fitting and, after a few minutes, got up to wander around the shop, checking out the suits on display, the accessory racks, and finally the fabrics themselves. Lucas was trying on the first cut of a wool winter suit when he noticed Bob talking to another one of the salesmen.

When Lucas was finished with his fitting, he found Bob draped in a pale blue crepelike material and looking squint-eyed into a mirror. Ted walked over, and said, "Mmm, I think we can do better."

"What does that mean?" Bob asked Lucas.

"It means that color makes you look like a fuckin' boxcar," Lucas said. "You ought to have them embroider Burlington Northern on your back."

"I might not have put it quite that way," Ted said. To Bob: "We should spend a while talking about your goals."

"My goal is to have a good-fitting suit that I can wear in southern Louisiana, because I've never had one of those in my life."

Ted considered that, and said to the other salesman, "Not one suit—I think two . . ."

They wound up spending three hours in the store, and when they left, Lucas, looking both ways before letting the door close behind him, said, "Well, that was a quick way to blow six grand. I'm proud of you."

Bob shrugged. "I've got a good job, I don't care about cars, don't gamble, don't chase too many women or use drugs . . . I've got a few extra bucks, and I've never had a suit that fit right, so why not?"

Lucas clapped him on the back. "Like I said, I'm proud of you—I'm serious. You, my friend, are gonna look terrific. You'll be able to hold your head up, even in New Orleans."

"I like that part about working around the gun . . . I never knew any of that shit. I'll tell you, though, I ain't spending four grand for a pair of wingtips."

Lucas said, "You're standing on a slippery slope, Bob. I predict there are wingtips in your future, but not for . . . three years. Once you go over, you'll never go back."

"I heard somebody say that about gay sex," Bob said.

"Almost the same thing," Lucas said. "They're very close."

17

Parrish arrived at Grant's house, and when Grant came to the door—the housekeeper had been sent home—he asked, "Who's here?"

"George," Grant said. "We're in the SCIF."

Parrish followed her through the house, past the heavy door to the basement, which silently slid closed behind them, and down the stairs. Claxson was spread across the sofa. He was wearing aviator sunglasses and an unwrinkled blue-striped seersucker suit; a fashionably battered leather briefcase sat at his feet.

Parrish took a seat, and asked, "What's up?"

Grant looked at Claxson, and said, "The electronics say he's carrying a big chunk of metal but no electronics, other than a cell phone."

"He's got a gun," Claxson said.

"Jesus," Parrish said. Then, "So what?"

Grant slid open her desk drawer, took out the 9mm, and laid it on the desktop. "Just good to know."

Parrish shook his head. "I'm not going to shoot anyone . . . I assume you're doing video or sound; I hope it spools to something you can erase."

"It does," Grant said. "Of course it does."

Parrish: "Okay. So what's up?"

"RITTER, IS WHAT'S UP," Claxson said. "It looks like the Marshals Service might have enough on him to put him in the truck that hit Smalls."

"And killed Whitehead," Grant added, "It's like I'm trapped in a circus. It all sounds good, then the clowns show up."

"How do you know this?" Parrish asked. "That the Marshals Service has—"

"I have a friend at the DOJ," Claxson said.

"So what do we do? Move Ritter out of here?" Parrish asked.

Both Grant and Claxson looked at him without saying a word, and Parrish finally said, "You're thinking of something more . . . permanent?"

"Not only that," Claxson said, "we're thinking that one of the three of us has to do it. Senator Grant and I took a vote, and you won."

"Wait!" Parrish croaked. "I've never done that."

"Yeah, but you can. Maybe you never had the opportunity," Claxson said. "I've seen you at the range. What's the problem?"

"It's . . . I've never done that."

"We're all in serious trouble here," Claxson said, standing up, leaning over Parrish. "Jim is a good guy but he's looking at life without parole if the marshals get to him. And they're close. They want him, but they want us more. If they break him, if they make a deal with him, all of us are done. He has to go. Senator Grant needs to be in a public place when he goes away, and so do I. That leaves you."

"I can't fuckin' believe this," Parrish said. "There's gotta be some other way."

Grant said, "There is no better way, not for George or me. If you get caught, well, too bad. Claxson and I'll say you'd gone rogue and we had no idea what you were up to. If you don't get caught, we've sealed off an existential problem. A problem that could kill all three of us."

"But . . ."

"No buts. It's decided," Claxson said. "Gotta be right away. Try not to step on your dick. Do that, and we'll throw you, and your dick, under the bus."

PARRISH ARGUED, but Grant and Claxson stonewalled him: it had to be done. Parrish left in a heavy sweat.

He'd never been an "operator," in the military sense of the word; he'd worked in supply, in logistics, even when he was with the CIA. If you needed to get a thousand M4s to Iraq by Monday, he could do it, though a few crates might fall off the back of the truck.

He'd known lots of real operators, though, and had provided expedited supplies for special operations forces. A dozen former operators hung around Heracles, coming and going without saying much. He liked to think he could hang with them.

And Claxson had seen him at the range: Parrish liked to shoot and was good at it. He liked the whole ritual of handling the weapon, cleaning it, the signature smell of the Hoppe's gun cleaner, the acrid odor of the brass brushes.

He left Grant's SCIF frightened—and exhilarated. Had to be done; and now he'd find out what he was all about.

He had some thinking to do as well: if they really and truly wanted to wall off the problem, he might go next. Something to worry about.

He called Ritter. "We may have a problem in St. Paul. We need to talk."

"Where?"

"My place."

WHEN PARRISH bought his Georgetown home, he'd bought the best address he could afford, which turned out to be a late-nineteenth- or early-twentieth-century town house that was structurally sound but internally a mess. He'd taken home-improvement classes at a community college and, over three years, had cautiously upgraded the place.

The project of which he was most proud of involved a closet. It had been in a bedroom, and he'd converted it into an office. He'd stripped off the molding surrounding the original door and replaced the door itself with a heavy metal-core blank that he'd fitted flush with the wall. He'd painted the blank to match the wall and attached a bookcase as a front.

This new door had a lock, six feet up from the floor, with a heavy bolt, which ensured that the bookcase wouldn't move no matter how hard somebody pushed or pulled on it. Because the lock was set right above one of the bookcase's shelves, it couldn't be seen except by somebody standing on a chair or an NBA center. Unlock the door, the bookcase swung out to reveal the closet.

Which was full of goodies. Parrish thought of himself as prepared, as an operator, as a survivor,. He loved the idea of a hidden room in his house.

He had two combat-style pump shotguns and two black rifles inside the closet, along with a dozen pistols, including two with suppressors; he also had an entire drawerful of knives, another drawerful of ammo, two compound bows with a hundred carbon fiber arrows, body armor, Delta-style helmets, a pair of night vision goggles, two tactical backpacks, three different kinds of camo uniforms, a variety of equipment bags, a gas mask, and even a straw cowboy hat. Much of it—not the cowboy hat—had been stolen during his Army tours in the Middle East. Since he was involved in logistics, he had no problem getting it back to the States.

None of the firearms were registered in Washington, so possession of them was a crime; he wasn't too worried, because the District was awash in guns. Still, if the cops wanted him for something else and tore the house apart, possession of the guns could land him in prison.

He selected one of the silenced pistols, a Kimber .45, his favorite. He was ready.

But nervous.

ONCE UPON A TIME IN IRAQ, Parrish had been on a convoy out of Baghdad headed north toward Balad Air Base. They were passing through a hamlet, an hour into the trip, when an improvised explosive device—an artillery shell—took out a truck three trucks ahead of his. There was one good lookout nearby—a two-story mudbrick building that stood in the shade of a copse of palm trees—and two real operators ran toward it while two more hosed down the exposed windows.

A moment later, there was a brief burst of gunfire from behind the building as the operators cut down a running man. Parrish, exiting the truck, could see there wasn't much more going on. Everybody was out of the trucks, and a medic was working on the injured up ahead. He saw the two operators moving around behind the building. He went that direction, where he found them standing over a downed man.

Parrish skidded to a stop, walked over, and looked at the man, who was bleeding heavily from multiple leg and stomach wounds. He asked, "He going to make it?"

One of the operators said, "Don't think so."

The second one asked, "You ever killed anybody, Jack?"

Parrish said, "No."

The man handed Parrish his M4. "Here. Go ahead."

Parrish took the gun, looked at the wounded man on the ground, who was looking up at him and rocking back and forth, his legs tight to his chest.

Parrish asked, "He's the guy who touched off the IED?"

"Probably," the operator said. "He tried to get rid of his cell phone, threw it over there." He nodded toward a clump of waist-high, trashy-looking palms. "We found it."

The first man held up the cheap cell. "No reason to do that unless he used it to trigger the bomb."

Parrish said, "Okay." He stepped back, turned the rifle on the wounded man. The man said, "No," and as Parrish focused on his heart area, the operator snatched the gun back.

"Jesus Christ, Jack, it was a joke." The operator was freaked. "Jesus."

The medics took care of all the wounded in the convoy, but by the time they got to the man he was dead. Just as well he was out of his misery, Parrish thought, as the medivac Black Hawks dusted off the bombing scene and headed for the hospital at Balad.

The fact was, there'd been nothing sexual about the situation, but Parrish got a hard-on when he thought about it. If only he'd had a chance to pull the trigger.

PARRISH TOLD RITTER to park two blocks away and to walk in, and to check for surveillance on the way. "There're always parking spaces behind the café, and you can get in and out of the lot without being seen."

"Why your place?"

"Because I stripped the whole house down myself and it's clean. We need to talk where nobody can hear us. With all the shit you guys have over at Heracles, I'd be surprised if there aren't microphones hidden in the office chairs."

"See you at nine," Ritter said.

Ritter was an athletic guy of average height, with black eyes, tight-cut black hair, and a dark Mediterranean complexion. In Somalia, at a short distance and wearing a *khamiis*, he could pass for a native, and had. Parrish had been told that Ritter and his twin brother had finished first and second in a Nebraska statewide high school cross-country championship.

Ritter left his car in the lot behind the Jitterbug Coffee & Café; Parrish was right, it was dark back there. If he ever needed to mug somebody for money, Ritter thought, he'd stake out the Jitterbug. The café wasn't cheap; it was full of prosperous-looking people with Macintosh Pros, and they all had pencil-necks.

Easy pickin's.

Ritter took fifteen minutes to walk to Parrish's house, circling the block twice. Been better, he thought, if only he had a dog; he wondered briefly if Washington had a pit bull rental agency.

He saw nothing moving. The fact was, if the marshals were watching Parrish, they'd probably be on a roof somewhere, or in an apartment across the street. They wouldn't be parked in a car where the cops might roust them.

Fifteen minutes after he left the Jitterbug, he rang the bell at Parrish's.

WHEN PARRISH bought his house, the floors were either wooden or covered with carpet. The carpet would soak up blood like a sponge, but the wood, always well waxed, would repel it. The wooden floor in the kitchen had been refinished for the sale; it was worn smooth but shone with the golden glow of old chestnut, and that was where Parrish decided he would kill Ritter.

Parrish didn't cook but had three cookbooks on a shelf under a kitchen cabinet. He put the gun between two of the books, cocked, safety off, a round of G2 RIP .45 ACP in the chamber.

There'd be no point in waiting, he thought.

When Ritter rang the doorbell, Parrish popped a chicken potpie in the microwave, turned the microwave on, and went to answer the door. The cooking pie would fill the kitchen with a homely aroma that might ease any suspicions in Ritter's mind. Parrish was more tense than he'd expected. He'd realized, as he got the gun ready, that if he screwed it up, Ritter would kill him.

RITTER SLIPPED INSIDE, and Parrish shut the door behind him, and asked, "See anybody?"

"No, but if you've got professionals watching you, I wouldn't. You think there might be somebody?"

"Not really, but since last week . . . we've got a problem. I'm cooking dinner. Come on back to the kitchen, and I'll tell you about it."

Ritter followed him down the hall to the kitchen. Walking with his back to Ritter made Parrish itch between the shoulder blades, but he focused on the job. In the kitchen, the potpie was beginning to heat up. Ritter said, "Smells good."

Parrish opened the microwave, and, as he did, he said, "There's milk, water, beer, and Pepsi in the refrigerator. Get me a Pepsi, and whatever you want."

"'Kay . . . What's the problem?" Ritter asked. As he answered, Ritter opened the refrigerator, the door swinging wide between himself and Parrish. Parrish pulled the gun out from between the books, and when Ritter shut the refrigerator, holding a two-quart carton of milk and a bottle of Pepsi, Parrish shot him twice in the chest, one of the slugs going through the milk carton, spraying milk over Ritter's face and chest.

Ritter staggered, looking blankly at Parrish, then he dropped the Pepsi and the milk and twisted and fell face-first to the floor, where he spasmed for several seconds and finally went quiet.

Though silenced, the shots had been loud in the small kitchen. Not loud enough for his neighbors to hear, but loud enough that Parrish's ears rang for a few seconds.

Parrish looked down at the body and felt some chemical flushing through his body. Not adrenaline, something else, something even more primitive, a kind of breath-robbing hormone, maybe a testosterone variant, whatever it is that makes warriors exult in a kill.

It produced a kind of . . . joy. Parrish stood still, closed his eyes, let himself feel it.

BEFORE HE'D LEFT Grant's house, and the SCIF, Parrish, Grant, and Claxson had talked about what to do with Ritter's body. Claxson had suggested taking it out into the woods somewhere and burying it. Grant said she'd let the professionals work that out but mentioned that she'd known of a situation where that had worked.

Parrish said he'd think some of something, but, in truth, he'd already thought of it: given the number of cops around D.C. and the surrounding countryside, he wasn't going to move a body any farther than he had to, and sure as shit wasn't going to stumble around in the woods, in the dark, with a shovel and a gunnysack.

He knew where the body would be going before he ever left Grant's SCIF.

PARRISH HURRIEDLY stripped all the ID off the body—wallet, telephone, Rolex, an Army ring with a blue stone—set it aside, took a contractor's trash bag out of the cupboard, knelt and pulled it over Ritter's upper body. Ritter began shaking again as he did that: brain cells dying. He pulled another bag over Ritter's legs, rolled the body over to look at the floor. There was a pink smear of blood mixed with milk. Parrish, scrubbing with household cleaner, wiped the blood and milk up with a paper towel, making sure he'd gotten it all. He remembered to pick up the .45 shells: once he was on the highway, he'd throw them out the window.

When he was done, he looked at the bagged body, then went on with the worst of it. The killing had been reasonably sanitary and drama-free. But if the body should be found, it would be best to delay identification as long as possible. He got a cleaver out of the hardware door and cut the third joint off each of Ritter's fingers, grimacing at the sound of the cleaver going through bone and tendon.

He set the severed fingertips aside on a sheet of Saran Wrap, carried them to the bathroom. He flushed three at a time down the toilet, four with the last flush. When he was satisfied, and still with the strength and energy from whatever hormone he'd stirred up, he dragged Ritter's body down the stairs to the garage tucked under the house and lifted it into the back of his Jeep.

Almost forgot: his own phone. He called Grant. She picked up, and neither of them said anything. After a minute had passed, he hung up and carried the phone upstairs and put it on the kitchen counter.

HE DROVE across the river to a brewpub called Applejack's Burger & Beer, which happened to be near a metro station. The place had no cameras overlooking its dumpster, no windows. He parked next to the dumpster, looked for people out walking, and, in another ten-second burst of energy, boosted Ritter out of the Jeep and into the dumpster, where he landed almost soundlessly on a pile of cardboard and garbage.

He'd taken Ritter's car keys and telephone. He crushed the phone under his foot, pulled out the battery, threw the pieces in the dumpster. Five seconds later, he was out of the parking lot and on his way back to Georgetown. He dropped the phone battery out the car window, along with the .45 shells, and after parking in his garage, and checking the back of the Jeep for any traces of blood, he walked to the Jitterbug Café, clicked the key fob, and spotted the flashing lights of Ritter's Mazda.

He drove the Mazda carefully to the metro station, near the body dump site, parked it, and took the train back to Washington, to Foggy Bottom. He walked home from there, a bit more than a mile.

A mile was nothing.

He whistled most of the way, fighting back the adrenaline surging through him while reliving the shooting mentally in split-second frames.

Nobody, he decided, could have done it better.

At home, he called Claxson on his cell phone. Claxson didn't answer, as planned. The call alone from Parrish's number meant that everything had gone well.

He hadn't liked seeing Jim go, but they'd sealed off the problem, and he'd gotten the thrill of a lifetime. He hoped to do it again someday.

18

When Allah wants to mess with a perfectly good murder, He doesn't hesitate.

Jasim Nagi, a moderately faithful Islamic man of Arabic descent born in Atlantic City, who carried with him the full faith and credit of the New Jersey accent, drove a garbage truck.

Not a humble garbage truck: it was a two-year-old, forty-cubic-yard McNeilus Front Loader painted bright green, and it took some skill to operate.

At six o'clock in the dawn's early light, Nagi maneuvered through Applejack's empty parking lot, picked up the dumpster, and when the load dumped in the cargo box, he heard a loud bang as something large and metallic hit the bottom.

He said, "Aaa . . . shit," in his best Joisey Shore accent, because he knew what it probably was: a piece of obsolete office equipment, like a printer. It had probably been thrown in the dumpster because the owner didn't want to dispose of it in an environmentally responsible way.

That also meant that if Nagi tried to unload it at the landfill without reporting it and got caught, he'd get stuck with both a fine and the printer.

Nagi went on with his route, had the first full load ready to go by nine o'clock. At the landfill, he told the supervisor at the gate that he probably had a big printer in his load, and the supervisor pointed him to a specific dump area, a laborer following him with a Kabota Front End Loader.

Nagi dumped the load, waited for the wave from the laborer. Instead, he got the white-faced laborer running down the side of the truck, calling, "You better get out here."

The printer was there, at the top of the load of foul-smelling garbage. Right next to a partially exposed leg, an expensive Salomon hiking boot still on the foot.

Nagi crossed himself, although he was a Muslim, because that's what you did if you were raised in New Jersey. To the laborer, he said, "This ain't good. Go get the boss."

THE COPS CAME, and the medical examiner, and over the span of two hours the body was exposed, photographed, and re-covered. The top of the torso was still wrapped in a black plastic garbage bag, which was packed away for a further forensic examination. The lack of fingertips was recorded, and the detective team working the scene noted that the body had probably been fingerprinted at some point and that the killer knew it. The crime scene crew checked the clothing for any kind of identification but found nothing.

When the cops were satisfied that they'd done everything possible at the scene, the body was moved to the Medical Examiner's Office. There, the clothing was removed and bagged for forensics, the body examined: it bore two tattoos. One was a generic American flag, but the other was Special Forces, with the designation ODA 331.

That information, with a photograph of the dead man's face,

was sent to the Army's Criminal Investigation Command, which, in the Army's idiosyncratic way, was abbreviated "CID," since "CIC" was reserved for the "Commander in Chief."

Two hours later, the CID came back with the information that the body was almost certainly that of former master sergeant James Harold Ritter, who had been subsequently identified by two of his former teammates. He had been honorably discharged from the Army a few years earlier.

The cops found a Virginia driver's license for Ritter, matched the photos, and went to his address in Arlington, where the apartment manager told them that the apartment had just been searched by federal marshals.

The cops eventually found Russell Forte, told him about Ritter, asked him about the search. Forte said, "I'll call the marshal in charge of the search and have him get back to you."

By that time, an autopsy was under way at the Medical Examiner's Office.

Nagi had pointed the Alexandria cops to the Applejack's parking lot, though he couldn't tell them for sure where the body had come from. Applejack's was a good guess, but it could have come from either of his next two stops as well.

The cops checked all three places but found no evidence of a murder in any of the dumpsters.

THE COPS FOUND FORTE more quickly than they might otherwise have because he had put in a request for all available information on Ritter. A history of being murdered was definitely information.

Forte called Lucas two minutes after he finished talking to the cops.

"Bad news, man," Forte said when Lucas picked up.

"What is it?" Lucas asked. He, Bob, and Rae were ambling along M Street in Georgetown because they didn't know of a more interesting place to go.

"Somebody murdered James Harold Ritter and threw his body in a dumpster. The body was found by chance. At a landfill. There's an autopsy going on right now, but the cops say he was shot twice, in the chest. Best guess right now is, he was killed last night."

"Oh, no. Ah, man." Bob and Rae stopped when they heard Lucas's tone. He turned to them, and said, "Somebody killed Ritter."

"The killer cut off Ritter's fingertips to prevent printing, but he was identified by a tattoo from his Special Forces group and then by matching photos with his license," Forte said. "There's not a hell of a lot more unless the autopsy comes up with something. That looks like a long shot."

"We better get over there—we'll need an address for wherever the autopsy is."

"Got that for you," Forte said. "And the cops want to talk to you."

"Listen, call the cops back and ask them to stay quiet about the murder . . . a couple of days. Ask for cooperation. It'd be best if this didn't make it in the papers until we've figured out what to do."

"I can do that," Forte said.

"WHAT HAPPENED TO HIM?" Rae asked.

"Somebody shot him to death," Lucas said. He told them the

rest of it, and they stood there, shaking their heads, as they heard the story.

When Lucas was done, Bob looked at Rae, and said, "Heavy-duty, girlie."

The three of them had been waiting for something to happen; they'd talked about pushing things harder but decided in the end to wait until they had the lab results from West Virginia, which were due any minute. They had spent the previous afternoon and that morning reading everything the FBI, the Marshals Service, and the Army could produce on Ritter, Parrish, and other employees of Heracles.

As they walked out to Lucas's Evoque, Forte messaged the address where the autopsy was going on.

"Manassas," Lucas said. "I don't know where that is."

"Over in Virginia," Bob said. "I think there was a big Civil War battle around there."

Rae: "I thought it was something white people kept in a jar, in the refrigerator."

THE DRIVE TO MANASSAS took an hour. The Medical Examiner's facility looked like an elementary school, and a detective named Roger Clark from the Frederick County Sheriff's Department met them at the front entrance. He said that the autopsy was nearly over.

"Whoever did it probably didn't know about the tattoo, because that got us an ID faster than fingerprints would have," he said.

"Do you know the time of death yet?" Lucas asked.

"Not yet, but we should know in the next few minutes. If you have the time, there's a conference room down the hall. I'd like to get a statement from you guys to put in my report."

"Sure," Lucas said. "We'd like to know the details of the discovery. In a landfill? Any idea where the truck came from?"

Clark filled them in on what they'd learned and asked to record Lucas's statement. Lucas agreed, and started with the accident that had killed Whitehead, and nearly killed Smalls, on through to the attack on Weather and the murder of Douglas Last. He also described Ritter's background and involvement with Heracles.

"Wow. You think that Ritter was in on it all?" Clark asked.

Lucas nodded. "This killing confirms it, as far as I'm concerned. The people who set this up knew we were getting close to him and couldn't take the chance that he might roll over on them."

"You have suspects . . ."

"Yes. A number of people associated with Heracles. They are professionals, and I doubt you'd get much from them, but I can give you names if you want to go talk to them."

WHEN CLARK was satisfied and had gone to check on the progress of the autopsy, Rae said, "If the locals go talk to the Heracles guys, that should give them a nasty bump."

"I'm counting on it," Lucas said. "But it would have helped to have Ritter as a hammer."

"The idea that we might try to use him that way, probably got him killed," Bob said. "I'm not feeling too good about that."

Lucas said, "Yeah. I hear ya."

CLARK CAME BACK a few minutes later, and said, "The doc will talk to us now."

The pathologist's name was Benjamin Woode; he was a fleshy man, with thinning red hair, who asked, "Why are federal marshals chasing this one?"

"Because we were asked to, and we have jurisdiction," Lucas said. "Did you see anything that might help?"

"Yes, a couple of things," Woode said. He carried with him the faint but peculiar scent of autopsy rooms: something like a butcher's shop, but with noxious chemicals attached. "He was shot twice, the bullets both penetrated the breastbone, one an inch or so above the heart, the other directly through it. And they made a mess of it. The slugs started coming apart as soon as they hit the victim. They were man-killers, designed to do just that. One passed entirely through the body. The core of the other one hung up on the skin of the victim's back. He was shot from the front, by the way, and there are extensive powder traces on his shirt and around the bullet's entry point, so the shooter probably wasn't more than five or ten feet away, if that."

"Can the slugs be identified?" Bob asked.

"That's not up to me; that's up to the forensics people . . . But they were in pieces, and one core is missing. What may interest you is that while one core didn't make it through the body, a few small pieces cut channels in the body and did penetrate through both the body and the victim's skin and shirt. If you can find the scene of the shooting, and it was inside somewhere, a good crime scene lab might be able to find those fragments in a wall. You probably couldn't see them at all unless you looked closely. They're tiny, like chips off a fingernail clipping. The killer might not have been able to clean it up . . . might not even know about it. If that turns out to be important."

"It could," Lucas said. "Do you have a time of death?"

"There's a limit to what we can say at this point, until we get some labs back."

"I know that, but what do you think?"

"He was still showing signs of rigor. He was shot last night. He's not twenty-four hours dead."

THERE WAS MORE OF THAT, but not enough to help identify the killer. When they'd finished talking to the medical examiner, they looked at Ritter's clothing, which had been separated and bagged. His wallet was missing, and a watch and ring were gone as well: they only knew about them because of the white they'd left on Ritter's tanned skin. The only thing the clothing told them was that Ritter habitually dressed in high-end outdoor garb and boots and that he wore a heavy leather belt designed to accommodate a holster: Bob knew that because he wore the same belt.

"The only difference is that he wrote his name on the back of his with a Sharpie or something," Bob said, turning the belt in his hands. "Probably because he spends time in a barracks, and everybody wears pistol belts; this is an expensive one."

Lucas glanced at the belt, which had an elaborate "James Ritter" written on it in black ink, with decorative dots preceding the first name and following the last to either end of the belt. There was also an "S."

"Must have had a lot of time to kill," Rae said, "him doing art deco design on his belt."

Lucas told Clark, "We're going to run over to his apartment, take another look. Won't need a warrant now. He'd have been driving either a Ford F-250 or a Mazda Miata roadster. We have both tag numbers. We need to get all the local patrol guys looking for it."

"We'll get that out, call you when we find it," Clark said. "I need to be there when you look at the apartment, though."

"You're welcome to come along," Lucas said.

LUCAS, BOB, AND RAE left for Ritter's apartment, with Clark trailing. On the way, Bob said, "The truck didn't look like it'd been driven all that much. Maybe we should have had it processed for DNA. Ritter was probably driving; we should look for traces in the passenger seat, see who might have been sitting there."

Rae said, "The FBI has that fast forensic DNA analysis going now. If we can get a team over there, they can have the results back tomorrow."

"Not a bad idea," Lucas said. "What we need is an FBI crime scene team at Ritter's, to check if he might have been killed there. I'll call Forte, see if he can get one moving. After that, they can hit the truck."

Bob said, "We need a new Ritter. Right now, we're back to zero."

"Always Moore and McCoy," Rae said.

"Yeah, they're up," Lucas said.

"Fuckin' Ritter," Bob said.

FORTY-FIVE MINUTES LATER, they pulled into Ritter's apartment complex, swung around back. No Miata.

"Probably not shot here. The killers wouldn't have driven it away," Lucas said.

Forte called. Chase had gotten the crime scene team moving.

WHILE THEY WERE WAITING for the FBI team to show up, Armstrong called from West Virginia. "You might want to have another hard talk with Ritter," he said. "We got test results back on the fabric samples from the truck, and they match the fabric samples from the logs exactly. It's apparently a kind of canvas used for martial arts mats. It's not common."

"Well, I've got some news about Ritter . . ." Lucas began.

Armstrong was astonished by the murder, and Lucas told him that the canvas samples were still in play if they could pull DNA out of the truck. "Hang on to that stuff, Carl. We'll get back to you."

"I feel like we're rolling, but I can't tell if it's uphill or downhill," Bob said when Lucas told them about Armstrong's lab results.

THE FBI TEAM showed up, the manager let them into Ritter's apartment, while the marshals and Clark stood around in the hall as the team took a preliminary look. An hour later, the team leader, Jake Ricardo, came out, and said, "We can't find any sign of a shooting in here. I don't believe he was killed in this apartment."

No murder scene. The first time the marshals searched the place, they'd been restricted by the warrant—they'd had to specifically list what they were looking for, and they'd been strictly held to that list because their justification for the search was fairly thin. With Ritter murdered, the FBI team could tear the place apart.

They did that.

The first significant find was two passports, hidden under a carpet edge held down with a strip of double-sided tape. One passport was British, issued to one Richard Carnes, with Ritter's photo. The other was American, issued to a David Havelock, also with Ritter's photo.

The second and final good thing was Ritter's laptop, which was sitting on a coffee table. They couldn't get into it because it was password-protected. Lucas asked them if they could get the laptop to their computer lab to break the password.

"That's in a different place, down in Quantico," Ricardo said. "I'll call them and see if they can pick it up. What about his cell phone?"

"Haven't found it," Lucas said. "We know he had one, because we got the number, and we know some places that it wasn't."

"When did he get killed?"

"Probably last night," Lucas said.

"What service?"

"Verizon."

"Okay. Verizon will have tracking data for him going back quite a while, and texts going back at least a few days. You gotta get some guys on them."

"Could you do that?"

"Our people can. Let me call another guy."

HE DID THAT, and then called the computer specialist at Quantico, whose name was Roger Smith. "I live up near where you are,"

Smith said. "I could stop by on the way home, take a look. If I can't do anything, I could bag it and bring it to the lab first thing in the morning."

"That'd be great," Lucas said.

"In the meantime, look for the password. Could be written anywhere, if he actually wrote it down. Which he probably didn't. Probably his mom's middle name."

"We'll look," Lucas said.

CLARK, the Frederick County detective, gave up first. "If there's anything else here, I'll be damned if I know what it would be. I don't think he left a note that says 'I'm going to Joe's house, and he might shoot me.'"

"No, but he might have left a trail to the house," Lucas said. "The FBI is looking at his phone records. Hang on a while longer, we ought to be hearing back from them."

They did, but not for an hour. An FBI tech called Lucas, and asked, "Do you have a cell phone or an iPad?"

"An iPad, in my car," Lucas said.

"Give me your email, and I'll send you a link. We've mapped his track for the twenty-four hours before his phone quit."

"When did it quit?"

"About eleven o'clock last night, over in Virginia."

"Where in Virginia?"

"There's a place called Applejack's . . ."

"That's where his body was dumped," Lucas said. "How long before I get the track?"

"About thirty seconds after you give me your email address."

LUCAS WALKED DOWN to his car, got the iPad, and walked back to Ritter's apartment, bringing up the email as he walked. The FBI file was simply a pdf of a Google map, with the track played across it in a red line, with ant-sized numbers attached to the track. A legend with the map showed the time for each number.

The track started at Ritter's apartment for eight hours—he was asleep—then touched at the Heracles office, where it stayed for a few hours, followed by a wandering line at noon—lunch, Lucas thought. The phone went back to the office in the afternoon, went out to a location in Arlington, touched at the office, went over to Georgetown in the evening, and looped back toward Virginia, where the signal disappeared.

Lucas got back to the apartment, and Bob, Rae, and Clark all looked at him. "Ritter was at home last night, and he drove over to a restaurant that's about a block from Parrish's house," he said. "There are some squiggles on the map, where he maybe walked over to Parrish's place. The phone goes back across the river to that restaurant, where the body was probably dumped. Parrish killed Ritter and drove him back across the river and dumped him."

"Good to know," Clark said. "That's better than Ritter driving himself back home, stopping to get a bite to eat, where he gets shot behind the restaurant by muggers and thrown in the dumpster."

"That's unbecoming skepticism," Rae said.

"Only because the Washington area has the best defense attorneys in the country, because it needs them," Clark said.

Rae was looking over Lucas's shoulder, and said, "Call the FBI phone guy, get Parrish's track."

"Of course," Lucas said.

He did that, and the phone guy said it would be another hour.

While Lucas was talking about the phone, Smith, the computer expert, showed up. He was a balding black man, who first took a long look at Rae, then used some electronic boxes to mess with Ritter's laptop. After a few minutes, it opened up. Lucas, looking over his shoulder, said, "Thank you."

"You're premature," Smith said. "Everything in here seems to be encrypted. Everything. All his email and a dozen or so documents. It's standard heavy business encryption . . ." He tapped the screen showing an icon for an app called SanderCrypt. "That means there's no possibility of reading this stuff without the key."

"Well, hell, what would the key look like?" Bob asked.

"Could be anything. Might not even exist anymore, if he memorized it, and of course now he's dead."

"What if he wrote it down?" Rae asked. "How many numbers would it be . . . or letters . . . or whatever?"

Smith shook his head. "Can't tell. It could be anything, but probably quite a few letters, or numbers, or symbols . . ."

"And you guys can't break it?"

"Nope. The NSA can't. Nobody can."

"So let's say he wrote it down? What should we be looking for?"

"Well, anything that's sort of out of place," Smith said. "Most people don't write 'Hey, diddle, diddle, the frog and the fiddle and the moon jumped over the plutocrat' on the typing tray of their computer desk. If you find something like that, it's probably a key."

"We've been all over this place, inch by inch, and haven't found anything like that," Lucas said. "Would it just be a regular sentence, though, instead of random stuff?"

"Oh, depends on how much he knows about computers. If it was that 'Hey, diddle, diddle' thing, and, say, thirty letters long, it'd be impossible for any computer to break through with brute force. At the same time, it'd be easy to remember," Smith said. "Most non-techies don't know that, so they create a long random sequence. But random sequences are a lot harder to remember, and they get written down. That's what you'd look for—random numbers and letters that are out of place, that don't connect to anything else."

"Haven't seen anything like that, either," Lucas said.

"Then you're SOL," Smith said. "I'll take the computer—let me know if you find anything. Maybe he's got the key in a safe-deposit box or something and you'll find it later."

"That seems unlikely if he has to use it," Bob said.

Smith shrugged: "You're right. With all the encrypted emails, it looks like he used it quite a bit." He paused, then added, "We had one guy who used the serial numbers on a dollar bill—ten numbers, two letters; once forward, once backward. He told us he almost spent it a couple of times. He finally tucked it into the back compartment of his wallet to make sure he didn't."

"That'd be impossible to see even if we had Ritter's wallet, which we don't," Rae said.

"Yeah. We didn't see it, either, with the dollar-bill guy," Smith said. "He told us about it as part of a plea bargain."

Lucas shook his head. "There's gotta be a way to break it . . ."

Smith shook his head. "Sorry, man. There isn't. That's the way of the world now."

SMITH WAS PACKING UP when the FBI phone technician called and said that Parrish's phone had been turned on at his house all evening. A few minutes later, the Arlington cops called and said they'd found Ritter's car a block from the Applejack's. The doors were locked, but the car appeared to be empty, with no bloodlike discoloration on the fabric seat. They'd tow it and open the trunk, but the Arlington cop said the trunk was more like a lunchbox than a cargo hold, and nobody could have squeezed a body inside, with or without fingertips.

"But there could be documents," Lucas said. "I want a callback as soon as you open the trunk."

"We'll call," the cop said.

19

Forte ran the passports through the relevant databases to see where Ritter might have gone with them; he called back after dinner to tell Lucas that both had been used for trips to Europe and back to the U.S.

"He didn't stay long—two days in France, three in Spain, for one of them; three days in France, two in Germany, for the other," Forte said. "I could be wrong, but I suspect he was validating the passports with travel. Used passports already carrying visa stamps are less interesting than brand-new ones, if you're working passport control. They've already been checked."

The next morning, Bob called after his workout, and Lucas told him that he was going out to walk around for a couple of hours. "I need to think, that's all. Figure out what we can salvage. Like you said, Ritter was our guy, and now we need a new one."

Lucas went back to Georgetown, which was close by and not a bad place to walk. He wound up in a diner, eating a short stack of pancakes with bacon, reading the *Post*. There was a short item on page three about the Smalls/Grant controversy, but with nothing new.

When he got the check, he paid with his last twenty-dollar bill, which was a mild surprise. He'd stopped using credit cards for small charges in unknown places—every exposure created another possibility of getting hacked—and so always carried a supply of cash. He rarely let the count get below a couple of hundred dollars. He left the diner with fifteen dollars and change, the lack of cash scratching at the back of his brain like a weevil on a cotton boll.

And he hadn't figured out the next step.

HE'D SEEN a Wells Fargo Bank a couple of blocks away and walked over. He put in his ATM card and punched in his code . . . and noticed the Braille dots below the operating instructions. He wondered why they'd put Braille on a machine where a blind guy couldn't find it easily.

A bell rang in his head.

He collected his cash, stuffed it in a pocket, and called Rae. "Go down to the business center, however that works—maybe you'll need to take your own laptop—and download a Braille chart that shows letters and numbers and print it out. I need you to figure out how it works—Braille, that is. You know, how to read it."

"You mean, with my fingers?"

"No, no . . . what each Braille pattern means—what letters they are, the numbers."

"Well . . . Okay. What are we doing?"

"Looking for the key to Ritter's laptop."

"It's in Braille?"

"Remember those weird dots on the back of his belt?" Lucas asked. He heard an intake of breath.

"Oh my God, you could be right. Why don't I download it on my iPad? I can do that in a minute."

"I won't have the belt in a minute, but the iPad sounds fine. I'll get back to you when I get the belt. Or we'll meet back at the hotel and work it out."

"I'll download it now. The Stump will be amazed . . . which he usually isn't."

"We don't know what we've got yet," Lucas said, "but this feels right. A code on his belt could be as long and random as he wanted, would be handy, anyplace, anytime, impossible to misplace, and not obvious. People who know Braille would never see it because they're, you know . . ."

"Blind."

"Right. And people who aren't blind probably wouldn't recognize the dots as a code."

"How did you recognize it?" she asked.

"Thought about it a lot . . . all the places I've seen different dot codes," Lucas lied. "The Braille idea sorta popped into my head."

"Someday you'll have to tell me the truth," Rae said.

WITH RAE GOING OUT on the 'Net to find a Braille chart, Lucas called the Frederick County medical examiner, identified himself, and talked to a Medical Examiner's investigator named Gates. "You have a body there, a James Ritter."

"Yup."

"I need to come over and see his belt," Lucas said. "It's a gun belt, made for wide loops, like on jeans."

"What are you looking at?" Gates asked.

"The back of the belt. There might be some . . . information . . . on it. That we can use," Lucas said.

"Really? I didn't see anything."

"It's my superpower," Lucas said. "I can be there in an hour."

"I could take photos with my iPhone and have them to you in four minutes, if that makes any difference to you," Gates said.

"Well—yeah, let's try it. I need the whole length of the back of the belt. I'm sitting on the side of a road in downtown Washington and I'll wait for the call."

"Not four minutes, though, more like seven or eight."

"I'll wait," Lucas said.

LUCAS WAS WAITING with his iPad when the photos came in seven minutes later, three of them, all tight and well focused, with a note that said, "From left to right. Are the dots a code?"

Lucas didn't bother to answer the question, sent "Thanks," and headed for the hotel.

Back at the hotel, Lucas found Bob and Rae waiting in Rae's room, and when Rae let him in, she waved her iPad at him, and said, "Bob and I have been figuring out Braille. It's simple enough. You still think it's Braille on the belt?"

"Sure looks like it to me," Lucas said. He turned on his iPad, called up the photos, and they all crouched over the room's desk, the two iPads side by side. Lucas asked, "How do we know which way is up or down?"

Rae explained, and Lucas said, "So you read them."

She did, and wrote each letter or number on a legal pad as they scanned the belt photos: there were twenty-four symbols: "c3cejd24lstpv319qubdo6g9."

"That's nothing but a key to something," Bob said.

LUCAS FOUGHT through the FBI bureaucracy to get on the line with Roger Smith, the FBI computer tech. "Do you have Jim Ritter's laptop handy?"

"It's in a lockup, but I can get it in a minute or two."

"I got some numbers for you," Lucas said.

"Hang on."

LUCAS HUNG ON, and Bob said to Rae, "If this works, I'm probably going to have to kiss Lucas's ass. You might not want to be here for that."

"No time for it anyway," Lucas said. "If this works, we need to get down to Quantico and check this stuff out."

Rae: "Why? We'll just have him email it to us."

Lucas rubbed his face, and sighed. "Shit. You know, deep in my heart, I don't understand that we don't always have to go places to get things anymore," Lucas said. "I was about to drive an hour over to the Medical Examiner's Office to look at Ritter's belt. The investigator sent me the iPhone photos in seven minutes. Kind of scizzes me out, the way it comes out of the sky now."

SMITH CAME BACK to the phone, said, "We're up and running. What's your best guess?"

Lucas read the string of numbers and letters to him, and the tech typed them in, and said, "Nothing."

"Maybe it's backward, or whatever," Lucas said.

"Or maybe I mistyped something. I'm going to read them back to you," the tech said.

He did, and, toward the end of the string, said, "ddo6g9."

Lucas said, "Wait. Wait. Toward the end of the string, it should be bdo, not ddo . . ."

The tech said, "Wait one . . ." and then, "Shazam! We're in."

"I could come down and look at it, but if you could send the stuff, it'd be a hell of a lot quicker."

"I can send it. What's that chick's name, the one working with you?" Smith asked.

"You mean Rae?" Lucas looked at Rae.

"Yeah, the pretty one . . . the basketball player."

"Rae." To Rae, quietly: "He kinda likes your looks."

"Well, naturally," she said.

Smith: "Gimme her email and yours. I'm going to send her a string like the one you sent me . . . a different one, of course . . . and I'll send all the texts and emails in one long file to *your* email. We'll keep them separate so nobody can see both at the same time. You'll need to enter the code to read them. It's a onetime code, nobody else will be able to use it after you do. Not even you. Of course, if you open the files on your computer and save them in plain text, and somebody takes the computer away from you, they've got it."

"I'll open it on my iPad. I got Touch ID," Lucas said.

"Didn't this Ritter guy lose his fingers?" Smith asked.

"Yeah," Lucas said. "I won't do that."

"Gimme Rae's email."

"Don't hit on her," Lucas said.

"Hey, I'm with the FBI. Fidelity, Bravery, Integrity—FBI."

SMITH SAID IT WOULD TAKE a while to put a file together, and they sat and restlessly watched a Nationals game for twenty-five minutes, then Lucas's iPad dinged, and the file came in. A minute later, a string of letters and numbers came in for Rae: "Hey, sugar bun, I'd gr8ly like 2 take U out 4 a drink someday."

"That can't possibly be the code," Rae said.

Bob: "Sure it is. Remember what he said about using regular sentences as keys? And what Lucas told him about hitting on you? He's delivering the encryption code and hitting on you at the same time."

"He's not a bad-looking guy, either," Rae said. "Tall. Intelligent."

"Bald," Bob said.

Lucas said, "Jesus, Rae, just type the fuckin' thing into my file."

She did, and the new file opened up: twelve documents and thirty emails.

"Not much," Rae said.

"Ritter was disciplined," Lucas said. "Probably cleans out stuff he's not using."

"Even though he knows we could never crack the encryption without the code?" Bob asked.

"Even then," Lucas said. "If you got something you don't need, get rid of it." He thought about the Ritter bank statement he'd flushed.

BUT RITTER WASN'T PERFECTLY DISCIPLINED.

The longer files contained details of shipments to Libya,

Niger, and Iraq from Heracles—there were no details of what the shipments might be—that Ritter, McCoy, and Moore would be escorting to their final destinations. There were names of recipients and places mentioned, along with notes on briefing times, and, occasionally, enigmatic labels that seemed to Lucas to be cautionary: "Maziq is reliable and knows his way around, and he's always got protection, both physical and political, so you'll be okay there," and, "You can't count on Jibril to back you up if push comes to shove (which it won't). Be aware that he's belonged to four different militias that we know of, and they're not friendly with each other, so he's a guy who's willing to change beliefs like he changes his shorts. If he changes his shorts . . ."

Another one said, "Every time the cases are out of your sight, check the seals when you get back. Even when you get off the plane. This shit can't get pieced out or we're in trouble."

A third one said "Beware the OGA, they're thick in there."

"I wonder what the OGA is?" Lucas asked.

"I know that," Bob said. "It stands for 'Other Government Agency,' which means the CIA."

"Got it."

"The FBI needs to see this," Rae said. "What about the emails?"

Most of the emails were cryptic. They came in from several people at Heracles, but mostly said things like "We still on for two?"

Then they found the maps.

Lucas clicked on an email titled "Here" and, when he opened it, found two satellite blowups of tight areas of West Virginia. One had a dot on what appeared to be the intersection of a dirt lane and a back road less than half a mile from Smalls's cabin above the South Branch of the Potomac.

The other displayed a "path" that went from the point of impact, where Ritter's truck hit Smalls's Cadillac, to the back road above the cabin, to the spot where the logs that had been on the side of the truck were dumped.

They all read it, half disbelieving, until Bob tapped the screen where the trail intersected with the back road. "This is a scouting report, setting up the attack. Somebody was set to watch Smalls—here. When they left the cabin, he would call Ritter, in the truck, and walk out to where the truck was going to pick him up—here. He'd be picked up, and they would drive out to the place where they dumped the logs. After that, it was over the hill and back to D.C."

"Look at the time stamp," Lucas said. "It was, what, five days before they hit Smalls? They must have been watching him, and knew he'd be going up there with Whitehead."

"You don't get that just by watching," Rae said. "They bugged him."

The email had gone from Moore to Ritter.

Lucas said, "We need to tell the FBI guys about this. Then we go bust Moore. He's toast. We got our new guy. The only question now is, do we put him in a cell or wire him up?"

HE FOUGHT through the FBI bureaucracy again, finally arriving at the desk of Jane Chase's assistant. The assistant said that Miz Chase was in a conference. Lucas said, "This is quite important. Go into the conference, right now, and tell her the U.S. Marshals are calling with information she'd want. She'll know what you're talking about."

The assistant hesitated, then said, his voice pitching up with mild exasperation, "Well, I'll do it, but I hope you're not getting me in trouble."

"I promise, I'm not."

Two minutes later, Chase said, "Hello?"

"Agent Chase? This is Lucas Davenport, the U.S Marshal from the meeting—"

"I remember," she said, her voice dry as desert sand. "What do you want?"

"You're aware that one of our targets, James Ritter, was murdered?"

"I was informed of that, yes. Your man Forte called."

"We seized Ritter's laptop . . ."

"Which I understand is heavily encrypted."

"Yes. The other marshals and I cracked the code this morning. We have a number of documents about shipments from Heracles to Libya, Iraq, and Niger, although it doesn't say what the shipments were. But it looks to me like it might be stuff they don't want anyone to know about. From our perspective, the more important document apparently locates a suspect named Moore at Senator Smalls's cabin and also pinpoints the location where the logs we found with paint from Smalls's Cadillac on them were dumped. We're thinking of busting Moore right away. The question is, do we drop him in a cell or see if he'll wear a wire for us? Or might the FBI have a different idea altogether?"

"Wait. You cracked the encryption code? I was told by experts that couldn't be done," she said.

"Yeah, well . . . what can I tell you? We're marshals."

After considering that, she said, "I'm jammed up in the early afternoon, but I'll clear my schedule for later on. Be here at four o'clock. You'll be met in the lobby. Bring the documents you've found with you. We will have some of our specialists look at them."

Lucas told her that the computer guy at Quantico could have them to her in seven minutes, and she said, "Excellent. I will retrieve them from him. Your diligence is to be commended. We'll see you here at four."

She hung up, and Lucas said to Bob and Rae, "There is a woman not just with a stick up her ass but an entire fuckin' tree. With branches."

Rae said, "You gotta be straight to get as high up as she is with the feebs."

"Like you," Lucas said.

Rae said, "Nah. I just gotta be willing to shoot any dumbass motherfucker stupid enough to run from me. Which I am willing to do. And I have to take care of the Stump, of course."

"For which I'm eternally grateful," Bob said.

LUCAS CHECKED his cell phone. "Four o'clock—three hours. Maybe I'll work out. Too hot to go shopping."

"Take a nap," Rae said. "Or I could drive down to Quantico and meet Smith for a drink. He could give me a back rub. I could use a good rub."

Bob said, "I've been thinking . . ."

Rae: "Oh-oh. You know what I told you about that."

"What's the 'S' on Ritter's belt?"

Lucas said, "What?"

"There's an 'S.' Right at the end of the code. If the dots are a code, maybe the 'S' is, too."

Lucas got out his iPad, called up the photos of Ritter's belt. Bob was correct about the "S," written in the same black ink as the Braille dots, although Lucas was not certain whether the symbol was actually an "S." The initial, or symbol—or whatever it was—was rendered in open-ended double parallel lines, with one side of the initial/symbol shorter than the other. "It's more like a shape than an actual initial. It's like an S-shaped road," Lucas said.

"That's dumb. Who'd have to remember an S-shaped road?" Rae asked. "What good would it do you?"

"Maybe a river?" Lucas suggested, and Rae shook her head.

They sat and stared at it for a while, and Lucas said, "Fuck it, let's think about it."

A second later, Bob said, "You know what it looks like? It looks like the trap under a sink. Like maybe someplace you'd hide something small. A thumb drive, for instance?"

Rae and Lucas looked at each other, back at the iPad, and Rae said, "Goddamnit, we didn't look. Now we've got to go back over to Ritter's. And be back here by four."

ON THE WAY, Lucas called Russell Forte, told him about the meeting with the FBI. Forte said he'd be there, and O'Conner would probably come along to add weight. When Lucas finished the call, he made another to the manager at Ritter's condo complex, asked if they had a maintenance man. They did. "We need him to do some plumbing," Lucas said.

The maintenance guy, a phlegmatic man with watery blue

eyes, was waiting for them when they arrived. He said they might not have seen everything, but they'd seen most of it, no longer curious about why three feds in suits showed up to have him take a sink apart.

They started in the kitchen, found nothing in the trap.

In the bathroom, he looked at the trap, and said, "This has been taken apart a few times, but not by me. And I'm the only one authorized to do it."

The maintenance man took off the looped section of the pipe, stuck his finger into it, and popped out a plastic tube about the length and diameter of Lucas's little finger. The ends were wrapped in tape.

He handed it to Lucas, and said, "Radiator hose tape. So water can't get in. Couldn't put it in the kitchen because garbage going down could push the tube along and clog the sink. Nothing goes in this sink but water, soap, and whiskers."

While the maintenance man put the sinks back together, Lucas borrowed Bob's Leatherman tool to cut the tape off the plastic box. That done, he pulled the box apart and took out a flat, odd-looking key.

"Safe-deposit box," Rae said. "This should be good."

LUCAS CALLED FORTE. "I need a couple of clerks and another warrant, and I need them in a hurry." He explained, and Forte wasn't sure they'd need the warrant because Ritter was dead but decided that having a warrant when they didn't need it was better than needing a warrant when they didn't have it. "I'll write it up and get it."

The clerks started calling banks in the area, using three

names: Ritter's own, and those on the two passports they'd found under the rug. One of the clerks found a David Havelock at a Citibank a half mile away. Forte wasn't much farther away than that, at the Marshals Service headquarters, and said he would meet them there with the warrant.

Lucas said, "Let's go," and they were out the door and into the heat. They arrived at the bank ahead of Forte, got to the branch manager, and told her what was about to happen. "The warrant's fine," she said, after looking at their IDs, "but I'll need to call a man to drill the lock."

Lucas took the key from his pocket. "We have Ritter's key, and also the passport he used to get the box under false pretenses."

The woman looked at the passport, and the key, and muttered, "Yeah, it's one of ours. It's a big box. I think I remember this gentleman. He's a nice-looking fellow."

"Not so much now," Rae said.

FORTE SHOWED UP, sweaty yet well dressed, and produced the warrant. "You know I don't do this so much, come to the scene. I'm more of an intellectual than a street guy."

"We all know that, but it never hurts an office guy to add to his street cred," Rae said.

"Hadn't thought of it that way," Forte said. "I should start packing heat." They all looked at him, and he added, "Okay, maybe not."

They followed the manager into the vault, along with the women who managed the registry and safeguarded the master keys. The box opened on the first try, the woman pulled it out, said, "Heavy. Let's take it to a viewing desk."

The desk was in a private niche. They sent the bank people away, gathered around as Forte popped the top, looked in, and Bob said, "Oh boy."

The box was filled nearly to the top. The first layer, six or eight inches thick, was a mass of documents in English, French, and Arabic. "Contracts for delivery," Rae said, thumbing through them. "Guns. Oh my God, antiaircraft missiles."

"Ritter was keeping the docs for self-protection, his cover-your-ass files. Just in case," Lucas said.

"Looks like it's gonna work, too, if we're right about who killed him," Rae said. "Maybe not for self-protection, but revenge."

Under the first layer was a thin, flat plastic box, identical to those that Lucas had for his fishing tackle. Inside were two dozen thumb drives.

The third layer consisted of cash—hundred-dollar bills and five-hundred-euro notes—and gold coins, and three more passports. They did a quick count of the cash, and an estimate of the gold, and Forte, looking at his cell phone calculator, said, "He was looking for a rough equivalent of a million dollars in cash. The five-hundred-euro notes make it more compact."

The eighty gold coins added a bit more than a hundred thousand dollars to the total.

RAE WENT BACK to the lobby and got a cardboard bank box from the manager. Forte filled out a return on the search warrant, signed it, the manager took it away to xerox, and then they put everything inside the box and carried it out to Forte's car.

"Got thirty minutes to get to Hoover," he said. "We could be a bit late, especially if I drive slow. And I will. Holy cats, a million dollars in the footwell. Maybe I'll be *really* late, drive out to Reagan and get on a plane to Panama."

"Think about the wife and kids," Bob said.

Forte said, "That's what I was doing."

20

Forte's boss, Gabe O'Conner, was waiting for them outside the Hoover Building. He saw the box that Forte was carrying, and joked, "Money?"

Forte said, with a straight face, "Over a million, we think, though we didn't have time to work out the exchange rate on the euros. Or the current price of gold."

O'Conner looked from Forte to Lucas, to Rae, to Bob, and back to Forte. "Are you shittin' me?"

"Might not be the most important thing," Lucas said. "We took it out of Ritter's safe-deposit box; there are a lot of CYA docs in there, apparently about illegal weapons sales."

"You guys find . . . interesting cases," O'Conner said. He looked at his watch. "Let's go. Russell, talk to me about this while we walk up. I don't want to be late, but I don't want to be the complete dumbass in there, either."

Forte started talking, and didn't stop, even when their escort showed up. He talked fast—and in paragraphs, Lucas thought. If you'd typed out what Forte said, you could have published it as an essay. He continued all the way to the conference room, with O'Conner nodding steadily like a bobblehead doll. The conference room was still empty, like the first time they were there, until Jane Chase and her retinue of suits showed up, Chase carrying a thin aluminum attaché case.

As they were arranging themselves in their chairs, Forte stood up, plunked the mass of documents on the table. He followed that with the thumb drives and passports, added the stacks of cash, and finally the pile of gold coins, and sat back down.

"Where did you get it?" Chase asked.

Lucas smiled, rubbing his nose as cover. They weren't asking "How much?" or even saying "Oh my God" but instead "Where did you get it?" The gold and cash weren't enough to impress this particular bunch of bureaucrats.

Forte looked at Lucas, and said, "You talk for a while."

LUCAS STARTED with Ritter's laptop and the encrypted documents, explaining how the code had been concealed—though openly—on the back of Ritter's gun belt. Then he explained Bob's sudden comprehension of the "S" design on the same belt and finding the safe-deposit box key.

One of the suits with Chase, a woman, said to Bob, "You thought it was a drain? Why would you think that?"

Bob said, "Well, it looked like one. The design."

The woman said, "I don't think I've ever looked at a drainpipe."

"Probably not a do-it-yourselfer," Bob said. "I've looked at quite a few of them. They're kind of interesting, if you really get your head around them."

The woman said, "Huh."

LUCAS EXPLAINED that they hadn't had time to go over the documents from the bank, "But it looks like Ritter was accumulating material that would give him some protection if Heracles, for whatever reason, ever decided to sell him out," Lucas said. "There's a lot of stuff about arms sales, including antiaircraft missiles, and the implication seems to be that the sales were illegal. Or at least irregular."

"What are you planning to do with it?" Chase asked.

"I was planning to give it to you," Lucas said, "all of it," and Chase showed a tiny smile of satisfaction. "We have a particular focus: the assassination attempt on Senator Smalls. If you could have your legal people process this stuff—quickly—and give us an idea of the ramifications, we'll use it to confront a couple of the guys who were involved in the deliveries. We need to turn them. It'll have to be swift: they know we're coming, right now, and they've already lined up attorneys for the main suspects. We've talked to two of them, and they told us to go . . . You know."

"Go fuck yourselves?" Chase said crisply.

"Exactly," Lucas said. "We didn't have a lever."

"Who do you want to go after?" Chase asked. "Specifically?"

"Four names," Lucas said. "You have them all: Claxson, Parrish, Moore, and McCoy. We think we could bust Moore right now, with a good chance that it would stand up. If you looked at that map in the encrypted documents . . ."

"Yes, I did," Chase said. "That was the ambush at Smalls's cabin."

"Exactly."

"You might get him with that, and with the other circumstantial stuff, but it's thin," she said.

"Which is why we need somebody else to turn on him. To turn on all of them. You might find that somebody in these documents." He patted the pile of paper in front of Forte. "If we don't, we'll have to talk about the possibility of giving a break to somebody who has probably actively participated in at least two murders, and, depending on who killed Ritter, possibly three murders."

Chase winced: "I'd hate to have to do that."

"So would I."

CHASE FLIPPED THROUGH the documents, pulled a cell phone out of her attaché case, punched a couple of buttons, and said, "Can you come down here?"

She clicked off, and said to O'Conner and Forte, "I'm going to have my assistant count the money and the gold and give you a receipt that you can file with your warrant return." She turned to Lucas. "I will have him copy all the documents so that you can have them to read. Don't lose them. We'll talk again tomorrow, after I've had a chance to digest their content."

To the other suits she said, "You all should get in touch with anyone expecting you this evening. We're going to be here for a while."

They all nodded without protest.

Chase's assistant poked his head aound the door; he looked like what Lucas thought a Dartmouth grad should look like. "Yes, ma'am?"

COPYING THE DOCUMENTS took half an hour, with a couple of extra clerks working on it. Lucas collected the copies, and he and Bob and Rae got ready to leave. Documenting the money would take longer; it was not only being counted, it was also being xeroxed, bill by bill, so that the Marshals Service would have full paper documentation of each and its amount. Forte would wait for that. O'Conner had already left, saying, "Great work, guys."

Lucas and Forte agreed to talk in the morning, and as Lucas, Bob, and Rae were leaving, Chase's assistant poked in again, and said, "The amount, with today's exchange and sales rates, would be one million thirty-five thousand six hundred and twenty dollars. And fifty-two cents."

"There's a vacation home for you," Bob said.

Chase, who'd gone back to her office while the clerical work was done, caught them in the hallway.

"I wanted to tell you that I appreciate what you people have done," she said. "This is very useful. We've tried to monitor this kind of activity in the past, but so much of it is done secretly, and is classified, and so many documents are encrypted, or simply burned, that we've had a hard time finding a wedge in. This could be it. This really is something."

"Don't forget about the assassination attempt," Lucas said. "The other stuff may be good, but that's what's going to wind up on the *Post*'s front page."

"We're aware of that. I will be talking to you tomorrow about putting a headlock on some of the Heracles employees," Chase said. "Don't expect it at the crack of dawn, though. We've got some fairly tedious procedures to go through over here. I'm going to try to shortcut them by talking to your friend Deputy Director Mallard, but I don't know if he'll buy in."

"Tell Louis if he doesn't, I'll kick his flabby ass," Lucas said.

"Yes. I'll be sure to tell him that," Chase said, with a second rare smile.

21

As Lucas and the marshals were meeting with the FBI, Claxson pulled John McCoy and Kerry Moore into a back conference room, shut the door, and said, "We've got a problem. Maybe all three of us, but you two in particular."

McCoy and Moore glanced at each other, and Moore asked, "What's the problem?"

The two younger men looked alike and, at the same time, not alike: both were an inch short of six feet and stocky, athletic, with tanned, nut-hard faces and hands. While McCoy was a strawberry blond, Moore had dark hair. The way they moved made them look like big-league second basemen.

Claxson took a deep breath and exhaled in phony exasperation. "It's Davenport. He's back here . . ."

"He ditched his wife?" McCoy asked. "Nice guy."

"His wife is home and recovering. There was a newspaper story in the St. Paul paper; a columnist named Soucheray says he was talking to a cop and the cop told him that they're now treating Last's death as a homicide, not a suicide."

Moore said, "Shit. How . . . ?"

"The Soucheray column says Last had a heart problem. He couldn't run half a block. Whoever hit Davenport's wife's car ran a couple of blocks—and fast. You know how Jim could run."

"Goddamnit," McCoy said. He stood up, walked around his chair, brushing a hand through his hair, and sat down again. "Nobody told us. That's the kind of shit we had to know. Bad intel can kill us."

"Yeah, well, Davenport's back, and you know what happened next. Jim Ritter gets killed. We got an autopsy report off the Medical Examiner's files . . ."

Claxson had that report in his hand and pushed it across the table they were sitting at to McCoy. "Looks like Jim was waterboarded and then shot up close, in the heart. Executed. He was looking right down the barrel when they pulled the trigger."

Moore was incredulous. "You think Davenport and the marshals did that?"

"There's no proof. All we know is, Jim disappeared and turned up in a landfill. But he was tortured first, and Davenport was here and he's a killer. He's killed eight or nine guys as a cop, and some of the killings were seriously questionable. He's always done the hard-core stuff, which explains some of it . . . The point is, killing isn't something that worries him."

"We made a mistake when we went after his wife," Moore said to McCoy. "When I was married, if somebody had gotten rough with Jeannie, I would have killed him."

McCoy flashed a grin, and said, "Fortunately for that guy, he was only fuckin' her."

"Bite me," Moore said, but he laughed. He then stopped laughing, and said to Claxson, "Maybe it's time to get a job somewhere else. Like Niger. Go up the river for a couple of years."

Claxson said, "That's one option. The other option is, get rid of Davenport. We didn't want to do it because it'd attract attention, but Davenport is the only one who's got the personal . . . animus . . . to keep pushing this thing."

Moore was skeptical. "So we put a .338 through his heart from six blocks away? That'd get some attention—and since they're looking at us anyway . . ."

Claxson shook his head. "Can't look like a pro killed him. Has to look like something else. An accident, a mugging, anything. We're still thinking pushing him downstream a couple of months would probably get us out of it."

McCoy and Moore looked at each other again, and McCoy said, "So if he just got sick—I mean, like really sick . . ."

"You got something that'll make him sick?" Claxson asked.

"No, but somebody might," McCoy said.

Moore was shaking his head. "That's bullshit. We don't know how to do that. The thing is, we got that lady on the books, the one riding with Smalls. If we get caught, if we get identified, we're looking at the needle. If we're gonna kill him, we do it when we got an exit plan. I'm not sneaking into some fuckin' hotel without good intel, not knowing where the cameras are, and try some goofy idea like gassing him or giving him chicken pox or something."

McCoy said, "You're right."

Moore said to McCoy: "I'm sayin' Niger." He looked at Claxson. "Unless you got something good in Syria, or with the Kurds."

Claxson said, "We're talking about the White House. We put this chick in there, knowing what we know, we can get anything we want. Anything. You want ten million bucks? No problem. Twenty million bucks? No problem."

"Unless she knows a couple of more guys like us to remove that problem," Moore said.

Claxson shook his head. "Never'll happen. Money is easy. Killing all of us would be way too hard. And dangerous."

They sat and looked at one another for a while.

Claxson stood, picked up the autopsy report, and said, "Think of something. And I'll try to come up with something. Worse comes to worse, we give you a jar of malaria pills and you go on up that river."

Claxson headed for the door, but before he got there, McCoy said, "Hey. Jim's got a twin brother. Heavy hitter, right? He's like a major or a lieutenant colonel, did some work with Delta? I think they were tight, the brothers . . ."

"Lieutenant colonel," Claxson said.

"What if we sicced him on Davenport? He gets caught . . . no skin off our asses."

Claxson raked his lower lip with his upper teeth, thinking, and said, "That could be it. He wouldn't even have to kill him, if he beat the shit out of him or something. Anything that'd slow things down, take the heat off, get people to move on."

"How do we find out when he gets here? The colonel?"

Claxson shrugged. "We'll check and see if Jim's parents were notified. I'm sure they were, so we'll call them up and offer to fly them here. Jim's will says he wanted cremation, and burial at Arlington, and it'll take some time to set that up. We'll offer to take care of the Arlington paperwork, but the cremation can take place as soon as the medical examiner releases the body. Anyway, his folks should know when the colonel gets here and where he'll be. We'll brief him . . . point him at Davenport. If nothing happens, nothing happens."

"Hard to believe that nothing would," McCoy said.

"He's not one of us," Moore said. "He doesn't think like us. You can't predict."

"What if one of us . . . did something, but made it look like the colonel?" Claxson asked.

McCoy shook his head. "Wouldn't do that. If he takes out Davenport, he takes his chances. But I won't frame some innocent guy who spent years over in the sand."

Moore held up a hand, and McCoy slapped it.

Claxson shook his head and left—from the hallway beyond the door, he called back, "I'll talk to the colonel."

WHEN HE WAS GONE, Moore stood up and went to the door, looked down the hall to make sure Claxson was gone, closed the door and sat down again. He leaned across the table to McCoy, and said, "Man, we gotta get out of here. This ain't gonna work out, no way, no how."

"I think we got some time . . ."

Moore shook his head. "No we don't. If we kill that cop, everything is gonna get worse. If the colonel kills the cop, we'll still get blamed. We're tied up in the biggest clusterfuck in the world."

"If we can make it through, though, the reward—the White House . . ." McCoy began.

Moore interrupted: "If we disappear, and she makes president, we can come back for the reward. With what we know—"

"You'd try blackmailing the fuckin' President, and fuckin' Heracles, and the fuckin' guy who was Army and CIA and would have an office in the White House? Are you fuckin' nuts?" McCoy asked.

"We could. We'd have time to figure out how to make it work." Moore leaned forward across the table, got right in McCoy's face, dropped his voice to a barely discernible whisper, and asked, "You want to know the worst of it? What I think I figured out?"

"Do I want to know?" McCoy asked quietly.

Moore stayed with the whisper. "I don't think that marshal killed Jim. I think somebody here did. Maybe Claxson. Maybe Parrish. You know how they're always talking about guns, how they did something here, did something there? When they don't have any more use for us . . ."

"Ah, man."

"I'll tell you something else. I spent the morning packing up," Moore whispered. "I got couple of good passports and bought a ticket to Bogotá. From there, I'm flying to Rio, and from there to South Africa, and I'm gonna grow a beard along the way, and then I'm going north. Niger, Nigeria, Libya—there's a couple of mining companies up in the Congo would take us on . . . there's a shipping company outta Perth that hires security guys to ride their ships up the east coast of Africa, to protect them from pirates. The money's okay, you don't spend a nickel aboard the ships, and you don't walk through any passport controls with facial recog."

"Ricky did that, the ship thing. He said it bored his brains out," McCoy said.

"Ricky didn't have our problem," Moore said.

McCoy tilted his head back, looked at the ceiling. "Let me think about it."

"I'm leaving tonight," Moore said. "I'm inviting you to go along. There are some empty seats on the plane; I looked. We could get your ticket on the way. I got a long drive, and you could help out on that."

"Where you driving to?"

"Won't tell you that until you're in the car," Moore said.

McCoy got pissed, and he snapped, "You think I'd turn on you?"

Moore said, "Keep your voice down. Man, you're not diggin' what I'm saying. I'm sayin' that if things go wrong—and they've been doing that since we took the run at Smalls—we could go down for murder. That's bullshit. With everything that happened, it could be a federal case, and the feds got the needle. I've trusted you with my life, but if they said, 'Tell us about Moore or we're gonna strap you to the table and give you the shot,' I'm not one hundred percent sure what you'd do."

"Thanks a lot, good buddy," McCoy said.

Moore exhaled in exasperation, and said, "I'll trust you with one important fact. I'm rolling out of my driveway at eight o'clock tonight. I can't wait any longer than that if I'm gonna make the drive. I'm leaving all the furniture and everything else I can't get in my safe-deposit box. If you don't want to come, set up a new Gmail address, and when I land where I'm going, I'll drop you a note—if you're still walking around free."

"Let me think about it," McCoy said.

22

Lucas, Bob, and Rae spent the evening in Bob's room, plowing through the Xerox copies of the documents found in Ritter's safe-deposit box, as well as the encrypted documents found on his laptop. The docs mostly consisted of bills of lading, along with handwritten notes by McCoy about the contents of the shipments and their recipients. There were also photographs of these people, men in military dress, or partial military dress, which appeared to have been taken surreptitiously with cell phones.

They quit at ten o'clock, and Lucas hadn't been back in his room for more than the time needed to pee, take off his shoes, and turn on the television, when he heard a knock, but across the stub hall, the room he'd had the first night.

He picked up the PPQ on his way across the room, eased up to the door, plucked the spitball out of the peephole, and peeked out. A dark-haired woman was facing the other door. He couldn't see much of her because she was short, no more than five-four.

He popped open the door with his left hand; he kept the PPQ in his right, turned away from the door—he didn't want to frighten her if she was a hotel employee. Startled, she turned quickly, and he realized that she had no mouth or nose, only black eyes and eyebrows. About the time he realized she was wearing a military desert camo face mask, he also saw her long-barreled pistol coming up, a pistol with a wicked-looking silencer, and he slammed the door, and fell on his back, as the first slugs smashed through it.

He rolled to his right, toward the bathroom door, and fired off a single shot, and three fast shots smashed back at him through the hall door, but now he was in the bathroom and he fired another shot through the door. The incoming shots were loud, silencers reducing the sound of the blasts but not eliminating it. His outgoing shots, on the other hand, were deafening. The incoming shots stopped, and a door slammed, and he thought she was probably running.

He got on his knees, ready to fire, cracked the door, saw that the stub hall was empty. He got to his feet and took three fast steps down the hall and, as he did, heard perhaps fifteen full-auto sound-suppressed shots in the main hallway, then three fast, noisy pistol shots, another brrrp of full-auto, and then sudden silence.

He cracked the door to the outer hallway, and Bob shouted, "Lucas! Lucas!"

Lucas shouted back, "You guys okay?"

"We're okay. She's down the stairs."

Lucas stepped into the outer hallway and saw Bob, barefoot, in a T-shirt and white boxer shorts. He was pointing down the hall, and Lucas looked past him toward the exit sign. Seconds later, Rae, wrapped in a bathrobe, burst into the hall with a gun in her hand, saw the two men, and shouted, "Where'd he go?"

Bob and Lucas shouted at the same time, "*Woman*. Down the stairs."

Rae and Bob started running toward the stairwell, and Lucas, running behind them, shouted, "No, no, no, Bob, stop!"

Bob and Rae kept going, and Bob shouted over his shoulder, "She'll get away."

"Stop. Stop, goddamnit!"

Bob and Rae, now uncertain, slowed as Lucas caught up to them, and said, "You really want to go into a concrete stairwell with an assassin who has a machine gun?"

Bob and Rae looked at each other, and Rae said, "Maybe not."

"She's gone anyway," Lucas said. "She had a suppressed pistol and a machine gun. She's some kind of pro, and she'd have a getaway set up. Let's find out if anybody's hurt, see if the security people have any video."

"And maybe call your man Russell and see who's gonna pay for all this shit," Rae said, waving down the hall.

Lucas looked, saw the carpeting covered with plaster dust and soundproofing, the walls scarred with bullet holes, with more holes in the wall at the end of the hallway. A man poked his head out of a room, saw three people with guns, slammed the door.

Bob was talking fast, riding the adrenaline wave. "She had an MP9. It's a rare gun, I've only seen one before this. She had it on a sling under her jacket. I saw it coming up and jumped back, and she hosed down the door. I fired three shots down the hall without looking, hoping to hit her." He looked down at the carpet. "No blood. When she fired that second burst, I heard her kick the door open . . ."

"Got lucky," Lucas said. "She thought I was in my original room . . ."

"Gotta call the cops right now," Rae said, "or they're going to show up with their own machine guns, and we're the only people around they might think worth shooting."

"Right," Lucas said. "Let's do that."

Another door popped open, a woman looked down the hall, and shouted, "What happened?"

"You okay?" Lucas called.

She was. Bob put on some pants, and he and Lucas ran down the hall, knocking on doors, checking to see if anyone had been hurt. No one had been.

LUCAS WAS NEVER SURE how many D.C. cops showed up, but it looked to be about thirty, right on the heels of the on-duty security man. The full-auto was what had drawn them in, thinking *terror attack*. They'd gotten a couple of dozen reports of the shooting before they even got the call from Rae, who told the 911 operator that there were marshals on the scene and, as far as they knew, nobody was injured.

Lucas called Forte, who listened to Lucas's story, then said, "This is now officially out of control. This is now officially nuts. This is now officially about six hundred pounds of paperwork."

"Get to it tomorrow," Lucas said. "Right now, it looks like we'll be up half the night with the D.C. cops."

"And the FBI and DHS. You can't shoot up the Watergate pie without getting a whole lot of fingers in it."

AT FIVE O'CLOCK in the morning, Lucas, Bob, and Rae gathered in Lucas's room, and Lucas said, "She was wearing a camouflage face mask; I've seen them in pictures of soldiers in Iraq. All I could see were her eyes, and her body, but I think I've seen her before."

Rae: "Where?"

"That girl in the photo at Ritter's place. The one where she's turning away because somebody's taking her picture."

"You think . . . she's with Heracles?"

"I don't know, but she knew what she was doing," Lucas said. "If she'd come to the right door, I'd be dead right now."

Bob nodded, and said to Rae, "You know what that would mean? No more Business Class, no more suites. We'd be back at Motel 6."

"Let's not even think about that," Rae said, shivering, wrapping her arms around herself. "Tourist Class—the Walk of Shame."

"We're not there yet," Lucas said. "But I'm worried."

JANE CHASE didn't call in the morning—she'd warned them she might not. Lucas, Bob, and Rae were rousted out of bed at nine o'clock to be interviewed by three Homeland Security guys, accompanied by a D.C. cop and two FBI agents. They were gone by noon, having extracted everything that Lucas, Bob, and Rae knew by ten o'clock but insisting on going over and over the same territory for the next two hours.

"Excuse me, but those guys wanted it to be a terror attack," Rae said.

"If you don't have the occasional terror attack, what are those guys going to do for jobs?" Bob asked.

"There you go," Lucas said.

At one o'clock, Lucas called Chase's office number, but nobody picked up, and he left a long message about the firefight at the Watergate. They got sandwiches at a Subway, and the three ate lunch in Lucas's room.

"You see the reporters out there last night?" Rae asked. "We're national news everywhere. We're probably all over CNN and Fox right now."

Lucas turned on the television, surfed the news channels, and on the third click found a reporter, standing outside the Watergate, talking to a woman who'd either seen or heard something. "They were shouting in Arabic, clear as day, *Allahu Akbar* . . ."

"Aw, man," Rae said, and Lucas turned it off.

"Homeland Security is handling it," Lucas said. "Or their PR department is."

THEY TALKED about the documents from Ritter's safe-deposit box and concluded that while there may have been illegal activity at Heracles, it wouldn't directly help them with the Smalls investigation.

"I'd need a lot more background to even understand the documents. I mean, I know all the words, but I don't know what they're saying. If you know they shipped twenty cases of used/surplus full-auto SAWs, what does that mean? Is it illegal? I don't know," Rae said. SAWs, Squad Automatic Weapons, were belt-fed light machine guns. "The fact that Ritter saved the paper suggests there's something wrong, else why would he save it? If it's all legal, there wouldn't be any difference between shipping a SAW and a grilled cheese sandwich."

"There's something wrong with it," Bob said, "I promise. That's why Jane Chase said they'd have some specialists look at it." After a moment, he said to Rae, "I'd like to get one of those SAWs for our equipment bag. Remember that dipshit Willard pecking away at us with that .25? Think about stepping out there with a SAW and powdering his whole fuckin' trailer."

They both laughed, thinking about it, and Lucas shook his head, and said, "Jesus Christ, guys, try to hold it together, huh?"

LUCAS'S PHONE RANG. He took it out of his pocket, looked at the screen, and said, "Speak of the devil and she calls you."

Lucas put the phone on speaker, and they all bent over it as Chase came up. "We've been working through the documents. We can make a strong case against Heracles for illegally exporting these weapons," she said. "They show end-user certificates issued to approved users—national governments, mostly, along with a few militias in North Africa—but Heracles personnel delivered the weapons to different buyers altogether, including some groups on our FTO lists."

"What's an FTO list?" Bob asked.

"FTO is an acronym for Foreign Terrorist Organizations," Chase said. She said lists were maintained by the State Department.

"What are you going to do?" Lucas asked.

"The documents implicate Heracles, Flamma, and Inter-Core Ballistics, which are all interlocking. The men who actually delivered the weapons are the low-hanging fruit. We can pick them up right now and try to turn them. We plan to do that. Today. We invite you to come along; two of the men implicated are McCoy and Moore, who you want to squeeze for your Smalls investigation."

"This is dang quick for the FBI—no offense," Rae said.

"None taken, but you're right. For us, this is quick," Chase said. "We have a problem. Two of the most critical documents, the clearest cases, will fall under the statute of limitations in a matter of a few weeks. That's unfortunate, but it is what it is. So, we're going to pick up McCoy and Moore and three other men today, interview them separately, and use their statements, if any, to launch a raid on Heracles, Flamma, and Inter-Core tomorrow morning. Frankly, we're planning to use the possibility of a murder charge, those that you're pursuing, to motivate the men we grab today to make a statement on the gun diversion case. We're waiting now for warrants for both the arrests and for searches of their apartments."

Lucas: "Wait—you're not going to promise them immunity?"

"No. Not at this point anyway, and most likely never," Chase said. "But these papers open the possibility of putting the whole illegal weapons trade under the microscope. We're talking about hundreds of possible deaths, maybe thousands, not two."

"Ah, Jesus," Lucas said. "Did you talk to Mallard about all of this?"

"Yes, and he's with us," Chase said. "He thinks you're a great guy and all, but he said, and I quote, 'Get me the guns, and fuck Davenport.' The f-word was his, not mine."

Lucas said, "I understand, but I might have to oppose you on some of this."

"We'll be talking to your director," Chase said.

"And I'll be talking to Senator Smalls," Lucas said.

Chase said, "Lucas, please, I'm telling you—no, I'm *asking* you—if you want to fight us over the process, that's fine. But please don't do anything until tomorrow. Please! We're putting these men under heavy surveillance, and we plan to pick them up after they leave their offices this afternoon or tonight so they can't warn the Heracles people. They'll want to bring their attorneys in, but when we begin questioning them, we're going to use what we get for the warrants for the raid on Heracles. If you break this whole thing into the open before we get the warrants, there'll be some bonfires in the Heracles offices tonight. It won't hurt you to wait a day."

Lucas thought about that, and said, "Okay. I won't talk to anyone until after your raids."

"Thank you. We . . . thank you. Somebody will call you in an hour or so when we're ready to launch."

"Will you be there? For the arrests?"

"I won't be making the arrests myself. I'll be observing."

"See you there," Lucas said.

BOB SAID, "Good, we're gonna do something. These guys . . . I don't think we need to go in heavy. Maybe keep some shit in the truck, but, basically, civilian dress."

Rae nodded, and Lucas said, "Take your Glock."

"I take my Glock when I go to bed," Bob said.

TWO HOURS LATER, Chase's assistant called, and told Lucas that Chase was on her way to monitor a surveillance team that was tracking McCoy in preparation for his arrest. "We believe McCoy will be leaving Heracles around four o'clock, and we will keep him under surveillance until we can pick him up. You're welcome to observe. She knows you're also interested in Kerry Moore, but we've been unable to locate him. We will serve search warrants on both of their apartments later this evening."

"Where is Miz Chase now?" Lucas asked.

"She's on her way. She'll be in a communications car at the corner of Wilson Boulevard and North Veitch Street. If you go around the corner on Veitch, we've reserved parking for members of the group."

LUCAS DROVE, with Rae in the passenger seat, Bob in back. Lucas normally didn't like to ride with other law enforcement officers because too often everybody wound up wanting to go to different places. In this case, they'd be more observers than an action team, so it was unlikely they'd need to split up.

On the way over, Lucas said, "Her assistant said they expect McCoy to leave around four o'clock. I think they're doing some electronic monitoring. I don't know how, but they're doing it."

"Wonder where Moore is," Rae said. "Hope he's not in a landfill."

"Don't even think that," Lucas said.

TRAFFIC WAS already tightening up as they crossed the Potomac into Arlington. They turned the corner off Wilson onto North Veitch and found a line of large sedans and two Chevy Yukons parked on the right side of the street, and a man in a suit who waved them away from an open parking space. Lucas pulled in anyway, got out, and held up his badge: "U.S. Marshals, here to meet Miz Chase."

The man nodded, and said, "Okay. White Yukon."

Chase was in the passenger seat, and Lucas, Bob, and Rae

piled into the empty second row of seats, squeezing Rae in the middle. Lucas asked, "Where are we?"

"We're looking at five men: Luther Franklin, Ray Shelve, Arnold Buckram, and your two, Kerry Moore and John McCoy. I'm worried about Moore; we've picked up some chatter from Heracles, and they don't seem to know where he is, either."

"You're monitoring Heracles?"

Chase turned her head to glance at him, and said, "We have some . . . resources in place."

"Hope he's not dead," Bob said. "They kill both McCoy and Moore, we marshals be suffering some serious butthurt, Smallswise."

Chase looked over her other shoulder. "What? Butthurt? Is that a marshal technical term?" First hint of a sense of humor.

THE YUKON'S DRIVER was a serious young agent with a Caucasian-colored earbud in one ear, which made Lucas wonder whether the feds had other ethnically correct monitors. The man said, "Franklin's leaving Heracles, and McCoy is with him . . . They're talking . . . They're splitting up. Ben's on Franklin, Clark's on McCoy."

Chase said to Lucas, "McCoy's meeting his personal attorney at the Corner Bakery Café. He made the appointment this afternoon, and he made it walking down the street from his office, like he didn't want to be overheard. We plan to approach both men at the same time. We arrest McCoy and give a National Security Letter to his attorney."

"I don't know what that is," Lucas said.

"It's like a gag order. It'll keep him from tipping off Heracles, should he be inclined to do that. We can do it administratively, but the director herself has to approve. That's why we're running late today. It took a while to get that done. The lawyer—his name's Roy Bunch—can challenge it in court, but by the time he does that we'll be all over Heracles. Bunch has a general practice that has included some criminal law, and we're hoping he'll agree to come along with McCoy when we take him in."

"Where's this café?" Bob asked.

Chase gestured over her shoulder with her thumb. "On the corner . . . There's a Dunkin' Donuts on the other side of the street, around the other corner . . . You've got time—you know, being cops and all." Second hint at a sense of humor.

"I could go for a couple of those powdered jellys," Bob said.

Rae: "You probably will."

The young agent muttered, "McCoy's in his car. He's headed this way."

Chase: "There's no parking. As soon as he gets to the corner, one of our cars will pull out and leave a space for him. When he gets out of his car, we take him. Then we'll go down to the corner and fetch his lawyer. If he's not there yet, we'll wait. But his office is across the street, so he should be on time."

"Still got time for donuts?" Bob asked.

Chase: "Seriously?"

"Seriously. I'll get a bag and wait on the corner. You can wave when he gets close. Rae can wait down at the other end of the block. In case he runs and gets past your guys. He's supposed to be tough."

"He won't get past our guys," Chase said.

"He sure as shit wouldn't get past me or Rae," Bob said.

Chase said, "Whatever," and Bob and Rae got out of the car, and as she was getting out, Rae said to Bob, "Get me a chocolate cake donut."

"'Kay."

They split up and hurried away from the Yukon. Chase watched them go, and said, "It's a little hard to take them seriously."

Lucas said, "If there's a problem, McCoy won't get past them. They do this for a living. Rae was a starter in basketball at UConn. She has a degree in art history. Bob wrestled for Oklahoma State and finished third in the NCAA tournament his senior year, which means he lost just once. He has a degree in social work."

"All right," she said.

THEY SAT IN SILENCE for a few minutes, saw Bob walk around the corner with a bag of Dunkin' Donuts in hand. He walked far enough down North Veitch that he couldn't be seen by a car coming up Wilson, and he waited. At the other end of the block, Rae perched on the hood of a Mustang.

The young agent said, "He's here."

Two cars ahead of them, a sedan pulled out of its parking space. Chase said, "Here we go."

A Toyota 4Runner turned the corner, moving slowly, and Chase said, "That's him."

McCoy spotted the parking space, rolled ahead of it, backed in. A moment later, as he was getting out of the car, FBI agents climbed out of the cars ahead and behind him. McCoy saw them and did exactly what Lucas had done during the attempted mugging outside the tailor shop: he sprinted away.

A burly FBI agent tried to step in front of him in the street, but

McCoy juked, juked again, stuck out a fist, and smacked the agent in the face—just as Lucas had during his almost mugging—and without hesitating, ran back toward Wilson Boulevard, and Bob, with a string of FBI agents chasing after him.

Bob was standing there, a ring of powder on his upper lip, a jelly donut in his hand, and McCoy, paying no attention to him, tried to blow on by.

Bob stuck out his other, empty hand and clotheslined him. McCoy went facedown in a heap on the sidewalk, and Bob put one heavy foot on his head.

In the front seat, Chase said, "Indeed."

A few seconds later, the scrum of FBI agents arrived, and two of them squatted over McCoy's body, bent his arms behind his back, cuffed him, and pulled him to his feet.

Bob still had a half-eaten donut in his hand. Chase said, "Wouldn't want to fight the guy who finished first."

"Got that right," Lucas said.

LUCAS, CHASE, RAE, and the young agent walked around the corner to the café, Rae finishing her chocolate cake donut, the young agent carrying an envelope. They looked inside, and Chase said, "That's him. In line."

McCoy's attorney was a thin man, balding, the remaining hair, gone white, cut tight. He wore gold-rimmed glasses, a rumpled gray suit, and was carrying an attaché case. He was waiting patiently behind two young women, who were discussing the menu with the counter clerk, and Chase took his arm, held up her ID, and said, "Mr. Bunch? I'm Jane Chase with the FBI. Could we speak to you for a minute?"

She guided him out of line, and Bunch asked, "What's going on?"

Chase said, "We've arrested your client John McCoy. We're holding him around the corner in a car. We are serving you with an NSL, a National Security Letter." The young agent handed him the envelope.

"I know what an NSL is," Bunch said, as he took the envelope. "But why?"

"Because your client is being held on a national security issue. We'd appreciate it if you could walk around the corner with us and advise your client of his rights and consult with him about what he should do this evening. We are taking him in for questioning."

"How did you know we'd be meeting? Have you wiretapped me?"

"We have a warrant to cover Mr. McCoy's phone calls. One of his calls went to you. But we were not monitoring you specifically."

"Better not have been," Bunch said. Then, "Where's John?"

"Right around the corner," Chase said, "like I said. Would you like to get a cup of coffee before you talk to him?"

Bunch looked down at his shoes, thinking, eventually nodding. "All right. I better get the coffee."

23

McCoy and the other three Heracles employees arrested that evening were interrogated in four separate oversized FBI interview rooms by four separate interrogation teams, with Jane Chase moving among them.

Lucas, Bob, and Rae were not invited to the interrogations themselves, but each of the rooms was equipped with a discreet video camera, and they watched McCoy's interview on a high-resolution screen in a separate observation room.

McCoy had been checked by a doctor for physical injuries after being decked by Bob, but the doc found only a few developing bruises, and McCoy agreed that he wasn't badly injured. The interviews were two-part, with the interrogation teams first asking a series of questions, then Bunch and McCoy adjourning to a secure conference room to talk privately.

McCoy was willing to confirm some of the information in the documents hidden by Ritter but volunteered no further information, denying knowing anything about the attack on Smalls and Weather or the related murders of Whitehead and Last. When asked about Ritter's death, he said, "Everybody knows that the marshal did it—Davenport. Jim was waterboarded and executed because Davenport thought Jim attacked his wife."

The FBI interrogator said, "Mr. Ritter wasn't interrogated. He wasn't waterboarded. He was shot twice, in the heart, a few minutes after talking with Mr. Parrish."

McCoy: "I've seen the autopsy report."

"So have I. It doesn't say anything about waterboarding because it didn't happen," the fed said. "I don't suppose those documents were given to you by either Mr. Claxson or Mr. Parrish, the very people who'd have the most to gain from Mr. Ritter's death?"

McCoy sat back, his tongue trailed across his lips, and he asked, "Parrish? What does Parrish have to do with it?"

The interrogator said, "Give me a minute." He disappeared out the door, leaving McCoy and Bunch in the interview room. A few minutes later, Chase stuck her head in the door of the room where Lucas was watching with Bob and Rae, and said, "Lucas, we think we could use you in the room with McCoy. We want you to give him your theory of Ritter's death."

Lucas nodded. "Sure."

LUCAS WALKED DOWN the hall to the interview room, where the interrogator was waiting. The interrogator asked, "You get the idea?"

"Yeah. Give him a reason to turn."

Lucas followed the interrogator into the room, and McCoy looked up, frowned, and said, "Hey!"

Lucas said, "Nice to see you again, John."

McCoy said, "What?"

"The way you reacted to the FBI guys, I thought maybe you'd taken a lesson from me, outside that tailor shop."

McCoy shook his head. "I don't know what you're talking about. You killed Jim."

Lucas took a chair across the table across from McCoy, and said, "Couple of things. First, you knew who I was. You've never seen me before except outside that tailor shop unless you've seen some photograph or have been doing surveillance on me. How'd you know who I was when I came through the door?"

McCoy said, "Fuck you."

Lucas said, "Second, I didn't kill Jim Ritter. The most likely candidate for that is Jack Parrish. The next most likely candidates are you and Moore, because we know you're willing to murder people, and Ritter might have looked like the weak link. We were about to pick him up on the assassination attempt on Senator Smalls and the murder of Cecily Whitehead. He knew that, and he was probably looking to Claxson or Parrish for help. One or both of them decided to get rid of him altogether."

"That's bullshit. They wouldn't—"

"Sure they would," Lucas said. "They're not soldiers like you guys. They're weasels. Suits. Bullshit artists. I have a cop friend back in Minnesota who'd call them douchenozzles. They not only would kill Ritter, they'd kill you. I'll tell you, John, if Mr. Bunch manages to get you bail, I'd stay far, far away from those guys. They'll kill you in a minute."

McCoy shook his head, and turned toward Bunch, who shrugged.

Lucas continued. "I think you know all this, by the way. I wouldn't be surprised if you had a whole bunch of documents and other evidence stashed somewhere to cover you if they start giving you a hard time. Like Jim Ritter did."

"Jim didn't—"

"Sure he did. More than a million dollars, and a bunch of documents that are going to hang you and Moore and Claxson. The feds here hate to go to trial without being a hundred percent sure of a conviction. They've got you—you're toast, man—but you might still make a deal for leniency if you help them out."

"You're looking for a turncoat."

The interrogator sighed, and said, "John, you know, you use words like 'turncoat,' which makes you sound like a good guy holding out against a bunch of terrorists. Something admirable. What you're really doing is, you're protecting a bunch of murderous criminals." He leaned across the table, and asked, "Have you ever heard of Inter-Core Ballistics?"

McCoy glanced at his attorney, who said, "Don't answer if you think it might be a problem. We can talk first."

But McCoy said, "Yeah, I've heard of them, but that's all. I never had anything to do with them."

"I believe you," the interrogator said. He told McCoy about Claxson and Parrish fixing the sale of inferior armor to the military. "That's the folks you're protecting, John. There are dead soldiers out there, but these guys made a buck off it. Is that where you're at?"

"Fuck no. I'm not sure I even believe you."

"I got the paperwork, if you want to see it," the interrogator said.

McCoy turned to Bunch. "We need to talk. Again."

LUCAS WAS WALKED BACK to the viewing room, and Rae said, "You look good on TV. Maybe you oughta be one of those talking heads. Interview the Kardashians and shit."

McCoy and Bunch were out of sight for fifteen minutes, and when they returned, Bunch said, "We'd like to see some evidence about this Inter-Core company. We'd like to see it tomorrow. We're done for tonight. No more questions."

McCoy was taken to a holding cell, and Bunch made arrangements to return in the morning. "We'll ask for bail, and we hope you will recommend something reasonable," he said. "If you do that, I expect we'll be able to provide at least limited testimony about Heracles and its activities, if what you say about this Inter-Core company is correct."

"We'll see you in the morning," Chase told him.

LUCAS, BOB, AND RAE went back to the hotel, had a late dinner, agreed that the investigation was looking up, and headed off to their rooms.

Lucas was on the last ten pages of Hiaasen's *Skinny Dip* when he took a call from a clerk at the front desk. "Marshal Davenport, we have a gentleman down here who wants to talk to you. He's a colonel in the Army—um, a lieutenant colonel." Lucas knew only one lieutenant colonel, Horace Stout, whom he'd interviewed about Parrish. Had he told Stout that he was at the Watergate? Maybe. He said to the clerk, "Okay. Give him the room number, send him up."

Five minutes later, there was a soft knock on the door. Lucas glanced at his watch: almost eleven o'clock. Bob and Rae were the early-to-bed, early-to-rise sort and would already be in bed. The last time Lucas got a nighttime knock, he'd almost gotten shot. The PPQ was sitting in its holster on the nightstand. Lucas slipped it free, got to his feet, and trotted to the door.

Another knock, harder this time.

One good way to get shot, he'd read in a novel somewhere, or possibly an airport survivalist magazine, or maybe he even made it up himself, was to look out the peephole of your hotel room. The killer on the other side, peering back through the hole, would know precisely where your body was and could shoot you through the door.

Sounded more like a novel; not that survivalist magazines were any less fictional.

In any case, he plucked the spitball out of his peephole and looked out. He could see a man's shoulder, but that was about all.

Leaving the chain on the door, he brought the muzzle of the gun up, cracked the door, and was startled enough to take an involuntary step back: James Ritter was standing there. Lucas had seen the very same James Ritter dead on a slab at the Medical Examiner's Office. Unquestionably dead. He blurted, "What the fuck . . . ?"

The man showed both hands: empty. "I'm Tom Ritter," he said. "Jim's brother. His twin brother."

Lucas took a moment to absorb that. "Oh, Jesus, you scared the hell out of me."

Ritter nodded, without smiling. "I understand . . . You Marshal Davenport?"

Lucas was still befuddled: Tom Ritter was an exact duplicate of his brother, and Lucas had never encountered anything quite like it. "Uh, yeah."

"I need to talk to you."

"How'd you find me?"

"I asked around Heracles, and some guys there had an idea

where you might be. I came over and asked at the front desk. Can I come in?"

"Are you carrying?" Lucas asked.

"A gun? No."

Lucas took off the door chain and backed away from the door, kept the PPQ pointed to one side but still up. "Yeah, come on. Push the door shut behind you."

Like his brother, Ritter was short, muscular, tanned, and dressed in outdoor clothing—a long-sleeved blue cotton shirt, covered by a blue linen sport coat, tan nylon/cotton cargo pants, and light hiking boots. Lucas began to pick up some differences: James Ritter had a scarred face from a shrapnel wound, Tom Ritter didn't but carried the same military look.

LUCAS SAID, "Take off your jacket before you come in."

"I don't carry a gun. Not in the States."

Lucas said, "Take your jacket off anyway."

Ritter did, stepped into the room, nudged the door closed with his foot, and did a pirouette so Lucas could see that he didn't have a gun holstered at the small of his back. "I've got some questions, and I might have some information you need," he said, when he was looking at Lucas again.

Lucas had backed up to the desk. He said, "Sit on the bed. I'll take the chair." Sitting on the bed would make a hidden gun harder to get at. Lucas sat on the edge of a hard-seated office chair. Ritter might well have been a computer programmer, or a life insurance salesman, but he didn't look like that. You had to have experience as a cop to notice he bore the wound-spring look of a man who could hurt you.

When Ritter was sitting on the bed, his jacket across his lap, Lucas asked, "Who told you where to find me?"

"I've got a story about that," Ritter said. He was younger than he looked, Lucas thought: the tan put on a few years and some wrinkles, but Ritter was not yet thirty-five.

"I'm listening," Lucas said.

"I'm an Army officer, Third Stryker Brigade Combat Team, Second Infantry Division, in Afghanistan. I was granted leave to bury my brother."

"That's . . . rough. Maybe even rougher with a twin."

"Yeah, it is. Hard even to explain how rough it is. It's like you lost a leg. Non-twins wouldn't understand," Ritter said in his quiet voice. "The people over at Heracles say you shot him."

"I know what they're saying. It's horseshit. Your brother was our best way into our case. I don't want to sound . . . insulting . . . but he was small fry. The last thing we wanted was him dead. The people who killed him are responsible for murdering three people now—two of them completely innocent. The third was your brother."

Ritter watched Lucas for a minute or two, judging him, and asked, "What do you know about waterboarding?"

Lucas said, "Nothing. I was going to look it up on the Internet tonight, but I forgot. We were told by a source that Heracles is passing around some fake autopsy papers that say he was waterboarded, but he wasn't. If you check with the ME, the medical examiner, he'll tell you so. Heracles was trying to convince people that I killed Jim."

"But you were pissed about what happened to your wife, and you're working for Senator Smalls . . ."

Lucas nodded, and said, "Yes. I'm more than pissed about my

wife, I'm . . . if I was sure I found a guy involved in that, he might fall down a couple of flights of stairs. But I wouldn't kill him. I wouldn't kill him especially if it was your brother. Like I said, he was about our only entry into the case, but he was nowhere near the top of the food chain."

ANOTHER BIT OF SILENCE, then Ritter asked, "If you didn't kill Jim, do you have any idea who might have? Specific names? Anything at all?"

Lucas said, "I'm not ready to talk about that—we've got an ongoing investigation."

Ritter looked around the room, appraising it as if for ways to defend it, and said, "I looked you up on the Internet. You're a rough guy, huh?"

"I have my moments," Lucas said. "What are we talking about here?"

Ritter said, "I was passing through Kuwait when I heard about Jim and caught a flight back home. I've got fourteen days. You gonna find the killer in that time?"

"I could if I could get some leverage on somebody involved," Lucas said. "Now, tell me how you knew where to find me . . . or even what my name is?"

"I called some people. I went over to Heracles Personnel. I guess you've already been looking at them."

"Yes, we have," Lucas said.

"I know people at Heracles, ex-Army guys, friends of Jim—and tapped into the rumor mill. Word is, some guys have been involved in questionable actions here in the States. I've got names, not easy to get, but I'm . . . trusted, to a certain extent."

"They weren't questionable actions, Colonel," Lucas said. "The first attack was an attempted assassination of a U.S. senator and the murder of a completely innocent woman. The guys who did it, including your brother, I'm sorry to say, knew what they were doing—that they'd kill her along with the senator. The second attack was an effort to get me, personally, off their backs. They did it by going after my wife—and by the cold-blooded murder of an innocent man. Do you know about all of that?"

"Yeah, I was told about it, and I read a newspaper story." Ritter put his jacket aside and stood up, looked around the room again, and Lucas said, "Sit back on the bed," and he did, but asked, "Why?"

"Because if you have a hideout gun, it'll be harder for you to get at." Lucas had put the PPQ on the desktop, letting his hand rest a couple of inches away.

"You're nervous."

"Shouldn't I be?" Lucas asked.

"Maybe, I guess. The guys you're looking at, they're the real thing. They've all been over in the sandbox both as military and as private contractors. If you get in their way, they'll flat put a hole in your head. But I'm not one of them."

"That's comforting."

Ritter looked down at his thighs, rubbed his nose, looked up, and said, "Look, a guy named Claxson . . . You're looking at him?"

"Yes."

"He told me you were probably the one who killed Jim, and he told me why—your wife. Said Jim was waterboarded and then executed . . . that sounded funky to me. I should tell you that after I talked to Claxson, I cornered the medical examiner, and he said there was nothing to indicate that Jim had been waterboarded or tortured in any way, that nothing like that had been put in the autopsy report. But the report Claxson showed me specifically mentioned the waterboarding. I asked myself why that would be."

"Claxson wanted you to come after me."

"That's why I came up here empty-handed, no gun. I wanted to hear what you had to say."

"Then you probably know who killed him," Lucas said. "And why."

"I'm not sure about the why. He wouldn't have talked."

Lucas thought about it, and said, "Because he'd become a problem. If your friends at Heracles are up to date, they'd know—and you probably now know—that we found some logs out in the countryside in West Virginia. They were used to protect the side of your brother's truck when they pushed Smalls's Cadillac off the road and almost over a bluff. If it had worked, it would have looked like Whitehead and Smalls accidentally ran off the road, hit a bunch of trees, and landed in the river. It's a fuckin' miracle that Smalls didn't die along with Whitehead. If he had, there would have been nobody to talk about a second vehicle."

Ritter said, "You're saying it was a good plan, should have worked, but the targets caught a break?"

"Yes," Lucas said. "Their problem—your brother's problem—was, we'd located his truck. You could see the damage where the logs had been tied to the side, and some other forensic evidence that was convincing. If we got him for murder—and we were about to do that—maybe he'd give up the other people involved in return for leniency. We're more interested in those other people than we were in James . . . Jim . . . He was the trigger. He was paid. We want the people who hired him."

"He wouldn't have given up anyone," Ritter said. "Jim was loyal to his pals. Almost pathologically loyal. It was about all he had left, after his time in the military and with Heracles. He'd gone to jail, before he'd let a friend down. Or died."

"But would all of those people have known that? They are not the kind of people who think in those terms . . . Not people like Parrish or Claxson. They take care of themselves."

"Claxson . . . if he had to make a choice between himself and his own kids, if he had any, his kids would be dead meat," Ritter said.

Lucas poked a finger at him. "Exactly. Those are the guys we want. We'll take the triggers, too, but they're not the ones who are driving this thing, the assassination attempt."

"Do you know the other people involved in these . . . actions?"

"I think I do," Lucas said. "I think there were two more triggers, two more managers, and somebody who pulls the whole train."

"Would that be Senator Grant from Minnesota?"

Lucas tipped his head. "Where are you getting this?"

"Like I said, I know these guys, and they know me and trust me. When I was fishing around, I heard all kinds of things. You couldn't take any of it to court; it's all rumor, but rumors from guys who are professional intelligence operators, and their rumors are better than most. There are some hints that if things work out, Heracles could have its own office at the White House."

THEY LOOKED at each other, then Lucas took his hand away from the PPQ and rubbed the back of his neck, and asked, "How far can I trust you? To hear what I have to say and not spread it around? Even if it'll help you understand what happened to Jim."

"I wouldn't tell a soul," Ritter said. "I mean that: nobody would hear a word from me, of what was said in this room."

Lucas looked at him for a couple of beats, and Ritter added, "Look, I went to the Academy. I'll be a general someday, if I don't screw up, and so far I haven't. Jim didn't finish college, joined the Army, took an entirely different path. He wound up with Delta. He was over there way too long, maybe killed too many people, including, you know, civilians. Women. Kids. His circle got too tight; he'd die for the people in the circle, but, outside it, he didn't give a shit about anything. That pushed him out of the Army. He killed one too many people who didn't actually need it. The Army gets fussy about stuff like that."

"So he signed up with Heracles?"

"Yes. And he went right back to killing. I guess he was a bad guy, in the end, but he was my brother. And he was close with the Heracles operators—the operators, the guys around him, not the managers. If you told them to kill him, they were like Jim: they wouldn't do it. They might kill the guy who asked."

Lucas shifted in the chair. "That's interesting."

"Yeah?"

"Yes. I need to find somebody who knows what happened, or

has a good idea about what happened, but would be loyal to Jim."

Ritter nodded. "Now, tell me the truth: did Senator Grant buy these hits?"

Lucas said, "I can't prove it, but I believe so. I believe she worked through Parrish, who is one of her aides and works with the Senate Intelligence Committee."

Ritter shook his head in disgust. "Parrish is tight with Claxson. I can give you names of people who can tell you that, if they decide to, people who work with Heracles but were close to Jim."

"That would be a great help, if we ever get to to a trial," Lucas said.

"Are you going to get Grant?"

"If somebody gives her up."

"That's the only way?"

"That's it," Lucas said.

"Well, shit." Ritter grunted, slapped his thighs, and said, "I'm going to stand up now. I don't have a hideout gun—or whatever you cops call them. I'm leaving."

"Where are you going?"

"I'm in a BOQ over in Arlington, but I'm moving to a motel tomorrow. My parents got here from Nebraska this afternoon . . . They're falling apart . . . My mother is . . . My father's mostly taking care of my mother. I'm trying to take care of both of them."

"I understand. Let me give you an email," Lucas said. "I need a secure email from you, if you have one."

"Of course I have one," Ritter said. "Not even the Army knows about it."

WHEN THEY'D EXCHANGED emails and cell phone numbers, Lucas asked, "When will you be talking with your friends again? Over at Heracles?"

"I'm going out to lunch with a couple of them tomorrow," Ritter said. "We're all talking about what happened to Jim. People are worried about Heracles and what's going on there. They're worried that if there's trouble, some of it will stick to them. Word is, some of them have already split. Left the country."

"Will you call me if you hear something?" Lucas asked. "I don't know what your situation is over there. I don't want you to get hurt."

"I'm not ready to sign up as a spy—and I really don't want to talk to the FBI. I'm talking to you because in the stuff I read, those newspaper stories from Minnesota, you sounded like a guy I could deal with. If the FBI gets involved, if they detain me on suspicion of anything, I'm not going to get my stars. I'm not going to make colonel. My career will be over. So I've got to be careful."

Lucas nodded, observing Ritter's escalating intensity. "If these guys go after Smalls again, how would they do it?"

"I don't know." Ritter threw up his hands. "They could do it a million different ways. I know a SEAL who specialized in snatching Arab terrorists off their tea stools, hurting them bad enough that they couldn't resist, or trigger a bomb hidden in a vest, while the rest of his team covered him. He could put a man on the floor, with broken bones, in two seconds—literally. Two seconds. I saw him do that. There are all kinds of techniques—they could run Smalls off the road again; they could break his neck and throw him down the stairs in his home; they could kill him with alcohol poisoning or an overdose—and never leave a mark on him. They all have some level of sniper training. Jim wasn't the best at it because, basically, he wasn't a sniper, but he could put a .338 through your chest at a thousand meters, if he had time to think about distances and angles and it wasn't too windy. There are guys at Heracles who *are* snipers, and they work at it all the time. They like sniping *way* better than sex . . . If you were sitting at a desk by a window, they could hit you from a mile out."

"Okay. But be careful. If you hear anything operational, call me right away. I've got some hard-core guys here myself, and I can get more if I need them." He thought for a moment, and added, "If you hear any more about Jack Parrish, he could be key. Or John McCoy. Or Kerry Moore. And Claxson, of course."

"I know those names, McCoy and Moore, from asking around. They're the ones, huh?"

"Yup, I think so." He almost told Ritter that four Heracles operators, including McCoy, had been arrested, but he didn't trust the man quite that much. Instead, he said, "One more thing. Jim apparently had a girlfriend—or a girl he was friendly with anyway—slender, very good shape. She knows how to get a rare concealable submachine gun, and knows how to use it and isn't afraid to. Looks, to me, like a pro."

"What'd she do?" Ritter asked.

Lucas told him about the shooting in the hallway, and Ritter said, "Oh, jeez, that was her? It's all over the news . . . They say nobody was hurt, though."

"No, but she scared the shit out of quite a few people, including me."

"I can't tell you much about her. I've met her, once, and she didn't want to talk to me. I think she and Jim were in bed together, but she didn't want people to know it."

"What's her name?"

Ritter shook his head. "She was introduced to me as 'just Suzie.' Jim seemed to like her—a lot. Like marriage a lot. Made me happy, made me think we were getting him back, so I pried. I can't swear to any of this, but I believe she's covert CIA, the division called SAD/SOG. Special Activities Division/Special Operations Group, which is their paramilitary wing."

"They have women working with them? Combat types?"

"My understanding is, they do. I know Suzie spoke fluent Arabic. You know how cool that would be, a small woman speaking perfect Arabic, dressed in a *niqab,* with a gun in her underpants? She could go anywhere, and nobody would pay any attention to her. I suspect that's what she did, and maybe still does."

"Tried hard to kill me," Lucas said.

"Then you are a lucky man," Ritter said. "Those folks don't miss much."

"She had some bad intelligence," Lucas said, "but it was goddamn close."

WHEN RITTER WAS GONE, Lucas got out his laptop and wrote a long report to Russell Forte about the interview, saved it but didn't send it. Forte might be worried about possible illegalities being sheltered by the Marshals Service, and Lucas didn't want to get involved in that argument.

Not yet.

WITH THE REPORT SAVED, he settled back on the bed, dimmed the lights, and closed his eyes. There were several tangled thoughts stalking around his mind, and he needed to get straight with them.

Tom Ritter had emphasized how dangerous the Heracles operators could be. He'd also talked about how loyal they were to each other—not so much to the managers but to fellow operators.

Yet, something was going on—Jim Ritter had been killed, and Kerry Moore had disappeared. Either Claxson—the guy with two loaded pistols on his desk—or Parrish could have killed them. Or—a new thought—so could have Taryn Grant.

Grant might be unlikely, he thought after some consideration. Whoever killed Ritter picked him up and threw him in a dumpster, and Ritter, a muscular man, had probably weighed a hundred and eighty pounds. Grant would have wanted to move him quickly, out of a car and into the dumpster, but he was too heavy for one woman alone. Lucas doubted Grant would have exposed herself legally to direct involvement in a murder. And even if she had commissioned the killing, somebody else had probably carried it out.

If you bought Tom Ritter's feelings about personal loyalty, the killer wouldn't have been McCoy or Moore. If it were neither of them, it would have been Parrish or Claxson, or perhaps some third party Lucas didn't know about yet.

And here was the big problem: whoever it had been, Lucas could see no clear route to implicate Taryn Grant. None of the major actors would see any benefit in selling her out. To do so, they would have to admit they had been conspirators in murder. Even that might not be enough to get her.

Further, Grant's money would be available to fund the best possible legal defenses for her associates. If she had a real shot at the presidency, there was a possible pardon downstream for those associates, if worse came to worse.

If what he feared came to pass, getting Taryn Grant might not be possible.

Not in the ordinary way.

24

Jane Chase called the next morning as Lucas was shaving.

"We're going to arrest Claxson this morning. Between the documents and what we'll get from McCoy, we can arrest him on several counts of illegal trading of restricted weaponry. That will take care of the statute of limitations problem. We've got search warrants for both his businesses and his home."

Lucas: "What'd you give McCoy?"

"Nothing, at this point. Bunch showed up early this morning—"

"It's early this morning right now," Lucas objected.

Chase said, "Lucas, it's ten o'clock. I've been here since six. Anyway, Bunch spent an hour talking with McCoy. When he was done, Bunch suggested to one of our attorneys, a DOJ guy, that McCoy could provide detailed information about various weapons shipments and that he got specific, and possibly illegal, delivery instructions from Claxson himself."

"Then what are you going to give him?"

Chase hesitated, said, "Bunch is looking for immunity for any possible crimes deriving from involvement with employment with Heracles, Flamma, or Inter-Core Ballistics."

"Well, Jesus, Jane, that could mean involvement in the attack on Senator Smalls and all the subsequent murders," Lucas said.

"You know how Smalls is going to take that? He'll go on the Senate floor, and he'll have a crucifix and nails with him, and you'll be the one nailed to the cross."

"Well, McCoy denies any involvement with the murders. Bunch says those can be attributed to Ritter and persons unknown. Frankly, Lucas, with what you've developed so far, no prosecutor I know would try McCoy for murder. Claxson won't admit to knowing anything about the murders; Ritter's dead; and Moore—we don't know, he may be dead as well."

"So McCoy walks?"

"He won't walk. We've got him on the weapons stuff with or without any additional testimony. He'll do time—we're going to tell Bunch that we want between ten and fifteen years on the weapons charges. He won't take that, but he'll take five. McCoy'll only get that if he hangs Claxson. Otherwise, we take him to trial and ask for fifteen."

Lucas said, "Then you've got to go after Claxson hard. You've got to talk about a deal to implicate Parrish and Grant."

"He won't take a deal," Chase said. "He'll go to trial and hope to beat it. If he doesn't, and can't win on appeal, he'll try to deal on the sentence. You've said it yourself—the only way he could implicate Grant would be to admit that he set up at least two murders, and maybe three. He won't do that. It will be hard enough to get him on the weapons. He'll try to drag in CIA and military operators for the defense, and they'll resist on grounds of national security."

"Ah, shit," Lucas said. Chase waited him out, and Lucas finally asked, "What are you doing today? Other than arresting him."

"The searches. You and your team are welcome to observe," Chase said. "We'll be at McCoy's town house, and Heracles and

Claxson's office, grabbing files, and Claxson's house. The warrants are in hand; we've got teams on the way. I'll probably go to Claxson's house to get a feel for what he's like."

"I'll tell you what he's like: he keeps two loaded automatic pistols on his office desk."

"Doesn't surprise me."

"Remember what I said about Smalls and the crucifix."

"It won't be me that he goes after—it's the attorney general who'll be fronting this, and I doubt that Smalls would take her on."

Lucas said, "Give me Claxson's address."

CLAXSON LIVED off the heavily wooded Kurtz Road in McLean, Virginia. The house was a stark, red-brick three-story structure that sat back on a large lot, ten or fifteen feet above street level. There was a two-door double-car garage at the end of the blacktopped driveway, and two stone pillars at the front door. Four SUVs crowded the driveway, and a man with the air of a junior FBI agent leaned against one of them, smoking a cigarette.

"'Mistah Kurtz, he dead,'" Lucas quoted as he rolled by, looking for a place to park.

"I know that," Rae said. "*Heart of Darkness*. I'm surprised you know it, being, you know, a hockey puck."

"Actually, it's from 'The Hollow Men' by T. S. Eliot," Lucas said. "'This is the way the world ends / This is the way the world ends / This is the way the world ends / Not with a bang but a whimper.'"

"Bullshit," said Rae. "*Heart of Darkness*."

"Nope, 'Hollow Men.'"

"Jesus, now I got to look it up," Bob said. He took his phone out and started typing with his thumbs. There wasn't enough space to park in the driveway, so Lucas found a place a couple of hundred feet down the street where he could pull all four wheels off the pavement. As they got out of the truck, Bob said, "Ah, got it."

"Who wins?" Rae asked.

"I do," Lucas said. "I know the whole poem."

"And I know the whole Joseph Conrad novel practically by heart," Rae said.

Bob said, "You're both right. Conrad wrote it, Eliot quoted it as the first line of his poem."

"I was right first," Rae said.

"Eliot's poem is far better known," Lucas said.

Bob said, "Shut the fuck up, both of you. We're cops, not some literary, you know, fairies."

"Well, I'm not anyway," Rae said. "Lucas is the one who quoted the fruity poem."

THE CIGARETTE SMOKER was fieldstripping his Marlboro, as they walked up the driveway, and he snapped the filter into a hydrangea bush. "This is an FBI undertaking," he said, carefully checking them out. "I suspect you know that."

"U.S. Marshals," Lucas said. "Jane Chase should have cleared us through."

"If you're Davenport, Matees, and Givens, she did." He looked at his watch. "She should be here in the next few minutes."

THE IMPRESSION Lucas had of Claxson's house was rugs and cigars. A thin odor of smoke hung in the entry hall like a signal of masculinity, a dozen oriental carpets in a variety of sizes spotted the russet-colored plank floors like high-dollar islands. The place had been done by a decorator apparently told to make it into a British men's club, with everything but spittoons.

"Wooden boxes," Bob said, and when Lucas looked around, he noticed lots of antique boxes.

"And mirrors," Rae said.

There were a dozen FBI agents inside the house, slowly taking it apart. They were mostly looking for documents but hadn't had much luck. A Bureau locksmith had failed to open a wall safe in the study—the house, naturally, had a study, two walls of bookcases, an oil portrait of a woman on a third wall, and the requisite cut-stone fireplace on the fourth. The safe was hidden in one side of the fireplace.

A tech bypassed the password on a Dell computer, but except for routine business docs—more bank statements—all documents were encrypted, everything else cleaned out by the same Win/DeXX program that they'd found on Ritter's desktop.

They'd taken Claxson's iPhone when they arrested him, and now they found a second phone in one of the many wooden boxes. The same tech said, "The phones are locked. No can go there. Six digits, four chances, a million possibilities."

One of the agents told Lucas, "He's like the Ritter guy—he's got a safe-deposit box somewhere, under a false identity, with all the good stuff."

Bob said, "We found Ritter's safe-deposit keys in the sink trap in the bathroom."

"Already looked there," the agent said.

An agent clumped up the basement stairs, holding four black rifles by their slings. Rae asked, "Full-auto?"

"These are," the agent said. "He's got seven gun safes down there, thirty-five rifles of various kinds, twenty-two pistols."

"He's an arms dealer," Lucas said. "He'll have got permits for everything."

CHASE SHOWED UP a few minutes later, got a quick briefing from the agent heading up the search. To Lucas, she said, "Not much at his business, either. They were careful about documents. I suspect that the stuff we got from Ritter was emailed to him as encrypted documents, but after decrypting, Ritter broke security and printed it, instead of wiping it clean, and hid it as insurance."

Lucas said, "We talked to Claxson's PA when we went to his office the first time . . . older woman, maybe ready to retire. Any chance of getting her here?"

"What for?"

"So Bob, Rae, and I can intimidate her. Bet she knows his phone code."

Chase gazed at Lucas, said, "We have her. Haven't arrested her, but we've detained her. I could bring her here . . . to answer questions about his lifestyle and so on. She's already intimidated."

"Park her in the parlor, let her sweat, and then we'll drop in on her."

"I'll make the call," Chase said.

THE PA'S NAME was Helen Oakes. Lucas, standing at a front window, watched her walking up the driveway two steps ahead of her FBI escort. She was wearing a conservative gray suit, and he remembered that she was wearing gray the first time they'd seen her: not a woman given to flamboyance.

Bob and Rae were watching an FBI search team guy rolling up rugs, and Lucas called to them: "She's here. Let's get out of sight."

They hurried into the study, and Chase met Oakes at the front door and took her to the living room.

Rae told Lucas what she'd learned about Claxson's rugs: "They're okay, not great. Most of them made in India. The rug guy told me they look better than they actually are."

They were still talking about the rugs, and the guns and the mirrors, and the antique boxes, and the two Japanese swords racked near the door, when, ten minutes later, Chase poked her head in the room, and said, "I worry about this, so . . . go easy as you can."

Lucas nodded. "Sure."

WHEN LUCAS, BOB, AND RAE walked into the parlor, Oakes was seated on a beige, Italian-looking couch, knees tight together, elbows tight to the ribs, purse in her lap, held with both hands. She was frightened.

Rae dropped on the couch beside her, a few inches too close. "Ouch!" she exclaimed, reaching under her jacket and pulling out her Glock. She leaned across Oakes and, with noisy clatter, dropped it on the end table, its muzzle pointing toward Oakes. To Oakes she said, "Shit gets up my back, know what I'm sayin'?"

It wasn't a real question, and Oakes didn't answer. Lucas took a chair facing her, and Bob dragged over another chair, its legs scraping across the plank floor with a tooth-rattling screech, until he was also too close to her.

Lucas said, "Miz Oakes . . ."

Bob: "Jesus, Lucas, call her Helen—we're all friends here. That is your name, right? Helen?"

Oakes nodded, flinching away from Bob.

Lucas said, "Okay, Helen. Look, we don't want to frighten you, and you're not required to tell us anything. We won't arrest you at this point, but you are in serious jeopardy."

"That's the fucking truth," Rae said. "He ain't bullshitting you, babe . . . Excuse the language."

"Everybody, shut up," Lucas said. "I'm talking."

"Yez, boss. I always do what white people tell me," Rae said.

"Shut the fuck up, both of you, and let Helen talk," Bob said.

Lucas continued. "Helen, your boss is going to prison for a very long time. Probably for a couple of decades or more, if we get him for these murders. I'll be honest and tell you we aren't all that interested in you. You're small fry. We're interested in Claxson and some of his military operators. If you stonewall us and we give up on you . . . we could easily throw you in the same bag. We know you must have had intimate knowledge of what was going on in there, since you're so close to Claxson—"

"I was his PA!" Oakes wailed, opening her mouth for the first time. "I handled his schedule and travel reservations, but I didn't do any of the business stuff."

"Oh, horseshit," Rae said.

Lucas snapped: "Rae, I don't want to have to warn you again."

"You ain't warned me the first time, cracker," Rae said. To Oakes she said, "I can tell you from personal experience, honey, that you don't want to fuck with the FBI. Those coldhearted motherfuckers drop you in a hole without thinking about it twice, and not even remember you're there after they throw you in. Claxson's going down for thirty. You don't want to be in that bag."

"C'mon, Rae," Bob said, "don't be trying to scare her." To Oakes he said, "Even if they put you in prison, well, federal prison, especially for women, isn't that bad. You get three hots and a cot and good medical attention."

"Not the only kinda attention she'd get," Rae said, lifting her eyebrows. "Some of them rug munchers can get right up in your lap."

"C'mon, Rae, goddamnit," Bob said.

Lucas raised his voice. "Again, everybody shut up." To Oakes: "Claxson's computers are all encrypted. Do you know his private key?"

"No, I . . . I don't. Nobody knows that but him. It's long; I've seen him entering it on his computer, moving his lips when he's doing it. It's like he's typing in whole words. And he's not referring to anything—he's got it memorized."

"That's bad," Rae said. "Is everything in code?"

"Most everything," Oakes said. "That's why I don't know anything . . . It all goes back and forth in code because it's mostly classified. I know they ship armaments from one place to another, but all these details are in code. That's not what I do."

"You do his travel," Lucas said. "Did you arrange his airplane flight to Omaha?"

She hesitated, then said, "I knew he was flying."

"Do you know who was with him?"

The hesitation again. "No, but I got four box lunches. I have no idea who they were for, but one of them could have been Carol."

Lucas, Bob, and Rae all glanced at one another. "Who's Carol?" Lucas asked. "Is that a woman?"

She nodded. "Carol Ruiz. I don't know that she went, but she was buzzing around that day, before George—Mr. Claxson—left. We don't see her very often—she doesn't work for us—so . . . I don't know that much about her."

"Are they intimate?" Bob asked. "George and Carol?"

Oakes frowned, repeated, "Intimate?"

"You know," Rae said, "is George slipping her the pink piccolo? The ol' skin flute?"

"Oh . . . no. No! Carol mostly talks to the guys. I think she's an OGA."

Lucas: "She's a spook?"

"Careful where you go with that," Rae said to Lucas, "I don't like that spook shit." She glared at Oakes, leaned into her. "You don't never say 'spook,' do you?"

"I never . . ."

Lucas said, "Hmph, Carol Ruiz. We'll take a look at her."

"Don't mention my name, please. She's . . . scary."

"We'll try not to," Lucas said. He took his notebook and a pen from his jacket pocket, flipped the notebook open, wrote "Carol Ruiz." "Can you tell me what she looks like?"

Oakes said, "She's shorter than I am and I'm five-six. She's thin, like a marathon runner or something, that's what she looks like. Black hair, dark eyes. Doesn't laugh much. In my opinion, she's . . . not quite right. She looks at you funny . . . Please don't tell her I gave you her name."

"If we have to use your name, we'll make sure Ruiz knows you're protected by the FBI," Lucas said. "To get back to Claxson, I understand that his encryption code is a long one, but his phone code wouldn't be. Either four or six numbers, right? You must know what that is."

"I . . ." She began to cry.

Lucas let her go for fifteen seconds, then said, "Helen? Don't lie to me. You can tell me that you refuse to answer, but you can't lie to me. That's a crime, and I'm not lying when I say that."

"He does lie a lot, but not about this stuff," Rae said.

"Please don't tell him," she said, and sobbed again.

"We'll do the best we can to keep it private . . ."

"It's 312415 . . ." Lucas wrote it in his notebook as she recited it.

"How'd you figure it out?" Rae asked.

"I sit beside him when we're in a car. I've seen him do it a hundred times and I . . . just remember it. He didn't try to hide it because . . . it's like I'm not there . . . most of the time."

Lucas stood up. "We'll need you to wait here," Lucas said. "Your escort will come pick you up."

"Please don't tell George I told that to you. I'm . . . afraid of him."

"Like Carol Ruiz?" Bob said.

"Well, Carol's different. Carol's crazy. George is only mean. You can deal with mean. You can't deal with crazy."

LUCAS STEPPED OUT of the parlor and into the hallway, and Chase, who was standing there, listening, out of sight, said, "Mr. Claxson isn't the only one who can be mean."

Lucas said, "There are three people dead that we know of, and maybe four if Moore was killed. We weren't even mean enough to give her bad dreams. Let's go try the phones."

The FBI tech had bagged the iPhone in transparent plastic. He left it in the bag when he turned it on. Chase read the number from Lucas's notebook, the tech punched it in, and the phone opened up.

"We need printouts of everything," she said to the tech. "Like, now."

"Yes, ma'am," he said. "What about the other phone?"

"Maybe he only has one code to remember," Chase said.

The tech shrugged, got the bag with the second phone, and tried the code. The second phone opened up.

Chase said to Lucas, "It was still mean, but I forgive you."

SHE WALKED AWAY to talk to somebody else, and Lucas said to Bob and Rae, "Carol Ruiz sounds a lot like Suzie, who shot up the hotel."

"She does," Bob said. "But is it Carol or Suzie?"

25

Grant was walking a California venture capitalist through the Senate Office Building when Parrish called her. The VC was wearing an antique Black Sabbath T-shirt, black jeans, and a black linen jacket, and, at the back of his scalp, a small but prescient pink spot; Grant expected that the next time she saw him, he'd have a shaved head. He had the rattlesnake charm of the typical VC, plus money and connections. The connections were the important thing—she was building her network, and if the presidential primaries came down to California, she needed them.

The call from Parrish was an irritant. She told the VC, "One second—I have to take this," and stepped away from him. "What?" she snapped into the phone.

"We've got a problem with the subcommittee," Parrish said. "We need to talk in a secure facility."

Emergency code: the subcommittee was Heracles and Claxson and the operators.

"I can do it at noon," she said. "Meet me at my hideaway."

"Sooner would be better."

"How long will the meeting be?" she asked.

"Fifteen minutes?"

"I can give you fifteen at ten-thirty," she said. "I'm scheduled at eleven."

"See you then," Parrish said, and hung up.

Grant reached out and put her hand on the VC's arm, turned him back toward her office, leaving her hand on his arm as they walked. She *would* fuck him, if necessary. "You know the problem with the Senate? It's like being nibbled to death by ducks. There's never a second during the whole darn day that somebody doesn't want to talk to you—and, most of the time, doesn't need to. People want to talk to you, so they can say, 'I was talking to Senator Grant yesterday,' and then they start lying."

The VC nodded. "I get the same thing. Some guy running a two-bit start-up wants to say he talked to you so he can spread the word that there might be some interest in whatever he's peddling. 'Nibbled to death by ducks'—I'll remember that."

U.S. SENATORS are each assigned hideaways in the Capitol, unseen by the public or the press. Only the senator has a key to his or her retreat, which are routinely checked for electronic surveillance. Not as secure as Grant's SCIF, but close.

Since Grant was a junior senator, her hideaway was in the Capitol basement, a windowless room barely large enough for a desk with a computer on it, an office chair, two wooden visitor's chairs, a worktable, and a small office refrigerator. If she lasted for another term and got lucky with senatorial turnover, she might actually get a place with a window. Of course, if everything worked out right, she'd have a big oval-shaped office before that happened.

GRANT ASKED, "What happened?" as she dropped into her chair.

Parrish took one of the wooden chairs. "The FBI hit Heracles this morning."

"Ah, shit."

"They detained Claxson. Claxson didn't say anything, asked to speak privately to his lawyer. They said he could, from his SCIF. He did that, and he called me, all of it on our burners, but we ran his burner through a shredder, so we should be clear there," Parrish said. "He could talk only for a couple of minutes, but what I get is, the feds found Ritter's safe-deposit box and took out a bunch of documents about some . . . irregular weapons deliveries. Nothing to do with us, not directly. Since it was Ritter, I expect your friend Davenport is out there stirring up trouble."

Grant pointed a finger at Parrish. "But . . . But what if it's Davenport trying to turn Claxson on the Smalls thing?"

"That was the second thing that occurred to me."

"The first thing was worse?"

"Well . . . I've been involved in some of Claxson's sales. It was a while back, but I was either already working for you or about to start working for you."

"Ahhh . . ."

"Wait, wait—I don't know that any of the documents involve those transactions. They might, but that would be purely unlucky. Still, I thought you should know about it. And that Claxson's been arrested. If Davenport's trying to turn him . . ."

"Would McCoy or Moore be willing to solve that problem? The Claxson problem?"

Parrish was shaking his head. "I can't find either of them. I asked Claxson, and he said Moore dropped out of sight yesterday or the day before. He may be on the run. McCoy is still around, or was yesterday afternoon, but nobody's been in touch with him since then. I cruised by his town house, didn't see anything unusual, but I didn't see his car, either. He may have been picked up, or, like I said, he may be running."

"Coming apart," Grant said. "The whole deal's coming apart. How much do Moore and McCoy know about me?"

"Nothing more than your name," Parrish said. "Basically, they know I work for you, and that I'm friends with Claxson. And I don't care what Davenport suspects. As long as Claxson keeps his mouth shut, they can't get me. And if they can't get me, you're fine, too."

"I'm not fine," she said. "I'm in trouble here. I mean, if the FBI has Claxson on illegal weapons deals, it's possible that they could even get him on murder charges, depending on where those guns went. If they went to Boko Haram, God help us. Especially if they can get some of his operators to testify against him. Claxson might desperately need someone to deal. That would be you and me. Actually, it'd be me. I'm the big fish."

They stared at each other, and Parrish said, "So . . . ?"

"Your sources may decide you're toxic. Before that happens, you have to find out what's happening with Claxson. Specifically, what the feds have got on him, if he's in jail or going to jail—all of that."

Parrish said, "I already made some calls. I'm friendly with Claxson's PA. I'll catch her somewhere this afternoon and find out what she knows. And she usually knows everything that goes on in that company."

"Careful," Grant said. "She's an obvious source for the FBI as well. You might be talking to her and find out she's wearing a wire or something . . . maybe under surveillance."

"I can handle it," Parrish said.

Another ten seconds of silence, then Grant asked, "If Claxson has to go away, could you handle it?"

"I was afraid you'd ask that," Parrish said. "I'll do some research. I've been over to his place—it's over in McLean—any number of times. There's woods behind his house, and he likes to barbecue on his back porch. And he likes to sit out there and drink. If the worst happens . . ."

"Are you good enough for that?"

"The shooting wouldn't be a problem, the getaway might be. Like I said, I'd have to do some research."

"You'd better do the research," Grant said. "Don't move without signaling me. But do the research."

WHEN PARRISH WAS GONE, Grant worked through it and realized that if Claxson was going down, Parrish probably would as well. Parrish had worked with Claxson on several deals involving Army procurement and major weapons deliveries. Like Claxson, Parrish would be looking for somebody to deal, and he only had one choice likely to clear him out of a prison term: Senator Taryn Grant.

She walked back through the Capitol to her official office, brooding about it. She had twenty staffers in Washington, twenty more in Minnesota, and one of her Minnesota people was in town to brief her about a series of polls taken in the past two weeks on rural issues. She wanted to think, but she didn't want to break her schedule, either, didn't want to appear in any way disturbed.

She took the meeting: numbers and more numbers, and all the numbers said that she was still strong in Minnesota despite Smalls's efforts to screw her. They'd come to the question-and-answer segment when her chief of staff stepped into the room, leaned over her, and whispered, "Jack needs just a moment. He's in your office."

"Let's take a break," she told the polling group. "Five minutes."

In Grant's office, Parrish handed her a piece of notebook paper on which he'd written "Claxson will be held overnight but will ask for bail tomorrow, and he's expected to get it."

She nodded, and wrote a note back: "We need a way to get face-to-face at a secure site and work this out. Not my SCIF, I don't want him near my house. Someplace the cops won't have bugged." When he'd read the note, she took both pieces of paper and pushed them into her shredder.

26

Claxson's phones held only one gift.

The iPhone, basically, was a long list of phone contacts, but with nothing recorded from recent calls—the phone was apparently wiped clean after each call, other than the list. Chase pointed out the one-button app for that.

"Lots of politicians have that app," she said.

The phone wasn't in Claxson's name; it was registered to a Gerald D. Wilson.

The second phone, an off-brand burner, didn't have that app. On the day after Claxson admitted flying to Omaha, he made two calls, and received two calls, all on the same anonymous T-Mobile burner phone.

With the phone numbers in hand, Chase jacked up the FBI phone experts. A half hour after they'd opened the phones, she told Lucas that one of the calls was to Clear Lake, Iowa, two more were from and to St. Paul, and the final one went through a tower west of Des Moines.

"That's when they hit Weather and Last," Lucas said. "Clear Lake is on the Iowa border, right off I-35, on the fastest route to the Twin Cities from Omaha. The last one was on I-80, on the way back to Omaha. That ties him directly to a murder."

"But doesn't prove it, unfortunately," Chase said.

"Oakes made four lunch boxes for the flight out," Bob said. "That's Claxson, Ritter, McCoy, and Moore."

"Unless one of them was Suzie or Carol Ruiz," Lucas said. He turned to Chase. "We need to ask McCoy who Suzie is. Or Carol Ruiz. And if they're the same person."

"We don't have a deal yet, but he's been giving up that kind of information—filling in the employee list."

"She might not be an employee," Rae said.

"We'll ask," Chase said. "I'll make a call."

"Let me in to talk with him," Lucas said.

MCCOY WAS DELIVERED to an interview room in the Hoover Building from an Arlington lockup at the insistence of both Chase and Bunch, McCoy's lawyer, a happy confluence of requirements. He was escorted by two marshals. One of them recognized Rae from a training program, and asked, "You guys are running an investigation? How'd that happen?"

She nodded at Lucas, and said, "Political pull. It's corrupt, but we fly Business Class."

"Are you shittin' me?"

BUNCH AND MCCOY were locked up to talk privately for a few minutes, and, when they were done, Lucas, Chase, and a Department of Justice prosecutor named Steve Lapham went in, along with the two marshals. Lapham told Bunch, "We have a number of questions for both you and Mr. McCoy regarding arrangements for testimony. But before that, Marshal Davenport has a question for Mr. McCoy that has no potential legal liability for Mr. McCoy, as far as we know."

Bunch said, "Ask. We'll decide whether he should answer."

Lucas asked McCoy, "Do you know, or have you seen, a woman known either as Suzie or Carol Ruiz?" He described her, and McCoy said, "I've seen a woman who George called Carol who looks like that, but I don't think that's her real name. I think it's fake, and somebody told me she's a NOC, a chick with a non-official cover working for the CIA or somebody else, I don't know who."

Bob asked, "You think she'd know where to get a silenced submachine gun?"

McCoy shook his head. "I don't know, I might be able to, but I'd have to dig around for a while, and I'm not sure I could. I was more of a meat-and-potatoes, M16 kinda guy."

Rae asked, "Would this chick have been hanging out with Jim Ritter?"

McCoy thought for a minute, said, "Yes, she did. I think they were—what do you call it?—an item? For a long time. Jim said she was a girl he could trust. I saw them once over at the Last Minute Grill, by the airport. I didn't interrupt. I figured Jim was flying out, they were saying good-bye, but I was wrong. She was the one flying out . . . and they might have been worried, the way they were holding on to each other."

Lucas said, "Huh."

"I'll tell you one other thing," McCoy began, but Bunch put a hand on his arm, and asked, "You're sure?"

"Shouldn't be a problem," McCoy said. "Maybe get a few more brownie points. I speak some Arabic. She speaks perfect Arabic.

The one time I saw her at Heracles, she was talking to this Syrian guy like they were old friends, and, I'm telling you, I thought she was Syrian."

Lucas had nothing more to ask, but he said to McCoy, "We've tracked the phone that Claxson used to call you boys on your way into the Twin Cities to hit my wife and murder Last. If I were you, I would sign anything that Mr. Lapham gives you, because, if you don't, you're looking at thirty years in Stillwater Penitentiary after the feds get done with you."

McCoy gave him a sullen look, shuffled his feet, and said, "You ain't from the Chamber of Commerce, huh?"

THEY WERE GETTING toward dinnertime, and Lucas, Bob, and Rae went back to the hotel, agreed to work out for a while and go to dinner together. When he was back in his room, Lucas called the number that Tom Ritter had given him.

"Marshal Davenport . . . I've only got a minute. We're filling out papers to get Jim buried at Arlington. Lots of paperwork. It takes forever."

"I'm calling about Jim's girlfriend . . . Suzie. I'm now told that she might also go under the name of Carol Ruiz, and she might work for the CIA or some other agency and speaks perfect Arabic. Does that still sound like her?"

"Maybe," Ritter said after a bit. "I only saw her that one time. We were at a party, all military or ex-military people who worked in the Middle East. Jim invited me to come along. I didn't hear Suzie speak Arabic, but there was a minute where a couple of guys were speaking Arabic, and she suddenly looked at them, and I got the impression she knew what they were talking about."

"Know where I could find her?" Lucas asked. "I need to talk."

"No, I don't," Ritter said. "I could ask around."

"I'd appreciate it. She's been seen at Heracles, so people there know her."

"All right, I'll ask. Should I give her your phone number?"

"Yes. I was on the wrong end of that submachine gun, so she probably wouldn't want to meet me at McDonald's."

"Why do you want to talk?"

"I want to find out if she was hired to shoot me up or if she did it because she bought Claxson's line of bullshit about me torturing and shooting Jim, if she tried to kill me because she loved Jim."

"I'd like to know that answer myself," Ritter said. "I'll start making some calls."

AFTER DINNER, Bob needed to catch up with people on the Internet, and Lucas and Rae got Lucas's car and drove across the river to a Barnes & Noble bookstore they'd seen while driving around Arlington.

"I'm getting tired of the 'Net," Lucas said, as they crossed the river. "You can't separate the facts from the bullshit anymore. The constant carping drives me nuts . . . Did I ever tell you that I supervised the construction of our house?"

"Never did," Rae said.

"Well, I did, and it was interesting," Lucas said. "Sometimes I wish I'd become an architect. I used to go out on the 'Net for tips, on this one particular building site. I still check it sometimes.

The last time I looked, there was this flame war about politics. At a construction site. I mean, why? Is there a difference between a left-wing and right-wing two-by-four?"

"I made the mistake, commenting on a story on the *Wall Street Journal*'s site, of mentioning that I'm black," Rae said. "I started getting that 'you people' shit. Can't avoid it."

The bookstore was located in a California-style outdoor shopping center. After they parked, they got cups of coffee at Starbucks and split up to look at books. Since he was living in Washington temporarily, Lucas browsed the politics section and wound up with *Dark Money* by Jane Mayer, then hit the magazine rack, while he waited for Rae to finish browsing.

They were back at the Watergate by nine o'clock. Lucas had finished the Hiaasen book, and set it aside to ship home, and had started the Mayer, when the call came in from an unknown number.

A woman with a light soprano voice: "This is Wendy."

"Wendy who?"

"Suzie . . . Carol. What do you want?"

"I didn't shoot Jim Ritter," Lucas said.

"Then who did?" The question was as much a confession that she was the hotel shooter as he was likely to get, Lucas thought. She continued. "Don't bother scrambling your tech guys—I'm talking to you on an old burner. I'll throw it in the garbage as soon as I take the battery out."

"I understand that you're one of the people who knows all about that kind of thing—burners and taking out batteries," Lucas said.

She didn't reply to that. Instead, she repeated, "Who shot Jim? Specifically?"

"I have several suspects," he said. "And, by the way, I don't have any techs looking for your phone."

"I forgot, you're a marshal, you don't do tech. Anyway, if you think Jim was shot by Moore or McCoy, you're wrong."

"You're sure of that?"

"Absolutely. Put it this way: those guys risked their own lives to keep Jim alive, and he did the same for them. After that, they're not going to shoot him in cold blood."

"Tom told me the same thing," Lucas said. "Did Tom tell you that Claxson bullshitted him on the waterboarding thing?"

"Yes. Claxson lied to me, too. If it's a lie," she said.

"It is."

"You think he did it?"

"No. We don't think it was Claxson himself. Although I think Claxson could have set it up."

"Parrish, then."

"I'm not sure. Do you know Parrish?"

"Yes. If he did it, it was because he was told to do it. Parrish is a bullshit artist, a fixer. He might be able to do it, if you squeezed him hard enough, but he wouldn't like it. He wouldn't want to. Not because he'd be killing somebody, but because he might get caught. Or might fuck it up and get shot himself."

"Okay."

"That leaves Senator Taryn Grant." Lucas didn't say anything, and after six or eight seconds Wendy said, "You're a U.S. Marshal, so you don't want to say that."

"It's complicated," Lucas said. "Did you look her up?"

"Yes, and I looked you up, too. You think she was involved in some murders in Minneapolis, but you weren't able to get her on that. Senator Smalls thinks she tried to assassinate him. You think Jim was one of the people in on that silly fuckin' stunt."

"Jim was involved, for sure," Lucas said. "He was one of the triggers, but he wasn't doing it for himself. His orders came from someone else, and since he worked for Claxson . . . But what would Claxson get from killing Smalls? Nothing that I can figure out. We need to find somebody who needed to get rid of Smalls."

"You say that but you won't say her name," Wendy said.

"Like I said, it's complicated. I don't really know who I'm talking to."

"Let me give you a hypothetical," Wendy said. "Do you think a person like Grant, with her personality, could pull the trigger?"

"I don't want to get involved in hypotheticals," Lucas said. "I do know that a lot of people have died around her, people who might have obstructed her ambitions."

"Huh. Then you think she could. Okay. From what I've read about the Minneapolis situation, you obviously think she was the one giving the orders in those killings." Again, Lucas didn't reply, and she asked, "Are you going to get her?"

"I'm beginning to doubt it," Lucas admitted. "To do that, we'd have to jump through a lot of evidentiary hoops, and she's got an ocean of money for lawyers. Our only hope is to get Claxson or Parrish to talk to us. But if they do talk to us, they'd be implicating themselves in multiple murders."

"So you won't get her."

"I'll be as honest as I can be: I'm not sure we'll get any of them. Not for murder. Not for killing Jim, or the others. We had hard evidence that Jim was involved in one murder, when Senator Smalls was run off the road, but Jim's dead now. We don't know exactly who was with him, although we have some evidence that Claxson was directing the murder in St. Paul and the attack on my wife. McCoy and Moore may have been involved in that, but we have no hard evidence against them, and they won't admit it . . . And we can't find Moore. He may be dead, too. We're still trying, though. We should know in a week."

"All right," she said. "You got anything else?"

Lucas hesitated, then asked, "Have you seen the actual autopsy report on Jim?"

"No. Tom told me about it. He was shot twice."

"Listen, Wendy . . . I want you to know, this wasn't just a shooting. It was a cold-blooded murder done by somebody who Jim thought was a friend. The crime scene analysis suggests that when he was shot, he was holding a carton of milk. His face and shirt were soaked with it, like a bullet went through the carton. He didn't even have a chance to throw the carton, or even drop it. Then they cut off his fingers . . ."

"What!"

"They were apparently trying to keep him from being identified. They actually identified him from a Special Forces tattoo. Then, you know, they threw him in that dumpster . . ."

Wendy broke: Lucas could hear her sobbing. "I'm sorry. I thought you knew all this."

She sobbed for several more seconds, then said, "Tom said he was shot, he didn't say any more, only that he was shot . . ."

"I'm sorry," Lucas said again.

"Oh, God," she said. "I gotta go, I gotta . . ."

"Was that you in the hotel?"

"The hotel . . . the hotel . . . I don't know what you're talking about," Wendy said, and she hung up.

She definitely was at the hotel, Lucas thought. All in all, it had been a worthwhile conversation, though it would be a while before he knew that for sure.

27

Lucas was a night owl and exercised at night. Bob and Rae got up early, and because they knew Lucas liked to sleep in, they worked out in the morning. That got the workday nicely coordinated, as Lucas woke up, and Bob and Rae got back from the gym, at the same time, and, a half hour later, they were all at breakfast together.

Chase called while they were looking at menus, though they never ordered anything other than pancakes or waffles.

Claxson, Chase said, would be released on bail that morning, probably before noon. "Bail will be set at four million, all cash, plus his house. His lawyer says he can produce the cash from an investment fund; they agreed on the house. There are some restrictions: he's not allowed back in his office or house until we finish processing the searches, which are still going on; he's got to give us the combination for his home safe before release; and he's got to wear an ankle monitor."

"If he decides to run, he'll cut the monitor off, and we'll never see him again," Lucas said.

"That's a possibility," Chase said. "But we're willing to take that risk because we know where his resources are and where he'd be likely to run to, and we told him that and we think he believes us. We've also done an analysis of his income, and we suspect he may be hiding assets offshore. Still, giving up four million and his house, which is worth another one and a half or two, would take a big piece out of him. We think he'd be reluctant to forfeit all of that . . . at least, not yet. And the ankle monitor has a built-in GPS, which means we'll be able to track him, step-by-step, wherever he goes. We didn't mention that to him—"

"He certainly knows."

"Maybe, but this is an FBI special made to look like it's obsolete, which it isn't. We're quite interested to see where he goes and who he talks to. We'll have a surveillance crew nearby when he makes his move. Not on top of him, but close enough to surveil him without him knowing, see who he might meet with. Close enough that if he cuts that monitor, they can take him."

"He's a spy kinda guy. He'll be looking for the surveillance," Lucas said.

"But with that GPS monitor, we never have to follow him. We never even have to see him. If we can't see him, he can't see us," Chase said. "Besides, he might not think we'd expend those kinds of resources on him, a full team."

Lucas said, "Hmm, I guess we'll see."

"What's the Marshals Service going to do?"

"Don't know," Lucas said. "I'd like to talk to McCoy again, go back to him about the woman who shot up the hotel. I'd like to know more about her."

"If you find out anything, tell us," Chase said.

"And if Claxson moves, please let me know."

"I normally wouldn't do that with another service," Chase said, "but your team has been valuable enough that I will. I'll connect you up with our surveillance crew—the daytime leader is Andrew Moy. I'll give him your number. He gets off at eleven o'clock, and I don't know who the overnight team will be yet, but I'll let you know about that, too."

"Thanks. My guys here have a lot of surveillance and tracking experience—basically, that's what they do. If we don't have anything else going on, we might hook up with your crew. At least until we put Claxson to bed."

WHEN LUCAS got off the phone, Bob asked, "What are we doing?"

"Mostly waiting," Lucas said.

He told them what Chase had said, and Rae said, "If I knew we might be pulling surveillance, I'd have gotten a few more magazines last night."

"We could still do that," Lucas said. "We could swing by the store, go over to Claxson's place when they open the safe, then go talk to McCoy."

"Not gonna be much that the FBI hasn't gotten," Rae said. "Claxson wouldn't give them the combination to the safe if there was something in there that would hang him."

"I know, but what the hell else have we got to do?"

"Maybe time to go home," Bob said.

"Could be," Lucas said.

THEY WERE talking that over when Porter Smalls called on Lucas's burner phone. "This is just a heads-up," Smalls told Lucas. "I'm coming through Washington today. I've got an event I've got to go to tonight, big-money people."

"You think it's safe?"

"Oh, yeah. When the party's over, I'm going out to the airport, getting on a NetJet to Los Angeles. By the time somebody figures that out, I won't be in L.A. anymore. And I've still got those cops with me as security. I'm gonna have to come back to work after the recess, so hurry up and nail Taryn."

"We're trying," Lucas said. "Things have gotten complicated."

"How complicated? Anything that's gonna hurt?"

"Not you, no. Is there any way you could be at Kitten's apartment tonight? I could give you a rundown on everything."

"Yes, but early. Let's say six."

"See you then," Lucas said.

When he hung up, he said to Bob and Rae, "We've got a bunch of errands to run. But let's pull together our thoughts, what else we might do, and talk about going home."

"Bummer," Rae said. "I would prefer a more definite conclusion."

THEY RAN ERRANDS all day. They found out that Claxson's will left all of his money to the National Infantry Museum at Fort Benning, apparently not having any other heirs deserving enough to leave money to; and that he carried disability insurance but no life policy. He had a small album of nude photos of himself with a dozen different women, with space for more. There were photos taken with groups of men in a variety of military gear; there were photos taken from hotel balconies. And there were two American passports, both in his name.

"Nothing wrong with having two passports," one of the FBI agents said. "Back in the day, I had to travel to some Arab countries that wouldn't let you in if you had a visa stamp from Israel, and since I often had to go to Israel, I had two passports. Lot of people did."

The FBI had an interview scheduled with McCoy, and they drove over to the Hoover Building to sit in. During the morning, a sullen-looking cloud layer moved in, and a soft drizzle began to fall. All they learned from McCoy, that was new, was that he was well traveled and often took loads of guns to small, out-of-the-way countries. His lawyer Bunch wouldn't let him talk about anything Lucas was really interested in.

Claxson made bail at one o'clock in the afternoon. The FBI wouldn't let Claxson back in his house until the searches were finished, so he checked into the Ritz-Carlton at Pentagon City. The FBI wouldn't let him have his car, either, until they'd finished processing it, so his lawyer drove him to a Hertz agency, where he picked up an SUV.

Andrew Moy, running the surveillance crew, told Lucas at four o'clock that Claxson had spent the day in his room "probably with a burner that he got from his attorney" except for two trips to the hotel's restaurant. On one of those trips, Claxson had a Cobb salad with shrimp, which told Lucas that the feds were in Claxson's shirt pocket. Moy assured Lucas that Claxson hadn't seen them. "But, I gotta say, he might assume we're here even if he can't see us."

AT SIX O'CLOCK, Lucas walked through the drizzling rain to meet with Smalls at Kitten Carter's apartment. After shaking hands, and offering Lucas a beer, Smalls said to him, "Tell me every goddamn thing."

Lucas did. They talked for an hour, and, as they finished, Smalls was pulling a tuxedo out of a garment bag. "Hate these fucking conventions. But it's either conventions or spending my own money to get reelected."

"Well, Jesus, you wouldn't want to do that," Lucas said.

When he left Smalls, Lucas walked back to the hotel, picked up Bob and Rae, and called Moy, who said that Claxson was still at the Ritz.

"Now what?" Bob asked.

"Gonna watch the ball game," Lucas said.

"Mind if I hang out?" Bob asked. "I mean, unless you're going to be laying around naked or something."

"Absolutely," Lucas said. "Rae?"

"I'm gonna go read," she said. "Call me if anything happens. I'm so fuckin' bored that if I knew where the local muggers hang out, I'd go over there for a stroll."

Rae read, Lucas and Bob settled in for a Nationals game, and, at nine o'clock, Moy called. "Claxson's moving. He's moving fast."

TEN MINUTES LATER, Lucas, Bob, and Rae were in the Evoque and running hot, Moy calling every couple of minutes to give them updates. At first, Moy thought Claxson was headed back to his house. "Wonder if he thinks he can get in? The place is sealed . . . He can't be dumb enough to go in anyway, can he?"

"Maybe he's going to throw a Molotov cocktail through the window," Bob suggested.

"You don't really think that . . ."

CLAXSON WASN'T GOING to his house. He drove past McLean, where he lived, and continued west to the town of Great Falls, still on the Virginia side of the river. "One of my people passed him," Moy said. "He appears to be alone."

"He must know he's being monitored, even if he doesn't know you're following him," Lucas said. "He can't be going somewhere he shouldn't."

"You wouldn't think he would," Moy said. "By the way, we've notified Agent Chase. She's on her way."

"Is that normal?"

"No, but this is getting some attention at the Bureau. She wants to be on top of everything because, well, that's just the way she is."

"You're saying she's a bureaucratic climber?"

"No. She's very . . . conscientious," Moy said cautiously.

"Okay," Lucas said.

Five minutes later, Moy called back. "He's getting off the highway." And five minutes after that, "He's pulled into a house off Chesapeake Drive. We're running the address." And five minutes after that, "The house belongs to Charles Douglas. He's Heracles's main company attorney."

"Okay," Lucas said. "Shoot. I was kinda hoping he was running for it."

"MAKES SENSE HE'D TALK to the company attorney after what's happening at the company," Bob said, as they drove toward Great Falls. "Claxson must know it's too late to bug Douglas's house. Nice safe place to talk."

"I'd kill to know what they're saying," Lucas said.

"We could sneak up to the house and put our ears to the window," Rae said. "Done that a few times."

"Can't do it in this neighborhood," Bob said. "I've been looking it up on my phone, and it's one of those richie rich places. Sneaking through backyards could be bad for your health."

"The other thing is," Lucas said, "if we got caught listening in to a private conversation with his attorney, we could go to jail ourselves."

MOY HAD SET UP an observation post a block from Douglas's house, in the driveway of a neighbor, where they were hidden from the road by a screen of oaks. They'd gotten the spot easily enough: Moy pulled into the drive, leaned on the doorbell until the owner came to the door, showed him his ID, and asked if they could park there "on a matter of national security."

The neighbor had many questions, none of which were answered, but agreed to let Moy's team wait in the driveway. Before Lucas, Bob, and Rae arrived, one of Moy's minions, dressed in camo and wearing night vision goggles, snuck off through the trees, set up across the road from Douglas's house with a radio and a chicken salad sandwich. They couldn't bug Claxson's attorney, but there was no law against watching him.

LUCAS, BOB, AND RAE arrived fifteen minutes after Moy. Moy, an Asian American, had a West Coast beachboy accent and hard angles in his face. "Nothing happening," he said. "We got a guy a hundred feet out with a direct view of the house."

"How far away are we right here?" Lucas asked.

"According to my Google Earth, about two hundred and ten feet, if you run out the driveway and down the street," Moy said. "In a straight line, a hundred and ninety-one feet, but of course there are a lot of trees between here and there. And it's dark."

They sat and waited in four different cars. A while later, a fifth car pulled up, and Moy walked over to it, a door popped open, and he got in. He was in there for two or three minutes, then all the doors opened, and Jane Chase got out of one of them and walked over to Lucas's Evoque. She was wearing jeans and a long-sleeved black shirt and running shoes, the first time Lucas had seen her when she wasn't wearing a dress. "Nothing happening," she said.

"I know," Lucas said, as he got out and eased the car door closed. Bob and Rae got out to join the huddle, and Chase gave them a couple of paragraphs on Douglas's background. "One of those lawyers who got rich writing bills for Midwestern congressmen," she said. "Sent lots of government defense money out that way."

Moy jogged over to them. "Larry says there's a car coming down the street, moving slow."

He was carrying a radio but listening through earphones. He listened for a few more seconds, and said, "It turned into the driveway . . . Okay, two people are getting out . . . Looks like a man and a woman . . ."

Lucas felt sudden apprehension. "What's the woman look like?"

Moy repeated the question, said, "Can't tell, it's too dark. And Larry's not positive it's a woman but thinks it is. She's wearing a hooded black rain jacket . . ."

"Aw, Jesus," Lucas said.

He looked at Bob, who said, "Suzie?"

"I think so."

"We gotta get down closer," he said. To Chase: "I think it might be the woman who shot us up at the hotel. I don't like the idea that she's here with Claxson because—"

"Larry says they're inside," Moy said.

Seconds later—three or four, no more, Lucas thought—they heard a series of whumps, like you might hear if somebody fell down the stairs in your house.

Lucas pulled his gun, and Chase said, "What?" and Bob said, "That was gunfire," and Rae yanked open the back hatch of the Evoque, and as Lucas and Bob ran toward the opening of the driveway, she pulled out an M4 and a thirty-round mag and slammed the mag into place as she ran after them.

28

Taryn Grant stood in the bay window at the back of her Georgetown mansion, watching the drizzle deflect off the multicolored foliage and the red-brick walkways of the sprawling garden she never thought to sit in. In the middle of a densely built world capital, she felt alone: not only was she alone in the house, and would be for the rest of the day, she couldn't even see the city. She could see a few windows in the gabled roof of her next-door neighbor, but that was it. Other than that, she might be out in the Minnesota countryside.

The temperatures were in the low seventies, low enough that she shivered in the cool air, after the long string of stultifying hot and humid days. But the rain—she liked the idea of the rain. The rain was like a sign.

Time to roll the bones, she thought. Everything would ride on this night.

The idea was . . . arousing. In a sexual sense. She took a deep breath, feeling the heat between her thighs, turned away from the window, and walked through the kitchen to the basement door, to the SCIF, walked down the stairs, got her pistol from the desk.

The gun was a Beretta 92F, once owned by a security man who'd killed for her and was now dead himself. He'd picked the gun up after a firefight in Iraq, had taken it off the body of a dead intelligence officer who'd made the mistake of popping up from behind a wall at the wrong split second. In movie cop terms, the piece was cold as ice.

She carried the Beretta up the stairs, stopped in the kitchen to pick up a plastic mixing bowl and a bottle of dishwashing liquid, which she took back to the laundry room. There, she popped the magazine and thumbed the fifteen rounds out on the top of the dryer. She poured the dishwashing liquid in the bowl, dropped the rounds in. Using a dishrag, she scrubbed each round clean until the brass shone like a new gold coin, eliminating any possible fingerprints. That done, she rolled the rounds out on the dryer again and washed the bowl in the utility sink.

Next step: she took a bottle of bleach from the cupboard, poured it in the bowl until it was two-thirds full, and dropped the rounds in. She let them sit for a minute, then gingerly picked each one out with a paper towel, dried it, and lined them all up on a paper towel on the dryer top. The magazine went into the bleach for a minute. She took it out, again handling it with a paper towel, patted and waved it dry. No more DNA.

When the fifteen rounds and the magazine were thoroughly dry, and yet again with paper towels, she pushed the cartridges into the magazine and loaded the mag back into the pistol. She finally put the gun in a new garbage bag.

None of that technique came from the CIA or the Intelligence Committee. It was all hot off the Internet.

SHE CARRIED THE PISTOL back to her bedroom, where she lay on the bed for five minutes, working out the exact sequence of events, while getting her courage up and fixing it steadfastly in her heart. What did the Buddha say? *Do not dwell in the past, do not dream of the future, concentrate the mind on the present moment.*

When the moment was clear to her, she packed an overnight case with jeans, a black cashmere sweater, a hooded black nylon rain jacket, sneakers, and a leather shoulder bag with the gun inside. Her murder gear. On top would go a travel kit, fashion blouse, jacket, slacks, and shoes for the following day.

She showered, did her makeup, dabbed a bit of Tom Ford Black Orchid on her earlobes, the inside of her wrists, and at the top of her spine. She dressed in a notable emerald Versace summer gown, which subtly displayed her long legs through a shifting slit, and by seven o'clock was in a taxi headed to the Park Hyatt, where the U.S. Public Hospital Association was holding its annual summer soirée. And where she'd reserved a suite for the night.

By seven forty-five, right on time, she was in the room. She retouched her makeup, shook out her hair, got her jeweled clutch purse with the plain black burner phone in it, and, at eight, walked into the ballroom. Almost the first person she saw, off to her right, dressed in a black tuxedo, was Porter Smalls.

And Smalls saw her, displayed a white flash of teeth—not a smile, a grimace—and turned away. She headed left and began working the crowd.

PARRISH CALLED at ten minutes to nine. Grant glanced at the phone, and said to the doctor she was talking with, "I'm sorry—I have to take this."

"The President?"

"I don't think the President wants to chat with me," Grant said, laughing. "We do have our small differences."

She stepped out in the hall, walking toward the elevators, and said, "Yes?"

"On my way. Ten minutes."

"How about the other guy? Where is he?"

"He's closer. He aims to get there right at nine-thirty."

In the allotted ten minutes, she transformed herself in her room. She pinned her hair up, got into her jeans, sweater, sneakers, and hooded nylon jacket. She pulled on a pair of thin leather gloves, took the Beretta out of the shoulder bag, jacked a shell into the chamber, made sure the safety was on, and put it back in the bag, under her purse, the grip up where her hand could fall on it easily.

She left her regular phone on the dressing table. That done, she checked the hall, hung a "Do Not Disturb" sign on the door, took the elevator down to four, and, from there, the stairs down to the street level. Several people were in the lobby as she hurried through, her head covered by the hood, her face turned away as best she could manage.

Parrish was waiting. He popped the door of an anonymous Toyota sedan, she climbed in, and they were off. "This isn't your car," she said.

"It's a Hertz. I don't want my car seen at Charlie's house."

"Which could be traced . . ."

"Yeah, if I'd rented it under my own name, which I didn't. I'll take it back, they'll rent it again, and by the time anybody could trace it, there'll have been five more people inside."

"Paranoid, are we?"

"You're not paranoid when people are out to get you. And people are definitely out to get us."

CHARLIE DOUGLAS, Heracles's principal attorney, lived in the town of Great Falls, a tedious drive at rush hour, but only a half hour at nine o'clock. They drove most of the way in silence, Grant with what felt like a hand squeezing her heart. Douglas lived in a white pillared house on Chesapeake Drive, two stories high in a center section, with lower wings to either side. An American flag hung vertically from a rack on the second floor, with an overhead light to shine on it at night. The house itself was set above the road in a dark forest of scattered pines and looming deciduous trees—oaks, Grant thought.

"George said to look for the flag," Parrish said, as he turned into the driveway.

"Anybody here besides us four?" Grant said. "I don't want anyone else seeing my face."

"Nobody. I don't want anyone to see me, either. Charlie's a widower; he said his housekeeper is gone at six o'clock." Looking at the black SUV parked in the driveway, Parrish added, "George is here. He told me he rented a Land Rover, which is a George thing to do."

He parked, and Grant said, "What I'm mostly worried about is blackmail. If they record us, if there are cameras . . ."

Parrish was shaking his head. "There won't be. Nobody could afford to have this on the record, any kind of record, anytime."

Grant let Parrish lead the way to the front door, which opened as they walked up. Douglas stood there, a glass of whiskey in his hand. He was an older man, slightly stooped, with thick white hair and heavy eyebrows, each as long and as wide as Grant's little finger. "Come in," he said.

They stepped inside, Douglas sticking his head out and looking both ways as if he expected a busful of FBI agents to land on his doorstep. He stepped back inside, locked the door.

"When George was turned loose, one of the conditions was that he wear an ankle monitor," Douglas said. "They'll know he's here, but why shouldn't he be? And we really do need to talk business."

Grant: "There's no chance that it can monitor the conversation, is there?"

"No, that would be illegal," Douglas said. "It would threaten their whole case."

Grant nodded, and Douglas led the way to the living room, where Claxson was sitting in a leather chair, another glass of whiskey by his hand. Grant doubted that she'd be offered one. Douglas asked, "Would you like a drink? I have a split of champagne, unless you like a nice snort of Jack Daniel's."

So she'd been wrong about that. She was still behind Parrish, ten feet from Claxson, with Douglas off to her right, walking toward the liquor cabinet.

Grant didn't bother to reply. She had her hand on the pistol; the pistol felt electrified, as the checkering on the grip bit into her hand. She'd flicked off the safety as they walked down the hallway from the front door. Now she pulled it out and, with no hesitation, shot Parrish in the back between the shoulder blades.

The muzzle blast was like a slap on the head, though slightly muffled by the carpets, drapes, and soft furniture. Parrish pitched forward onto his face. Claxson shouted something she didn't comprehend and tried to get out of the leather chair, rolled slightly to his left, eyes wide, and she shot him in the chest and side—two quick taps—from five feet.

Douglas had the crystal whiskey glass in his hand, and he pitched it at her head. She pulled her head back, got splashed with the whiskey. Douglas blurted, "Please don't," and she thrust the pistol at him and shot him twice in the chest.

Parrish and Claxson were dying but alive. Claxson had a pistol and had managed to claw it out, but it had fallen from his hand, as he faded, and now lay on the floor beside him. Grant stepped over to him and shot him twice in the head, stepped back, shot Parrish twice in the head, and finally went over to Douglas, who appeared to be dead, but she shot him in the forehead anyway.

She'd heard of people who'd been terribly wounded but had survived, so she took time to check each of the bodies: they were all clearly gone. As she bent over Parrish to retrieve his car keys—she'd drive the Toyota back to Washington—there was a bright flash of car lights, coming fast, and somebody at the door, pounding.

She froze. FBI? Davenport and the marshals? No way to get to Parrish's car. She turned, ran to the back of the house, opened a door on the far wall of the darkened kitchen, and stepped out onto a deck.

The steady drizzle continued, and she ran across the back lawn and stepped through the row of trees at the back of the house. She was nearly blind under the canopy of trees, the starless sky offering no light, the headlights from the cars in front of the house and the glow of lights from within waning dramatically as she moved deeper into the woods.

Then a spark, a light of some kind, barely visible, two

hundred yards away, maybe more, blinking on and off, occluded also by individual trees as she moved past them.

She heard a splintering crash from the front of the house and realized that somebody had broken through the heavy front door. She moved deeper into the woods but, unable to help herself, stopped and looked back.

Douglas hadn't pulled the drapes on the side window in the living room, and Davenport was there, in its brightly lighted rectangle, like a man in a painting, moving toward the bodies, a burly man next to him, as well as two women—one white, one black—and she could now see Davenport shouting something and waving to the black woman, who was carrying a rifle, and she disappeared out the front door.

An insane rush of anger flooded through Grant, seeing Davenport there like a target in a shooting gallery. Without stopping to consider, she raised the pistol and fired three shots at the window and saw Davenport and the white woman go down.

She turned back to the spark of light she'd seen just before. It was a long way away, several hundred yards at least. She dropped the gun in her bag, and with her hands in front of her face to ward off unseen tree branches, she jogged toward it, tripping once, twice, three times, but she managed to stay on her feet.

She kept her eyes on the light, and eventually it grew closer and sharper. Somebody shouted behind her, yet the voice was hushed. The steady patter of the drizzle off the forest leaves, she realized, had the effect of muffling the shouting.

She moved on toward the light, came up behind a house. A different light went on nearby—motion-activated, she thought. There was no further activity.

Had to keep moving, she thought. She ran to the front of the house and out to the street. The street curved back toward Chesapeake, where she didn't want to go, and the other direction seemed too dark. A cul-de-sac? She wasn't sure, but she had no choice and ran that way, only to discover that it was.

But there was another spark of light across the lawn and through more trees, a couple of hundred yards to her left and away from Douglas's house. She crossed the lawn, entered the trees, nearly fell again, eventually worked her way out to another street. This one had more houses, and she ran down the blacktopped road. With the solid footing, she could move faster. The house with the light she saw had three cars parked in the driveway, and she went on by.

She could follow the road guided by the lights coming from the houses on either side, and now by the sky overhead, which was light gray rather than almost black when obscured by trees overhead. She stepped in a hole, stumbled, caught herself, ran on. There was more shouting behind her, now distinctly distant, and, even farther away, the wail of a siren.

She hadn't panicked. Not yet. But she could feel it clawing at her throat, trying to choke her, but she pushed it down. The farther she could get from Douglas's house, the safer she should be. And the woods, always lapping at the sides of the road, provided impenetrable cover if she needed to hide from a passing car.

But they would find her, sooner or later, if she didn't get completely clear, and now. With three dead and the shooter loose and on foot, they'd be putting up roadblocks, bringing in an army of cops to walk the woods.

The sound of the siren was coming from behind her but still distant. She'd gone a half mile or more, jogging and walking fast, when a garage door began rolling up at the house that she'd just passed. She stopped at the side of the road and watched as a small car, a green-and-white Mini, backed out of the garage. The garage door rolled down, and in the light she could see only a single person inside the car, small, probably a woman.

At the end of the driveway, the car turned toward her. She flipped down her hood to show her blond hair, and as the Mini slowly approached, she stiffened one leg to simulate limping and waved at the vehicle, which slowed some more, and Grant could see an elderly woman's face peering out at her.

The car came up, stopped beside her, and she limped around to the passenger side. She already had the gun in her hand. When the driver's-side window rolled down, the old lady said, "Is there something—"

Grant shot her in the face.

The car started to ease forward, the car in gear but the woman's foot apparently still on the brake. With the street gradually inclining upward, Grant was able to reach inside the window and grab the door latch and open it. She had to struggle to stay with the car, as she unlatched the old lady's safety belt and pulled her out on the street. Then Grant was inside.

She'd lucked out: the car had an automatic transmission. She put it in park, got out, ran back to the woman, dragged her body to the side of the road—she couldn't have weighed a hundred pounds—and threw it under a spreading evergreen shrub. As she did, the woman's phone fell out of her pocket. Grant crushed it underfoot and kicked it into the brush.

Back in the car, she drove slowly out to a main road, the one Parrish had driven in on, and turned back toward Washington. A mile down the road, two cops cars sped past, their lights flashing and their sirens screaming, into the murky darkness. Followed by a third, and a fourth, but no ambulances. She almost got lost twice, thinking about Davenport and the Watergate. There was a public garage at the Watergate.

SHE PARKED THE CAR at the Watergate forty-five minutes after leaving Great Falls. As she was getting out, she noticed a green bottle in the door pocket: hand cleaner. She rummaged around the inside of the car, found a packet of tissues, soaked one in the cleaner, which was mostly alcohol, and used it to wipe down the steering wheel and gearshift. She pulled her hood up, got out of the car, wiped down the seat, closed the door, locked it, and walked out to the street.

The Park Hyatt was a half mile away. She moved quickly, without running, up New Hampshire Avenue to 24th Street, north on 24th. She checked for cops, dropped the gun and magazine, separately, into sewers; it was still raining, and water bubbled over both as they disappeared through the grates and down the culverts.

At the Park Hyatt, hood still up, water trickling down the jacket, she caught an empty elevator and ten minutes later was back in her room.

Her hair was a mess, and she smelled like raw wet oak bark and the whiskey Douglas had thrown at her, and she was still sweating. She combed her hair out, hit it with a dryer, jumped into the shower, used the hotel soap to scrub herself down for a full two minutes. She had several small cuts on her hands from tree branches, but her face was clear. Out of the shower, she checked her hair and fluffed it with the dryer again, did a quick rework of her makeup, covered a scratch on the back of her hand with more makeup. The five quick dabs of Black Orchid. Her black clothing was locked in the overnight bag, to be dumped as soon as she could safely do it. She'd been gone an hour and a half, needed to mix, needed to be seen.

A lot.

She closed her eyes, took several long breaths, calmed herself. *What would the Buddha do?*

Her heartbeat slowed, a smile on her face, she was out of the suite.

SHE WALKED BACK into the party, heart pounding a bit more. She got a drink, swirled it around her mouth simply to saturate her breath with the odor of alcohol. She talked briefly to more hospital people—three women and two men—a couple of Minnesota congressmen, and finally, hunting around, spotted Porter Smalls, hooked into some conversations, and let herself be pushed in Smalls's direction. She got close, blundered into him when she suddenly turned, spilling a little of her drink.

Smalls: "Whoa. Almost knocked me off the bluff. Excuse me—I meant, off my feet."

Grant threw back her head and fake laughed, reached out and grabbed Smalls by one of his blue-green tourmaline shirt studs—chosen, she thought, to precisely match his eyes, the vain motherfucker—pulled him close, and muttered into his ear, "I knew what you meant, you piece of shit. You keep telling people I was involved in your drunken fuckfest, I'll hand you your ass."

Smalls tipped his head back, laughed, leaned close, muttered, "Get your hands off me, you murderous cunt."

Grant was laughing with him, and they broke apart, both satisfied. Smalls got to call her a cunt to her face, and Grant had him as a witness to her being present at the tail end of the party, in a conversation neither one of them would forget.

Smalls was exactly what she'd wanted: the most credible witness imaginable.

29

Lucas and the others ran down the driveway and along the dark street and saw a man come out of a house across the street from what must've been Douglas's house. The man saw them coming, shouted, "FBI," and Lucas shouted back, "FBI, Moy team," and the man turned away and ran up Douglas's driveway, stopped, and shouted back, "I think I heard gunshots."

"You did," Lucas shouted, as he ran up the drive to the front door, with Rae now right behind him, with her M4, and Bob a few steps behind her. How long had they been running? Less than a hundred yards, but in the night and rain? Fifteen seconds? Longer?

Lucas snapped at Rae, "Cover me."

She already had the rifle up, and Lucas went straight to the front door and began pounding on it. Nothing inside moved that they could hear, and the door, a heavy slab of walnut, didn't even tremble in its frame. Lucas stepped back and kicked it as hard as he could. It shuddered but didn't give.

Bob said, "Get out of the way. Get out of the way," and the big man kicked the door, the door buckling with the impact. He kicked it again, and something splintered. A third kick knocked the door open enough that Lucas could follow the muzzle of his gun through. As he did it, the surveillance team's SUVs began roaring into the driveway, their headlights flashing across the front of the house.

The first body was on the floor right in front of Lucas, and he shouted, "Man down."

He kept his pistol up, felt Bob moving to his left, covering the hallway that led to the right wing of the house. Rae was moving to cover the hall to the left wing, and Lucas squatted by the body. "Parrish," he said. Parrish was clearly dead, one eye open, one closed, two bullet wounds right in the middle of his forehead, another hand-sized blotch of blood on his back. In a half crouch, Lucas went on, glanced back, saw an FBI agent with a helmet and night vision goggles coming up behind him, a pistol in his hand.

"Don't shoot me," Lucas said, and the fed grunted once.

Up ahead, two more bodies were sprawled on the floor. Lucas called, "Two more down." He quickly checked them: Claxson and an older man, who must be Charles Douglas, both shot at least three times, both dead.

Lucas said, "Goddamnit."

Rae stepped beside him, and said, "Suzie? Carol? Wendy?"

"I dunno. Probably."

Chase came up, staring, openmouthed, at the bodies. "My God . . ."

Lucas said to Rae, "Listen, let's clear the house. You and Bob take the wings, I'll go that way." He gestured toward the back of the house. "But I think she's running."

And to Chase Lucas said, "Jane, I think she's running, I think she's in the woods. We need a lot of cops out here."

"Got it," she said.

Moy had just come through the door, and she turned to him, and said, "Andy . . ."

THE WINDOW at the side of the house blew out, and Lucas batted Chase to the floor, as he went down himself, Chase screaming, "I'm hurt! I'm hurt!"

Lucas crawled over to her, and asked, "Where?"

She said, "Leg," and grabbed her left leg below her butt. And when she took her hand away, it was red with blood.

Moy was still standing, staring, and Lucas shouted, "She's in the woods. Get some guys out there—the night vision guy. And we need an ambulance—right now."

Chase was staring up at him, eyes full of pain, and she groaned, and Bob dropped to his knees beside her and dug into a pocket and came out with his Leatherman tool, and he flicked out a blade. He said to Lucas, "Roll her over, I'll cut her jeans."

They rolled her over, and Chase groaned again louder. Bob cut a slit up the back of her jeans, and two more at right angles, until he could peel the denim back and they could see the wound. The shot had gone in through the back of the leg and come out the front, just missing the bone. The wound was bleeding heavily.

Bob, as calm as he might have been addressing the Kiwanis Club, said to Lucas, "Through and through. Not pulsing."

Chase asked through clenched teeth, "Am I gonna be okay?"

Bob said, "Yes. But it's gonna hurt, both now and later. Believe me, I know."

A fed came running through the door with a first-aid kit the size of a suitcase, knelt beside Chase, and popped open the lid. "I'm gonna plug the holes, put pressure on the wound."

Lucas patted Chase once on the shoulder, and said to Bob, "Clear the house. Let these guys take care of her."

Rae took the left wing, Bob took the right, Lucas went straight ahead into the kitchen. He stopped halfway in. What? What was it? Out the kitchen window, he could see high-powered LED flashlights playing through the woods and hear the plaintive wail of sirens. The sirens were too clear, this far back in the house, and he moved through the kitchen and found the back door standing open. She'd run through there into the dark, he thought.

Maybe.

He spent five minutes working through the back of the house, joined by one of the feds. When it was cleared out, Moy came up, and said, "We've got the streets covered, but it's harder than hell to see anything in the dark and the rain. It's been twelve minutes. If she made it out to a road, she could be a mile away."

"Gotta keep looking," Lucas said. "We don't know if these were executions or a gunfight. She could be wounded."

Moy was doubtful. "Haven't seen any blood except from the dead guys."

"Gotta look anyway . . . think about the after-action report. If you don't do everything, they'll be on you like a hot sweat."

"Ah, shit. I'll push the search," Moy said. "I'll do everything. Get the crime scene team down here."

LUCAS WALKED through the kitchen again, stood by the back door, looking out into the trees and at the flashlights searching through them.

Rae came up to him. "House is cleared."

"Where's Bob?"

Bob called, "Right here," and he came through the arched

doorway from the front room. "What are we doing? I could go out to the roads . . ."

Lucas shook his head. "I missed something. I saw something when I came into the kitchen, and it was important, but I don't see it anymore. Look around . . . What do you see?"

The two of them looked carefully but saw nothing relevant. Lucas went back out of the kitchen and then walked back in, looking for whatever he'd seen the first time, but, again, he didn't see it.

A minute later, an ambulance pulled into the driveway, and two EMTs hustled through the door. They looked at the FBI man's first-aid work, pronounced it good, and lifted Chase onto a gurney.

Pale as a piece of computer paper, she saw Lucas, licked her lips, said, "They told me I'll be okay."

"Maybe better than that," Lucas said. "A guy told me once that an FBI agent shot in a firefight gets extra career points."

She revealed the tiniest of smiles, said, her voice rasping and near a whisper, "It's absolutely ridiculous to be thinking about that . . . but I already did."

Lucas gave her arm a squeeze, and the EMTs took her out.

WITHIN A HALF HOUR of the shooting, thirty local cops were combing the woods and stopping cars within five miles of the Douglas house.

Lucas told the local chief of police: "She came in a car that's still out in the driveway, and she ran out through the trees. She's either holed up in the woods, getting hypothermia; or she cracked a house, killed the owners, and has taken their car; or she hijacked a car on the street, killed the driver. If she got a car, she's god-knows-where by now."

"We're looking with everything we've got," the chief said.

Rae had gone out in the woods with the searchers, came back soaking wet. "Nothing. You figured out what you missed yet?"

"No. I keep going back to look but don't see it anymore, whatever it was."

"Maybe a brain fart," Bob suggested.

"Don't think so. It felt too real."

AT TWO O'CLOCK in the morning, the police chief told Lucas, "We might have a problem. There's an old guy here who said his wife went out to a grocery store sometime after nine-thirty and she hasn't come back. He can't get her on her phone."

"Ah, Jesus. She's gone, she's dead," Lucas said.

"Don't tell me that," the cop said. "Please don't tell me that."

THE THREE MARSHALS were on the scene until four in the morning, until there was nothing more to see or say, and the FBI crime scene crew told them to go. There were still cops in the woods, and they'd be there through the next day, the chief said. There was no sign of the old woman or her car.

Lucas got Russell Forte out of bed to tell him what had happened.

"Oh my God," Forte said, and a woman's voice in the background demanded, "What happened? What happened? Is Sara okay?"

They agreed to talk the next morning.

LUCAS, BOB, AND RAE were halfway back to Washington, and the after-shooting was setting in. Bob was nearly asleep in the back, Rae was glassy-eyed in the passenger seat, when Lucas braked and pulled the Evoque to the side of the road.

He shifted into park, put his hands on the steering wheel at ten and two o'clock, and leaned his forehead against the wheel. Rae asked, "What? What? You okay?" echoed by Bob in the back, "What's going on?"

"I figured out what I didn't see in the kitchen. I didn't see a fuckin' thing," Lucas said.

"What?"

"I smelled it," he said.

Rae: "What?"

"When I was investigating Taryn Grant back in the Twin Cities, I interviewed her several times, and one time got in her bedroom after she was robbed . . . Well, never mind about that. Anyway, she uses a heavy scent, a perfume called Black Orchid. Kind of funky. I got a whiff of it when I ran into the kitchen, Just a whiff, but I know I'm right."

"You're saying . . ."

"That wasn't Wendy in there. That was Taryn Grant. She killed them all. Everybody who could take her down."

BOB AND RAE DIDN'T QUITE BUY IT.

"There was the smell of the gunpowder—that's what I noticed—and the smell of blood. And the odors from the forest outside. And then Chase got shot . . . It'd be impossible to pick out a dab of perfume," Rae said. "I mean, I'm wearing perfume and I can't even smell myself."

"I smelled it," Lucas said.

"Even if you did, a jury would never convict," Bob said. "It's useless as evidence."

"Ah, you're right, you're right," Lucas said.

"We need some sleep," Rae said. "Let's get some sleep and think about it in the morning."

"You *are* correct about one thing, Lucas," Bob said.

"Yeah?"

"Yeah. That old lady is dead."

30

Forte called early, eight o'clock, and the first thing he said was, "They found the old lady about thirty feet from the end of her driveway, under a bush. Your shooter, Suzie—whatever her name is—apparently flagged her down as she was coming out. Shot her in the face."

"It wasn't Suzie," Lucas said. "It was Taryn Grant."

Long silence. "Lucas . . ."

"Yeah, I may be full of shit." The memory of the scent was beginning to fade. "Last night, I was sure of it."

He explained, and Forte reacted the same way Bob and Rae had: "You might be right, but it's useless."

"Yeah, I know. So what do I do next? Everyone we had tagged on the Smalls thing is dead. All dead except Grant."

"And you don't have a thing on her," Forte said. "Might be time to wrap it up. I'm sure Smalls will be happy enough."

SMALLS WAS. Lucas called him on the burner, woke him up in a West Coast hotel. Lucas told him what had happened, including Taryn Grant's Black Orchid scent trail, and Smalls said, "I almost hate to tell you this, Lucas, but Grant wasn't there. She was in the same ballroom I was in—I actually had a spat with her."

"She was there the whole time?"

"Well, the party started at eight. We avoided each other, but I saw her several times. Toward the end—sometime before midnight, I guess—I actually spoke to her. Called her a cunt."

"Nice," Lucas said. "I expect we'll be hearing about that, if I ever get her on a witness stand."

"Hadn't thought about that," Smalls said. "But, anyway, you're not going to get her on a witness stand. I'll tell you, though, I'm a happy man. You got the killers. They're all dead."

"One disappeared, might still be on the loose. Either that or he's dead, too."

"If he's alive, would he be a threat?"

"No. If he was one of the killers, which we couldn't prove, he was being paid by Claxson or Parrish. I'm sure he wouldn't have been directly involved with Grant. I think Grant's happy to be out of it. She wouldn't send him after you again."

"Then let's call it a day. This has been quite satisfactory, Lucas. Go home, kiss your wife and children, spend some time at the lake."

"No, wait, wait, Senator. Think for a minute. When did you see Grant last night?"

Smalls thought, and said, "Well, I definitely saw her right at the beginning. She looked good, I admit. Green dress . . . I saw her a couple of more times right after that. And I saw her at the end . . . You know, I can't remember seeing her halfway through the reception, and she was highly visible. Let me ask around. Huh . . ."

His voice trailed off, and Lucas said, "Yes, ask around."

LUCAS CALLED Jane Chase in her hospital bed and she picked up instantly.

"I didn't think you'd be answering," Lucas said. "You should be all doped up."

"Nope. It's a workday. I'm sitting here at Reston Hospital with a major pain in the ass, if you'll excuse the vulgar language."

"I can handle it," Lucas said.

"I'm sure you can. Anyway, I'm working. I'll probably be here for another two days, they tell me. You heard about Mrs. Woods?"

"The old lady? Yeah. I knew she was dead. Knew before we left last night."

"Andy told me."

"I've got something to tell you that nobody believes but me," Lucas said, "not even Bob and Rae. And Senator Smalls told me to forget it and go home."

He told her about smelling the Black Orchid. She asked a couple of questions, then said, "Well, if it hit you like that, I think you're probably right. I have a small stock of perfumes, mostly lighter, like Chanel No. 5, because of the office environment. Some people are allergic to scents. Anyway, I tried Black Orchid when it first came out, and it was too strong and lingering, maybe too masculine. It stays in the air."

"But it would be useless in a prosecution."

"Unless there was a lot of other evidence."

"All right," Lucas said. He rubbed the side of his face. "I've gotta go shave. Listen, Jane, I hope your ass stops hurting and you get back on your feet. You're a good cop. You'll do well."

"Thank you. I'll tell Deputy Director Mallard that you said hello."

"Don't really have to do that," Lucas said.

"I know, but it gives me another chance to chat with the deputy director. Make him aware of the bandage on my ass."

Lucas laughed. "You *will* do well."

TOM RITTER CALLED. "There are rumors of a massacre."

Lucas said, "Guy named Charles Douglas, Claxson, Parrish, all shot to death, probably by a woman. There are some people at the FBI who would be interested in talking with Wendy . . . Suzie . . . whatever her name is."

"It wasn't her," Ritter said. "My folks and I went out to dinner last night, and she came with us. She got over to my folks' motel about, mmm, six-thirty or so, and we were out until after ten. They had an emergency board meeting over at Heracles this morning, and word from there is, the shooting took place around nine-thirty."

"That's right. Anybody besides you and your folks talk to Wendy?"

"Sure. Let me see, there were at least three servers, counting the bread guy and the drinks lady. And Wendy bumped into somebody she knew . . . I could get his name, if you need it."

Lucas sighed. "No, I don't need it. I'll call my FBI contact and tell her that I checked around, and Wendy's whereabouts last night is accounted for."

"Thanks. She was Jim's girl, you know?"

"I'd like to talk to her again," Lucas said. "If you see her, tell her to give me a call."

"I'll do that, if I see her again. I'm headed back to the 'Stan soon as I can get a plane out," Ritter said. "We got all the paperwork done, Jim will be cremated, but it'll take a few weeks before the ashes are interred at Arlington. They've got quite the waiting list."

"Good luck, Colonel."

"Same to you. One last thing. Was it Grant?"

Lucas didn't hesitate. "Yes."

"You're sure."

"Yes."

LUCAS, BOB, AND RAE spent the day making statements for the Great Falls Police Department, the FBI, and the Marshals Service. The interviewers at the FBI and Marshals Service both said that Smalls had called to make his own statement, about asking Lucas to initiate an investigation into the assassination attempt.

That, Bob remarked as they left the FBI building, seemed to have a cooling effect.

"Not that we did anything wrong," Rae said.

"I thought we did well," Bob said. "Lucas?"

"I'm not happy, but it is what it is," Lucas said.

THEY HAD A LAST DINNER that night. Bob and Rae planned to fly out early the next morning, before Lucas got up. Rae said, "We're leaving for the airport at six. Don't bother to come out and wave to us."

"I promise I won't," Lucas said. His plane was at one o'clock. He added, "But you're flying Business Class, right?"

"We are," Bob said. He placed his hand on his chest. "Be still, my beating heart."

SUZIE/CAROL/WENDY called at ten. "I heard all about it," she said. "Tom was worried that you might be coming after me. I wasn't there."

"I know. I mostly wanted to make sure you were straight on the death of Jim Ritter. What caused it, who caused it, all that."

"I think I got it. You believe it was Parrish. So do I."

"Yes. Not long before we think he was killed, he was within a couple of hundred feet of Parrish's house without any reason we've been able to find for being there," Lucas said. "The phone track looks like he walked around the neighborhood, maybe to check for surveillance."

"Why would he do that? Nothing wrong with talking to Parrish, not at that point." Lucas didn't reply, and she added, "Unless Parrish asked Jim to check because he was planning to kill him and didn't want anyone to see Jim go into the house."

"I think that might be it," Lucas said. "A crime scene crew is going to take Parrish's house apart, and they may find out what happened there. Look, you knew Jim, I didn't, except through research and some observation. It seems to me, though, that if Parrish had given him even a hint of what was coming, Jim would have torn him to pieces."

"Yes, he would have," she said.

"So I think what happened was that Parrish completely surprised him, asked to see him for some innocuous reason, and Jim was standing there, chatting, friendly, maybe drinking some milk, and Parrish pulls a gun and kills him. That's the way I see it."

After a moment, Wendy said, "Parrish wouldn't have done it on his own. So there's still one person out there, and you won't get her." Her voice had pitched higher, was almost squeaking. Lucas realized that she was crying but trying to talk through it.

"She's nuts, she's a killer, but nobody would ever say she's stupid," Lucas said. "She's got some guts. She went to Douglas's house and executed three people, her whole plan blew up, and then she murdered her way out of trouble, killed Old Lady Woods, got away with it, and used Senator Smalls as an alibi, which might have been the neatest touch of all. I doubt she even thinks about it anymore. In some ways, I've got to admire her."

"A good op is a good op," Wendy agreed, her voice almost back to normal. "And you don't think the cops are coming after me?"

"Nah. I told them you were accounted for last night, that I got that from a source I trusted but won't disclose. And I won't. They might figure out who you are and want to chat, but there won't be much urgency to it," Lucas said.

"I'll think about that," Wendy said. "Have a nice life, marshal."

"Wait, wait. Tell me the truth, goddamnit. That was you at the hotel, right?"

"I don't know what you're talking about," she said, and hung up.

31

The night was hazy with heat and humidity, creating fuzzy balls of light around all the streetlamps visible above the garden wall. Taryn Grant was alone in her house, moving around in a silky black camisole and thong. The air-conditioning was pounding away—the place would be intolerable without it—but she didn't like the dry cold and had opened two small side windows to let in some of the night air. A Backstreet Boys album, *Never Gone*, played from hidden speakers; the Boys had been her favorites since high school, and still were.

The Senate.

The Senate was a political circus, but that had been true for quite a while. She didn't care, as long as she could continue to push her profile higher.

She had a champagne flute in her hand, holding a drink favored by her mother. It looked like champagne but was actually an inch and a half of Bollinger champagne with a double shot of Stolichnaya vodka, traditionally called a Stoli-Bolli. A delicate, feminine-looking drink that could kick like a mule.

After she'd drunk about half of it, she thought about the senator from Colorado. He was talking about running for the presidency. And there were some good reasons to think he was viable. Grant didn't want to murder him; she would like to keep him intact long enough to run on the ticket with her as her vice presidential candidate.

Put a cowboy hat on him, peel off some of the redneck votes that the Republicans had been counting on.

As far as murder went, she didn't think about that long rainy night in July anymore. She'd been frightened for a few days, but then not. No cops came calling, no FBI. None of those people—the dead people—amounted to much, scratching around for their petty little retirements, playing with their guns. And the woman she shot? Well, she was just plain old.

There was nothing left of that night: the weapons, the ammo, the clothing, the witnesses, the victims—all gone forever.

She drifted toward the bay window that looked out over the garden. She could smell herself, the delicate scent of sweat and a hint of that morning's Black Orchid. At the window, she looked over at the neighbor's house. Only the peak of a gable was visible, with its single window, always, before tonight, totally dark. An attic, she'd thought. Tonight, there was a very faint light glowing in the window.

She was wondering about that when the 300-grain .338 slug ripped through her heart.

Grant felt no impact, no pain. She did feel herself falling, wondering for the seconds of the life remaining to her why that was. Then she was on the floor, her shoulder and head landing on a very fine Iranian carpet. The champagne flute landed on the same fine carpet, bounced once.

The last thing Grant registered was the flute, sparkling in the overhead lights, unbroken, elegant . . . innocent.

And she was gone.

LUCAS WAS IN HIS GARAGE, working with Sam, his son. It was time, he'd told Weather, to start teaching his kid some shit. He had two immediate projects in mind. One was cleaning up the engine on an elderly twenty-five-horsepower outboard motor, including the installation of new spark plugs. The other was the construction of a simple wooden box, which involved the use of a tape measure, a compact table saw, an electric drill, screws, a sander, and varnish. They'd decided to start with the box and had gone to a specialty lumber store, where they picked out some nice one-inch walnut planks.

When finished, the box would be given to Weather as storage for her piano sheet music. They'd measured and cut the first planks when she came to the door, and said, "Porter Smalls is calling. He said it's important."

Lucas took Sam inside with him, didn't want him out there alone, maybe thinking about using the table saw to cut the planks himself.

He'd left his cell phone inside specifically to avoid calls. Weather handed it to him, and when he said, "Hello?" Smalls asked, "Have you heard?"

"Heard what?"

"Somebody shot Taryn Grant last night. She's dead as a doornail."

"Hang on a second," Lucas said. He turned to Weather, asked, "Could you get me a Diet Coke? This is gonna take a few minutes."

"What happened?"

"Porter says somebody shot and killed Taryn Grant last night."

"Oh my God," she said, her voice hushed, and she went to get the Coke.

Lucas sat down, and said, "Tell me."

SMALLS DIDN'T KNOW all the details, but he had friends in the Justice Department who'd leaked a few of them. At about eight-fifteen the night before, an elderly couple had been watching Anderson Cooper on CNN when a woman dressed all in black, wearing a black balaclava, sunglasses, and gloves, had appeared in their media room and pointed a gun at them. Because of the total body coverage, they couldn't even tell the FBI what race she was. She'd told them that she didn't want to rob them, or hurt them, but simply wanted to look out a window.

She'd marched them into a bathroom that faced the street, made them sit down on either side of the toilet, and had handcuffed them together with their arms wrapped around the toilet. She'd searched them for cell phones, found some newspapers and magazines, taken some bottles of water and a bottle opener, and a couple of pillows, and left them.

Some long time later, they'd heard a single rifle shot. The old man had been a hunter and knew a rifle shot when he heard one. The woman had come running down the stairs, opened the bathroom window, and told them, "If you yell for help in the morning, somebody will hear you."

Nobody actually did, but they had a housekeeper who arrived at nine o'clock. She found them, called the cops. They told the cops about the single rifle shot; the cops were horrified to learn that Senator Taryn Grant lived next door.

"They went over and pounded on the door," Smalls said, "they got her chief of staff to come over with a key. They found her dead, on a very expensive Iranian carpet, shot once in the heart. That's all I know."

"Wonder if it was somebody from Heracles?" Lucas asked.

"No idea. But it was a professional hit, no doubt about that."

LUCAS HAD PUT the cell phone in his pocket, he and Sam were back in the garage, with Weather closely watching Sam operate the table saw, when he felt the phone vibrating.

Jane Chase: "Have you heard?"

"Porter Smalls called."

"This sounds exactly like the woman who attacked you at the hotel," Chase said, the excitement riding close beneath her dry tone. "Do you know anything at all about her?"

"No. I eventually got three different possible names for her, from the Heracles people, but I doubt any of them were real."

"This is going to cause endless trouble," Chase said. "The Senate's going totally insane and we're right in the bull's-eye."

"Jane, some advice: stay away from it. Find something else to do," Lucas said. "You won't find this woman. She apparently worked with Heracles, and for the CIA, and is probably back in Iraq, or Syria, or one of those places, by now. If she belongs to the CIA, do you think they'll give her up as the person who assassinated a senator?"

She thought for a second, then said, "It does sound unlikely."

"And when the Senate starts looking for an FBI scapegoat, you don't want to be the one standing there with your dick in your hand."

"Certainly not," she said, tempted to laugh at his metaphor.

"Now that that's settled, give me a few details."

She told him the same story he'd gotten from Smalls, with a couple of extras. "The crime scene team recovered the bullet. It's a 300-grain .338 slug, fired from a .338 Norma Magnum. She was hit very precisely. The assassin was shooting from an attic window in an adjoining house. She shot from a stack of books sitting on top of a table; she was sitting in an old wooden chair. She either didn't eject the brass or she picked it up."

"I don't know the gun—is it an exotic?"

"Couldn't get one across the counter at Walmart, but you could probably order one there," she said. "So it's uncommon but not exotic. We're trying to trace all sales, but there'll be a whole bunch of them, and secondary sales and trades . . . It's impossible."

"Once again: stay away. This is a professional job. You won't get her," Lucas said.

"And I certainly don't want to be standing there with my dick in my hand."

"Atta girl."

When he hung up, Weather said with a certain tone in her voice, "Sounds like the two of you got pretty close."

Lucas nodded. "Yeah . . . If we were living in Baghdad, I'd probably make her my second wife."

Weather kicked him in the calf, said, "Oh, sorry, I slipped."

LUCAS HAD BEEN HOME for two weeks. In that time, the FBI had torn Heracles to pieces, and it appeared that the company was about to be indicted on dozens of charges, from illegal weapons trafficking to illegal contacts with foreign terrorist groups, having provided both material and training support. The blight had spread to other contactor companies as well. The operators turned by FBI investigators had worked with several of those companies in addition to Heracles, and with criminal charges hanging over them, they were eager enough to take deals in return for information.

Lucas didn't have a clear idea of how it all worked. The FBI was a swamp, and unless you were in it, it was impossible to tell precisely who was doing what. He'd called his friend Deputy Director Louis Mallard to ask a few questions, and it appeared that Jane Chase was right in the middle of it all.

JOHN MCCOY gave up everything he knew about Heracles but admitted to no knowledge of murder. He took a plea deal and would spend two years in a minimum security federal prison, which Lucas knew he could do standing on his head. Nobody had heard anything of Kerry Moore. Some thought he'd been murdered, like Jim Ritter; others thought he'd run. When asked, McCoy shook his head, but one perceptive interrogator thought he might have looked amused.

AN FBI CRIME SCENE CREW detected tiny pieces of copper in the walls of Jack Parrish's kitchen and matched them to the bullet fragments taken from Jim Ritter's body.

SENATOR SMALLS asked around quietly, a few friends, and told Lucas, "You know what? I can't find anybody who talked to her halfway through the party, only at the beginning and at the end."

"Toldja," Lucas said.

LATE THAT NIGHT, on the same day that Taryn Grant was found dead, Lucas took a third call. There was a whistling sound in the background, and when Lucas asked about it, Tom Ritter told him it was satellite noise.

"I'm calling on a satphone. I'm sitting on a bench, on a nice bright day, at Bagram Air Base."

"Is that—"

"In Afghanistan? Yes," Ritter said. "Listen, I heard about Grant. It's on the Internet here."

"They're interested in Wendy. Or Suzie or Carol, or whatever her name is. Maybe. I didn't have much to say about it, but they'll be pushing McCoy."

"Think they'll come to me?" he asked.

"I don't think so. You're out of it, given where you're at. They might have some questions about Jim, but . . ."

"I haven't seen him a lot in the past few years," Ritter said. "Don't know much about his love life."

"Stick with that," Lucas suggested.

"Tell me what happened," he said. "All I know is what I've seen on the Internet news feeds."

Lucas told him what he'd gotten from Smalls and Chase, and, when he was done, Ritter said, "Oh boy. It does sound like her, doesn't it?"

"Yeah. But it's not my case anymore," Lucas said. "Or yours."

"Stay loose, Lucas. You ever get to Afghanistan, give me a ring," Ritter said. "We'll go get some fried chicken. They got good fried chicken here."

"I will. If you hear from Wendy, tell her to give me a ring."

A COUPLE OF DAYS LATER, Lucas was sitting in his backyard with Virgil Flowers, waiting for the charcoal briquettes to get right for the steaks. Flowers had come up with Sam, the youngest child of his girlfriend. Flowers's Sam and Lucas's Sam were the same age, were amazed that they shared a name, had rapidly become friends, and were playing their version of mixed martial arts–croquet, while Lucas and Flowers sat in lawn chairs and talked.

They were drinking Leinenkugel's and discussing child care when Lucas's iPhone dinged with an incoming call from an unidentified phone.

Satellite noise. Then Wendy said, without preface, "I've been thinking about it. And I've been thinking about you. You believe I was involved in that shooting at the Watergate Hotel. Why didn't you ever come after me?"

"We *were* looking for you . . ."

"No, you weren't. Or if you were, you weren't looking very hard. The media was going wild, Homeland Security was issuing press releases every five minutes—all of them wrong—the FBI was running in circles. The one group that might have given me trouble, which was you and your marshal friends, never came looking. You didn't come even though you knew some people I was friends with. You never squeezed Tom, you never really squeezed John McCoy, you never squeezed Claxson or the lady who worked for him . . . Why was that?"

"We don't have the investigatory resources to throw around like the FBI does," Lucas said. "Or like Homeland Security. Whatever happened at the Watergate, it didn't seem likely to have much connection with our main objective, which was to find out who tried to murder Senator Smalls."

"Oh, bullshit, Davenport. Nobody came to the Watergate and shot the place up by accident, not with a machine gun," she said. "You had to know there was some connection."

When Lucas didn't say anything, Wendy demanded, "Were you grooming me?"

"What?"

"When you got Tom to give me your phone number, did you want to talk so you could manipulate me . . . Were you grooming me to kill Grant?"

Lucas let that hang in the air, then said, "I don't know what you're talking about," and hung up.

"What was that?" Flowers asked.

"Unfinished business," Lucas said. He picked up his Leinie's, took a swallow, and added, "But it's finished now."